PRAISE FOR
THE CHOSEN SHELL

The Chosen Shell opens at a time of profound change in the nation and the Catholic Church. Its young heroine, Celie O'Rourke, is caught between a desire to live a life of divine purpose and a yearning for human love and connection. Author Katherine Sartori, once a nun herself, follows Celie's journey from vulnerable adolescent to empowered adult with sensitive and poignant prose, while offering readers a fascinating glimpse inside monastic convent life. Although Celie's transformation is rooted in the turbulent 1960s, her story offers a stirring and ultimately uplifting message that transcends that era.

—**DeAnna Cameron, author of *Dancing at**
the Chance* and *The Belly Dancer*

The Chosen Shell by Katherine Sartori, is an intimate, insightful and ultimately explosive exploration into the life of a young woman who is both naïve and full of faith. Her journey leads her into the convent, where light is too often mixed with darkness and innocent trust becomes tragedy. Ms. Sartori, a former nun, shows great courage in exposing a shameful truth that tradition and church "loyalty" have hidden for centuries. I would make this book required reading for any young woman who is considering taking vows.

—**Matthew Anderson, Dr. of Min., author of *Brother**
Matthew: One Disciple's Love Story* and *The Prayer Diet.*

Why couldn't I put this book down? *The Chosen Shell* isn't just a story about a nun, it's about a young woman who desperately needs to find her place in the confusing world of the '60s. Growing up in a supposedly ideal, Irish-Catholic family, Celie misses out on the love and acceptance all girls need. So she embarks on a journey, seeking to quench a deep need . . . Well, suffice it to say that *The Chosen Shell* made me recall my own deep sorrow. It is truly a universal story set against the backdrop of one of our country's and the Catholic Church's most turbulent eras.

> —Pam Rocke, Board of Trustees, Center for Spiritual
> Living, Capistrano Valley, California

In *The Chosen Shell,* Katherine Sartori masterfully weaves an intricate, multi-layered story about relationships, disappointment, betrayal, and a young woman's determination to rise above it all.

> —Kathy Pratt, author of *Let Them Have Cake* and *Miss Dairy Queen*

The Chosen Shell is the illuminating adventure of a nun's struggle to find her true identity against the backdrop of the turbulent '60s, a fascinating look into monastic life and struggles that most of us know nothing about. A rich and personal story.

> —Catherine Singer, Award Winning Photographer—
> www.catherinesinger.com

The Chosen Shell is a fascinating peek at life as a young nun in the 1960s, seen through the eyes of the main character, Celie. Despite her nun's habit, I connected with her many struggles and her ultimate triumph.

> —Cindy Cooksey, Artist—www.cindycooksey.com

Katherine Sartori treats us to an amazing story about a young woman who seeks to understand the meaning behind an inner call from God. Joyfully, Celie becomes a nun, but after several years other things begin to tug at her. Passion and courage are required of her before she can follow the dreams of her heart.

> —Teri Winters (Terrill Smith) author of *Dancing Near
> the Edge* and *Motivating the Bad Attitude Kids.*

THE CHOSEN SHELL

THE CHOSEN SHELL

A Novel

KATHERINE SARTORI

Dream Traveler Press
Los Angeles

The Chosen Shell is a novel with poems by Katherine Sartori

Published by Dream Traveler Press

First Edition, October, 2012

Publisher's Cataloging-in-Publication
(Provided by Quality Books, Inc.)
Sartori, Katherine.
The chosen shell : a novel / by Katherine Sartori.—1st ed.
p. cm.
ISBN 978-0-9883746-0-7
ISBN 978-0-9883746-1-4
1. Augustinian nuns—California—San Francisco—Fiction. 2. Elementary school teachers—California—San Francisco—Fiction. 3. San Francisco (Calif.)—Fiction. 4. Psychological fiction, American. I. Title.
PS3619.A755C46 2012   813'.6
QBI12-600197

Printed in the United States of America

Book design by 1106 Design
Cover by Katherine Sartori, Pamela Mason, and Graphicz X Designs
Author's Photo by Jennifer Palmer, www.petitefeetphotography.com

DEDICATION

For my husband Joe Sartori,
who has believed in me and this story for many long years.
Because of his tireless help, constant caring and encouragement,
I am finally sharing it with others.

ACKNOWLEDGMENTS

Our life decisions and accomplishments are forever influenced by those around us. My efforts to write this novel are no exception. Therefore, I want to thank several of my friends and all my writing critique partners whose close readings, suggestions, positive feedback, and constant encouragement helped me to complete this book, especially: Diane Schochet, Kathy Pratt, Terrill Smith, Darlene Glass, Judy Cheek, Susan Klaren-Hatzenbuhler, Claudia Alexander, Ph.D., DeAnna Cameron, Pam Rocke; my editors, Barbara Ardinger, Ph.D. and Tracy Gantz; and my life coach, Dr. Matthew Anderson.

CHAPTER 1

A DIFFICULT GOODBYE

August 1963

Celie O'Rourke peered out the living room window. For a moment, she couldn't breathe. Mike was parking his red and white '57 Chevy in front of her house. She hadn't seen him in three weeks, not since they'd broken up. She raced to open the door.

He was tanned, his pale hair bleached brighter by the southern California sun, his eyes a translucent blue. As usual, he wore faded jeans and a T-shirt. She had always marveled at his rugged good looks—powerful shoulders, square jaw, the ridge of his nose strong and perfect, eyelashes the random colors of straw. He stood there on the porch holding a long white box, his chin jutting out a little, his full mouth a grim line. It seemed like ages since she'd seen him.

Celie looked at his face and knew he was hurt. She didn't know what to say. She felt only guilt. To keep her hands from shaking, she clasped them together and offered a tentative "Hi."

At first, he wouldn't meet her gaze, but finally his eyes darted in her direction. "I . . . I wanted to give you something before you left."

"Come in," she said.

He didn't touch her, barely looked at her.

Cripes, he's acting like a total stranger! We went steady for two whole years.

Sitting down on the old green armchair, he shoved the box into her hands. "Here's something to remember me by."

She lifted the tissue paper and found twelve long-stemmed, crimson roses. "They're beautiful!" She moved toward him, but thought better of it

1

and, trying to keep her voice even, said, "Mike, you don't have to worry. I'll never forget you." But she knew he wasn't listening. She studied his face as she sat down on the couch nearby.

"I didn't believe you'd go through with it." He was stumbling over his words. "I don't understand, Celie. I just wish I could keep you here."

The long pause stretched on, a seemingly timeless void, and Celie overheard Mom talking to her older sister, Maureen, in the kitchen.

"Father Walsh just called," her mother was saying. "I love his sense of humor. Such a dedicated man. Another funeral tomorrow. I guess he can't do without Celie and Rosemary helping out in the choir. He's always counted on you girls."

Why does she treat Father like he's the next Pope?

Outside, Celie's younger brother Stevie started to squeal.

"Stop that racket!" her father growled. "You hear me?"

Great! Another horrific scene.

Trying to block the noise out, she held Mike's gaze and struggled again to find words to explain her decision and her feelings, which he found impossible to comprehend. She'd tried before, but it hadn't done any good.

Ever since Mom had asked her six months ago if it was true that she was planning to follow her cousin Rosemary and go off and become a nun, Celie had been alternately disturbed and ecstatic about the fact that her mom approved of her decision to dedicate her life to the church. Mom even seemed proud.

But how could she explain to Mike that this was something she felt compelled to do? Felt—no, maybe "knew" was a better word—that she must follow God's call and help the people He placed in her path. She'd always wanted to make a difference, to help those in need. She tried to be gentle.

"I still love you, Mike, and I guess you don't understand this, but I *have* to try it. I know it hurts you. It hurts me, too. Believe me, I've felt such an ache for you these last few weeks. I've missed you. Even so, I can't explain it, but I feel God is calling me to this vocation."

He looked at everything in the room except her. "But you could be so important right here. With me."

She wanted to interrupt, but held back.

Mike's probing went on, like searchlights piercing the darkness.

"I thought you wanted to get married," he said, "and have a slew of kids like your mom. Didn't you?"

"No. I've never wanted to be like her."

"Since when?" Then, almost under his breath, "I just think they got to you."

"What's that supposed to mean?"

"You know. All those vocation pitches they make all year, every year. You've heard them ever since you were in first grade. They need more nuns and priests, so they talk it up constantly. It's as never-ending as their sermons on the Sixth and Ninth Commandments."

She instantly dismissed his sarcasm about the church's incessant warnings about sins of impurity and shook her head. "No. It's not like that."

"You sure? Jeez, we get a sermon on 'the mysterious call to become nuns and priests' at least three times a year at Sunday Mass, not to mention the annual retreats. C'mon, Celie, the nuns spend months recruiting for religious vocations at your high school. Every spring. Like clockwork."

She wouldn't look at him.

"And what about Sister Pauline?" he asked. "Don't tell me you haven't felt pressure from her, especially these last two years. They're all *very* serious about signing up seniors."

The bitterness in his voice was almost palpable. What could she say to make him understand?

She leaned toward him, one hand fingering the petals of the roses in the opened box. "Sister Pauline has been a wonderful friend to me. She's been there for me all through high school, cheering me on to pull top grades. If it hadn't been for her, I never would have won the state writing competition. So don't put her down."

"I don't give a damn about her!" He stood up and headed for the door.

Celie followed him. "Please, I have to do this. You've got to accept my decision. My memories of these past two years with you have been the absolute best. All I can tell you is that I will never, ever forget you. Do you believe me?"

Stretching his arm out to push the screen door open, he glanced back at her. His voice was so low she could hardly hear it.

"I don't have to accept anything."

He marched down the driveway, yanked the car door open, got in, slammed the door shut, jabbed the key into the ignition, and drove off.

She leaned against the front door for support, holding her body rigid, swallowing her tears. She watched him drive away, then closed her eyes and listened as the tailpipe's roar faded to silence.

"Celie, I forgot to tell you," Mom's cheery voice shattered the silence. Not wanting anyone to see her crying, Celie had retreated to her room.

Mom was standing in the doorway, holding the vacuum. "Guess who called?"

Celie had seen her hovering nearby when Mike told her goodbye. Mom had never turned the vacuum on, though; she'd been listening to them the whole time. Celie cringed.

And Mom chattered on, "Father Walsh needs you and Rosemary to sing at church. I don't know what he'll do when you're gone." She came in and dusted Celie's bureau as she talked.

Celie couldn't say anything. She tried to push away the anger that wrapped itself around her so she couldn't breathe. She didn't trust her mother's words, never had. As a familiar lightheadedness came over her, she reached for the wall, inhaling deep breaths. Most of the time this helped.

Now Mom was dusting photos of Celie and her two sisters. "An unexpected funeral tomorrow has put him in a bind."

"I told you before," Celie began. "I have to—"

"C'mon, Celie. He doesn't need you till ten o'clock."

"Mom, I still have to pack everything and find some time to buy my shoes. We leave in two days, and I'm not ready. I want to help Father Walsh, but—"

"Please! You can't disappoint Father this one last time. I've told you over and over, you worry too much. Everything will get done. You're always tense. So much like your dad. Besides, when Father just called again, I couldn't say no to him. I promised him you'd be there."

Celie turned her back, the dizziness growing behind her eyes.

Mom wasn't finished. "Besides, Rosemary said she'd be happy to help out. Your cousin's always so generous."

Celie bolted for the kitchen, wooziness clouding her vision. She gulped deep breaths. The tests they'd done years before had never gotten to the root of these strange spells.

The noisy timer ticked away on the stove, clocking the minutes. She knew Dad would charge in here if she didn't hang up soon. *He's so unreasonable.*

After lying down for a while to quell her dizziness, she'd risen and forced herself to return her friends' phone calls. Paulette and Dennis were out. Dennis' mom said he was playing baseball. So what else was new? She'd finally gotten through to Rosemary, though. Her cousin's normally stoic voice rang with excitement.

"Have you packed your trunk?"

"Your time's almost up!" Dad bellowed from the living room.

She winced. "No, I haven't bought everything on the list yet. I still have to get towels, a comforter, and my shoes. Let's go downtown together this afternoon, okay?"

"Fine with me," said Rosemary. "I'm down to the wire, too."

"Hey, did you notice? Everything has to be white, except for the black nylons and the granny shoes. The shoes will be the hardest to find because my feet are so wide." Celie watched the timer's dial move as she talked. Five more minutes. And there was Mom rummaging through the refrigerator. Celie knew she was listening to her phone conversation.

And now her older sister, Maureen, pranced into the kitchen, going on and on to Mom about her new classes at Pasadena City College. Celie put her hand over the phone's black mouthpiece. "I can't hear!"

Maureen was always rude, but, as usual, Mom never said a word to her. As she came nearer, Celie glared at her sister again, then turned her back and huddled in the farthest corner of the tiny kitchenette. She pressed a finger into her right ear to drown out the noise. Would they ever leave her alone and give her some privacy?

"Are you excited?" asked Rosemary.

"No. I guess I'm anxious, but I haven't planned this since third grade, like you. Who's driving you up to the Motherhouse? I've heard that Santo Domingo might be hard to find in those hills. It's a little town."

"My mom and dad are driving," Rosemary said. "He's pretty good with maps, so we'll find it. Is your whole family going?"

"Just Mom and Dad. Eight of us in the old Rambler would be insane."

"Your station wagon's not that ancient. It's a '58." Rosemary suddenly changed the subject. "Hey, wasn't the going-away party neat? I've never had a surprise party."

"Yeah," Celie said. "So many kids showed up. Even Sister Pauline and my English teacher."

"I heard them. Boy, were they laying it on."

"They just want me to continue writing. I wonder if I'll have time in the convent."

"'Course you will. You can turn in all the poems and short stories you want in your English classes. We're not going to another planet, Celie."

"Hey, I've got an idea. Why don't we visit Sister Pauline one last time? After we finish shopping?"

"I'm up for it," Celie said.

Rosemary babbled on. "I still have to buy my shoes, too, and towels and. . . ."

Huddled by the window, Celie tried to listen to her cousin, but the noise of her younger brother and two little sisters playing outside distracted her. The girls had tied a rope around their brother's neck and he was barking. Mollie, only four, patted Stevie's chestnut hair, and Jody, age nine, commanded him to sit and put his paw up in the air. Then they tugged at his leash, trying to lead him down the driveway on all fours.

He'll break out of that game in no time, Celie thought, *and treat us to one of his famous tantrums!*

As she watched, Mollie climbed up on Stevie's back, dug her heels into his sides, and slapped his backside. "Giddy-up, giddy-up," she shouted. At the same time, Jodie began to tug hard on her brother's makeshift leash.

Celie opened the kitchen window. "Get Molly off, Jodie. It's not safe. Now!"

Jodie ignored her and instead called to her brother, "Go down the driveway."

Stevie was squirming under Mollie's weight. "No, no!"

The noise was drowning out Rosemary, "Yeah," she was saying, "we're leaving at dawn on September seventh—"

Stevie's cries blended with a chorus of piercing wails as Molly toppled over onto the lawn. The timer rang. Dad charged through the kitchen on his way outside. "Get off that phone, Celie!" He slammed the back door and started breaking up the little kids' squabble outside. Mom followed him.

Rosemary was still talking. "What time are you going to leave?" she asked.

Dad charged in again. "Celie, you're not off yet?" He opened the refrigerator. "Damn those kids! Drive me nuts! I need a beer." He grabbed two cans of Schlitz and left the kitchen again.

"Rosemary," Celie said into the phone, "I can't hear you. And I've got to get out of here! I'll meet you downtown in front of the movie theater at 2:30."

As she turned around to put the telephone receiver into its cradle, Maureen snatched it from her. "My turn!"

That's it. Celie stomped out of the kitchen.

Her sister's voice followed her. "What's with her?"

Celie turned to listen, but she already knew her mother wouldn't stick up for her. Celie saw her through the window, lifting Mollie into her arms, while Stevie banged his legs on the lawn, shrieking. Dad bent down and yelled at her brother, shaking his finger in his face. They were all in for it now. Dad would be riled at everyone all day and all night.

Celie retreated to her room. It was always like this. Chaos. No one listening. The tumult never seemed to end.

All eight of them were crowded into their small stucco house in a working-class town called San Gabriel, near eastern Los Angeles. Telephone wires, the quaint street lamps Celie loved, orange trees, and neatly mowed rectangular lots lined the suburbs of this post-World War II neighborhood of one-story tract homes. The Kennedy era was in full swing, and kids like Celie's brother and sisters looked forward to their favorite black and white TV programs: *Leave It to Beaver*, *The Mickey Mouse Club*, and *Father Knows Best*. And Celie had to admit it, she still watched *American Bandstand* sometimes after school.

Celie shared her cramped pink bedroom with Maureen and her other older sister, Colleen. Down the hall in her parents' room, Mollie slept in the crib, and Stevie and Jody used the bunk beds in the tiny back room.

Now Celie's eyes roamed over the wallpaper that Mom, Maureen, and Colleen had picked out, with its large masses of roses in garish shades of red and pink climbing up all four walls. She hated it, but they'd never allowed her much say about decorating.

Maureen's homecoming queen pictures filled the shelf above their old mahogany dresser. The one exception was a photo framed in gold of Celie's senior prom. She gazed once again at the floor-length lavender gown that accentuated her tiny waist, at her hazel eyes made up perfectly, and her auburn hair swept up in a bevy of curls. And Mike, more glamorous in his black tux than she'd ever seen him before or since. She'd felt like a princess that night.

She pulled her eyes away from the photo and began counting Colleen's softball trophies, which filled the end of the shelf. Seven. A year older than Celie, Colleen was caustic at times, but her moods often changed suddenly and her wacky spirit invariably made the whole family laugh. She wasn't home today, but was off with her latest boyfriend. Dad couldn't stand him. But for as long as Celie could remember, there'd been a ruckus between Dad and Colleen.

She could hear Maureen finally hanging up the phone in the kitchen.

Thank you, God! In a minute, Maureen would go out, and Celie might actually have some privacy. Sometimes she wondered if anybody even knew she existed. *Mom's a snoop, but she never listens when I try to talk to her. Just endless chitchat, constant interruptions, kids crying, or that awful silence.*

She rolled over and looked at the portrait taken last Easter of the whole family. Everyone in the parish thought the O'Rourkes were the perfect Catholic family.

If they only knew.

The phone rang and Celie ran to answer it. The house was finally quiet. "Hello?" She heard a muffled sound like someone breathing. "Mike?"

"Celie." His voice sounded soft, hoarse. "I love you. Goodbye."

Her hand trembled as she hung up the phone.

CHAPTER 2

ANOTHER GOODBYE

"I'm going to miss our good times around Sister Pauline's piano," Rosemary was saying. "She's such a comedian. Can you believe how many music and chorus awards she's won?" Rosemary was talking non-stop, which was rare for her. She was usually a reserved, quiet girl, a high-achiever who usually didn't travel in the same circles as her cousin.

The girls had finished shopping, and now Rosemary was driving toward their high school and the convent nearby, still babbling on and on. They were going to say goodbye to Sister Pauline before they left for the Augustinian Motherhouse in northern California.

Let her talk, Celie said to herself. *I can't think, let alone say anything.* Mike's words were echoing over and over in her thoughts. *I love you. Goodbye. I love you. Goodbye.*

He'd never said it before. In fact, no one had said they loved her, in a long time. But no matter how many times she'd told Mike she loved him and wished he would say it, too, he'd never reciprocated. He was quiet by nature, a guy who showed he cared, not one to shower a girl with words. She understood. But now that she was leaving, he'd finally divulged his feelings, laid himself bare, as if by revealing his love for her he could make her change her mind.

Rosemary kept talking as she drove in the heavy traffic. "I was flabbergasted when I found out. She's won not just local awards, but nationals, too. Weren't you surprised, too?"

Celie glanced over at her friend and nodded vacantly, sitting with her arms folded tightly over her breasts, letting the memory of Mike's precious words tumble through her mind again, like a waterfall emerging from a hidden spring. She turned away from her cousin and reached for her purse, fumbling for a Kleenex to wipe away the tears burning her eyes.

Rosemary didn't even notice. A meticulous driver, she watched the oncoming cars carefully before maneuvering the car to the left. "Sister Pauline is like that, though," she chirped on. "She'd never say a word to us. If it weren't for Sister Maria spouting off—well, no wonder we always won the annual diocesan chorus club prizes."

She braked at the next intersection. "And guess what? Sister Pauline will be coming up to the Motherhouse every few months next year. She's on a special Augustinian committee."

"Really?" Celie couldn't care less what Rosemary said. She'd been looking out the window the whole time, seeing nothing. *I've got to get him out of my mind.*

Rosemary found a parking space. "Here we are!" She pulled the key out of the ignition and gathered up her sweater.

Putting her hand on the door handle, Celie silently admonished herself. *I have to stop this. Please, God, help me stop this.*

She'd known since a mysterious moment of revelation last November that she must follow God's call. Praying in the chapel during the high school retreat, she'd heard His voice penetrating her soul, knowing with certainty it wasn't her own. It was Another. She'd never felt anything like it, before or since. In the following weeks and months, though, she cried herself to sleep, trying to convince herself that no matter what Mike meant to her, God had offered her an illustrious path. After all, *any* woman could bury herself in a little house in the suburbs of L.A., have a bunch of kids, and spend her life living through them. To become a nun was different. Her decision would have far-reaching, significant consequences.

As she climbed out of Rosemary's VW, she thought of the clear mountain lake where she'd vacationed every summer since she was little. She'd often flung pebbles into that lake. She'd always loved the ever-widening ripples that moved across the sparkling surface. It suddenly came to her—this would be her life. God had called her to influence thousands of people as an Augustinian nun, especially children. She'd lead others to self-fulfillment, to inner healing, to a realization of their own unique importance. God's all-encompassing love was far more important than choosing love in marriage.

Still prattling, Rosemary walked ahead. "It'll be so neat to see Sister Pauline once in a while at the Motherhouse. I'm sure going to miss her, especially when I play my guitar." She waited for Celie at the convent door.

"Yeah."

Rosemary smiled as she pressed the doorbell. "C'mon, Celie, cheer up. At least if we see her every couple of months, we can have one of our famous sing-alongs. I'd die if we had to give that up."

Celie faked a smile. "I know."

CHAPTER 3

A POSTULANT'S FIRST DAY

September 1963

Celie couldn't decide whether the massive buildings on the hills looked friendly or forbidding. Her dad turned off the freeway and drove them up a long, winding lane to the Augustinian Motherhouse. Mom was very quiet beside him, and Celie fidgeted in the back seat. Huge olive and cypress trees lined the road, and the fruit orchards beyond filled the spacious fields on both sides. It was so different from her cramped San Gabriel neighborhood.

She was tired after the eight-hour ride from southern California, an ordeal thick with silence except for the radio station Dad finally chose, one that played his favorite songs by Nat King Cole, Al Martino, and Perry Como. She'd never spent this much time alone with her parents. It felt strange.

Finally, Dad parked the car and they all got out.

As the bells began to toll, Celie joined more than thirty other girls and their parents on a wide green lawn in front of a large Spanish-style chapel. A portly nun with a ruddy face and a bright smile motioned for the girls to form a line and go inside. Celie hugged and kissed her mom and dad, picked up her small suitcase, and followed Rosemary. Her cousin's cheeks were rosy, her expression radiant. Celie wondered why she didn't feel the same excitement. All she felt was a strange numbness.

When the nun opened a gigantic oak door, the first thing they saw was the life-sized statue of St. Augustine. Next, they followed the nun through a large, dim parlor filled with vintage couches and chairs set in clusters and down a hall lined with sepia portraits of Augustinian nuns. The monastic Order dated back to the 13th century, but the congregation Celie was joining had been founded in Europe in the early 1800's. Celie stopped for a moment in front of a framed map of Austria to locate the old town where the congregation of nuns had originated many decades before. After walking through another massive doorway, they stepped onto a meandering path in a garden courtyard. The nun put her finger to her lips, signaling they must now keep silent. Then she ushered them into another sizeable room, where stacks of black garments lay folded on every table.

"I welcome you on this, your entrance day, into our venerable Augustinian convent," the nun said. "Here you will dedicate your lives to Christ and to serving others, as He did. Ladies, please take off and put aside your secular clothes. We will keep them for you, but we hope you will never need them again. Start by putting on the long black stockings and the shoes you brought with you. They may look outdated to your young eyes, but they are sensible, and that is all you'll need now." She picked up one ebony garment and unfolded it. "Please put on this floor-length black skirt, blouse, and small cape. You will probably want to cut your hair later, but for now, you can pull it back tight and fasten your veil with bobby pins. When you're ready, we will say a short prayer and go to the chapel. This is the day you've been waiting for, the day you will offer your life completely to God for the first time!"

Celie was full of anticipation, but her stomach still felt hollow. Minutes later, correctly dressed, she marched with the other girls, two by two, down the wide marble aisle of the chapel as an organ played *Panis Angelicus*. This church appeared so different from what she was used to in San Gabriel, with its monastic stalls on the left and right sides of the aisle, stalls filled with nuns facing each other instead of church pews facing the altar in front. Surreptitiously, she scrutinized the nuns' faces, looking for a teacher she might recognize. After all, these Augustinians had taught her for twelve years. But no one looked familiar. *How disappointing.*

Seated on the hard wooden bench now, Celie admired the glistening blues and reds in the stained glass windows, then stole a glance toward the back of the building. It was empty. Only when she noticed the balcony above did she spot all the parents crowded together. Mom and Dad were barely visible, and it was only now that she realized she would not see them again for a long time. Perhaps in five or six months they'd make the trek up here again, but it would probably be much longer. Celie scrutinized her mother's grim face and noted that her father had put on his sunglasses. *That's why they were so quiet when I said goodbye. Maybe they'll miss me after all. At least Dad might.* Celie gritted her teeth to hold back tears.

After the nuns' prayers and hymns ended, Celie and the other Postulants (as the girls were now called) walked out of the chapel. She glanced up at Mom and Dad once more, knowing she could not even wave. This was the beginning of her new life as a nun.

Dinner was an austere experience, as they ate in complete quiet while a nun read about the life of a saint Celie had never heard of before. First, they had assembled around a giant U-shaped table, which hugged the walls of the stark white room. The portly Sister had called it a *refectory*. When the meal of jello salad and beef stew was served, Celie eyed the salt and pepper shakers, but they were just out of reach and no one noticed her need. The older nun had warned earlier that they could not ask for anything to be passed to them during meals. Instead, they must focus, not on their own desires, but on those of others. Celie decided she had to put up with the stew's bland taste. This would be her first sacrifice as an Augustinian.

With dinner finished and the dishes washed in basins at each table, one solemn bell rang out, signaling, though it was only nine o'clock, the beginning of Profound Silence, which would last the entire night. The Postulants lined up again, and the same portly nun led them outside and up the hill to a much older wooden building, which housed their dormitory. Celie stepped into the strangest room she'd ever seen. Lines of beds filled the gigantic room, each bed with a number hanging from the steel poles that surrounded it. White cotton curtains that looked like sheets hung from the poles and separated the beds. *It looks like a hospital ward from a 1940's movie*, Celie said to herself. Near the beds were small nightstands containing only two drawers, and on top of each was a sizeable metal pitcher sitting inside a large basin. Celie wondered what these were for. Didn't they have running water here?

Celie was assigned to bed 614. Not remembering what the nun had said earlier, she watched the others for a few minutes, then drew the curtains around her bed and undressed, hanging her black uniform on a hanger. Finding a long white nightgown in one drawer of the nightstand, she put it on. Carrying toothbrush, soap, and washcloth, she tiptoed over to the community washroom, to wait in the long line. When she'd finished washing her face and brushing her teeth, like the other Postulants, she ran to get her pitcher and filled it with cold water for tomorrow. Finally she recalled what the nun had said, "You must use the pitcher and basin in the morning. The bathroom is not large enough for everyone." Celie pictured herself at five a.m., dousing her face with icy water in the dark, her second sacrifice as an Augustinian.

At last, the older nun whispered good night and turned off the light. Celie lay in the shadows, listening to the strange sounds of creaking beds, coughs and sneezes, a whimpering across the room, then someone blowing her nose, not once, but three times. Celie wondered why she wasn't crying, too. *I'm in a total fog.*

She gazed up through the dormitory's one uncurtained window and saw the stars. Focusing on them as she prayed, she felt her body begin to relax. Those twinkling lights in the sky were the only familiar sight she had seen all day, a welcome comfort despite the numbness that still gripped her. She wondered why Sister Pauline had never told her what to expect here. The oddities she'd found today . . . yes, they shocked her, and so far, everything seemed much more grim than friendly.

She hoped tomorrow would be a better day, and the day after, too. She closed her eyes and prayed. "Dear God, I want to please You in the weeks ahead. Your will, not mine, be done."

CHAPTER 4

NEW CLASSES, NEW FRIEND

Immediately after entrance day on Sunday, Celie and the other Postulants started college classes that included scripture study, theology, church Latin, and philosophy, a heavy course load. But Celie wasn't worried. She knew she could suffer through them all, because her favorite, English composition, was also part of her class schedule. Since the Bay Area was only a half-hour away, Mrs. Halloway, a professor from UC Berkeley, taught all English courses at the Motherhouse. Rumors whispered that she was very tough on her students, especially freshman.

After turning in two in-class writing assignments during the first week, Celie eagerly waited for the professor's grades on Friday. A rare glow suffused her body and traveled all the way down to her toes when Mrs. Halloway started class by reading not just one but both of Celie's papers aloud, pointing out "the excellent techniques Miss Celia O'Rourke uses."

All week, Celie had noticed a seemingly perennial smile playing on the olive-skinned, brown-eyed girl named Lupe, who sat near her in English class. But now Celie couldn't help but notice that her smile had disappeared. When Celie got up to leave, Lupe was still clutching her paper. As everyone else moved on to their next class, Lupe remained in her chair, staring at the ominous F that hung in the paper's margin.

Celie lingered until the professor had left the room, then approached her classmate. "It's okay," she whispered. "You'll do better next week." She laid her hand on the girl's shoulder.

Lupe pulled away, slapped her paper down on the desk, and folded her arms. "That's easy for you to say! Mrs. Halloway raved about your writing.

She read your poem *and* your story to the class. And I'm sure she'll read more. I, on the other hand, drown in English every year and I always will." She turned, scooped up her books, and started for the door.

"Wait," Celie said. "What if I help you?"

Lupe shook her head. "You can't do anything. Besides, I don't even know you." Her voice was defeated, flat. "I tried and tried all through high school. Every teacher hated my style. If you can even call it a style. Anyway, Ol' Halloway didn't lose any time telling me how much she hates my writing. And you know what? I detest writing. Always have."

"Well, I'd love to show you a few things about writing. But only if you want to. I'd like to get to know you, too. Might be fun." Celie's voice was barely above a whisper, but it was firm.

Lupe turned around, her eyes forlorn. "You'll really help me?" She hesitated. "I guess it couldn't hurt." As if someone had pulled up a window shade in a dark room, her face brightened. "Thanks."

In the weeks that followed, Celie divided her time between finishing her own English assignments early and trying to get Lupe started on hers. But it wasn't easy. Lupe had no interest in creating stories or poems, something Celie couldn't understand. As she watched her new friend in class, Lupe always looked so intense, so interested, but after class, when Celie referred casually to something Mrs. Halloway had said, Lupe's face went blank. Obviously, she'd been faking it throughout the entire class, lost in her daydreams. *How can anyone with that kind of imagination not be able to write?* Celie wondered. Finally, in exasperation, she confronted her friend.

Lupe was incredulous. "You think I have an imagination?"

"Of course you do. Everything you think about during class is material for your next story. Put those thoughts in some kind of order and let your creativity run free. C'mon. What were you thinking about today? You were off on a cloud somewhere. I saw that glazed look in your eyes. You may fool Mrs. Halloway, but you don't fool me."

Lupe stared at Celie. "You've found me out. I've been doing it for years."

Celie grinned. "Yeah, I figured. Maybe that's why your grades haven't been all that great."

"You might have something there," Lupe said, her copper brown eyes turning serious. "I'll try to start by writing down some of my fantasies today. Okay, Teach?"

"Okay! I think we're finally getting somewhere."

After that, every Friday afternoon the two Postulants studied the compositions Mrs. Halloway handed back. When everyone else had left the room, Celie would almost grab Lupe's paper out of her hand and skim it. "C'mon, let's go up on the hill behind the tennis courts and delve into this deeper," she'd say. "You're going to be a writer, after all, Lupe Gonzalez, if it's the last thing we do!" Off they'd go to their favorite spot under the eucalyptus trees, the silver leaves glistening in the breeze as they pored over Lupe's ideas, words, and phrases, turning them into a compelling story. And week by week Lupe's papers gradually improved.

As Lupe's skill and confidence grew, Celie realized her friend needed her help less and less often. One day Lupe said, "Hope I don't hurt your feelings, Teach, but I don't think I need you as much now." At the end of the semester when Lupe showed her the B+ she'd earned, Celie felt an overwhelming sense of pride.

CHAPTER 5

CHRISTMAS GIFTS

December, 1966

Today was the last day of classes at Immaculate Mary Elementary School (IME) before Christmas vacation. Celie planned to collect the children's tests in a few minutes, whisk them off to the playground for lunch, and lay out surprise Christmas goodies for a holiday party this afternoon.

She looked out at the sea of faces before her, fifty-five second graders, bent over their desks, pencils in hand, finishing their reading quizzes, which were always a challenge for the children who spoke only Spanish at home. Many came from immigrant families who had fled dictators in Central and South America as well as from Castro's Cuba. Celie had worked hard to help them master phonics and vocabulary skills during these first three months of the school term.

Manuel, one of her favorites, sat right in front of her desk. Everything about him was round, his chubby face, his black eyes, his stubby fingers, even the tiny medal of the Virgin Mary that hung around his neck. He'd entered the class a month late, unable to speak one word of English.

On that October day, just two months ago, the boy's mother had knocked on Celie's classroom door. Mrs. Cruz was diminutive in size, only reaching Celie's shoulder. Her black wool crepe dress was tailored, its high collar trimmed with lace and its hem falling to about three inches below her knees. Her ebony hair was swept up tightly in a bun, and though her face looked tired, she wore clear red lipstick. Her only ornaments were her small gold earrings and a tiny golden crucifix around her neck. In stilted English, she told Celie how the family had recently left Cuba in the middle of the night with only the clothes on their backs. Then she had abruptly changed the subject, her voice emphatic. "I want him learn English good. Not like me. Please, help, Sister Celia."

Celie couldn't forget the urgency in Mrs. Cruz's jet-black eyes nor the dark circles that rimmed them.

The school day was over, her empty classroom finally quiet. As Celie unplugged the multi-colored blinking lights on the Christmas tree and drew the blinds, she heard a soft knock at the door.

When Celie said, "Come in," she saw Manuel walk into the room, leading his mother by the hand, his other fist pulling along his little sister. Manuel's father followed with measured steps, taking off his charcoal felt hat and nodding respectfully as he stopped at Celie's desk.

"Hello, Sister." Celie recognized the black dress and earrings, but now a smile lit Mrs. Cruz's face. "Sister Celia, we come and wish you Feliz Navidad!"

"Feliz Navidad to you, too!"

Manuel's father nodded as he silently presented her with a large Christmas gift wrapped in dark blue foil with a silver bow. Celie noted how gnarled and dry his hands were, and how his eyes sagged with weariness. Both parents bowed ever so slightly.

"We thank you for help you give our son," said Mrs. Cruz, while Manuel hovered near Celie and the Christmas box, but Mr. Cruz stood off to the side. Celie couldn't help but notice that his dark suit was carefully pressed, his white shirt starched, and his old-fashioned shoes gleamed with new polish. She also noticed that the cuffs of his pants and the sleeves of his jacket were slightly frayed. A miniature gold crucifix decorated his lapel.

Manuel's parents beamed as the small boy spoke up. "You like, Sister? We wrap it special." He pointed at the gift. "For you." His mother's hand closed over his stubby finger.

As Celie unwrapped the present, Manuel wadded up the paper, being careful that no scraps fell to the floor. His little sister still hung onto his right hand, playing with the discarded ribbon. Inside the box was a dark brown desk blotter made of genuine cowhide leather.

"How exquisite!" Celie exclaimed. "You shouldn't have."

"We bring from old country." Mrs. Cruz' voice was sad. "It is our business there, but not now."

Celie saw dejection fill Mr. Cruz' eyes then as he gazed at the floor.

Mrs. Cruz brightened. "Gracias, Sister Celia. Manuel improve so much his English! God bless you. Feliz Navidad!"

Trembling, Celie grasped Mrs. Cruz's hand, then reached for Mr. Cruz's hand as well. "Thank you so much," she said.

These parents, she thought, were a model of courage and sacrifice. How could she accept praise from people who'd given up their homeland to find freedom and education for their little ones in the U.S.?

As Mrs. Cruz picked up her small daughter and the family moved toward the door, saying their goodbyes, Celie couldn't help watching the girl wrap her arms around her mother's neck and nestle her head there, her large brown eyes staring back at the young nun. Celie looked away; then her eyes rested on Mr. Cruz's hand reaching for Manuel's. The boy's face lit up with an angelic smile as he followed his parents out of the room.

Celie shut her eyes as the door closed, determined to banish her wistful thoughts. She must set a solid boundary between the lives of ordinary people and her own. She'd chosen a celibate life, answering God's call, and "her children" would be innumerable—fifty-five second graders this year, at least fifty next year and every year after that.

She glanced up at the clock. Four-thirty. She gathered her teacher's manuals together and rushed across the schoolyard to the convent kitchen.

Today she'd promised to help Sister Rosarita prepare homemade tortillas for the twelve Augustinian nuns who lived in the beige stucco house on Trenton Street in the heart of San Francisco's Latino neighborhood. The tiny nun spoke mostly Spanish, so Celie, hungry for companionship, had learned several Spanish words. Their conversation was stilted as they prepared tonight's simple meal.

All too soon, the period of religious silence began, and Celie hurried from the kitchen to chapel to chant Vespers with the other nuns. By the time dinner—stringy beef and vegetables called "St. Augustine's stew"—was over, with its solemn reading of the life of Saint Theresa of Avila, Celie felt so jumpy she headed back to school to hit tennis balls against the playground's backboard.

The evenings in San Francisco had been cool and damp this week, and the long muslin folds of her white religious habit stuck to her wet skin and perspiration dripped into her eyes as she practiced her forehand. Blinded for

23

a moment by the schoolyard lights, she swung into her backhand stroke and pounded the tennis balls again and again. Fierce emotions erupted inside her—excitement and doubt, fear and elation—all jumbled together, propelling her forward and backward, as she hammered the ball with all her strength. Exhilaration flooded through her as she controlled its trajectory. Soon she was twisting back, reaching for a lob she'd created, then rushing toward the backboard for the ball, moving in rhythm as it bounced. The white coif that covered her shorn hair and framed her face was soon drenched, but Celie didn't care. She loved this time of night. And she loved to manipulate the ball with her racket, trying all the different shots she knew.

The other nuns were upstairs in the convent, putting last-minute items into their suitcases and getting ready for home visits they'd been looking forward to for years, even decades.

Celie had packed her things a week ago.

Even three years and three months away from home seemed like a long time to her. Though she was nervous, she also felt lucky that the Order's Rules were finally changing. For the first time in centuries, Augustinian Sisters everywhere in the world, herself included, would be allowed to spend the holidays with their families.

Every nun Celie knew was eager for the Ecumenical Council's second session to begin again in Rome. This Council was the cause of the Order's recent changes. They'd been hearing for months how religious orders everywhere were testing out the new Vatican II directives, which promised more freedom and enabled the nuns to become closer to the Catholic laity they served.

Celie pummeled the tennis ball again. She needed this exercise. So invigorating! Yet she yearned for someone to practice with, someone who would challenge her and engage her in this exhilarating, athletic dance.

CHAPTER 6

IMPENDING CHANGES

At eight o'clock, Celie entered the recreation room with the other nuns, where they were free to talk for an hour, as long as they "kept their hands busy," according to the Augustinian Rule, "with sewing or mending." Recently the Rule had relaxed a little. Now TV programs were allowed, and Sisters Celia, Rosarita, and Adele sat down to watch *The Ed Sullivan Show*. The singers, dancers, jugglers, and puppets helped them forget the hideous scenes of the ever-present Vietnam War that they'd witnessed earlier on the evening news.

Sullivan over, Celie began to tell the other nuns about a new film she'd seen, *Doctor Zhivago*, which was filled with images of stark Russian winters and wild spring daffodils. Restless during the past few months, she had attended a special viewing for Sisters in the San Francisco Diocese instead of working on lesson plans like the others at Immaculate Mary Convent.

But Celie didn't dare describe the scenes that had affected her so strongly. Sitting in the darkness of the theater, she'd felt her emotions surging as she watched Yuri and Lara's powerful, forbidden love, suppressed for so long, emerge against the tumultuous backdrop of the communist revolution. Maurice Jarre's balalaika theme haunted her, especially at night as she lay in bed. Images of Lara in her scarlet dress trimmed in black lace invaded Celie's thoughts, hot excitement growing within her as she pictured the lecherous Kamarovsky wiping wine onto Lara's lips, then forcing himself on her. . . . Celie lay in the dark, unknown passions coursing through her as she remembered Lara enfolded in Yuri's arms, his mouth devouring hers. Celie's breath quickened, unwanted feelings overwhelming her as her fingers began stroking forbidden places. Finally, perspiration covering her body, a crescendo of release overcame her and she lay spent, hoping for the distraction of sleep.

But this was a grave sin, and in the morning revulsion plagued her. As a teenager in the dark confessional, she'd confessed it often, but once she entered the convent, she had promised God perfect purity. Nevertheless, she seemed helpless to stop herself, no matter how many times she pleaded for God's forgiveness for her sins.

As the nuns asked questions about the film, Celie began a guarded retelling of the plot, but just then Sister Gerald, the convent's Superior, interrupted.

"Sisters, I have some exciting announcements. Most of you will be visiting your homes for two weeks over Christmas vacation, so I'll share them with you now."

Celie couldn't take her eyes off this charismatic nun, a recognized dynamo in the congregation. No taller than five foot four, Sister Gerald carried her muscular frame like a Cherokee princess, her shoulders thrown back in a statuesque posture demanding attention. A smattering of freckles dotted the woman's imposing nose and high cheekbones.

"The parishioners of Immaculate Mary Church," she began, "are planning another Italian Night dinner. We can't turn that invitation down, now, can we?" Her face broke into an impish grin, and the room began to hum with comments.

Celie looked forward to these church get-togethers, when the ladies in the parish stirred giant pots steaming with perfect Italian sauce. She loved to listen to them joke about the antics of their many children. Their stories reminded her of the families of her childhood friends.

Sister Gerald, her brown eyes snapping, broke up the room's prattle with another announcement. "Now, Sisters, for the most important announcement." A hush came over the room. "Our Vicaress General has finalized the changes for our religious habit. Give me a few minutes and I'll change into a sample of our new garb and show you, in person, how we'll look in the near future." Amid the nuns' exclamations of surprise, she gave a conspiratorial grin. "I'll divulge one detail before I go. The white coif that covers our hair will be no more."

Everyone began to talk at once.

Not hide our hair? How strange it would be, Celie thought, to take the coif off for good. She imagined how the older nuns might feel and giggled to herself. *Probably make them feel naked!*

Sister Gerald went on in a more cautionary tone, "The Vicaress General has decided that the new habit won't be ready until next year, but it will not become mandatory then. Those who would rather wear our traditional attire may do so. For a while."

Then she disappeared as the nuns' comments continued to buzz around the room.

Celie exchanged excited remarks with those in her set, but she couldn't help overhearing the negative comments in the circles around her. Some of the older nuns were completely against this sudden, new-fangled relaxation of religious rules and the modernization of Catholic liturgy, especially the introduction of English instead of Latin at Mass. The Ecumenical Council now underway in Rome had demanded these new adjustments.

Celie and most of the younger nuns, however, were eager to try the Augustinian Rule Modifications of 1966, even if they might lead to turmoil. The Vatican's changes, Celie had read, would allow nuns everywhere a wider range of apostolic work. Maybe, she thought, the chance to work in other areas besides teaching. Some religious communities were already permitting members to choose different careers, like social work among prisoners or ministering to the poor. More liberal notions, such as Sisters earning money or living in apartments, were even being discussed on television news programs, but most of the Augustinians Sisters Celie knew were worried about these new "left wing" ideas. Celie wasn't sure yet how she felt.

This new religious garb was also part of *aggornimento*, or "bringing up to date," as Pope John XXIII called his program. The Pope was urging all Roman Catholics to embrace the *spirit* of Jesus' teachings and modify the Catholic Church's emphasis on rules, sin, and rigidity.

Celie was both energized and nervous about facing so many changes at once, but she was also very eager at the prospect of a new habit. It hadn't taken her long to discern how parents and students alike stiffened and drew back from her when she came near. She was convinced that the traditional

Augustinian habit created an unhealthy distance between her and the children she taught and the people of the parish.

Sister Gerald reentered the room and glided around the nuns. She was dressed in the same white muslin habit they were used to, with front and back scapular panels and the cape-like bib called a gimp they'd worn over their shoulders for years—but her dress was *much* shorter. It fell just below her knees.

So much leg showing! Celie saw several nuns put their hands over their mouths, disgust written in their eyes. When she glanced over at Sister Lupe, she breathed a sigh of relief. Lupe looked like a cat who'd snared a mouse. Celie moved next to her, so they could share their mutual delight.

"I know you're used to our ankle-length habit," Sister Gerald was saying in a loud voice, "and our thick black stockings, which almost no one ever sees. . . ." As she went on, her voice fell into the gentler, syrupy tone that only Sister Gerald could create.

As Celie watched, her Superior finessed the older nuns individually, inclining her head to show each one respect as she passed out flyers with an artist's rendering of the new garb. "We're planning to issue secular nylons like these to replace the black stockings." She raised one leg a few inches. "Our shoes will be plain black pumps with stacked heels. They're comfortable and not nearly as expensive as the ones we're wearing now."

Quiet enveloped the room.

"And this shorter black veil will be a lot less trouble than the long, starched one that's always so hard to maneuver, especially on windy days." She moved her head and touched the new veil that only grazed her shoulders. "But as you can see, the white coif will disappear and our hair will show, but only above your forehead and at your temples." A low murmur rolled around the room. "And," she patted the right side of her skirt, "this is one change I'll miss. Our large black rosary will be eliminated." She raised a small beaded rosary. "But it doesn't mean you can't say the rosary and meditate, as we've done for centuries. You can carry it here." She put her hand in her skirt pocket and her smile gleamed as her eyes slowly encompassed everyone in the room.

Someone began to clap, and many others joined in, but most of the older nuns hid their hands under their white scapulars.

28

From the sparkle in her Superior's eyes, Celie surmised that Sister Gerald was as eager as she was for these changes to commence. Celie made her way through the chattering women. She hadn't seen or spoken to Sister Gerald in three days. They'd grown closer over the last twelve months, ever since the older nun had supervised Celie as she taught the lessons she'd created for her second grade class. Celie couldn't wait to get more details about their new religious apparel. Before she reached Sister Gerald, however, the solemn bell announcing the Augustinian Rule of Profound Silence signaled the end of Recreation.

Darn! Now I can't talk to her till tomorrow!

The Rule strictly forbade speaking to another person during the night. No one was allowed to communicate until Recreation, the next morning, which came only after solemn prayers and an early Mass.

Celie had only broken this silence rule once and she would never forget her penance. For seven days, she'd knelt at the entrance to the refectory with her finger over her lips as over a hundred nuns stared and filed past her on their way to breakfast, lunch, and dinner. She had lost face, and feelings of failure clung to her afterwards. *Never again.*

Disappointed now, she folded her hands under her scapular, found her place in line and cast her eyes down as she'd been taught, and obediently followed the others to chapel for the solemn chanting of Compline and Matins, the final night prayers of the Divine Office.

The tiny sanctuary candle gleamed, reassuring Celie of God's presence. Entering the small church, the twelve nuns separated into two lines, one group going to the wooden stalls on the right side, the others, including Celie, kneeling and facing them on the left. Next, Sister Gerald's golden voice intoned the ancient Latin Gregorian chant, *a cappella*, and answering her lofty vibrant strain, all the Sisters rose and began to sing the undulating verses of the Psalms that echoed back and forth, like the rhythm of waves surging toward the shore, then receding.

Celie couldn't help it. Her trepidation about her impending home visit seeped into her thoughts and flowed out and upward in her clear alto voice as she sang this melodious prayer with the others. Laying her worries at the Lord's feet, she mentally translated the Latin words of David's Song into English.

This I declare, that He alone is my refuge,
my place of safety. . . . He is my God.

For he rescues you and protects you. . . .
He will shield you with his wings!

They will shelter you . . . you don't need to be
afraid, nor fear the dangers of the day. . . .

For he orders his angels to protect you wherever you go.

For the Lord says, because he loves me, I will rescue
him; I will make him great (PSALM 91:2–14, NLT).

CHAPTER 7

CHRISTMAS HOME VISIT

December, 1966

As the train jolted to a stop, passengers crowded around the exit. Minutes later, new passengers flooded the aisle, trying to find seats. Celie closed the journal of her poems as a young mother with two children sat down across from her. The woman's black sweater was smudged in front. Her eyes were slits, and an infant nestled in her arms.

Celie couldn't take her eyes off the baby. As he kicked, his little foot tossed off a blue sock, showing his tiny pink toes. Celie reached out to pick up his sock and pull it back on his foot, her fingers lingering there.

The woman's frazzled smile met hers. "Thank you, Sister."

Celie bent her head slightly, hiding her hands underneath her long apron-like white scapular. "Hello."

The second child, a small boy, squirmed at his mother's side and tossed a Golden Book on her lap. The gesture reminded Celie of her little brother Stevie, years ago. Then the infant began to wail and the woman rummaged around in a bag sitting near her feet.

"May I help?" Celie asked, as the train started up.

The mother's eyebrows rose in surprise, but she nodded yes.

Celie reached down to pick up the baby bag and searched inside. She felt a tug on her long white habit and looked down. The little boy was silently demanding her attention. She smiled at him and held out the bottle she'd found in the bag. "Give this to Mama?"

Distrust clouded his eyes, but he reached for the bottle. Then the dimple in his cheek deepened as he gave it to his mother.

"Thank you, Sister—?"

31

"I'm Sister Celia."

"Pleased to meet you. I'm Marie. Handling all this is a challenge," she sighed, "but you seem pretty experienced. With babies."

"I took care of my younger sisters and brother when I was growing up." Celie changed the subject. "Are you going home for Christmas?"

"Yes. My husband just went to Vietnam, so we'll stay with my folks. It's his second tour." The woman's forehead wrinkled, though pride infused her voice.

"I'll keep him in my prayers," Celie said.

"Thank you." Her face brightened. "Actually, I have it easier than a lot of Army wives. My parents are excited about us coming to live with them, and my sisters can't wait. They love to spoil these two." She nodded toward her children. "Are you going home, too, Sister?"

"Yes. It's been a long time since—"

"I bet your family's thrilled."

"Yes." Celie hesitated, trying to smile as an inexplicable melancholy overtook her. "I hope so. . . ." She lowered her gaze again as she'd been trained to do, and heard her Novice Mistress' admonitions floating through her mind. *Augustinian nuns must always walk and talk quietly, and practice custody of the eyes, to rule out worldly distractions, in order to engage in continual prayer.*

At the same time, she found herself examining the folds of her habit. She lifted the crucifix attached to the large rosary hanging from her belt, and, hiding it under the scapular, laid it on her lap. *Please, God, let this visit be happy and fruitful, according to Your Will.* But the baby's cries distracted her.

The young mother immediately rose from her seat. "Sometimes walking up and down does the trick."

Celie watched her take the little boy's tiny hand and guide him up the aisle, while jiggling the baby in her arms at the same time.

. . . the life I chose not to pursue . . .

The train's rumble went on, and soon a male voice called, "Santa Barbara!" Celie nodded goodbye to the young mother who now held her infant tighter as she gathered up her possessions and stood up. After the sliding door opened, she led her little boy down the steps and off the train. He waved back at Celie, and she waved to him.

The train's wheels churned forward again. A few minutes later, the glittering, blue ocean outside became a welcome distraction. The sight of the waves, swirling and crashing, shifted Celie's thoughts back to her childhood. Chasing waves, building sandcastles, the smell of seaweed mixed with salt air. Somewhere out there, dolphins played. She'd glimpsed them once when she was very young.

The sight of the beach evoked other memories, too, memories captured in her carefully selected shell collection, now hidden in a drawer in her convent cell. The last time she'd chosen a shell had been the night she told Mike she was going to become a nun.

A trapped fly suddenly buzzed and flailed where the panes of the train's window overlapped. Celie hated that sound. Flies had often invaded the room she shared with her sisters at home, tormenting her when she longed for sleep in the stifling heat. Though her father had screened the house and ranted to everyone about "closing the damn screen door," the constant in and out of her siblings gave the insects easy access. She'd no sooner drift into a slight sleep filled with angels and fairy godmothers than the noise of a struggling fly would force her back to reality.

Now Celie pushed the window up to free the fly, but it was stuck. As she watched it struggle, her annoyance strangely began to fade. She felt sorry for it, doomed to spend the rest of its short life trapped between transparent barriers, its curled black legs almost motionless.

Celie averted her gaze and stared out at the giant oaks punctuating slope after slope of green hills as the late afternoon sun cast an unearthly glow. A formation of birds flew overhead, dark silhouettes against the sky. Leaning back on the seat and feeling the rhythm of the rails soothing the chronic ache in her shoulders, she closed her eyes. Words began forming in her mind—a common occurrence when unwanted emotions seeped through the layers of her reserve. She dozed.

When she awoke, the words emerged again, framing themselves into a poem. She found her pencil and opened her journal. She had to ensnare them before they vanished:

Golden hills hide empty homes of wrens and deer,
Shifting sands toss half-shells on the beach.

Earthen lairs lie bare of furry beasts,
Labyrinthine warrens lead to who knows where . . .

Upon the day
when creatures reach out to return,
will welcome await?
Will family recognize, respect, hold harmless, hug?

Or will the kin in old house walls, so used to needy, stumbling
    steps,
close off
and not accept,
when young migrate to sacred homes
beyond the place
where they grew up?

Would Dad and Mom treat her differently? Would Colleen and Maureen? Her younger siblings? Would they finally listen to her? Her students and the parents at the parish always nodded politely to her, as if she lived up on a pedestal, her words drops of holy water gracing their lives. She didn't deserve it. Did they actually believe she was sacred and wise? Maybe it was her habit that mesmerized them . . .

The countryside was giving way to the San Fernando Valley, then the crowded cities of greater Los Angeles, which were more familiar to Celie. But the rusted cars, rickety fences, trash-filled streets, and houses boxed together surprised her. This wasn't the Southern California she remembered. A sad feeling she couldn't quite name began to throb in her shoulders once more.

As the train pulled into Union Station, she saw a familiar figure standing in the distance on the platform. The train slowed, and she leaped up to wait by the door before it creaked to a stop, her packages and carry-on bag in her arms. She glimpsed her father again through the window. He'd promised to take off early to pick her up near where he worked in the office of a local factory, "keeping the books straight," as he called it. He was wearing a white shirt, striped tie, and a dark blue suit, but his wavy black hair was streaked with new gray strands.

Home, where the seven remaining members of the O'Rourke family lived in a Spanish-style house with red-tiled roof on the fringes of eastern Los Angeles, was about forty minutes away now.

Celie rushed toward her dad, dropped her bundles, and wrapped both her arms around him. His shoulders were hard and tense, his voice quiet, "Hi, honey, how was your trip?"

"Incredibly slow. But then I've never been known for my patience."

His smile wavered as he gently pushed her back to look at her. "It's still hard to get used to you in that outfit, with your hair all covered. The freckles on your nose are the same, though." He touched its tip lightly.

Surprised at his brief show of affection, she felt a glow deep inside. He'd always been so reserved and strict when she was growing up. She and her sisters had attributed it to his Marine years. *Semper Fi* was his favorite phrase. He had served in Japan when Celie was a baby.

He gathered up her suitcase now and turned toward the parking lot. "C'mon," he called back to her. "The Beast is over here."

She flashed him a smirk. "I can't wait."

"Okay, enough insults. Don't know why you kids hate my station wagon. I think American Motors is a good brand."

"Somehow I've heard it all before, Dad," she said with a grin, noticing a faint twinkle in his eyes.

He was silent on the short ride home. Celie had never known him to be any other way. Except on the rare occasions when he gave one of his famous philosophical lectures on how you should live your life, he only talked politics or baseball. She'd never forget his fatherly speeches about faith and morals that included Legion of Decency film ratings, church catechism answers expounded for an hour, and, of course, teenage dating rules. She still knew all his worn out clichés, like "Don't kid yourself" and "Be a leader, not a follower." He demanded strict manners at the table, too.

Just to break the silence and see what would happen, Celie introduced a new topic. "My class is doing really well."

"Oh? That's right. Your mother gives me your letters. Second grade, isn't it? Good."

"The parents surprised me with Christmas gifts—they're so grateful their children are learning English. Some have lived in the U.S. for just a couple of months."

"That's great, honey."

Silence again.

She tried again. "How're Maureen and Colleen?"

"Maureen's so wrapped up in her college classes she hardly ever leaves her room. 'Cept for that sorority. We never see Colleen. She still goes out with that good-for-nothin' Don. He's only gotten himself kicked out of three schools—"

"And Mom?"

"Still smokes too much. But she sure is good with the budget. Can't believe how she manages to squeeze it to buy everything. Your mother's quite a woman." He turned to look at her. "Oh, and she said to tell you—she won't be home till dinnertime."

Celie felt a little lightheaded. She tried to quell the nausea that always followed.

Her father was still speaking. "A meeting down at the church. She's doing a good job working for Monsignor Walsh. He was promoted. Did you hear?"

"Oh, no, I didn't. When?"

"Few weeks ago. Big celebration at the parish. Five hundred parishioners showed up. Your mom was head of the committee. Quite a wing-ding."

"That's great." Celie was mildly aware that Dad was talking more than usual. She rolled down her window and tried to take deep breaths. In elementary school, she'd experienced recurring dizzy spells, even fainted several times, but the doctors had never found the cause. Mom had told her over and over to ignore it. One day Celie had overheard her telling Aunt Lorraine, "I think it's Celie's way of getting attention." Now she gulped in the air, hoping if she calmed down, the vertigo might pass.

When they drove up, the house appeared much smaller than she remembered. Like the houses she'd glimpsed from the train, its white stucco was blotched with new gray patches, its shutters faded. But the square patch of crabgrass in front was green and manicured and neat. She turned to her father. "Your geraniums and camellias are blooming up a storm. Like always. Who mows the lawn with me gone?"

He stopped the car. "I recruited Jody and Stevie. They're old enough. I've got Stevie digging up the dandelions, too, but he sure throws a fuss. Maybe it's time to give Mo that job." He sounded bushed. Dropping her off at the front sidewalk, he drove the car up the long driveway into the garage.

As Celie walked up the steps and opened the front door, it occurred to her that only guests ever used this entrance. Family and friends always used the back door. Her stomach clutched at the thought.

She surveyed the house as she entered and saw a new, chrome-legged table and chairs in the kitchen nook. But the turquoise-green furniture and matching flowered wallpaper in the living and dining rooms were the same as ever. Had the sofa always been so tattered, the cushions so flaccid? Not even a Christmas tree was up, and the rooms smelled smoky. Her dad came in, carrying her suitcase.

"Seems deserted," she said. "No Christmas decorations? Where is everybody?"

"Don't know. Your mom's hardly ever home. Nobody tells me all the comings and goings around here. Remember? They'll be back eventually. Put your things in your old room. You haven't seen our new den since we fixed it up. C'mon back when you're ready. Help yourself to the fridge, too."

His shoulders sagged as he poured himself a large goblet of red wine. Then he disappeared, and Celie was home alone.

CHAPTER 8

A WELCOME HOME?

Mom tugged at the sash of her blue checked apron and tied it behind her. "You look *so* exhausted, dear. How was the long train ride?" She put her arms around Celie, clasping the black belt that hung around her daughter's waist under the long white scapular. "Why, you're skin and bones. Can't be eating enough. And it's been *so long* since we've seen you."

Celie listened to her mom's standard exaggerations and inhaled the rancid odor of stale cigarettes. Mom's cheek felt cool but soft as she squeezed Celie hard.

She pulled away. "I haven't lost any weight, Mom. And you and Dad came up to the Motherhouse last summer."

Now Colleen and Maureen burst through the back door and converged on their younger sister. "Hey, look who's here!" First Colleen hugged her, then Maureen.

Maureen turned to their mother. "When's dinner?" she asked. "I have a meeting tonight. Sorority stuff. A mixer with one of the big frat houses. Like my outfit?"

Maureen had barely glanced at Celie. She was busy holding up her new purple sweater to show it off, asking Mom to touch its soft angora.

"It's lovely, honey," their mother said. "Dinner will be soon. Tuna casserole, and it's all made. I just have to put it in the oven. Come and show me what else you bought."

As Mom and Maureen hurried out of the den, still chattering, Colleen flounced down on the vinyl couch, as far away as possible from their dad,

39

who was sitting in his corner chair sipping wine and watching the game on TV.

"So, Celie," Colleen drawled, "what's new in the land of nuns and priests?"

"Don't be disrespectful," Dad said.

"I'm not. Jeez, I can't even joke around." Colleen tossed her patent leather heels off, pulled her feet up, and folded her arms around her knees.

Dad's voice was like gravel. "That's a new sofa. How many times have I told you not to put your feet on it?"

"It's not new. We got it second-hand," Colleen mumbled. Suddenly she got up, picked up her heels, and strode out of the room.

"That girl—" Shaking his head, Dad left, too.

Celie sat back on the couch and watched the TV flicker. The fuzzy picture refocused as L.A. Lakers, their brown muscled legs and flashy gold uniforms, streaked across the screen. She remembered the games she'd watched in this room with Mike, his arm slowly sliding behind her shoulders, his fingers grazing her arm. Causing a shiver whenever he touched her—

Dad walked back into the den, carrying a martini this time. Celie stifled a gasp. She had never seen him drink more than two beers or a glass of wine, twice a week at the most. He settled back into his chair, eyes glued to the TV, which suddenly flashed to a "breaking news" report. Hippies like the ones Celie had glimpsed once in San Francisco were marching with large placards around a fire. The police were dragging them away from a screaming crowd, even strong-arming some with batons. *So violent.* Celie couldn't watch anymore.

"So, Dad, how's work?"

"See that? Those slackers are burning the American flag! I don't care how much they're against the war—"

Celie recognized that crazy stare. She'd seen it when she was little, way too often.

He took a swallow, then sucked on the green olive. "Look at those—"

"Do you think we'll decorate a tree while I'm home? You know, get into the Christmas spirit?"

"Ask your mother."

She remembered that growl, too.

She got up and wandered into the kitchen, where Mom and Maureen were still talking. There was a new, red cat clock on the wall, its solemn eyes moving back and forth, impassively examining the family scene. If it could talk, what would it reveal? *Creepy.*

Maureen looked a lot like Mom now, Celie decided, with her dark brown hair cut short. Except she'd lost weight, and her slim hips filled out her jeans perfectly, not the way Mom's pants pulled at her thighs. Celie listened to their brief conflicting views about the latest mini hemlines, and suddenly it dawned on her that everybody but Dad spoke in sentence fragments, something she'd never noticed before. Trivia seemed to fill the air—half-spoken bits of conversation wedging their way in between rushed comments.

A forgotten feeling began to envelop her, a sort of cool, transparent distance that separated her from them. It was as if she were living in a bubble. Invisible. The sensation urged her on toward her old haven, her bedroom.

But suddenly Maureen waved her hands in front of Celie's face. "The last thing *you* need to know about is short skirts," she said with a laugh. "Don't you love our new color scheme?" She swirled around, pointing at the white walls accented with crimson, the white print curtains, and the enameled red cupboards. The black and white tiled counters looked the same, though. "Bet this is quite a change from your convent." Waiting for her sister to reply, Maureen pulled out a chrome chair with a red cushion, sat down and spread out checked placemats on the gray Formica table.

Holding herself rigid, Celie nodded. *Better not say too much.* "Looks neat," she said approvingly. No one ever challenged Maureen's artistic opinions.

Maureen stood up. "I have to put these new clothes away." Had she even heard Celie? "Hey, Celie, why don't you pitch in? Set the table."

But Mom interjected, "Maureen, I need you to go to the store. And pick up Jody and Stevie, too. They're at the park."

"Where'd Colleen go?" Celie asked.

"Oh, I'm sure she went to lie down." Mom was washing pots in the sink, gazing out the window. "That girl works hard, you know. She gets up before seven and takes a bus all the way into L.A. to work for those attorneys. Doesn't get home until six. They must be pleased. Did she tell you about her big raise?"

Celie thought about the convent bell tolling at five every morning. *What's the big deal about seven o'clock?* But she bit her tongue.

41

Mom was still talking. "Honey, did I tell you about your cousin Sally? Now *she's* a redhead that turns heads. All grown up. You wouldn't recognize her from that scrawny kid. Tall, slim, *and* stunning. Going to law school, too, but she's still active at St. John's parish. Says she wants to be an ecclesiastical lawyer. Whatever that is."

Celie listened, pressing her lips together as she always had while Mom praised everyone else but her. Her fingers grasped her rosary under her scapular, and it occurred to her how consoling the silence at the convent could be.

Mom headed to the dining room, spreading out a tablecloth while she enumerated the exciting men in Sally's life as Celie opened a cupboard, lifting out the old Melmac plates. Mom walked back into the kitchen to find Dad pouring another martini. When he left without a word, Mom stared silently out the window at the steel garbage cans.

Celie could hear the cat clock ticking, ticking . . .

"I need to do something about—" Mom began, then, "Celie, go get Colleen, would you? I want her to put the trash out and take the clothes off the line. Oh, no! I forgot to make a salad." She opened the refrigerator. "Hmm. Well, I've got pineapple and cottage cheese. Ach, I didn't remind Maureen to buy lettuce."

"Okay." Celie set the last dish on the table and slipped away.

She found Colleen hiding out in the bedroom, reading a magazine Celie'd never seen before. The front cover said *Cosmopolitan*. Her sister didn't look up.

"Don't be upset," Celie said. "Dad is Dad. But he does seem more tired. And more crotchety than I remember, too."

Colleen put the magazine down, slouching on the bed. Her nylons lay in a mound on the floor. "Easy for you to say. He's tons more spaced out than when you lived here. You don't know the half of it."

Celie sat down. "What do you mean?"

"He detests his job. But that's nothing new. He's drinking much more. So I steer clear of him. And Mom's never home. She wants Maureen and me to do everything. You got out of here just in time. Good planning, Celie."

Celie nodded. "Yes, I noticed his drinking. But you've never gotten along with Dad." She patted her sister's shoulder. "I love your new image, though. It's really professional. How're the attorneys treating you?"

"Good. I like secretarial. Got another raise, too."

"Yeah, Mom was raving about it a minute ago."

"She was? She's never said a thing to me, and Dad just spouts his endless one-liners. 'Don't kid yourself,' 'Money won't make you happy.' Et cetera, et cetera." She smoothed her knit green skirt over her thighs and picked up her black heels. "I feel so young around those L.A. lawyers. But these suits make me seem older."

Celie pointed to her high heels. "How do you ever walk in those spindly, pointy-toe things?"

"Wanna trade, like we used to?" Colleen's face broke into her old grin. "C'mon, let me try on your granny shoes."

"I can't set foot in yours. Hurts my feet to look at them."

"Oh, c'mon, you're always so proper. Ever since you put that habit on, I don't recognize you anymore." She placed one of her shoes against Celie's foot. "'Course they'd be more 'in' without those ugly black nylons."

Celie took off her high-buttoned shoes, and Colleen paraded around in them admiring herself in the full-length mirror. "What a trip! These low stacked heels are just too weird." She flashed her grin again. "I don't know. . . . What do you think? I *guess* I prefer mine. Now, you walk in *my* heels."

Celie shook her head, but got up anyway a minute later to please her sister. She took only a few steps in Colleen's shoes, but soon took them off. It was all too foreign. She'd never worn such high heels, not even to her senior prom. Wasn't the style back then. Good thing, too. Her five-foot, seven-inch frame had always worried her. But Mike was six foot two, so there had been nothing to stress about.

She ran her fingers down the long, pointed heels. "Do you walk on these all day?"

"All day."

"Dinner's ready!" Mom's voice reverberated down the hall and into their bedroom.

It was Celie's turn to grin. "I guess Mom hasn't lost her screech."

"No. Vibrant as ever." Colleen's blue-green eyes shone, and Celie noted how striking she'd become. Her new Cleopatra eyeliner and mascara accentuated her thick eyelashes. Rosy cheeks and a buxom figure, but not chunky like Mom. Dark eyebrows, trimmed and lined, and curly short hair teased high in the latest bubble cut. Her coloring was like Dad's, though otherwise they were worlds apart.

"*Vibrant.* That's Mom." Celie winked. "I like your adjective."

They switched shoes and headed for the bathroom to wash up.

CHAPTER 9

A FAMILY DINNER

"So how does it feel to be home?" As Maureen ladled two small tablespoons of casserole onto her plate next to a large mound of salad, Colleen caught Celie's eye from across the table and mouthed the word "diet."

"I can't answer that yet, but ask me again in two weeks."

"So weird. Seeing you in those big, heavy clothes. Aren't you hot?" asked Stevie, now a fidgety ten-year-old.

"That's the way nuns always dress, Stevie," Mom said. "I just talked to Sister Superior down at church yesterday. Now *she's* a model nun, if I ever saw one. The parish adores her."

Celie studied her fork and spoon. She might as well be one of the crowded lilies in the dining room wallpaper. Mom was really laying it on now. Celie remembered how many times she'd listened to these stories, the interminable accolades her mother laid at the feet of people she hardly knew. Maybe the furniture had changed a bit here, but everything else seemed pretty much the same.

Her mother's words droned on, "Even *she* said it's not easy being a nun. She admitted it's probably the hardest challenge God can ask." Mom turned her head. "Oh, and by the way—Celie, are you listening? I never know for sure . . . always a daydreamer. Since you were small."

"Yes." Celie could feel an old tension settling into her back and across her shoulders. Daydreaming was anathema in the O'Rourke family. "I'm listening."

"Well, the whole parish knows you're home. They'll want to talk to you when we go to church on Sunday."

"Don't you get to show your hair ever?" Jodie cut in. Almost fourteen, she flipped her long brown surfer bangs behind one ear. "I mean, is your hair still the same? Just as red and just as—"

"Straight?" Colleen grinned.

"Always straight as a board. Grandpa's cliché," Maureen chimed in. "Remember when we were little, Colleen? She screamed when Mom curled it. Never forget the first time Mom used that new Toni Home Permanent on Celie. She cried all day, squealing, 'The smell's in my eyes.' Over and over. How can a smell get in your eyes?" Maureen exchanged a smirk with Colleen.

Celie remembered that acrid odor well and how her eyes had burned for two days. She must've been only five when she got that first home permanent. She'd wriggled around on the kitchen table gasping for air, afraid she couldn't breathe, while her sisters held their noses and laughed at her.

Colleen scrutinized her plate, but Maureen turned toward Mom. "The Toni Home Permanent never did any good, did it? Everyone said Colleen and I looked like Shirley Temple, but Celie's hair would never curl. Grandpa O'Rourke was right. Straight as a board."

As everyone else in the family snickered, Celie tried to force the corners of her mouth up. *But why try?* No one was looking her way. They were talking about her as if she weren't there, anyway. She wished she could magically vanish. She remembered how many times she'd made this same wish, right at this table. *No, nothing's changed here.*

Maureen wouldn't quit. "Not to change the subject, but has anyone told you who just got engaged? His first initial is M. Bet you can't guess."

Celie grabbed her glass of milk, but it tipped over. *Great! Now I've done it. Why did I have to sit next to Dad? He hates messes at the table. Always has.*

A massive white puddle spread out next to his coffee cup. Everyone was suddenly silent. Dad sipped his martini, glaring ahead, as Mom popped up, ran over to his place with her napkin, and mopped up the milk. "No problem, no problem," she murmured.

His eyes were impassive, but he puckered his lips and exhaled through his teeth.

"No one *we* know," Maureen went on, "Mike's fiancée, I mean." Celie had forgotten how relentless her older sister could be. "I heard she's nothing to look at. Big surprise. He was never very particular."

Celie gripped her glass hard. She wanted to throw it at the wall across the room and watch it splinter all over her sister.

Mom was still sopping up the milk puddle with napkins. "Yes, well," she said, "what was he going to do? I forgot about that. And Celie's hair too." She hurried back to her place and served up more tuna and noodles to Stevie, her words rising and falling as if she were talking to kindergartners. "Sure gave me trouble. Celie was the only one who didn't have natural curls. I'd dress you girls up and create all your ringlets, easy as could be. But Celie? Her hair always drooped. Spoiled the whole picture of us on Sundays." Finally she looked at Celie. "Well, you don't have to worry about that anymore, do you?"

Mollie, who was eight years old now, interrupted. "I never spill my milk anymore, do I, Mama? Does *my* hair droop, Mama?"

"No, *you* haven't made a mess in a long time and I'm so proud of you, Mollie. Of course your hair doesn't droop."

Maureen wasn't finished. "So, Celie, what do you think about M?"

Celie shook her head. She knew they were trying to trap her. She steadied her voice. "I've chosen a new life. Why shouldn't he? That was over three years ago, anyway."

She spent the next few minutes pushing overcooked vegetables around on her plate while they talked about other things. She couldn't eat, but leaving food uneaten was against the rules—another family drama she wanted to avoid.

Thoughts of dinners in the convent refectory came to her mind. The nuns eating in silence while someone read a saint's inspiring life. She often finished early there, rising from her place to wash the others' dishes with one of the small hand-mops in the aluminum pans filled with tepid water and sitting on the tables. In the beginning, she'd worried if this practice was sanitary, but she'd never had any trouble eating. She'd never had trouble anywhere except in this house.

As if reading her thoughts, Colleen mimicked Mom's voice, "Better clean your plate, Celie!" She and Maureen tittered. "Remember how she wouldn't ever finish her dinner when she was little? You sure were stubborn, Celie." Another laugh, and Colleen ranted on. "When I think back, I can still picture you sitting in the dark in the dining room. We'd be ready for bed and you'd *still* be right here. You said you'd get sick if you ate your lima beans. Well, that was pretty lame. I thought you'd think up something more original. But you just sat there night after night. Did you ever taste *any* of Mom's desserts?"

No wonder she still refused dessert. The doughnuts offered after lunch at the Motherhouse never tempted her as they did the other nuns. Besides, the last thing she needed was a reprimand from her Novice Mistress at weigh-in time. She'd witnessed that scene often enough; too many Sisters put on alarming amounts of weight by eating not one, but several stale doughnuts each afternoon.

Maureen cut into Celie's memories. "You really missed out, you know." She turned toward the head of the table. "Mom, I can still taste your chocolate cakes and your lemon meringue pies. We had 'em every Saturday. You were such a great cook."

Mrs. O'Rourke beamed. "What do you mean, 'were'?"

"The whole kitchen smelled absolutely scrumptious," Colleen added. "I could hardly wait to eat your gingerbread. Celie, do you even remember Mom's desserts?"

Celie mumbled a sarcastic retort—she couldn't stifle it—and concentrated on the mound of noodles on her plate near the cold peas she still detested, though she always ate them now. Otherwise, the casserole meals served regularly at the convent weren't much different from her family's meals. Except for the hotdog buns the Motherhouse frequently served instead of real bread or biscuits.

Maureen leaned closer to Celie. "What did you say? We can't hear you."

"At least I didn't gain much weight as a teenager—"

"Now that's enough." Mom glared at Celie. "I'm surprised at you. Let's not go on about people's weight, girls. It's not charitable."

CHAPTER 10

A FRIEND FROM THE PAST

The doorbell rang and Mom rushed to the front door. She'd become used to Dennis's unexpected visits when Celie was in high school, but his appearance tonight was a real surprise.

"You're a little late, aren't you?" she chided him as she led him to the dining room. "We've already said grace. You've stayed away too long—your timing used to be better than that!"

Celie had known Dennis since they were both nine years old. Dennis' green eyes, upturned nose, and muscular frame overwhelmed her now with feelings of excitement and ease.

He grinned at Mom. "The best meals I've ever had were the ones I mooched here. But getting one always took a helluva lot of careful timing." He brought a chair over and stood next to Celie. "How're you doin', Red? I heard through the grapevine you were in town." He took a step back and studied her habit for a minute. "Wow, you sure look different."

Celie had weathered her family's sharp reactions to her appearance almost from the first day she'd entered the convent. Today, however, she was suddenly aware that, despite the habit she wore, she didn't feel like a nun around Dennis. She just felt like an old friend. She stood up to hug him. "You've changed, yourself," she said. "Taller, thinner, so tanned. How's the pitching arm?"

"Gettin' stronger all the time." He held it up, bent his elbow at a right angle, and flexed his bicep. Then he peered over Celie's veiled head and gave her dad a playful salute. "How's it goin', Mr. O'Rourke?"

Dad's face beamed, his first real smile since Celie had come home. "Fine, Dennis. Have a seat and tell us your Dodger news. Join me in a drink."

"Can't, Mr. O'Rourke. I'm in training. But thanks, anyway."

To the O'Rourkes, Dennis was a celebrity since he had signed with the Dodger farm team right after high school. Now, as Mom and Dad urged him to talk about the baseball team, he told story after story and answered their questions all through dinner. With head bowed, he trudged around the dining room showing them exactly how he'd walked off the mound after a lost game. He pantomimed all his various pitches in slow motion and his favorite batting stance, too. Sitting down again, he spent more time describing his latest homerun, then elaborated on his most cherished memory, the first day he'd put on the uniform.

"I'll never forget it." He nudged Celie, sitting beside him, kidding her like old times. "It was almost a religious ceremony," he said. "Now I know why so many ball players frame their uniforms after they retire."

A lump of tuna casserole remained on Celie's plate, and now she noticed how the fork in her hand hadn't moved. Dennis was a Dodger now. She hadn't seen him in over three years, and she'd *never* seen him so excited.

He pulled photos out of his wallet and shoved them into her hands. Soon Celie was passing them to her sisters, who passed them on to Mom.

"Ooh," Mom gushed, "you're so handsome in your uniform!"

Celie squirmed. Mom's high, phony tone always jarred her.

But Dennis didn't notice. He talked on and on about a fourteen-inning game he'd pitched last year and told them how the team had doused him and everyone else in the locker room with cheap wine afterwards. He described the first day he'd walked—"scared shitless"—to the pitcher's mound. "No one was more surprised than me when I turned it into a no-hitter," he said, wonder still coloring his voice. He reminisced, too, about the hick towns the farm team played in and the shabby hotel rooms he stayed in, and how one day he had hurled ball after ball in the driving rain, mud sloshing around his cleats, only to lose the game in the last inning.

"But it's worth it," he concluded. "All the tired nights and dirty motels, the chilling cold and suffocating heat, traveling from one hick town to the next. It's worth it because finally, one day, you put on the uniform and you pitch a winning game!"

The grin Celie remembered so well lit up his entire face. He'd shared his baseball dream with her when he was ten years old. Now he was living it.

He turned to her. "Celie, it must be something like that with you, too. Right?"

She tried to smile, but it took several minutes before she could frame a reply. Then she quickly changed the subject, and, after the family finished dinner, Dennis hugged her goodbye.

Later that night, back in her old, familiar bedroom and relieved that Maureen and Colleen had both gone out, she changed into her long white nightgown. Gazing at Maureen's photos, still crowding the shelf above the dresser, she suddenly noticed her senior prom photo. She was sure she'd hidden the picture away in a box before she left home. Had Maureen or Colleen taken it out again? On purpose?

She would never forget her lavender formal, never forget the lace and the long, billowing skirt. The hairdresser had swept her auburn hair up, cascades of curls almost hiding her small tiara of sparkling rhinestones. She and Mike were standing close together, his arm around her waist, his tux accentuating his broad shoulders and blending with the shiny black Chevy that gleamed in the background. He'd borrowed his dad's car. Lean and brawny, he looked so much older than twenty and was certainly tall enough to make her feel feminine despite her height.

Celie touched her lips, remembering how he'd kissed her on prom night, and a surge of warmth ran through her body. She'd allowed Mike to caress her more than usual that night. When his hands had reached for her breasts, she had suddenly pressed in closer to him, his protruding desire filling her with urgency. But then she'd turned away, gasping with passion, her will not to sin stronger than these new sexual feelings. The pastor's interminable sermons still played in her head: *Girls are always responsible if their boyfriends become aroused. His mortal sin becomes yours, and you both face horrendous punishment in hell.*

Filled with desire now, she forced her thoughts away from that memory and focused on the prom photo again, studying the lavender carnation she'd placed in Mike's lapel and the striking purple orchid he'd slipped around her wrist. She'd never seen this exotic flower before that night. Yes, she would always remember—

But Mike was engaged now.

Celie turned away from the framed photo.

Switching the lamp off, she lay for hours trying to sleep, the day's conversations spinning around in her head like the carousels she'd ridden as a child. She looked up at the familiar framed picture of Christ, visible in the streetlight coming through the window. It had fascinated her when she was a girl. Back then, Jesus' eyes seemed to follow her, no matter where she went, making her feel safe, especially when night noises and nightmares frightened her. She squeezed her eyes shut now, clutching her pillow and her rosary, trying to figure out why she couldn't stop her tears.

It can't be Mike. I haven't thought of him in months.

Images of today's events still whirled through her mind. Dad, Mom, her older sisters . . . not much had changed. She'd just forgotten or maybe she'd hoped way too much, but she was still the target of ridicule by the whole family. Even becoming a nun would never change that. She understood that now. And when her sisters doled it out, she still faded away to nothing around them, like Alice's Cheshire Cat. Except she couldn't paste that enigmatic smile on her face anymore. All she felt was a recurring ache inside, an old wound that wouldn't heal.

Nothing's changed here except me. That's the difference. And Dad's drinking more.

But Dennis has changed. I've never seen him so happy.

Celie stared up at the shadows on the ceiling, letting her sisters' taunts push away the sharp edge of Mike's impending marriage. They'd made sure she knew. She turned over, trying to pray away a persistent feeling of rejection that clung to her like a disease. She tried suppressing her favorite memories, but they flooded back. Watching the sunsets as beach bonfires flared. Winning the state poetry award in her senior year. Cuddling next to Mike at hotrod races.

Yesterday on the train, she'd considered phoning him just to say hello. *That won't happen now.*

Amidst it all, Dennis' question resonated over and over in her mind. *It's worth it because finally, one day, you put on the uniform and you pitch a winning game! Celie, it must be something like that with you, too. Right?*

She hadn't been able to answer him, not really. She'd felt so empty. She'd tried to fake a smile, and when he'd pressed her for details about her life as a nun, she'd searched for something positive to say. Had he seen through her? Even if she'd found the right words, what could she tell him, other than the simple phrases she'd finally managed? How could she make anyone understand her life as a nun?

Then a completely new realization flooded through her. There was *so* much work and effort and activity in her life. But where was her winning game? *Where was her joy?*

CHAPTER 11

THE RETREAT

March, 1967

Celie tried to match her breathing to the soothing pace of the surf—an old remedy she'd learned as a child to banish the anxieties that made her feel dizzy. How else could she silence the questions swirling through her mind?

Sister Gerald had just parked the silver Pontiac in front of a rambling, Spanish-style retreat house by the sea. Celie knew her Superior was waiting for her to open the passenger door. But all she wanted to do was sit and listen to the waves. She hadn't heard their peaceful cadence in years.

The older nun carefully set the emergency brake, then took Celie's hand. Her fingers were warm. "Ready, Sister Celia?"

The words cut into Celie's thoughts. Her shoulders quivered.

"I hope you find your answer here," Sister Gerald said. "I'll try to accept your choice. Whatever it is." Her quiet tone calmed Celie as she flashed her familiar smile. "You're a natural," she added. "I've seen you in the classroom with the children, and I've seen how the parishioners warm up to you, too. You transmit *real* Christianity, Sister Celia." She paused. "I do know one thing, though. Decisions happen. You can't force them. Of course you're nervous, with renewal of your vows only three months away. But take it easy." She squeezed Celie's hand again. "Your decision will come in its own way, in its own time. Just relax, my dear."

Celie twisted on the hot vinyl seat and eased her hand away. This Cherokee woman's exotic good looks and mystical ideas intrigued her, yet they also made her feel uncomfortable.

Outside, a seagull took to the sky. Celie watched it soar and circle overhead. Wings spread wide, the bird coasted down, almost floating, to a jagged rock. It perched alone there, safe from the crashing waves. Perhaps in solitude, she, too, would find sanctuary. A line from the Bible she'd chanted that morning gave voice in her soul:

God, my rock and my refuge . . . the waves of
destruction surround me (2 SAMUEL 22:3,5, NLT).

Leaning her head back on the seat, Celie closed her eyes for a long moment. "Relax?" she said aloud. "I don't know what that means anymore. That's the trouble. I spend endless hours going over it all, back and forth in my mind. I feel guilty, too, that I'm even considering giving this life up. I try to sleep, but I wake up exhausted."

The older nun gave her a hug. "I know. Take your time, Sister."

Celie welcomed Sister Gerald's embrace. She'd never been close to her mother, and right now, more than anything else, she needed a mother's comfort.

"You've been in this life three and a half years," Sister Gerald continued. "You're not even twenty-two. You don't have to leave yet, and you don't have to decide this weekend whether to renew your vows for another year."

When Sister Gerald's arms tightened around her, Celie moved toward the door. "Thanks for your advice, Sister. I've got some serious thinking to do, and I'd better get on with it." She climbed out of the car, suitcase in hand, managing a weak smile as she waved goodbye, her black veil fluttering in the wind.

As a bent, wrinkled nun led Celie to her room, she glimpsed the sepia photographs lining the hallway. Turn-of-the century ladies in beribboned pompadours and flowing dresses and holding parasols trimmed with lace sat on a broad porch and gazing out at the ocean. *Sixty years ago, this Santa Cruz retreat house must've been a lavish California hotel,* she thought.

Except for a laywoman who glanced her way and then closed her door, the old house seemed empty now. Celie found her room restful but spare. An ivory chenille bedspread covered the single bed, and over it hung a crucifix made of driftwood. The mahogany floors gleamed and, hanging from a wrought iron rod, white lace curtains billowed in the ocean breeze. Celie's gaze converged on the only colors in the room, orange poppies and deep purple alyssum in a glass vase, wildflowers gathered from the surrounding hills. She'd glimpsed them on Pacific Coast Highway during her ride south from the convent in San Francisco.

She carefully unpacked her things and began to undress. She would be anonymous here among nuns, priests, and Catholic lay people. It was a way to free her thoughts so she could consider her future. Unlacing her granny shoes, she stepped out of them, then peeled off her thick dark stockings and stuffed them into the pockets of her long slip. Loosening the white coif that covered her auburn hair, she took it off and hung it, along with her white Augustinian habit and the large bulky rosary, in the closet. She smoothed out her black muslin veil and folded it away with her shoes and belt in the old chest nearby.

The sound of waves called to her. She splashed her face with cold water at the sink and quickly dressed in the pair of jeans and a navy top she'd secretly borrowed from the parish rummage sale box. Her outfit wasn't much different from the clothes she'd worn only a few years ago in high school. Grabbing an old madras jacket, she left the aging retreat house and climbed over the hilly sand dunes to the beach below.

No one was around. She ran to the sparkling surf and slipped her feet into the cold waves.

"So beautiful!" she whispered aloud. "Such a long time." The marbled green water eddied around her ankles as she watched the blazing sun begin its slow descent into the sea. A minute later, she spied a man way off in the distance, walking on the beach. Strange—he was wearing a business suit. He was tall, with broad shoulders. Soon he became a speck. Then the falling shadows erased him from the horizon altogether.

Invigorated by the salty air, Celie took a deep breath then began to search for shells, a pastime she'd cherished since childhood. But the sands were stripped clean today. Only stray pieces of brown and gold seaweed littered the beach. Disappointed, she sat on the warm sand to face her thoughts. So much to consider. . . . She started with her trip home at Christmas. Why had it changed her?

In two weeks, she'd managed to see everyone—her parents, her grand-parents, all four of her sisters, her brother, her aunts, uncles, cousins, and several high school friends. Everyone except Mike. But it was Dennis she remembered the most clearly. As she stared, unseeing, out at the dark water, her eyes filled with tears. How empty she'd felt after saying goodbye to him. Maybe hearing Maureen talk about Mike's engagement had plunged her into dejection, but even so, she couldn't forget Dennis' elation about being a Dodger.

What would he say if she described her life to him now? Although they'd been friends since fourth grade, he'd never understood her decision to become a nun. Neither had Mike.

Celie looked up at the smoldering red sky. Fingering the sand, she mentally reviewed her activities during the last few days at Immaculate Mary convent.

Her mornings always began at five a.m. with meditation in the chapel, followed by the slow melodious chanting of the Divine Office with the other nuns. An hour-long Mass ensued during which she prayed for all the virtues necessary to transmit God's love to her students. Her silent break-fast in the refectory came next, and then she hurried off to her classroom, where fifty-two squirming second graders scrutinized her every move. This week they'd huddled around her at recess, sharing their excitement over a captured lizard. One of them had showed off a new pair of shoes. They'd pleaded with her to play kickball, too, so she'd joined in the game, and the children had squealed with delight.

At 2:30 in the afternoon, the restless second graders she'd grown to love left for home. The classroom was lonely and quiet as she labored over end-less stacks of paper. Even so, she believed her many slow students deserved rewards for their efforts, so she corrected each paper painstakingly, affixing stars and stickers to every one.

On Wednesday, she'd visited her friend Sister Lupe, who lived fifteen minutes away at the Sacred Heart convent and taught second grade there. They'd shared stories and joked together about the antics of their students, then stole away to their favorite spot near the Golden Gate Bridge. As they breathed in the foggy salt air, they admired the glowing hour of dusk, the Creator's gift.

"We're so infinitely small compared to the vastness of the universe and God's Plan," Celie said to Lupe. "I have to keep reminding myself that my tiny hopes and troubles are nothing, because He offers me a glorious path every day."

But now the roar of a jet overhead cut her reverie short. It was dark. She studied her watch in the dim light, trying to decipher the time. Almost nine o'clock. Back at the convent, the Profound Silence bell would be tolling soon.

Relieved to hear the pounding waves instead of solemn chimes, she listened to the jet as it faded in the distance and stared up at the slice of yellow moon that lit a glittering path across the water. *This is the profoundest silence I've ever felt.*

God was very close to her here, and for the first time in many months, a mysterious peace filled her. She smiled, then meandered through the dunes, and climbed the stairs to the retreat house. She hoped for a good night's sleep.

CHAPTER 12

AN UNEXPECTED STRANGER

A strange noise startled Celie. She lay quietly in the thick darkness as the knob squeaked again and the door of her room opened. Her heart pounded as the shaft of light widened inch by inch. Terrified, she squeezed her eyes shut. She had forgotten to bolt the door! She was so used to her safe convent that it had never occurred to her that she could be in danger at a retreat house. She stiffened, holding her breath, then forced her eyes open again to make out the figure of a tall man. He moved nearer and, fumbling with his jacket, reached over to the nightstand and switched on the lamp.

Celie screamed. Her body went numb.

"Oh, my God! I'm so sorry!" His voice was deep. "I . . . I didn't mean to scare you. I thought this was *my* room." He tried to smile. "I must've opened the wrong door. So stupid of me."

He stepped backward, embarrassment all over his face. "I've frightened you. I'm so sorry. Can I do anything? For you?" His brown eyes, shaded by dense black eyelashes and unruly eyebrows, looked troubled. He bit his lower lip, and his hands formed tight fists.

Celie's heart was still thumping, but suddenly the whole incident seemed ridiculous. She giggled nervously. "Do anything for me?" She took a deep breath to calm herself and sat up in bed, pulling the covers up to her chin. Tears of relief filled her eyes.

He stood there for several minutes, still dazed by his mistake, then scowled and fumbled with his wristwatch. "Two thirty-five. An ungodly hour. I must've lost track of the time. I was up late walking on the beach. I was so immersed in my . . . in my—well, I obviously got the wrong room. Mine must be right next to you."

Celie couldn't say anything. The drumming in her chest had finally stopped. She saw his dark eyes narrow and distress crease his brows as he turned toward the door.

"I'd better go," he said. "I've obviously done enough damage for one night."

She could see that he was muscular, probably in his early thirties, and he was wearing a navy pinstriped suit and a classic white shirt. Only his loosened collar and tie implied a slight casualness. Despite the hour, his clothes were clean and pressed. Why would he be walking on the beach in the middle of the night? And why would he be staying at an old retreat house in this old California beach town?

He grasped the doorknob and turned back toward her. "Please. Can I make this up to you? I think they serve breakfast in the dining room at eight. Would you consider . . . joining me?"

She didn't know what to say. She stared at his face and the silence lengthened. He looked so troubled and contrite. She wanted him to relax. "Yes," she managed. "I'll see you then."

He nodded, and with an abrupt turn, he left and closed the door behind him.

Minutes later, Celie heard sounds coming through her bedroom wall, water running, a chair scraping across the floor, coughing. Lying in the dark, drifting off to sleep, she thought she also heard deep muffled sobs.

Such a distinguished, powerful man wracked by grief? Why?

Early morning light gleamed through the lace curtains in Celie's room, casting geometric patterns on the worn mahogany floor. She listened to the rhythm of the waves outside for a few minutes, then tried to loosen the knots in her shoulder with her fingers. She'd tossed and turned all night, distorted pictures of convent life tumbling through her dreams. Would she ever sleep soundly again? She strained to focus as Sister Gerald's words drifted into her mind again.

Decisions come. You can't force them. Relax this weekend.

She would take her Superior's advice and let the worries go.

The sound of the waves called to her. She slipped out of bed. Pulling the chenille bedspread into place, she stopped to stare at the driftwood crucifix that hung on the wall and, despite her uncertainties, offered a quiet prayer of thanks to God.

Donning her borrowed jeans and top again, she brushed her short hair till it gleamed, slipped into the jacket and zipped it up, and headed to the beach, notebook in hand.

It was nearly 6:30. She'd have plenty of time to look for shells before breakfast. She bounded down the old wooden steps and broke into a run as soon as she hit the beach. The sea was liberal with her gifts this morning. Dark jagged driftwood, shells of all shapes and colors, and amber seaweed lay on the smooth moist sand.

Suddenly she was a child again, searching for a new shell, the smallest, the prettiest. . . . She'd played the game for so many years, taking home one treasure every time and carefully setting it out on her bureau with the others, like trophies on display. Until her sisters came home and she hid them away. Each shell symbolized a wish held secretly in her heart.

Today she selected a white shell, which she knew to be called Sun-n-Moon. She studied it for several minutes, pulled out her notebook and a pencil out of her pocket and began writing.

Simplicity shell.
Only one half,
Bleached pure white inside and out.
Outside—rough and ribbed,
*   ridges curved,*
*   forced into parallel paths.*
Inside—satin smooth,
*   sea-shaped, cupped*
Ready to hold—
*   what?*

The shell seemed to symbolize her needs, her purpose. She stared at the words she'd written, then tore the page out, folded it, and tucked the poem into the shell. Right now, she couldn't think clearly enough to ferret

63

out its meaning, but as her fingers closed around the shell, she promised herself that she would give it more thought later. Suddenly the smell of crisp bacon and freshly brewed coffee coming from the retreat house roused her appetite. Laying the rest of the shells she'd collected back on the sand, she walked around the dunes and climbed the stairs two at a time. One thing was certain: she was hungry.

He sat waiting in the dining hall, which was filled with an odd assortment of laypeople. A reserved smile played at his lips as she strode past several tables to greet him. He stood up, serious, almost somber, holding his hand out to clasp hers.

She trembled, but managed to steady her voice. "Good morning."

Gesturing to the chair across from his, he pulled it out for her.

Unaccustomed to sitting with a man, she swallowed hard to quiet herself, willing him to start the conversation.

"I'm sorry about last night," he said. "I'm usually not so careless." Impatience laced his words. "I was immersed in my thoughts. I wasn't paying attention to details. Besides, I'm so used to hotel keys. It's strange they don't use them here."

"It's okay," Celie said.

He paused. "I hope you're not saying that for my sake." He searched her eyes for reassurance.

"Really, I'm fine. It was my fault too. I should've remembered to bolt the door." To set his mind at rest, she offered a smile. "You look different in the daytime, not like a cat burglar at all! But I have to admit . . . at two a.m. you looked pretty scary."

He finally laughed, his eyes turning gentle, the worry gone.

Silence filled the space between them and Celie clutched the menu, studying the sparse choices. When the pause lengthened, she awkwardly pulled out the shell she'd found on the beach and showed it to him. "I've always loved to gather shells. This one's beautiful. Don't you think? It's a little like a clam shell, but see the round, little cup it forms? Pure white inside. Elegant too. I wrote a poem about it this morning." She unfolded the paper.

"You're a poet?" he asked.

"A hobby, mostly." She put her index finger inside the shell, stroking its smooth, round cavity.

"Aw, c'mon."

"Well, I did win a couple of writing prizes in school," she admitted. "Writing poems is pure pleasure for me. A sort of a release." She turned the shell over. "This one is simple, yet full of contrasts. Rough, with definite ridges on the outside, and smooth, almost soft on the inside. Intriguing. I wish life could be that uncomplicated. We get so caught up in expectations, ours and others'. Don't we?"

He searched her face. "Yes," he said. "We do."

She wasn't used to his penetrating stare, but she sensed that he understood, and this surprised her. Twisting the napkin that lay in her lap, she turned toward the window and looked down at the sand dunes and the crashing surf below them. "Look at those waves. They must be eight feet high."

"Yes," he said, "but they don't intimidate the surfers out there, do they?"

They ate with slow deliberation, enjoying the serenity of the morning, sharing the eggs, bacon, and fresh strawberries that the tiny wrinkled nun brought to their table. She finally learned his name, Tony DeStefano. He was an engineer, an executive who managed hundreds of people at an aerospace company. Unwilling to reveal her identity as a nun, she gave him her secular name, Celie O'Rourke.

"So you're Irish," he said with a smile. "I should've guessed, with that auburn hair."

Celie flinched. *My hair again.* But his eyes were friendly. He wasn't being critical.

"You have an accent," she said to change the subject. "Where are you from?"

"New York. Grew up in Brooklyn. Now I live on Long Island. I'm out here working on a defense electronics project."

"And you decided to go on a retreat, too?"

"Not exactly. This time I wanted to combine business with a weekend of rest. When I told a friend I was coming to Santa Cruz, he suggested I stay here instead of the normal, run-of-the-mill hotels I'm used to. It may seem like a weird notion, but he raved about this place. And I think he was right. So far it's a homier atmosphere. More peaceful, too. The waves lulled me to sleep last night. And there's nothing like a morning run on the beach."

"What's your idea of homey?" she asked.

He gestured toward the door leading to the sitting room. "Yesterday after dinner, I saw a roaring fire in there—in a magnificent stone fireplace.

The food's home-cooked and better than I could get at any restaurant." He patted the stuffed arms of his chair. "This furniture reminds me of an old hunting lodge I used to visit in upstate New York."

"Don't you have to spend your time here in prayer and meditation?"

Tony shook his head. "No questions asked. I just said I needed some solitude." His dark eyes studied hers.

She turned away to look at the surfers again. "It sounds like you travel all the time."

"Only five days out of an average week. Well, okay, I'm exaggerating. It's not *that* bad. But you can imagine how excited I get about staying in swanky hotels. They don't impress me anymore." His voice took on a weary tone. "To me, a hotel's a cold, vacant room and hopefully a comfortable bed. But this place is different, and the nuns here are even friendly. They're sure different than the rough Irish sisters I knew as a boy." Without pausing, he pointed toward the beach. "And this sure beats the East Coast in March," he said. "The weather and scenery here are spectacular. I might stay here again next time I come to California on business."

As she listened, Celie studied Tony's face, sensing his loneliness. Her life was very different from his, yet she felt a strange connection with him.

"What about you?" he asked.

His question startled her. Should she tell him the truth? *He'll be shocked. Besides, he doesn't have a good history with nuns.* "I'm here on a weekend retreat," she finally said. "I live in San Francisco, and someone mentioned this was a good place to think things out and pray. I hope to find some answers here." She tried to smile, but couldn't quite manage it. Aware that her voice revealed her agonizing worry, she plunged ahead anyway. "Have you ever been faced with a decision that would change your life? That's where I'm at. It's no fun, believe me. I want to make my choice and get on with it. But I'm not there yet. It's painful."

Tony reached out and closed his hand over hers. "I know about choices."

His touch sent a shiver through Celie's fingers. She pulled her hand away and the moment shattered.

Tony looked away, toward the surfers.

She'd embarrassed him. She trembled inside, her own cheeks hot. She'd never felt drawn to a man like this. Hiding her turmoil, she coughed, picked up her glass, and gulped some water. "Well," she said, "I . . . I guess I'd better get up to my room now. I have to prepare my classes for next week, among other things. I'm a teacher." She fidgeted uncertainly, her hand still tingling. Then she stood up, though her legs wobbled as if they might not hold her up.

As she edged away from the table, he kept asking questions. Where did she teach? What grade level? Where had she gone to college?

"I know so little about you—" His full lips parted in a smile as his hand moved toward hers, just out of reach. She willed her hand not to move.

"Except you're a shell collector and a poet," he said. "I try to keep a running dossier of all the victims I burglarize." His teasing finally put her at ease.

She stood beside the table and let her hand rest on it for one more minute, then turned away. "I told you my name," she said over her shoulder. "Celie O'Rourke." Well, that was partly true. She could feel him studying her again, and it unnerved her. "I teach at Immaculate Mary School. Now I have to go, Tony. Thanks for a wonderful breakfast."

"I wish you weren't so determined to say good-bye," he said, getting halfway up. "I hope we'll see each other again."

"Maybe."

She saw him sink back down in his chair as she crossed the room.

As she climbed the winding stairs, she could sense him lingering below. She closed her bedroom door.

CHAPTER 13

REMEMBERING

Celie lifted her pen again and tried to write the letter, but only the words, "Dear Mom and Dad" were on the blank page. Distracted, she gazed out a window facing north and watched a squirrel scurry up the trunk of a nearby cypress tree and disappear in its branches. She looked past the grove of trees at the mist hovering along the cliffs above the beach. The ocean gleamed iron blue against a threatening sky. It seemed late, but it was only three o'clock.

Is he out walking on the beach? Shaking her head to banish the thought, she rummaged through her pockets, searching for the poem and the shell she'd shared with him. No luck. Had she left them on the table? He'd shown such interest. *I mustn't dwell on it.*

Pen in hand again, she found herself doodling. Circles. A tree trunk. After a moment, she dismissed her thoughts of the morning and bent her head to resume her letter. But instead, as had been her practice for years, she lost herself in creating a story.

Wooden Wheels

There was never any question back then. I was always last. Why did I even try to compete? They were always way ahead of me: my two older sisters, Maureen and Colleen, and Bonnie, the girl next door.

Roller-skating was the worst. I had the oldest pair of skates because hand-me-downs didn't just include dresses and shoes. They had uneven wooden wheels, dented in a couple of places.

Beginner skates, all right, meant to be slow. But I yearned for silver ball-bearing skates like theirs.

We'd start off together on the rough sidewalks near our old house where giant jacaranda trees shaded us from the scorching California sun. In seconds, I'd fall behind, though I skated much harder than they did. I'd huff and puff with drops of sweat running into my eyes, but when I peered ahead, it always seemed like their legs magically flew up after them. Soon the girls would become small dots, disappearing in the distance.

And that sound! That sort of buzzing-whooshing sound to their ball bearings, like the swish of tires on a rain-soaked highway.

But my wooden wheels didn't make much noise. I rolled along and, inevitably, got stuck in the sidewalk's grooves. Fast spurts to get ahead got me nowhere.

Forcing myself to pick up speed had its problems, too. Sooner or later, the skates would come off altogether and I'd have to sit on the sidewalk, undo the worn leather straps, and tighten the toe clamps around my feet again with my silver skate key.

Determined, I'd go off again, pushing forward with my right foot then my left, straining to see where the girls had gone, listening for those glorious steel ball bearings, racing and whisking on and on in the distance.

Dad said if I proved myself on the beginner skates, I could earn the silver skates for my next birthday. Mom, as usual, kept silent.

Months later, I did earn the ball bearings. But by then my sisters were on to other things: ballet, two-wheel bikes, catching bees.

My childhood was always about trying to catch up.

She reread her draft. No matter how she'd tried to belong, her sisters had always seemed out of reach. *Am I still playing catch-up? Still forcing myself to be what everyone else wants? To belong?*

The ticking of the alarm clock penetrated her thoughts like the irritating beat of a tin drum. Not quite four o'clock, and she *still* hadn't written her letter.

Enough remembering. It doesn't give me answers! Only confusing thoughts, pieces of an undone puzzle.

She slammed her notebook shut and stood up. Moving to the sink and the mirror above it, she fingered her hair, then ran a brush through it. Hard. She wouldn't wait for the tap water to warm up. She splashed the icy water on her face, dried herself, and rushed down the old wooden stairs to the sand dunes outside.

CHAPTER 14

AN OLD FRIEND

Leaving the dunes behind, Celie took a long, chilly walk on the abandoned beach. But she started shivering and began to run, heading back toward the retreat house. Her mood was as ominous as the sky. Why? She couldn't . . . no—she wouldn't think about the petulance festering inside her.

She found the public phone in the lobby of the retreat house and flipped through a phone book, looking for a number in Scotts Valley. Her fingers were shaking, but she finally dialed the number.

"Hello."

She tried to control the quiver in her voice. "Dennis? This is Celie."

"Wow! What a surprise! Where are you?" His eagerness reassured her.

"I'm right nearby. In Santa Cruz. When's spring training? I was hoping you hadn't left for Vero Beach yet."

"Next week. I can't wait for them to whip us into shape—you know me, I love the pain of baseball!"

Again, his relentless enthusiasm. She envied him.

"Say, how close are you, Celie? You sound like you're next door."

"About fifteen, twenty miles?"

"How about lunch?"

Celie's whole body relaxed. He was the friend she needed.

They agreed to meet, but before signing off, he said, "Hey, you seem a little sad. What's wrong?" He'd detected her mood so quickly.

"I just need a pal to talk to. Like old times. Okay?"

New freckles were scattered over Dennis' tanned face. He took off his baseball cap when he saw her, revealing a shock of thick brown hair bleached by the sun, but it was the sparkle in his green eyes and his familiar grin that warmed her all over. She'd been right to call him. No one knew her better than Dennis.

They'd been friends for thirteen years. His family had moved to California from Massachusetts. "That's why you have such a weird accent," she'd always said, kidding him since grade school. Back then, he used to walk her home every day and ride his bike over to her house on weekends. She'd be in the middle of Saturday chores, and he'd help her finish them. She'd dust; he'd vacuum. Or he'd mow the lawn while she did the edging. Once he came over while she and her sisters were repainting the blue shutters on their white stucco house. Dad handed him a brush.

"Hey, Mr. O'Rourke, does this earn me a baseball lesson?" Dennis wasn't shy.

Dad grinned. "Depends how long you paint and what kind of job you do. You know my work ethic: 'If you can't do a job right, no use doin' it at all.'"

Next thing Celie knew, Dad was out pitching to him, and giving him pointers on how to hold the bat. Dennis' dad was never around. His parents were divorced, one of the few broken homes Celie knew.

Later, when Saturday chores were done, the O'Rourkes piled into their old Hudson Hornet and drove to the high school athletic field, where they sat in the bleachers and cheered Dennis on as he batted and pitched.

Now he was grown up and successful, ready for spring training with the Dodgers.

The sun was breaking through the clouds, beginning its fiery descent, as they drove up the Pacific Coast Highway.

"I didn't recognize you at first," he said in a teasing voice. "But I like your new look. It's more like your old look than that nun's habit. That's why. And it's a nice surprise to see you're still Flaming Red." He couldn't resist using her grade school nickname. "I thought for sure they'd shaved off your hair."

She laughed out loud. "You don't believe everything you hear, do you? So medieval! They did away with shearing heads a couple of years ago." Teasing him helped her relax.

He laughed, too. "You need to fill me in on your modern *eck-you-men-ick-cal* life in the convent. I've never gotten the inside dope on it."

"That's what I plan to do," she said. "Ecumenical changes and everything else." But now she wasn't smiling.

"So why the new duds?" he asked. "Another change?"

"Yes," she fibbed. "I'm on vacation. So I decided to dress casual." Well, it wasn't a total lie. Lupe had shared a more shocking rumor with her recently—some members of their congregation had begun switching to secular clothes and had even secretly visited bars at night to listen to folk music!

"But think about it," Lupe had argued. "Parish priests take off their Roman collars all the time. And they're free to go wherever they want. Why can't we?"

But why hadn't Sister Gerald ever mentioned anything like this? Or given the nuns at St. Mary's convent permission to explore the secular world?

"How're your parents?" Dennis' question broke into her thoughts. He swung the wheel into a left turn and entered a busy intersection. "It was great seeing them again at Christmas."

"Dad's planning to retire from the factory in a couple of years," she said. "My sisters tell me he's been depressed because of his job and . . . well, he's drinking more than he used to. Sometimes he switches from wine to martinis after work."

Dennis gave a sympathetic murmur. "I hope his retirement works out."

"Me, too," she said. "He doesn't have any hobbies since he stopped playing baseball with you. So he's sure to drive Mom crazy. One thing he does, though, is read the paper, up one side and down the other. Whenever he reads about you and your team, believe me, I hear about it in their next letter."

Dennis turned off Pacific Coast Highway and pulled his red Mustang into Norm's, a popular 1950's-style roadside coffee shop. After they'd settled themselves in a booth, he came to the point. "Okay, Red, enough about your dad and his problems. What's eating you?"

She shrugged. It was hard to explain. "It's not so bad. I've just been sort of sad."

"C'mon, Red. You look depressed. Out with it."

She shook off her surprise. She'd forgotten how abrupt he could be. Had she made a mistake by calling him? "I guess . . . I . . . I . . . ."

"Yes?"

"Well, ever since I saw you at Christmas, I've been . . . more and more restless."

His eyebrows rose, but she went on, looking at the tiny jukebox resting on their table instead of him. "Your life sounds difficult," she said quietly, "but so exciting. My life isn't exciting at all. And lately it just seems . . . well, hard. Even though you say some parts of your training are the pits, the fact is you're ecstatic about being on the Dodger farm team. It shows all over your face."

Dennis played with his napkin for a minute, then gazed at her again. "Yeah, I love what I'm doing. And you're right. It's not easy. But what does that have to do with your life?" He rested his chin on one hand and twirled his fork with the other.

She began again. "I . . . guess I keep wondering why I don't feel the same way about being a nun. The truth is, it's been three and a half years now, but I'm . . . still restless. And I get depressed sometimes. No matter what I do, I can't seem to make the unhappiness go away."

He put his folk down and laid both hands flat on the table. "I'm sorry. I had no idea."

She waited. What more could she say?

He began slowly, choosing his words with care. "C'mon, Celie, you can't compare your life and mine. How can being a Dodger come close to being a nun? It's miles apart." He launched into a gentle lecture. "Sure, I left home, too, and I work hard at this dream. But I didn't give up all the other normal parts of living like you did. I drink, I smoke if I want to, I spend money, I travel, and I can do the club scene when I want. I come and go as I please pretty much, within the coach's guidelines. But that's not the case with you."

Celie listened, aware that she couldn't meet his eyes. Instead, she studied the gray and white pattern on the Formica table. When the waitress came, they ordered hamburgers.

Then Dennis continued. "Yeah, Red, I practice hard and fall asleep dog-tired. I don't have much time for myself. Traveling is no picnic, either. I stay in a lot of dives on the road. But the rest of my life is virtually normal. Face it, Celie. Yours isn't. You've given up almost everything."

She'd always admired Dennis' honesty, but now his words felt like an icy blast. She didn't agree with his last accusation. His opinions always seemed so black and white. Okay, she wasn't totally happy, but she wasn't one hundred per cent *unhappy*. Unable to reply, she sputtered for a moment, then crossed her arms and sank into the corner of the booth. "Everything?"

she said. "You think I gave up everything? I don't agree. According to you, my life is a humongous Lenten sacrifice. But that's not what I'm saying." Her voice sounded raw. She paused to calm herself down. "I've made lots of wonderful friends in the convent. If you could meet the girls I entered with—they're the cream of the crop and tops in their class. They're teaching me by example. How to think and question. How to tell others how I feel. How—"

"But—" He started to cut in, then waved for her to continue.

"I never knew what real learning was," she said. "All through school, I was always so tense about getting the best grades. But these girls aren't just interested in grades. They," she paused for the right word, "they *probe* for answers because they're curious about what really happened in history or why political events occurred. I've learned to raise questions, too. All the ones I was afraid to ask for so many years." She stopped.

"Wow," he said, "I haven't seen those hazel eyes of yours flare up in a long time."

She knew he was trying to lighten things up, but she rushed on, hell-bent on convincing him that she wasn't as discontented as he seemed to think. That was the trouble, she suddenly realized. Dennis always made up his mind too fast. Why had she forgotten that?

"At home," she said, "nobody ever wanted to listen to my questions, and in school I didn't dare ask any. But now, now I'm finally learning how to think! A whole new world is opening up to me. It's sort of exciting."

His eyebrows crinkled and his lips puckered. She read his face and felt his doubts, but she continued anyway.

"I have fun, too. We create songs together, and we hike in the hills, and I've discovered nature for the first time. The orchards near the convent are spectacular when they're in bloom. You've got to admit, in Southern California, it's wall-to-wall houses and people and sidewalks and tiny lawns. The closest I ever got to the environment was Dad's geraniums and rose bushes. I love the nature I've found! I've started sitting under the trees and writing poetry again, too."

Dennis put up his hand for her to stop. She was in for it now. "Okay," he said, "I get it. You've made some great friends, discovered nature, and you're doing some creative writing. But, Celie, be straight—is that why you joined up with those nuns? Wasn't it for a bigger purpose? I have a dream.

That's what keeps me going. But what about your dream? Everything you've talked about, you could get on the outside. So why did you really go into the convent? Besides, you were the one who said something was missing. Why are you staying?"

"I wanted . . . I want to help people." She knew her voice sounded too soft, too weak. "I've always wanted to help people, ever since Mom told me I have a calm, capable way—"

"For God's sake, Celie, what does being calm and capable have to do with being a nun? It's true. You are. But I know your mom. She could have been referring to any number of careers you could have chosen."

Celie's stomach tightened, and the muscles in her shoulders began tensing up again. Her whole body was beginning to ache. "I wanted to contribute something to this world, not take from it—"

"I know. 'Ask not what your country can do for you, but what you can do for your country.' You bought into that whole scene. JFK, the Peace Corps, Doctor Schweitzer—"

"What's wrong with that? Maybe I want to contribute something special to the world!"

"Well, if you ask me," he said, "you're not being honest. And you're not going for your own dream. You're living up to other people's expectations. I know what you've been exposed to." He clenched his fist. "I was lucky. Nobody *ever* considered me for religious life, so I got an opportunity to look at what *I* wanted, not what *they* wanted from me."

"What do you mean?" Her cheeks felt hot. "You act like a religious vocation is nothing but coercion, some kind of crazy conspiracy to make me do what *they* want."

"You mean you don't remember those recruiting sermons?" he asked. "All through school?"

She couldn't reply.

He wasn't finished yet. "And Sister Pauline? Don't tell me you didn't feel her influence, especially in your junior and senior year. Have you forgotten how she tried to get Mike to take someone else to the prom? No, you won't admit it. Those nuns and priests have it down. The church has been recruiting like crazy for years, just like the Dodgers."

Celie had heard the rumor about Sister Pauline trying to influence Mike, but she'd never believed it. And she'd never noticed such hostility in Dennis' voice before, either. She leaned toward him. "Sister Pauline is a dedicated Augustinian. Plus she was sort of a comedian back then. Always kidded me when I was down in the dumps. Encouraged me. She liked Mike. She just didn't want us to get too serious. She just wanted me to go for what I wanted, no matter what anyone else thought.

"And," she continued, her voice rising, "I am helping people. You should see the kids I teach. They're in this country only a few weeks, thrust into a totally foreign environment. Some can't speak one word of English, and I'm supposed to teach them to read. And I'm doing it! Without any real help! I never took Spanish, there's no speech therapist or foreign language expert available, and the textbooks I use are the ones *we* used in grammar school. But these kids are learning to speak English and they're sounding out words, too. Plenty of them."

Dennis made the timeout sign with his hands. "All right, all right, Red," he said. He smeared his last few French fries with ketchup and finished the rest of his burger. Celie could tell he was upset. She waited, aware that she was slowing her breathing to compose herself.

He wiped his mouth with a napkin and pushed his plate aside. "Okay, Celie, I buy it. You're helping people. I never doubted you would. But you've got to be happy down deep—feel it in your bones, in your gut. You know what I mean?" He folded his arms against his chest. "I never did get it. This God thing escapes me. Why do you have to give up all the things God gave you in order to do what He wants? If there's a God, would He want you to throw away your own happiness to make Him and others happy? Why does He want that? Even your dad wouldn't ask that."

She sat up straighter. This whole conversation had been a mistake. She looked down at her uneaten hamburger and took a deep breath. "But when you sacrifice for God, He gives you other blessings. Don't you see?" Celie knew her voice was too loud, but she didn't care.

The family in the adjacent booth turned around and stared.

She lowered her voice. "Like the Scriptures. One of my friends helped me discover things in the Bible I'd never seen before. Oh, I'm not referring to the Gospels. We've heard those at Mass for years. Now I'm seeing Christ's life in detail, how He treated people. Everyone. And I can't put the New Testament down. I've been studying the Book of Matthew lately—the stories are deep! I've started using Christ's parables for my religion classes, too. The children love it. And Sister Gerald, my Superior, has actually asked me to share the lesson plans I've created with other primary teachers in our local schools." She looked at Dennis's blank expression. Would he ever understand?

His voice was quiet. "Well, I guess there is some joy."

"Yeah," she said, "maybe there is. . . ."

CHAPTER 15

REASONS

It was early. Her eyes barely open, Celie checked the time again. Four-thirty. She got out of bed. Weary from no sleep, she walked barefoot toward the window and looked out, eager to find solace in the ocean she loved. She opened the window halfway and stared out at the black void, then discovered a profusion of stars. The chill breeze cooled her cheeks as she listened to the rhythm of the waves crashing against the rocks, then receding. The sea's cadence seemed to appease her inner tension, though her headache still throbbed. She raised both hands to massage her temples.

Why did she ache with such turmoil? Was she expecting too much? Her mother had always accused her of setting her expectations too high. Was she doing it again? But how could she expect Dennis to understand? No one understood when she tried to explain. *But I know I've felt joy as a nun. In spite of the restlessness I feel.* Everything she'd told him yesterday was true.

So why did she keep searching for a contentment that seemed to elude her? She'd followed every convent dictum, every tiny rule. She'd studied Sister Gerald and Mother Mary Lucretia for months, and she tried every day to emulate their holiness and become a model nun. Yet all her efforts left her wanting. She could not fill the void inside and she did not know what would satisfy her.

I can't stop my illicit fantasies and sins at night—they overcome me over and over again. I wonder if—has Mike forgotten me completely?

Her thoughts turned to her sister Colleen, married last month on St. Patrick's Day, now suddenly pregnant, her child due in January. Did Colleen ever feel incomplete? No, she'd described Don in her last letter as "the love of my life."

Was Dennis tormented by a restlessness he couldn't admit?

Desperate for an answer, Celie looked out at the star-studded night and repeated every childhood prayer she knew. Then she took out her breviary and began whispering the psalms. She mentally translated the words of Psalm 90, from the Latin she'd studied, laying her worries at the Lord's feet.

> *Thou art my protector, and my refuge: my God, in him will I*
>   *trust. For he hath delivered me from the snare of the hunters:*
>   *and from the sharp sword.*
> *He will overshadow thee with his wings, thou shalt trust.*
> *His truth shall encompass thee with a shield: thou shall not be*
>   *afraid of the terror . . . because thou, O Lord, art my hope.*
> *For he hath given his angels charge over thee: to keep thee in all*
>   *thy ways.*
> *In their hands they shall bear thee up.*

The prayer quieted her confusion, and peace suffused her.

She *did* sense an inexplicable pull to this vocation. She had always sensed a spiritual reality underneath life's humdrum, even more since she'd entered the convent. It was a magnetic force that lit up the world around her, no matter how depressing or futile life might seem. Like the sanctuary candle that burned in church and was never extinguished, it was mysterious and constant, not provable, but nonetheless real.

Celie pictured the Motherhouse grounds early in the morning, before light replaced night's shadows. She loved those dim hours of cold fog. As the dawn began its display, she slipped into line with the other nuns and walked toward the great mahogany doors that opened to the hushed splendor of the chapel. The shining candles on the altar always captured her attention and last week's golden day lilies and fragrant lavender adorning God's tabernacle lifted her heart, as the beauty of the flowers always did.

Morning meditation was a fertile time for her. When she read again about Christ's life and thought about the wonders He'd shown to others— healing their illnesses, rebuilding their hopes—she closed herself off from the world, and insights came to her. An unfathomable serenity overtook her when she pictured Christ. This was a mystifying time she couldn't explain.

But the reason she'd come to this life, to help others, to make a difference in their lives . . . did her vocation have any impact at all? *Why do I have to keep burying my memories of Mike? And dreams of having my own children?*

Yet she was reaching her students. Though their daily progress came slow, when they reached another milestone, mastered another concept, she was elated. Even watching them string sounds together to unlock a new word was thrilling. *They're like little seedlings*, she thought. *Seedlings who've been placed in my care, and I've found the best soil and a special place for them in the sun. It's as if I water them every day.*

But for weeks she'd seen little progress, despite her constant efforts, until, finally, signs of life appeared like a few green shoots pushing through heavy soil. Days wore on and the children kept learning, growing like eager little plants. Weeks passed, and the sprouts grew up into fledgling plants, reaching for the light. She was witnessing God's creative energy at work in the minds of her seven-year-olds.

Still standing by the retreat house window, Celie imagined the faces of her second graders. She saw Manuel, his eager smile and immaculate uniform. He'd made such wonderful progress since his first day. His parents were so proud.

Next, Enrique, who sat next to Manuel. Almost too chubby for his desk, Enrique looked up at her with dull, solemn eyes. He never talked or raised his hand. His gray uniform pants and white shirt were often wrinkled and stained with food from yesterday's meal. Last week while her students played at recess, she'd found a puddle of urine under his seat. This wasn't the first time. Enrique's mother had knocked on the classroom door later that day. "Sister," she'd said in a frightened voice, "he has a psychiatrist now." She'd given Celie a slip of paper. "Please call him today." Then she'd taken her son's hand and dragged him down the hall. The other children tittered—they'd taunted him about his accidents before—but Celie had held up her hand and glared at them.

In the evening, she'd dialed the number. "Doctor, I want to help Enrique. I'll do whatever you suggest."

His voice had been cool and professional. "You can't do much, Sister. A case like this is a family problem, and Enrique is the weakest link. Both parents are finally in counseling now. We need to find the underlying cause of their problems. Just give Enrique your warm understanding."

Celie had hung up, disappointed, but the next day she'd decided to give Enrique some special attention. Even though he had an aptitude for math, he'd been held back the previous year, and he still read laboriously, stumbling on nearly every word. But Celie knew he could make out the names of the children because of the folded paper nameplates that sat on each child's desk.

"Class," she had announced, "Enrique will now become the attendance monitor."

His pudgy face lit up. When the other pupils started to giggle, she stared them down. Meanwhile, Enrique ran to her desk, picked up the attendance sheet, and filled it out. As he handed it back to Celie, his somber eyes focused on the red pencil she held.

"You are right, Enrique. Record the number on the board, then take this report to the school office."

Enrique rushed to the blackboard, recorded the day's absentee figures and marched out of the room. Celie noticed that although no smile graced his face, his eyes were brighter, and his gaze followed her all day, plus he was alert, even during reading.

As these memories faded, Celie focused on the vague pink glow outside the window that flooded the sky and outlined billows of clouds hovering over the ocean. She could see the sandpipers near the shore pecking at buried clams and skittering away on their long pencil legs as oncoming waves spread their marble foam on the wet sand.

Celie's thoughts drifted back to her class again and she heard the sweet, mixed chorus of the hymn she'd taught them.

> *This little light of mine,*
> *I'm gonna let it shine.*
> *I'm gonna let it shine,*
> *I'm gonna let it shine,*
> *Let it shine,*
> *Let it shine,*
> *Let it shine.*

She could see Enrique and Manuel holding the shining white candles she'd brought to class and walking in procession with the other children, all dressed in white, down the main aisle of Immaculate Mary Church. When they reached the altar, they received Holy Communion for the first time.

She also remembered the scripture she'd taught them. The pastor had read the same lines at Mass:

> *You are the world's light—a city on a hill, glowing*
> *in the night for all to see. Don't hide your light! Let*
> *it shine for all to see . . . so they will praise your*
> *heavenly Father* (MATTHEW 5:14–16, NLT).

The images in Celie's mind remixed like a kaleidoscope, offering her new memories to ponder. Now she remembered her class retreat in her senior year of high school. Again, she heard Sister Pauline delivering a final lecture to a roomful of students, her message resounding like the chapel bells, echoing and re-echoing during that unforgettable week five years ago. *You can make a difference!* the nun had said. *You've been told all your life that God is your Creator, but think what this means. He's made a unique blueprint for you, and you're like no other person that ever was or ever will be. Imagine how much He wants you to use your special gifts.*

After hearing her words, a tranquil joy had enveloped Celie, filling the deep hole that ached inside her.

While praying in the chapel that night, she'd thought she'd heard God saying to her, *Celia, you must spread My love to hundreds of people.*

And now her thoughts shifted back to her junior year. Everyone had expected crucial announcements at the June assembly, and the whole school buzzed with rumors. Which seniors would win the coveted scholarships? The major sports trophies? Who was going to receive academic awards? And, most intriguing of all, who would enter the convent? The student body held its collective breath when Sister Pauline proudly announced, "Our most prominent senior, Mary Lou Walsh, homecoming queen and senior class president, has decided to become an Augustinian nun!"

Celie could still remember how she'd rushed home to share the news. "Mom!" she'd shouted, "Mom, no one could believe it! Everybody knows

Mary Lou's been going steady with the captain of the football team all year!"

Mom listened as she peeled carrots and potatoes for that night's stew, little Mollie playing on the kitchen floor.

"Everyone was shocked," Celie went on. "You could've heard a pin drop in the auditorium. Finally, Sister Pauline started clapping and everyone else joined in."

Her mom's reaction was still vivid. "I'm not surprised," she said, not even turning around to face her daughter. "Don't forget, Celie, Mary Lou has always been an extremely high achiever. Becoming a nun is the greatest challenge. I've always thought she was someone very special."

The admiration in her mother's voice reverberated in Celie's mind again as she gazed out the window. The golden sunrise was lifting the scene outside to a new brilliance, and now her memories faded. The seagulls were out in full force, calling to each other as they joined the sandpipers, all of them searching for food. The breeze even felt warmer now.

Celie opened her breviary to the psalms of Lauds, the morning prayer of the Divine Office. Facing the radiance at her window, she prayed, her soul finding comfort in David's ancient prayers.

CHAPTER 16

ANOTHER SACRIFICE

Sister Gerald finished her announcements to the nuns gathered around her in the recreation room and nodded in Celie's direction. "May I have a moment with you after Vespers?" she asked.

Celie had arrived back at the convent late on Sunday afternoon, half an hour before group prayers. She knew Sister Gerald was eager to find out how her weekend at the retreat in Santa Cruz had gone, so she had quickly found her way to her Superior's office.

"I'm going to go ahead and make vows," she had said, "temporary ones for one year." She had held herself erect, smiling resolutely. "I realized there are many reasons to persevere in my vocation, and I believe if I make the necessary sacrifices, God will do the rest."

Sister Gerald's eyes had shone with excitement. "I'm so thrilled you've decided to stay. Everyone in this life has temptations, times when struggle and restlessness plague our spirits. If you can endure those valleys filled with shadows, God will reward you with His blessings!"

Sister Gerald seemed to have an inner vision of the deeper meaning of life. Was her unique spirituality linked to her Cherokee heritage? Celie wasn't sure. But obviously, her intense mysticism was the result of many years of meditation, sacrifice, and effort. Only two years ago, Mother Mary Lucretia, Vicaress General of the Augustinian Sisters, had recognized her by appointing her Superior of the convent as well as principal of Immaculate Mary School. She was the youngest nun ever to be given these dual responsibilities.

She smiled at Celie now in her engaging way, her dark eyes almost mischievous, then she stood up to don the long black cape that every nun wore to Vespers. "I have a surprise for you," she said. "The Vicaress General and I want you to share your wonderful religion lessons, not only with all our teachers, but we've also decided to have them published! I want you to work on a set of manuscripts tailored for the primary grades in our schools across California. Who knows? Perhaps other Catholic schools will adopt them too." As Celie blinked in surprise, Sister Gerald continued. "You will be in charge of it, Sister, using all those beautiful lessons the parents have been raving about. This summer we'll maintain a schedule of daily meetings, you and I. That way, we'll have it published and ready for the primary grades by Christmas."

Celie was delirious with joy! *Her* writing published? *Her* lessons committed to the pages of textbooks and used by all Augustinians? Plus, she'd be working closely with Sister Gerald. What a privilege. She spent the next few minutes thanking her Superior. But then a nagging thought dampened her mood, and she couldn't help mentioning it. "I thought I'd be returning to the Motherhouse this summer. To continue my degree program. Everyone in my set will be there. My cousin Rosemary, uh, I mean Sister John Marie, and Sister Lupe, too."

Every summer the junior nuns in Celie's age group returned to the Motherhouse, where they'd begun their training, to take college classes. For months she'd been longing to see her "set," the name given to the girls she'd entered with. Summer school was a special time to renew old bonds, picnic in the hills of Santo Domingo, and suffer through assignments together. Celie sorely missed her friends.

Sister Gerald said, "No, you'll stay here in San Francisco. We can arrange for your work on the religion textbook to be an independent study. That'll add at least six more units towards your degree. You'll go to the Motherhouse briefly for the annual June retreat and to renew your vows, but you'll return here this summer."

Celie noticed that Sister Gerald had already planned all the details. *I can't disappoint her*, she said to herself. *Plus, I've always dreamed of being a published writer.* It was such an honor to be selected to author a series of books using her own ideas. It might even lead to other writing projects.

But she hadn't seen her friends for a year. "Who else will be staying here?" she asked.

"Sister Rosarita, Sister Adele, and you and I. It'll be more relaxed than during the regular school year. With so few of us, we can pray the Divine

Office privately and most of the time on our own schedule. We'll gather together in the chapel for morning meditation and Mass, and we'll eat our meals together. We always interact more with the parishioners in the summer, and we also tutor the slow learners from every class. You'll see how much more fulfilling it is, compared to the huge numbers we teach during the regular term."

Celie kept silent as she looked out the window.

Sister Gerald's voice rose. "And I've thought of another plus. You can obtain elective credit for your tutoring, too. You'll be well ahead of the rest in your set, as far as teaching experience *and* your college transcript."

The Vespers bell tolled, and Sister Gerald moved toward her office door. When she stepped into the hall, she turned around, put her hands on Celie's shoulders, and leaned forward to kiss her on the cheek. "You're very special to me, Celia. And to God. I'm so happy you've decided to make your vows. Your work this summer will please God immensely. Think what a contribution you'll be making by using your talents to help not only your students but hundreds of the others, too! God is blessing your talent and effort." Her fingers lingered a second, then she turned to lead the younger nun to chapel.

Celie was moved. Rarely did Sister Gerald expose her emotions so impulsively or deviate from her role as a Superior. Only when she'd driven Celie to the retreat house had Sister Gerald revealed a more personal interest. Obviously, her Superior was starting to trust her. She was lifting the walls of protocol to become her special confidante.

True, she would miss her friends at the Motherhouse, but God was only asking this one small sacrifice of her through her Vow of Obedience. Besides, she was determined to do whatever was necessary to make her vocation work. In return, God would reward her with the contentment she'd so vehemently described to Dennis.

Such an opportunity! To write and publish textbooks with Sister Gerald. *I can learn a lot from her,* Celie thought as she filed into the chapel with the other nuns. *Plus, she lives in God's presence most of the time. Maybe it'll rub off on me. Working with her will be a rare privilege. God's gift.*

As the chanting of Vespers began, Celie recalled her words to Dennis. "When you give up some things, you receive other blessings in their place."

CHAPTER 17

PROMISES TO GOD

June, 1967

Organ music thundered, and solemn hymns sung by two hundred nuns in procession echoed through the chapel. The altar, adorned in white and gold, glowed with candlelight, and cascades of ivory roses, mums, and baby's breath surrounded the sacred tabernacle. An ivory satin runner flowed down the ebony marble aisle to the chapel entrance.

Families were crowded into the small chapel's back balcony, Celie's parents among them, all of them waiting to see the young women pronounce the vows that would sever family ties forever and bind them to Christ, the Bridegroom. Some parents, like Celie's, boasted with pride about their daughters' decisions to become nuns. Many came out of love, but did not understand. Others didn't come at all, hoping their absence would dissuade their daughters from what they considered to be a mistaken, wasteful choice.

Celie cast her gaze downward, following the Rule, and slowly walked in procession with the others. Her hands, concealed beneath her spotless white scapular, were clenched together in earnest. "Oh, Father in heaven," she murmured, "shower me with Your grace. You want me to be Your Son's bride. I will give Him all my love and effort. I cannot do this alone. I am weak and often close to sin—only with Your help am I worthy of this calling. I will make my vows today for another year. Keep me strong in faith, obedience, and especially purity. Lead me from all temptations and replace the loneliness in my heart with Your love, so I may spend myself in Your service."

Behind Celie's set were several nuns who would make final vows, now that they'd completed five years of training. Ahead of Celie walked a number of Novices, and at the front of the procession came the Postulants, most of them only nineteen years old. This day marked one year of training for the Postulants, who would make their first vows today and receive their religious names. They would leave the chapel clothed in severe, black, floor-length dresses and return dressed all in white, Augustinian habits, coifs, and veils. They would file up to the altar again, where, amid incense and prayer, Father Zemmiti would place a crown of thorns on each head, symbolizing the Novitiate year ahead, to be filled with solitude, contemplation, and sacrifice.

Celie had vivid memories of her year as a Novice, when family visits and letters from home were strictly limited. Watching TV and listening to the radio were banned, too, and because all secular topics were removed from her college courses, she'd immersed herself in study of the Scriptures, and classes in religious philosophy and theology. Watching this new class of Novices, she recalled the day she'd pronounced her First Vows. Was it only three years ago? She had approached the altar, her thoughts focused on her new religious name. She'd submitted three choices to Sister Mary Matthew, her Novice Mistress. Novices could choose any name, masculine or feminine, as long as it was derived from a saint or a Biblical character. Mother Mary Lucretia, the Vicaress General of the Augustinian Sisters, made the final choice.

After Celie had mounted the altar steps, Father Zemmiti laid his hands on her head as his words rang out. "Cecilia O'Rourke, from henceforth you shall be called Sister Celia Marie, for now you are a member of the Order of St. Augustine." She had smiled at the priest, even as his wrinkled face frowned at her show of emotion. She'd quickly composed herself, but her heart warmed as she whispered her new religious name. "Sister Celia Marie." Mother Mary Lucretia had granted her wish.

Minutes later, she had donned the white Augustinian habit for the first time. She felt like the bride described in the Song of Solomon.

The voice of my Beloved, behold he comes. . . .
My beloved spoke, and said to me,
Rise up, my love, my beautiful one, and come
away. For, behold, the winter is past.

The rain is over and gone. The flowers appear on the earth. The time of singing has come, and the voice of the turtledove is heard in our land. Arise my love, my beautiful one . . . (SONG OF SOLOMON 2:8–13, WEB).

Today, Father spoke these same words again as each Novice, dressed in a new, pure white habit, moved toward the altar. The Biblical poem almost brought Celie to tears then she raised her voice with the others in the *Salve Regina* hymn.

Now it was her turn. Celie approached the altar with the other Sisters in her set, all of them dressed in white, veiled in black. Thirty-four young girls had entered with her almost four years ago. Fourteen had already gone home, by their own choice or the Order's. Twenty-one would profess vows for another twelve months. Then, next year in June, she would decide whether or not to take final vows.

Rosemary stood in a stall across the aisle from Celie now, but she seemed so far away. It wasn't the first time Celie wished she could feel closer to her cousin, who had been with her during so many family events, but she also knew they couldn't be more different. As each year of training passed, she had felt the chasm widen between them. A musician and highly intelligent, Rosemary still competed with Celie for grades, but even back in high school her horn-rimmed glasses and shapeless brown hair had always contrasted sharply with Celie's frosted lipstick and flip hairstyle copied from *Seventeen* magazine. Celie and Rosemary had attended the same schools since first grade, and here she was now with a religious name, Sister John Marie. Celie felt her cousin watching her as she stepped closer to the altar, but thoughts of Rosemary dissolved as she gazed at the sanctuary light that glowed near the tabernacle, all night and all day. "Stay with me always, Lord," she prayed. "'Not my Will, but Thine be done.'"

There was no crown of thorns this year. Now Father Zemmiti pinned a crown of flowers on her veiled head. Celie steadied her tremulous voice and spoke her vows. "I, Cecelia O'Rourke, renounce the world and all its pleasures, renewing my religious vocation again by using my religious name, Sister Celia Marie, as an outward sign of my fidelity to Christ as His Bride. For one more year, I solemnly promise God my sacred vows of Poverty, Chastity, and Obedience. I pledge further to do everything in my power through God's grace to keep the Augustinian Rule. I pledge my faith, hope, and love to You, my Lord, asking Your Divine Help to be a Sister worthy of Your gracious calling and to spread Your love to all with whom I come in contact."

She turned, walked near the altar, knelt in front of it, and then lay down on the cold marble floor, covering her head and entire body with her long black cape. She lay perfectly still as if dead, in stark submission to the God she loved. This was the *Venia*, the Augustinian custom, a symbolic act of negating the worldly self and consecrating oneself to God.

The solemnity over, Celie and all the sisters adjourned to the recreation room, where she accepted their congratulations. Sister Lupe enveloped her in a crazy bear hug, then held both her shoulders and looked her straight in the eyes.

"We did it, Celie! We did it again." She leaned closer and murmured in Celie's ear. "I bet Old Daggers never thought I'd make it this far!"

Celie could enumerate so many of Lupe's skirmishes. Her friend seemed destined to elicit the wrath of their Novice Mistress, Sister Mary Matthew, on a regular basis. Now she hugged Lupe and whispered back. "Who cares about what Old Daggers thinks. We're on our way, Lupe! I hope you have a fantastic year."

Sister John Marie approached her and leaned her cool cheek against her cousin's. "Congratulations, Sister Celia Marie. You look radiant."

Celie never knew how to respond to Rosemary's "flawless religious decorum," as Sister Mary Matthew called it. Since entering the convent, they'd been forced to relearn how they walked and talked, incorporating a stiff reserve she didn't feel. In addition, they regularly practiced "custody of the eyes" by casting their eyes down whenever possible. Her cousin embodied perfect compliance to the rules.

When Celie squeezed Rosemary in an affectionate hug anyway and said, "We're all pretty happy today, aren't we?" her cousin's response was predictably rigid. "Of course."

She's too detached, Celie said to herself, *and so kind. It can't be for real.* But why did her cousin annoy her so much lately?

Before she could pursue this thought, Sister Gerald moved into their group. "Sisters, my congratulations to you all." She turned to Rosemary.

"Sister John Marie, your performance was spectacular. You've come a long way. You do so well managing organ practice on top of teaching your classes."

Celie winced. Was she jealous of her cousin? *No way. Of all people.*

Sister Gerald passed over Sister Lupe with only a couple of words, then enveloped Celie in a hug. "Sister Celia Marie, congratulations to you, too. The Lord must be very happy with you today." Then she leaned closer and whispered, "You know how special you are, don't you?"

Sister Gerald's eyes were strangely compelling, and Celie felt drawn to this woman who treated her with such respect.

CHAPTER 18

FANTASY

When Mrs. Davies, the school secretary, handed her mail to Celie just as her tutoring sessions ended for lunch, Celie couldn't help but notice a mysterious glint in her blue eyes. It was odd to receive a letter here. The envelope was postmarked New York City and was addressed to Immaculate Mary School, Attn: Miss Celie O'Rourke. Who would use her secular name? The only items Mrs. Davies ever gave her were ads for textbooks and teaching magazines. She also noticed that this envelope was sealed. Obviously, the secretary hadn't thought to send the letter to Sister Gerald first.

The Augustinian Rule stated that mail was subject to censorship by the convent Superior. During the Novice year of training, the Mistress in charge prevented some letters from reaching the Novices, but after that year of isolation was over, Superiors rarely barred the nuns in their charge from receiving personal communications. But Superiors did retain the option to read every letter. The Rule said, *The Superior's duty is to prevent items of temptation from reaching the Sisters under her authority. They must take their responsibility very seriously, to guide and protect their Sisters always.*

It was a hot, stifling day. Celie climbed the stairs, eager to reach her cell and relax while she read her letter. Today had been uneventful so far. Up at four in the morning, she'd spent two hours writing a new chapter for the religion textbook before reciting the Divine Office privately in the chapel before Mass. Then she'd spent the rest of the morning in her classroom tutoring her second graders, although the room was at least ten degrees hotter than the schoolyard.

She kicked off her black granny shoes, took off her veil, and loosened the row of safety pins holding her white coif together on her head. She ran her hands through her hair, feeling perspiration on her scalp. After opening her window, she tore open the envelope. The first paragraph of the letter made her grin, but soon her smile vanished.

June 20, 1967

Dear Celie,

How is the famous burglary victim? In spite of the shock I caused when we met, I thoroughly enjoyed our breakfast together. I hope you did as well.

I'm planning another trip to California in the near future and hope we can meet. Perhaps for lunch. Or maybe we can drive to the wine country. My friends here in New York tell me that the Napa Valley wines rival even the French vintages.

Please call me (my business card is enclosed). Or leave a message with my secretary, if I'm traveling. I'll get back to you.

I hope you can make it. I expect to fly to California early next month; my stay will include the July 4th weekend.

Sincerely,
Tony DeStefano

What? Almost in a panic, Celie folded up the letter and forced herself to look out the window as she thought about this letter. She'd never expected to hear from Tony again. But, she asked herself, why was she so surprised? He had no reason *not* to contact her.

I won't answer, she decided. She stared at the wastebasket for several minutes, but then shook her head and tucked the letter into the middle of a novel on her bedside table.

Her cell was stuffy on this warm, humid day. Celie wiped her face, opened the window wider, and yawned. The shock of Tony's letter plus the heat suddenly made her feel sleepy.

I'll just lie down for a minute.

She stretched out on the plain white bed and closed her eyes. Visions of Tony driving through the countryside wafted in and out of her thoughts like the warm breezes soothing her in the stifling room. She saw him, tall and serious, driving a black convertible through the golden California hills.

And suddenly she was sitting next to him. Her long auburn hair was pinned high on her head, like she used to wear it, and a scooped-neck, emerald cotton dress covered her ample breasts and fell in soft folds just above her knees. When Tony stopped the car in a meadow shaded by silver-green eucalyptus trees, she turned to him and smiled, the aroma of the tree's musty leaves drifting through the air.

Half asleep, she held onto the fantasy as she lay on the bed and pulled her long white habit up to her waist. She reached down to stroke herself where she already felt a delicious warmth throbbing, a hunger she could not quell. Eyes still closed, she imagined Tony close, bending over her. She was lying on the grass and reached up for him, the faint, musky scent of him filling her with new excitement. His lips were soft, oh, so soft, as he kissed her ear then her neck again and again. His mouth moved down her body, feeding tenderly, until a delectable heat inflamed her. Moaning quietly, Celie felt a wet pleasure between her legs. Suddenly, she removed her hand and held back, but within seconds, a relentless longing forced her to reach down again. Rubbing herself gently with eager fingers, her breath soon turned into short gasps, and as the sweet momentum increased, she heaved up and down, up and down as she stroked until ripples of pleasure peaked and her whole body shuddered. Finally she lay still, every part of her relaxed.

"Oh, God," she said out loud, "dear God, I've never gone this far! And now with dreams of Tony! I've got to stop this." Her guilt sickened her, but her exhaustion overcame her and she fell asleep.

CHAPTER 19

GUILT, DAYDREAMS, AND QUESTIONS

She woke to the tolling of the Vespers bell. Visiting Sisters were joining them in the chapel today. Only five minutes to get ready! Quickly she changed into a freshly pressed habit, and ran down the stairs, but when she slipped into her stall, Sister Gerald was already intoning the beginning verses of the Divine Office. She glimpsed her Superior's inquiring dark eyes just before she bowed to the altar and found her own seat.

The chanting continued. *Dear God, I feel disgusted*, Celie prayed silently. *When I made my vows, I promised You I would never allow impurity to engulf me again. I am so weak! Can I live as a nun, knowing I'm violating my Vow of Chastity? Please, God, I'll try harder! Help me stop these feelings. Help me leave this horrible fixation behind. I beg You. Please forgive me.* She paused. *I . . . I simply cannot mention this in the confessional again.*

Celie would never forget the day, so many years before, when she'd forced herself to disclose this sin of the flesh, first admitting it to her parish priest in the shadowy confessional when she was only twelve. All through her teen years, she had confessed it repeatedly, hoping each time to rid herself of this repulsive habit. "Bless me, Father, for I have sinned. I lied once, I argued with my parents twice." Then, trembling, she'd say, "And I committed an impure act. Three times."

She always held her breath, hoping the priest wouldn't ask her the obvious questions. "What impure acts? Alone or with others? Child, did you get pleasure in touching yourself? Speak up, I can't hear you. Please explain."

Why did he have to know the details? He was the one whose sermons had convinced her she'd burn in Hell for these acts of impurity. But after he squeezed every detail out of her, all he ever said was, "This is a very grave sin. You must beg for Our Lord's help to stop. For your penance, say a rosary to the Blessed Virgin Mary and keep asking her help to become pure again."

The Gregorian chant swelled around her now, almost blotting her memories out, but she was so focused on her prayer for forgiveness (and, yes, the memories) that she almost missed her cue. Sister Adele, an older, motherly nun, nudged her, and, just in time, she met Sister Gerald in the center aisle, bowed to her and then to the altar. As the organ rang out, she intoned the hymn, *Panis Angelicus*, and the other nuns added their voices to the solemn hymn.

As they bowed at the altar once more together, Sister Gerald glanced at her. "What's the matter?" she whispered. "You look like you're in a trance."

"Nothing," Celie whispered back. "I dozed off in my cell. I guess I'm not quite awake."

"Well, wake up! I need your alto to liven up the choir." Had she winked at her before she returned to her chapel stall? Celie wasn't sure. Lately, her Superior had let her guard down, revealing hints of a more mischievous self.

The chanting went on, more brilliant today because of the visiting nuns' voices. Celie welcomed these slow melodious verses, rolling and billowing like pure white curtains rippling in the wind. She sang with a special urgency, hoping to be washed clean before God by the vibrant effort of her song. "Soon, very soon, Lord," she whispered, "I will force myself to go to confession."

Above her clear alto, the crescendo of Sister Gerald's soprano rose up like a soaring flute to the chapel's rafters. As the chant ended, Celie remembered their conversation just the other night. They'd joked about singing, Celie sharing with Sister Gerald how her dad's raucous Irish songs in the shower had resonated throughout their small house when she was a child.

"My father sang, too," Sister Gerald had said. "He took me with him almost every night to the beer joint near our trailer. I was just a bit of a girl. I'd sit on the bar, him holding my legs so I wouldn't slip off, and he'd announce to one and all, 'She's going be a famous singer.' So it went, me performing, and all of them clapping and yelling for more. My father was so proud." She stopped and Celie noticed her luminous, sad eyes as she looked off into the distance. Rarely did she talk of her past.

The first time she'd heard her Superior sing had been on St. Patrick's Day during her Novitiate. The older nun had visited their scripture class and presented a workshop on the New Testament. To this day, Celie had vivid memories of how Sister Gerald had breathed life into the gospel, describing Christ in such human, contemporary terms that Jesus seemed much more real to her. She'd wondered at Sister Gerald's insights and learned later that they stemmed from her command of Aramaic and Greek, the original languages of the New Testament. Fascinated, Celie had asked Sister Gerald several questions after class. That evening, Celie had made her way to the chapel filled with a new excitement and deeper understanding of Jesus, her Bridegroom. Afterwards, during their St. Patrick's Day party, Sister Gerald had settled next to Sister John Marie at the piano and sung the old, favorite Irish tunes with them, "Take Me Home Again, Kathleen" and "When Irish Eyes Are Smiling." Next, they'd swung into another favorite, "Danny Boy." But when most of the nuns faltered on the ballad's high notes, Sister Gerald's voice rang out above all the rest, her olive skin flushed with emotion.

As her last note faded, a hush filled the room. Suddenly her face broke into a wide grin, her dark eyes flashing. "Not bad for an Irish Cherokee, hmm?"

The next day, Celie had plied Sister Adele with careful questions, but the elderly nun gave her only a few crumbs. "Sister Gerald spent her childhood on an Indian reservation in Oklahoma. At seventeen, she moved to the heart of Los Angeles with her father. She never speaks of her mother."

Leaving the chapel now, Celie fell into line behind her Superior, and as the nuns turned to enter the refectory, Sister Gerald beckoned to Celie. "Let's work on the curriculum project tonight, okay? Until chapter seven is finished."

Celie nodded and took her place at the long, U-shaped table, and Sister Adele, standing at the lectern, began to read aloud from the *Life and Apostolic Labors of Venerable Father Junipero Serra*. The material seemed so dry and impersonal that Celie couldn't concentrate on it. She finished the lime Jello salad and the bland rabbit stew with dumplings. Salt and pepper might have spiced it up, but no one bothered to pass them to her. Oh, well, she was used to making these small sacrifices. She took two bites of dessert, apple strudel topped with cheese, and started drumming her fingers on the table. A visiting nun sitting two tables over glared at her, so she stopped.

She could hardly wait for the bell signaling dinner's end. She would slip in a question or two during her session tonight with Sister Gerald. She wanted to discover more about this talented, charismatic woman who had become her mentor and, yes, her friend.

The textbooks they were creating were beginning to take shape. Both women had brainstormed, then blended their ideas to map out the general scope and sequence of each lesson. Celie incorporated the chapters she'd already created for her second grade class, then came up with a detailed outline of curricula for other grade levels and began writing. The lessons would not only instruct children in grades one through five, but would also engage them in Christ's parables by offering activities to put His words into action. The writing process had become much more stimulating than she ever expected.

Every day in the early morning hours, she wrote her first drafts and Sister Gerald critiqued her work later in the day. Always sensitive to criticism, she had faced some difficult moments lately. The older nun seemed to be aware of her sensitivity, for she always ended her critique with at least one compliment. Her positive words were like a comforting salve on an open wound, and gradually Celie realized that her Superior understood her need for encouragement. So, in spite of some rough moments, she looked forward to their evening meetings, which often lasted until midnight.

Tonight, as usual, she sat across from Sister Gerald in her office, the pages of their manuscript spread out all over the oak desk. They'd finally finished working and were now indulging in cups of hot cocoa before ending their meeting and heading upstairs to bed. Sister Gerald set aside the latest Augustinian report she'd been reading to Celie. This was a new bulletin from Rome about the directives of the second session of the Vatican II Council.

"Pope John was a simple, down-to-earth leader who knew his flock intimately," Sister Gerald said. "He embodied not only the letter of the law but the spirit of the gospels, too. He was different from any Pope I can remember." Her eyes lit up with fervor. "He challenged the traditions of the Catholic Church, charging its leaders to study the true message of Christ and bring His kindness to every person. Pope John wasn't interested in the Church's emphasis on sin, punishment, and guilt. He urged both lay Catholics and religious orders to focus instead on imitating Christ's joy and love. I believe his directives to us as religious women still stand, even though his death four years ago created a void in the Council."

"And," Celie asked, "that's why you, as our Superior, interpret some Augustinian traditions and rules differently than at the Motherhouse?"

"What do you mean?"

A few weeks earlier, to Celie's amazement (and gratitude), Sister Gerald had told her they could dispense with the strict nine o'clock Profound Silence Rule. She had explained that as long as they were working on spiritual matters, Profound Silence could wait until the end of their meetings.

"Living in a branch house," she had explained, "is different from living at the Motherhouse, plus the spirit of Vatican II now allows many modifications of our rules."

Celie searched now for the right words. "I've been pleasantly surprised at how you apply practical matters to, for instance, the regulations of silence," she said. "Especially because I'll never forget my punishments at the Motherhouse for breaking Profound Silence. They were humiliating."

Deciding she could trust Sister Gerald enough to share her experiences, she pressed on. "It first happened back in the Postulancy, shortly after I entered. Sister Lupe and I were folding laundry together, separating everyone's underwear using our little number tags. You know, the ones we sewed onto our clothes when we first entered? Mine is 614. Well, old Sister Mary Matthew walked by, and we asked her what her number was—all I intended was to hand her her clothes—but she glared at us like we were headed straight to hell.

"Afterwards, both of us started every meal for a week on our knees. Like this." She demonstrated, kneeling and holding her forefinger to her lips. "Everyone stared at us. And we'd only uttered *one* sentence. The penance was mortifying. But poor Sister Lupe. She *always* ignited Sister Mary Matthew's disapproval. Couldn't seem to avoid it. I only had to suffer through that atonement once. Of course, I broke other rules and endured other punishments."

Sister Gerald nodded, then spoke in measured tones. "Certain beliefs and practices have been imbedded in the Augustinian Rule for centuries. Many need to be modernized."

Celie waited for more, but the older nun changed the subject. "Well, enough theorizing. Would you like more cocoa, Sister?"

Celie hesitated. She was half-afraid to mention a topic that had troubled her for a long time, but she plunged in anyway. "Sister, what about the whip? I was shocked when the Novice Mistress first explained it." That was all she dared to say.

Sister Gerald turned away, stood up, and headed toward the small hot plate sitting on her credenza. "There's at least a cup of cocoa left here," she said, not turning, "and I think it's still warm. How about a refill?"

Celie kept silent. Had Sister Gerald heard her question? The custom the Novice Mistress had described seemed so medieval. Inhumane. She tried again. "How does the spirit of Vatican II fit in with the Augustinian practice of self-flagellation?"

Sister Gerald turned and slowly swallowed the last drops of cocoa. Finally, she said, "You'll see, Celie. There will be some changes."

But she was not satisfied. "Sister Gerald, I just don't understand. I couldn't believe it when the Novice Mistress told us to use the whip at the beginning of Lent. But when we first entered, a girl in my set specifically asked about self-flagellation, and our Postulant Mistress told us it didn't exist anymore. She lied—"

Sister Gerald quickly snatched the cup out of Celie's hands and poured more of the steaming chocolate liquid, spilling some on her hand and the table. "Ouch!"

"Sister, can I help you?"

"No, no, I'm fine. I'll rinse my finger. It wasn't too hot." She wiped the mess up. "Sorry. There's none left now."

Celie didn't say anything because the older nun turned her back again. Then she went into the small bathroom adjoining her office and began washing their cups. When she returned, without a word she began to stack papers into piles. Not until she reached up to turn off the light did she reply. "Pain teaches us much, Sister Celia Marie. It makes us strong. I learned that from my father. To withstand severe pain without flinching is something to be proud of."

What? Celie followed her Superior down the shadowy hall and up the circular stairs to their cells, wondering about Sister Gerald's strange words. How could physical pain possibly strengthen her? Or anyone?

When she reached her cell, she quietly closed her door, then sat on her bed in the dark. Opening the drawer of her bedside stand, she found the small whip. She carefully set it in her lap and let her fingers trace a knot at the end of one switch to where the strand converged with others in a short handle. She fingered each of the knotted switches, one by one. "Kneel in your cell," the Novice Mistress had directed, "and use the whip every Friday in Lent to commemorate Christ's suffering on Good Friday."

Celie knew she would never forget the eerie sounds of her first night in the Novice dormitory. Back then, it looked like a hospital ward at night. Only white curtains separated the sisters' cells. After lights out, the rattle of the whips ricocheted around the room, the knotted cords hitting soft thighs and buttocks throughout the massive room. She had conformed, too, and felt the sharp bite of the lash. But even as she complied with the Rule in the following years, everything within her rebelled at the hideous idea of torturing herself to please God.

Tonight Sister Gerald had given her a chance to admit her true feelings, but she had not given her any answers.

As Celie sat in the shadows, Dennis' words came back to her, "Why does God want these things? Your own dad wouldn't ask that."

CHAPTER 20

A NEW KIND OF FRIENDSHIP

"How about a nature hike tomorrow morning?" Sister Gerald said to Celie. They were completing their work on the latest draft of the textbook. Sister Gerald's voice sounded tired but filled with concern. "You don't seem yourself tonight," she added. "Anything wrong? A walk in the hills might perk you up."

Celie looked up. "What hills? All I've seen here is wall-to-wall city."

"There's a gorgeous area right outside San Francisco," Sister Gerald replied. "Near Oakland. It shouldn't take more than fifteen minutes to get there. You *have* to see the sunrise from those hills. It's magnificent! We could recite the Divine Office together. And we can pack a breakfast, then take a hike, and be back by noon, so you won't miss tomorrow afternoon's tutoring."

Celie brightened. The thought of climbing amid the green grass and wild flowers lifted her spirits. "How did you know?" She stared at Sister Gerald, touched that the older nun sensed how much she missed the apple orchards and fields surrounding the Motherhouse.

Sister Gerald merely smiled. "Are you game?"

They set out before five o'clock the next morning. Darkness shrouded the city streets, but by the time they reached the Oakland hills, the first light of day was competing with the freeway lamps as the two nuns sped along in the Pontiac, like prisoners stealing a few precious hours of freedom.

They raced up the hill as fast as they could, though each was laden with supplies for a sumptuous breakfast. Sister Gerald clambered ahead of Celie, her lean, angular body more like a boy's than a grown woman's. She climbed easily, with a natural athletic gait that carried her higher in minutes. At the top of the hill, she stopped and looked down at the younger nun with her contagious smile.

Dawn's pink light was spreading across the sky when Celie caught up with her Superior. Standing together on the crest of the hill overlooking the Bay, they held hands and watched the drama of nature as it transformed night into day. Not a word was spoken as each nun, feeling the thrill of God's presence, reached for her breviary of psalms. Sister Gerald's full soprano intoned the first solemn lines of Lauds, and Celie answered her in clear alto tones. They chanted in Latin, but inwardly translated the verses, so they could meditate on the message of David's yearning for comfort in his hour of loneliness:

> *My eyes are ever looking to the Lord for help, for*
> *he alone can rescue me. Come Lord, and show me*
> *your mercy, for I am helpless, overwhelmed, in deep*
> *distress; my problems go from bad to worse. Oh,*
> *save me from them all! See my sorrows; feel my pain;*
> *forgive my sins. See how many enemies I have. . . .*
> *Save me from them* (PSALM 25:15–20, NLT).

These words spoke to Celie. Her deep guilt over her secret sins still haunted her.

As they finished, Sister Gerald turned to her. "We should sing Psalm 19, too. It's much more joyful." She pulled out a small, leather-bound book from her pocket and read:

> *The heavens are telling the glory of God; they are a*
> *marvelous display of his craftsmanship. Day and night*
> *they keep on telling about God. Without a sound or*
> *word, silent in the skies, their message reaches out to*
> *all the world. The sun lives in the heavens where God*
> *placed it and moves out across the skies as radiant*
> *as a bridegroom going to his wedding, or as joyous*
> *as an athlete looking forward to a race! The sun*
> *crosses the heavens from end to end, and nothing*
> *can hide from its heat* (PSALM 19:1–6, NLT).

"Yes," Celie said, "that psalm always lifts my spirits. It's so comforting."

"Comforting, yes," Sister Gerald agreed. "And so are you, my little Celie," Her smile was infectious and her dark eyes sparkled. She reached out and drew Celie into a warm hug.

Celie let herself lean against the older nun, suddenly surprised at her tears. As she cried softly, Sister Gerald stroked her neck and back. She lingered there, grateful for her friend's understanding.

"What's the matter, my Celie?" Sister Gerald asked. She handed her a white handkerchief.

"I don't really know." She was at a loss for words. Part of her felt so worthless and lonely, yet this kind woman, a woman so gifted and admired, actually thought she was special.

"Well, dry your eyes now. We've got more climbing to do." Sister Gerald got up and hitched up her long skirts so they hung unevenly around her knees. "C'mon! If you don't get going soon, I'll beat you to the top."

Celie watched her bound up the hill, her spare, muscular body traversing the tufts of weeds and large boulders up the trail. The rest of the morning sped by. They climbed until they were exhausted, then settled on the grass to enjoy the breakfast they'd carried. They ate buttered muffins with strawberries and drank freshly squeezed orange juice, laughing and sharing stories, their spirits high.

Afterwards, lying in the grass together, Sister Gerald gestured to Celie to come closer, but the younger nun was too tired to move. Instead, she turned on her side and faced the slope of the hill, watching the tall eucalyptus trees waving in the wind. Soon she felt Sister Gerald's fingers massaging her back. Though she was surprised, she relished the feeling of her friend's strong hands kneading her shoulders. Her tension began to dissipate, and her body finally relaxed.

Then Sister Gerald moved closer, and Celie felt an unexpected warmth inside as she responded to Sister Gerald's continuing touch. She wanted it to go on and on. She couldn't move. She closed her eyes, letting her body luxuriate in this languid massage. *Just for a moment, let this feeling warm me like the sun, all over and inside too.*

Fingers pressed the muscles of Celie's lower back, then touched her all over, in a rhythmic motion that consoled and mesmerized. Those fingers reached underneath the folds of her habit and stroked her skin and she couldn't think of asking her to stop. Then the fingers were stroking her thighs, hands teasing gently, and all she wanted was more. The older nun came closer, wrapping her arms around Celie's waist, entwining their legs . . . hugging her. Celie breathed in the earthy scent she'd grown so fond of . . . *and her breath on my cheek, her arms encircling me . . . it feels like the heat . . . the heat of Mike's touch long ago. Oh, God!*

What was happening? Celie felt confused, then horrified, then guilty. Her mind raced. Sensations flooding her body, she managed to move away. Finally, she broke free.

What's happening? How does this feel so—? But it was Sister Gerald. *What is she doing?* Celie scrambled to her feet, pasting a smile on her face, though inside she felt like cold marble. *Did I invite this?*

"Can you believe it? It's nearly noon." She knew her voice sounded too bright. "We'd better get back, or my second graders will raise the roof." Not looking at Sister Gerald, still lying in the grass, her habit disarranged, she quickly gathered up the remains of their breakfast picnic, then headed down the hill.

Minutes later, Sister Gerald followed without a word. All the way back to the convent, the silence hung between them.

CHAPTER 21

A WELCOME VISITOR

Using a fierce forearm stroke, Celie slammed the tennis ball against the schoolyard wall and then forced six solid backhand strokes before she battered another forehand cross-court and then raced back to create a lob. As the ball soared up into the sun, she heard clapping over near the classroom doors.

"Terrific form!" yelled Sister Lupe.

Breathless, she stopped and turned to see who her audience was, then bent down to retrieve the ball as it bounced off the wall.

A feeling like mellow wine suffused her at the sight of her friend. The last two weeks had been torture. During their evening meetings, Sister Gerald had been as friendly and vibrant as ever, as if everything were still the same between them, but Celie couldn't help feeling a mixture of revulsion and guilt, and yes, even attraction, toward the older nun. Nor could she help admiring the unusual talent and magnetism Sister Gerald displayed daily in the chapel, at recreation, during their writing sessions. But. . . .

Outwardly, Celie also pretended nothing had happened, but mostly, she doubted herself, wondering if anything had. Yet whenever Sister Gerald came near, she found a way to move away and the last few days had taken their toll. Her stomach was a hard knot, she wasn't sleeping soundly, and she had no appetite. Her mind was a maze of worry and self-loathing.

Seeing Lupe, she felt her body releasing all that pent-up tension. She ran across the schoolyard. Avoiding the usual hug, she held out both her hands to grasp her friend and swiftly brushed her cheek against Lupe's.

"You're a sight for sore eyes," she said.

Lupe's laugh rang out. "Well, you're just a sight. And you need a shower, too." Clowning, as always, Lupe pinched her nose.

Celie grinned back. "I don't care, Lupe Gonzalez. True friends accept the good with the bad! Hey, want to hit with me? There are some extra tennis shoes and a racquet around here somewhere."

"You talked me into it. I need exercise." Lupe followed Celie to the convent door, babbling all the way. "I'm getting so fat I can't stand myself."

Their scores were close. Lupe always gave Celie a workout. During their training years at the Motherhouse, they'd managed to spend some time on the tennis courts almost every Saturday. In the beginning, Lupe had won every game, but Celie loved a challenge and before long, she'd improved her game enough to test Lupe's skill. Today was no exception.

"You've been practicing," Lupe told her. "It shows. You're running me ragged!"

"I've only got a backboard here. What's the matter with you?" Celie shouted as she sent a deep lob across the net, driving Lupe to the end of the court. "You've got scads of people to play with at the Motherhouse."

"No time. Classes are unbelievable this summer." Lupe could barely talk she was so out of breath, but she managed a return, producing a drop shot that forced Celie to race forward to the net. "Tons of papers to write. And you know how I just *love* writing. It's been tough not having you around to help me." She dashed to the left to retrieve Celie's line drive, hammering it back out of bounds. "Whew! You got me. What do you say we take a break?"

Lupe had clearly not played for a long time. *She can't handle the idea of me beating her*, Celie said to herself. *A rest will give her a way out.*

"Yeah," she said aloud, "I'm tired too. So, how long are you staying?" She secretly wished her friend could stay with her all summer. Lupe's antics and teasing on the tennis court reminded her of her girlfriends in high school. Plus, she knew she could learn from her friend's persistent high spirits and her way with children. *It feels so natural to be with Lupe. So different from Sister Gerald.*

They set their racquets aside and walked to the drinking fountain.

"There's an in-service workshop over at Sacred Heart High School tomorrow," Lupe said, "and again on Sunday. The convent is crowded. Lots of the nuns signed up. So I thought of ME over here and you 'all by your lonesome,' and then I asked if I could stay overnight here instead. It's close enough that I can walk there in the morning." She tapped her forehead with her index finger. "Good thinking, huh?"

"Yeah." It was so refreshing to be with her old friend, with no mystery and no pretense. Celie had trusted her since the day they'd met.

Suddenly Lupe was standing still and looking at her. "What's the matter? You okay? I hate to break it to you, your tennis game's great, but you look awful."

Celie faked a grin. "I guess I've been working too hard." She tried to mask her deep conflicts and steer Lupe away from any concern. Underneath her friend's banter, she knew, Lupe had an uncanny gift for perceiving trouble in others.

Lupe nodded. "That curriculum project must be tougher than you thought," she said. "Now, if it were me, I'd be in the pits at the thought of writing so much, but it's your thing. So, is Sister Gerald becoming a slave driver? You were so excited when I last saw you."

Lupe was probing. She had grown up the oldest in a Mexican-Irish family of eight children and had taken over at a moment's notice every time her mother had fallen into epileptic seizures. Her easy chatter had always calmed her younger brothers and sisters afterwards. Years of discerning unease in her own home had given her a keen sense for identifying fear and worry in others.

"So what gives with Sister Gerald?" she was asking now. "It seems like she's always up on a cloud somewhere. Is she easy to work with? I never could talk to her. She always acts like my questions are trivial. Maybe they are. To her. But, gosh, to me, she's the one who's out in space somewhere."

Celie kept silent, so Lupe continued. "I'll never forget the scripture workshop when we first met her. Remember that? The way she talked, so dramatic and everything? It was great, but didn't you think it was, well, a little too much? And did you notice that other nun who was always hanging around her? What was her name? Sister Eileen." Lupe finally stopped.

Celie was careful with her response. "Now that I think of it, yes, I remember Sister Eileen. She came with Sister Gerald. I guess they were good friends."

"Yeah. She stuck to Sister Gerald like glue. They went everywhere together." Lupe's voice was filled with innuendo.

Celie turned to face her. "Lupe, why do you say that? The Vicaress General has recognized Sister Gerald many times. She's not only the youngest Superior to date, but she's also the youngest principal of all our schools. Plus, you can't deny it—she knows scripture backwards and forwards. And her voice. She could've been a professional singer." But though she defended Sister Gerald, Celie felt less conviction than she might have even a week ago.

"I don't know," Lupe said vaguely. "I just get weird vibes when I'm around her. I'm just wondering if you do. You see her a lot."

Celie could feel Lupe examining her face. She finally answered. "Well, sort of." Her voice was thin. "She has such a mysterious way about her. She's certainly not like any other woman I've ever known."

"Take my advice." Her friend's tone had turned serious. "Try to steer clear of Sister Gerald as much as you can. I'm not sure what it is—but she's trouble." Then Lupe switched topics. "Hey, why don't you get permission to come to the workshop this weekend? A professor from UC Berkeley is heading it up. The topic is Teaching the Problem Reader. You must have a few students in that category, right?"

Celie brightened. "Maybe my whole class," she said with a rueful laugh. "It sounds great. I'll ask Sister Gerald this evening."

One thing is certain, she added silently, *I've got to get out of here this weekend.*

Celie fidgeted in her seat. Just one more hour to go. The teaching workshop was stimulating enough, at least so far. But she jotted down a new stanza to a poem she'd been writing in her notebook and stole a glance at her watch.

Lupe, sitting next to her, gave her a nudge. "I've got enough ideas now to last a year," she whispered.

Celie managed to slip her a note just before the seminar director looked in their direction: *If we leave on time, do you want to take a ride to Golden Gate Bridge?*

Lupe signaled with an "okay" nod, though her eyes were riveted on the lectern where the speaker stood, not more than twelve feet away.

Celie marveled at Lupe's apparent concentration. *She play-acts so well. She looks so interested. I can't stand it.*

As the minutes ticked by, her mind began to wander again. Their college days together had been so much fun, especially all those times she'd helped Lupe produce her essays. She longed to return to those innocent days. She knew her friend's triumphs in writing hadn't extended to convent life. Lupe seemed to attract trouble. She washed her habit more often than once a week, which was forbidden. She regularly arrived late for chapel prayers. She had a habit of questioning her teachers too much, and she broke the silence rule way too often. Overall, her carefree, honest spirit grated on teachers and Superiors alike.

". . . and thank you for your attention." The day's speaker finished her presentation, and for some reason was staring at Lupe as she set her pointer to one side and closed her binder of notes.

When the participants rose to leave, Lupe poked her. "Hey, where did *you* go? I bet you found some great material for a new poem, right?" She winked, and Celie glanced at the speaker to make sure she hadn't overheard.

"Shhh."

"Okay, okay," Lupe whispered. "Want to see the Golden Gate, or are you going to rush to your typewriter?"

Celie grinned and pointed to her temple. "I can store it here and bring it back for a story or a poem anytime I want. Let's go!"

Neither of them wanted to miss the sunset over the Golden Gate Bridge.

CHAPTER 22

A SECOND INVITATION

"Sister Celia Marie!" Mrs. Davies tried to stop Celie as she dashed across the schoolyard.

Late for her tutoring class, Celie couldn't hold back her irritation. "What?"

"Special delivery letter, Sister. I'll leave it in your mailbox. Okay?"

"No, I'll take it. It must be important." She masked her curiosity as she turned to accept the letter. She'd never received anything by Special Delivery. She entered her classroom just as her students were settling into their desks. "Children," she said, "open your workbooks."

She noticed how they squirmed during the phonics lesson, and when she gave them a quick oral quiz, most of them missed half the questions. As the morning wore on, four students lost their places in the reading lesson, so she changed course and tried reading aloud to them, even offering a couple of her own zany poems, which usually perked them up. However, though faint smiles pulled at their lips, they still kept rubbing their eyes and fidgeting.

Celie decided that if she was going to squeeze any more out of them, they needed a break. "Okay," she said, with a glance at the clock on the wall, "let's call a halt to this." Her voice was bright. "Want to try a ten-minute recess?"

The children leaped from their desks. As they lined up in front of her, she patted their heads. "The cobwebs in your brains better be gone by the time you come back in here," she said. "Deal?" When they nodded, she said, "Now go play dodge ball."

Remembering the letter, she slipped over to the convent to read it in the privacy of her cell. She fumbled with the envelope and pulled out a sheet of paper.

June 28, 1967

Dear Celie,

My travel plans have suddenly changed, so I wanted to get this off to you as soon as possible. I haven't heard from you yet, but I'm hoping no news is good news and you've decided to see me sometime on the July 4th weekend.

The location of my engineering meeting has moved to Santa Cruz—a hotel right near the retreat house where we met. I have something for you when you come. A surprise.

My plan is to fly to the West Coast this afternoon, so I'll check in late Wednesday night.

Somehow, I know you'll come, if for no other reason than to walk on the beach and search for shells.

Hopefully,
Tony DeStephano

She was tempted. She thought back to the retreat and that first night, when she'd sat on the sand in the moonlight, watching the water and listening to the gulls calling across the waves. She'd felt so close to God. And the next morning she'd gazed across the breakfast table at Tony. It seemed so long ago, so unreal. Now she couldn't quite remember what he looked like.

With an effort, she pushed her daydreams away and hid the letter with the other one, inside a book on her bed stand. As she walked through the convent gate into the schoolyard, her students gathered around her.

"Sister Celia! Play with us, play with us." These Latin American youngsters were so affectionate, smiling and tugging at her long white skirt. Their shiny, eager faces surrounded her now, and their chubby hands pressed the large rubber ball into hers.

Rosa, the group's ringleader, led them to the stucco wall for a game of dodge ball. "C'mon," she ordered, "line up queeck! Before Seester change her mind."

They squealed with delight when Celie took her turn and hit Juan with an accurate throw. Dodge ball was their favorite game. "You out, Juan!" they shouted. "Seester got you out. In one throw!"

Celie raised one hand to get their attention, "Now, now, what did I tell you? No making fun of each other."

"Okay, Seester, we won't." Rosa glared at the others, then motioned to the group and they all lined up again.

Celie's skill at tennis came in handy at times like this. Screams and groans pierced the otherwise quiet yard as she eliminated one contestant after another. Finally, only Rosa was left. The tallest of the second graders, she was eight years old, still in second grade because she'd flunked first grade. Her thick, black hair trailed down her back and wisps clung to her perspiring face as she spun around and around, dodging the ball.

"Watch out, Rosa!" Celia gave the ball another pitch. "This is your last chance!" As Rosa twirled out of the way, it caught in her skirt.

The children screamed. "Rosa's out! Rosa's out!"

Celie ran forward and swept the little girl up into her arms with a wide smile, hoping to dissolve her tears before they appeared.

Rosa gave her a reluctant hug. "Seester, how come you throw so good?"

Celie hugged her tight. "It's a beeeg secret!"

Putting her down, Celie turned to the rest of the children. "Now line up for a drink at the fountain. Then we have work to do!" After everyone had a good, long drink, she hurried them back into the classroom to resume their reading lessons.

She was surprised at the children's quick progress this summer in phonics and comprehension. Helping each child individually was easier than teaching the immense group in her regular second grade class. This was her first attempt at tutoring small groups, and she loved it.

CHAPTER 23

A SHARED CONFIDENCE

Sister Gerald stood up when Celie came into her office for their regular evening editing session.

"Mrs. Davies happened to mention you received a Special Delivery letter today while I was at the San Francisco Teacher's Conference," she said. "Is everything all right at home?"

Celie hesitated for a moment, then dove into a white lie. "Yes, everything's fine. My sister wanted me to be the first to know the University of California in Santa Barbara has accepted her on a full scholarship. She's been attending the local community college, but now she'll be able to graduate from UCSB." As she spoke, she tried to assuage her guilt. She really wasn't lying. Mom had called last Sunday with the news about Maureen.

"That's wonderful!" Sister Gerald's sincerity made her feel worse about her fib. "Now that our home visit rules have changed, perhaps you could arrange to see her on the UCSB campus next fall. It's only about a five-hour drive from here."

"Really? I thought our only option was to go home. You mean we can visit our family in other places?"

"The new Rule of the Order states that the decision about the details of your home visits rests in the hands of your Superior, so. . . ." Sister Gerald's eyes twinkled.

Celie couldn't believe the congregation's rules had relaxed so much. She was thrilled at the thought of visiting a real university. "I haven't seen Maureen since Christmas," she said. "The campus is supposed to be right near the ocean."

"Why don't you plan to go and see her one weekend? Come to think of it, there's a conference on religious instruction this fall not too far from UCSB. Would you like to go? We'll need a publisher for the religion books we've been writing. You'd get to meet lots of people in the publishing business there."

Celie gasped. "That'd be unreal! I've always dreamed of becoming an author, but no one's ever taken me seriously."

"What have you written besides the fabulous lessons you turn in each week?"

"Well, just a collection of poems and short stories. But I'd like to write a novel someday, too."

"I didn't know that. This conference offers an opportunity to meet people in the textbook industry, both authors and publishers. But I believe there's an afternoon session for novelists, too. Perhaps even poets."

Celie felt a thrill of excitement at the thought of rubbing shoulders with anyone in the publishing business. "You can't imagine how fantastic that sounds!"

"Oh, I think I can. I happen to believe we should take our dreams seriously." Sister Gerald's dark eyes shone.

Without thinking, Celie asked, "Did you follow your dream?"

"Partly. I wanted to be a Sister when I was a little tyke. In those days, the Augustinians visited the Cherokee reservation every week. I always looked forward to it. They came with food, clothes, and books." She picked up the small, worn Bible that always lay on her desk. "I'll never forget one nun, Sister Imelda. She helped me learn to read, and she aided me in so many other ways, too. If she hadn't been there for me when I was very young, I don't think I'd be here now."

Celie noticed how her Superior bit her lower lip, then quickly wiped the edge of one eye. She was hearing this woman's very private secrets. Celie could hardly believe this talented nun had grown up amid such poverty and struggle. She wanted to reach out and comfort her, but all she said was "I've heard the older nuns talk about Sister Imelda. She's sort of a legend in the congregation, isn't she? You must've really looked up to her."

"An understatement. She was the closest I ever came to having a mother. My father left me alone a lot. Sometimes I was glad he did."

Now Sister Gerald stepped closer and opened the Bible to show Celie Sister Imelda's note and signature written in the front cover. "Even though she moved up the Augustinian ranks very fast, Sister Imelda found time to visit me when I was a teenager. She was always there for me. And a couple of times I phoned her, desperate for help. . . ."

The older nun suddenly turned away and stared out the window at the empty schoolyard. Without a glance at Celie, she continued talking as if her memories of Sister Imelda quivered before her like a mirage in a desert wasteland, "I used to watch for her from our little house when I was young. It wasn't much, believe me. A ramshackle hut at the edge of the reservation. Her old black Ford would drive in the gates almost every Saturday. I'd station myself at our kitchen door and race out to meet her as soon as I saw her. Once she brought me shoes to wear to school. She *always* brought books. And books are what saved me. One time on my birthday, she carried in a used record player and a stack of records. I was overjoyed! She knew I loved music, and even that young, I could sing. I must've played those records a thousand times. I memorized all the words and sang those songs until. . . ."

"Until what?"

"My father came home drunk one night. And smashed them all. I've never forgiven him. For some reason, I remember that incident more clearly than all the beatings he ever gave me."

The air in the room seemed to vibrate. Celie didn't know how to respond. She laid her hand on her Superior's arm.

The ringing of the telephone pierced the moment, wiping out the older nun's past. Resuming her role as school principal, Sister Gerald reached for the receiver. As the conversation lengthened, she interrupted the caller. "Sister Celia, this will take a while. I've tried to reach this parent all week. Can we postpone our meeting until tomorrow night?"

Celie nodded and closed the door quietly behind her. Sister Gerald's words still hung in her thoughts as she climbed the convent stairs in the dark.

CHAPTER 24

UNFORGETTABLE MOMENTS

"I've decided to reward you for all your hard work," Sister Gerald said. "I've poured us our usual warm cocoa, but I have a surprise. I guarantee it will add a zing to the chocolate flavor." Her eyes twinkling, she opened a cabinet near the coffee table and pulled out a bottle of Kahlua.

Celie was mildly shocked when her Superior added a little liqueur to each mug. She hadn't tasted liquor since her last high school party, a beer more than four years ago. When she was growing up, alcohol was scarce in the O'Rourke household, as her father had repeatedly told the story of his "drunken Irish uncle, a worthless loafer who wasted his life." She could only remember Mom and Dad having a highball with friends at Christmas time. Later, when she was in high school, Dad drank a glass of wine or two with dinner. His martinis were a recent addition. And now Maureen had written that he'd upped them to at least three a night. *She must be exaggerating*, Celie thought, but, regardless, she had always heeded Dad's warnings. *Take care of your body and your mind. Don't spoil the gifts God has given you. The last thing you want to do is lose your ability to control your life. Never give anyone the chance to say they saw you do something you can't even remember because you drank too much.*

As her father's words drifted through Celie's mind, Sister Gerald patted the couch beside her. "C'mon," she said. "Sit down and relax for a few minutes. You look exhausted. You tutor the children till two o'clock every day, and then you work on our textbook project, not to mention the fact that you get up before five every morning. My dear," she handed the doctored cocoa to Celie, "I admire your dedication, but sometimes you have to take time to enjoy yourself."

Sister Gerald was right. She was weary. Because she wanted to meet the November textbook deadline, she'd been driving herself well beyond her normal work schedule. This meant long hours, often working past midnight, to complete her tutoring work, her summer coursework, and the manuscripts. Besides, she said to herself, a little Kahlua in her cocoa was far different than the drunken high school parties she'd heard about.

Sister Gerald tried again. "Sister, do you realize you haven't taken a break in three weeks? It seems like you haven't smiled since then, either."

Celie managed a grin and sat down next to her Superior.

The older woman handed Celie a steaming mug. "I found the most wonderful album," she said. "I love the music." She pulled a record out of its jacket, then got up to switch on the turntable.

As Celie heard the familiar, haunting melody, her whole body stiffened, but then she drew in a deep breath and closed her eyes, luxuriating in the melody played on the balalaika. "It's 'Lara's Theme,' the soundtrack from *Doctor Zhivago*," she murmured. "I saw the movie before Christmas."

"Lucky you! I haven't seen it yet, but when I was shopping, that melody was playing and I couldn't resist buying the album. It's unforgettable, isn't it?" She hummed along to the music as she sat down on the couch again. "It's so seldom that we enjoy life's simple joys. We'll miss them, Celie, unless we force ourselves to stop for a minute and listen to their beauty." She leaned back, her mug in her lap, her mellow voice humming louder.

Celie remembered certain scenes from the movie only too well. The hot cocoa trickled down her throat and she savored the liqueur. Chocolate was her weakness and she loved coffee, too. The combination was irresistible.

When Sister Gerald got up to put on another record, Celie welcomed a refill. As she relished its flavor, an exhilarating warmth spread through her and she stretched out on the couch and began to unwind.

The music changed to rock and roll tunes.

Sister Gerald's voice was soft. "You probably remember these oldies from the late '50s and early '60s better than I do," she murmured as Chubby Checker's voice singing "Let's Twist Again Like We Did Last Summer" drifted through the room. When the song ended, tunes by the Beach Boys began, and Celie joined the older nun singing "California Girls" and "Good

Vibrations." The mood changed slightly with Fats Domino's "Blueberry Hill," and it changed again with an old favorite Johnny Mathis song, ". . . helpless as a kitten up a tree. . . ."

By now, Celie was lounging like a schoolgirl, with pillows tucked behind her, her body stretched out, the long white skirt of her habit forming a tent around her bent legs. Sister Gerald got up to refill their mugs but Celie didn't protest—she was feeling a contented buzz by now as her Superior put on some more albums of golden oldies. They sang on and on along with the nostalgic tunes, and she noticed vaguely that she was drinking wine now—out of a crystal goblet that sparkled when she held it up to the glowing lamplight.

Daylight was gone and only one small lamp lit the room. Celie's head felt fuzzy, her body languid and mellow, and she was hardly aware of how close Sister Gerald was, singing in the full, throbbing tones everyone loved.

"You must be tired, and tense," the older nun murmured as another song started. Sister Gerald moved even closer and began massaging Celie's arms and her shoulders. With a soft giggle, Celie reached for a refill as she blended her voice with her friend's, singing "Where Have All the Flowers Gone."

Celie was hardly aware of Sister Gerald undoing her coif and veil and taking them off. "I have to get comfortable," she whispered. Celie agreed. She would get comfortable, too. Letting her coif and veil fall to the floor, she accepted another full glass of Chablis. Now the romantic, sensual "Lara's Theme" returned, and Celie settled back against the pillows again and closed her eyes, slipping into a delicious reverie as Sister Gerald stroked her forehead and temples, fingering Celie's hair. Celie wondered if Mom ever fondled her hair like that when she was a child. She didn't remember. Still sipping her wine, she lay quietly, her eyes closed, filled with music and reverie, marveling at this new contentment. She faintly sensed Sister Gerald's arms reaching around her, releasing the fasteners of her tunic. She could smell the sweet, musky aroma of Sister Gerald's body.

Now the wine drew a filmy curtain over the dim room as Celie sank into a pleasurable darkness where she was only distantly aware of tangible realities. She heard the music; she heard Sister Gerald's incredible voice soaring above hers. Somehow her white tunic was on the floor now with her coif and veil, and she could feel Sister Gerald's fingers releasing all the tension in her aching muscles. She felt so warm and loved. It was as if a benevolent force were cradling her, bathing her in rich light. Sister Gerald was near, her hair touching her throat, touching her body, lightly teasing her, kneading and stroking her.

They moved together in a circle of irresistible closeness and warmth. Sister Gerald wrapped her in her arms. She pressed her lips to Celie's neck, and her throat, then her mouth moved down Celie's body and Celie began to groan with pleasure.

As Celie watched, as if in a dream, Sister Gerald dipped her fingers into Celie's wineglass and dribbled the wine onto her lips, her throat, her breasts. When Celie opened her mouth, Sister Gerald gave her one more generous swallow of wine, then her hands began searching out forbidden places, and Celie moaned, wanting more.

The rock and roll beat wailed on as her breathing and excitement mounted, reaching a crescendo that was totally new to her. Celie shuddered with pleasure after pleasure. At last, she lay spent as the music sang on. Vaguely, she felt Sister Gerald's arms still holding her. And then she slept.

CHAPTER 25

SHOCK AND ESCAPE

Holding both hands to her forehead, Celie tried to stop the throbbing. The first light of dawn was filtering through the blinds. *Where am I?* Groggy and lost, she blinked. She could see the outline of Sister Gerald's desk. But she was alone. *What happened?* Celie remembered only pieces of the night before. She sat up, trying to make sense out of the fuzzy visions reeling around in her head. *Where—what?* The smell of stale wine and liquor nauseated her.

She realized that only an old quilt was covering her body. Where was her habit? On the floor. Faint images of shocking intimacy crowded her mind. "My God!" Waves of revulsion seized her. Tears spilled down her cheeks, giving way to convulsive sobs.

What happened? How could I . . . how did this happen? "Oh my God, my God!" She lay back down on the couch, writhing in emotional pain. She wanted to die.

How did she make it to morning prayers? She would never know. What she knew was that she couldn't bear to look at Sister Gerald sitting calmly in the stall across from her. Morning prayers ended, she feigned illness and sought refuge in her cell, where she took a sleeping pill because all she wanted to do was erase her memories. Later in the day, frantic after she awakened, she phoned Sister Adele at a conference at the neighboring convent. She was afraid to approach Sister Gerald to ask permission to leave the convent and spend the coming July Fourth weekend at the old retreat house again in Santa Cruz.

"Sister Rosarita will be the only one here today," Sister Adele told her. "The others are attending various teaching conferences. Child, of course you can go. If you feel the need. You certainly don't sound yourself. The sea breeze will cool your mind and warm your heart."

In her frenzy, Celie hadn't been able to think of anywhere else to go.

"You can leave this afternoon," Sister Adele added. "Take the Pontiac. Mr. Gonzales has just finished tuning it and changing the oil."

Making sure her cell door was firmly closed, Celie began to shed her religious garb. First, she unclasped her leather belt and took off the large ebony rosary beads that hung from her waist to the hem of her long skirt. Next, she unlaced her granny shoes and kicked them off. Then she unhooked her thick, charcoal stockings from her garter belt and peeled them off. Standing up, she went to her small mirror over the sink. As she unpinned the black veil and white coif covering her hair, she noticed her ashen face.

"Oh God, forgive me," she prayed out loud. "And forget I'm running away, too. Dear God, I can't handle this mess anymore. I need some space or I'll go crazy."

Suddenly she thought of Tony. He might not show up. She'd never left him a message. *If I can just wander the beach alone,* she said to herself, *maybe I can sort out this chaos. What have I done?*

Up and over her head went the long muslin scapular that usually covered her habit like a pure white apron. Then she shed the floor-length tunic dress and full, cotton slip. The morning was hot. Her body felt clammy. Was it the unusual humidity or her agonizing turmoil?

She had to disappear while no one was around to see her because leaving the convent in secular attire was forbidden without permission, at least as far as she knew. Swiftly she threw the few pieces of civilian clothing she had borrowed from the thrift shop into her worn leather suitcase and slipped into the faded jeans, T-shirt, plaid jacket, and sandals she'd worn the last time. Then she tiptoed down the inner stairs to the garage where the Pontiac waited. Everyone was away this weekend. Sister Adele had assured her the car wouldn't be missed.

Ten minutes later, she was winding her way through the traffic on Army Street, bound for State Route 1 and Santa Cruz. Was she really leaving this torment behind? Her utter relief at escaping from Sister Gerald gradually seeped into her soul as she maneuvered the sedan onto the freeway. She'd never really planned to meet Tony again, but when she'd realized at Mass this morning this was the weekend he'd written about, a surge of liberation had flooded through her.

Maybe it was the idea of going back to last spring, of recapturing those wondrous moments of innocence and peace she'd found beside the ocean. Everything around her at the convent had turned into a nightmare. Though the air was still unusually warm, thoughts of Sister Gerald made her shiver.

The afternoon sun nearly blinded her as she steered the car west along the highway, commuters crowding the freeway. When dizziness threatened to overcome her and interfere with her driving, she opened her window wide and quickly took deep breaths of the sea air, trying to quell the nausea, forcing herself to pay attention to the road, to drive more carefully.

Back in control, more or less, she finally allowed herself to picture Tony. Would he come?

Stopping at a signal, she looked in the rearview mirror, surveying her pale face and copper freckles sprinkled liberally over the bridge of her upturned nose. She struggled to cheer herself, playing a childhood game, puckering her lips up in a grotesque grin. It was useless. Queasiness filled her stomach along with an exhaustion that clung to every limb of her body.

Deep inside, she felt a dead weight. She was a damaged bird with broken wings.

CHAPTER 26

TONY SHARES HIS SORROW

At last—there was the old retreat house below the distant cliffs, nestled snugly among tall pine and cypress trees. A peaceful calm began to seep through Celie as she drove. She kept glancing at the aging Spanish hacienda overlooking the sea. It felt like home, a truer home than the one she'd grown up in, a truer home than the convent or the Motherhouse. Yes, she was coming home at last.

The dinner hour was near as she pulled up and parked. She lingered beside the car for a moment, watching the dark foliage silhouetted against a russet sky and waving in the ocean breezes. She started up the steep steps leading to the retreat house, but unable to resist the call of the waves, she turned toward the ocean and ran down the hill to the surf below.

She stopped on a mound only a few yards from the foaming waves and tossed her borrowed pair of sandals aside. Her toes burrowed into the warm sand. The salt air invigorated her. She'd thought about this scene many times since last March, mostly at night, and then every muscle in her body would relax. Now, as the chilly afternoon breeze played with her auburn hair, she pulled the borrowed jacket more tightly around her shoulders. She gazed at the shimmering ocean, watching the gulls soaring high in the sky, then gliding up and around, back and forth, landing here and there to scavenge for bits of food.

It's like someone is offering me new life. She took another deep breath, welcoming the myriad scents of the seashore. Had it only been four months since she'd walked along this beach, trying to decide whether to renew her vows? "Oh, God, please forgive me!" she cried aloud.

She waded into the surf, dancing between the foaming rivulets to prevent her rolled up jeans from getting wet. She looked north up the coast below the retreat house. Then she saw him. There he was, way off, where lofty cypress trees above leaned out on overhead cliffs. He was a small figure, but she knew it was Tony. He was hurrying toward her. She held her breath as he raised his hand in greeting. Relief grounded her. She waved back.

No one else was on the beach except a black Labrador rummaging through the stray driftwood and seaweed. After a moment, the dog ran to her and began to lick her hands. She tensed and held herself stiff, so the dog lost interest, turning away to poke at the clumps of kelp, probably sniffing out some small sea creature.

"Looks like we have company," Tony shouted as he drew near. He was taller than she remembered.

Her heart suddenly began beating faster. She tried to smile, but gestured at the dog, glimpsing his eyes for only a moment before she looked away. "Yes, and I'm not too keen about it, either."

His eyebrows lifted. He came closer. "You don't like dogs?"

"I had a puppy a long time ago. I loved her, but she died. I don't like large dogs. When I was five years old, my dad brought home an Irish Setter. They called him Streak. He was three times my size, and he towered over my older sisters, too. After he knocked me down a bunch of times, I stayed inside and watched him race around the backyard like he was crazy. I was petrified to go out there unless he was tied up. I never heard the end of it from my sisters. They thought he—" She suddenly realized she was talking nonstop. Would he notice?

"Why?" he asked.

"Well, they're both older than me." She finally met his gaze. "Neither of them was a 'fraidy cat' like I was."

He smiled at her, his brown eyes soft, holding hers in a stillness that reached inside her and offered comfort.

As if starved for air, she breathed in his calmness.

He leaned down and offered a hand to the friendly, oversized puppy. After getting a good licking, he scratched under the dog's chin. "Hey, guy," he said, "you're nobody to be afraid of, are you? You just want some company, don't you?" He stepped back a bit. "Looks like he hasn't had a meal in awhile." Reaching into his pocket, he pulled out two packs of saltine crackers, which he gave to the dog. Then, picking up a piece of driftwood, he threw it off in the distance. The Lab scampered after it and brought it back, dropping it at Tony's feet. They repeated the game several times, and finally the dog raced off down the beach.

"You've made a friend," Celie said.

Tony was watching the dog, but his smile faded. "I had a dog myself for several years. In fact he was a black Lab, too, but older than this one. His name was Rex."

"What happened to him?"

"He got cancer last year. I had to put him down."

"Oh, how terrible for you."

"Yes. It was very difficult."

There was a long silence. Celie had to break it, so she changed the subject. "It's good to see you. What brings you out to California again?"

"Oh, business, of course—that defense project. And I guess I needed a rest." He paused. "I needed to get away from everything." The dog came racing back, and he reached down to pet it again. He stroked the dog's ears for a minute, then stood up and threw the stick with a severe kind of energy.

Celie faced him straight on so he could not turn away. Worry lines etched his brow and his eyes looked somber. "Is something wrong?" she asked. "You seem down." She grinned. "You're not the carefree burglar I remember."

He smiled briefly. "I just need some time alone here. Time to think and rest."

Her heart was aching for him. "You sound like me four months ago," she said. *Now, too,* she thought. "C'mon, I think dinner must be ready. Maybe a walk on the beach and a solid meal will make us both feel better."

She instinctively fell into step with him as they trudged across the sand. He held out his hand, but his strides outpaced hers, and her fingers only skimmed his, then slipped away, even though she jogged to keep up. Silence stretched between them and Celie's feelings of desolation began to take hold again. To distract herself, she pointed at the glowing sky, "Unbelievable sunset, isn't it?"

Tony nodded, keeping up his rapid pace. The dog trailed them, even following when they climbed the old wooden staircase leading to the retreat house. As the screen door slammed, the Lab settled down outside to wait for them.

They chose a table near the window. Only a few people occupied the dining room on this holiday weekend, since it wasn't a popular time for a quiet retreat. As they sat in silence after the same old nun had taken their order, Celie began to wonder if she should excuse herself after dinner to be alone, to sort out her tangled emotions.

Never adept at small talk, she attempted conversation by asking Tony to explain the two pasta dishes listed on the mimeographed menu. As he pronounced them in Italian, she listened to the lilting tones. "I've always wanted to learn Spanish, but Italian sounds so much more musical. I've taken five years of Latin, and you know what? It really is a dead language as far as helping my students. I wish I'd studied Spanish. Their families are recent immigrants from Cuba and Central America. Some of them start school speaking no English at all."

"I know what that's like," he said. "English is my second language. I didn't learn it until I started first grade back in Brooklyn." He stopped and looked straight into her eyes. His voice softened. "You look great. I'm glad to be here with you."

Her face suddenly felt warm. She tried to laugh away her embarrassment.

"It's been a long time since I've seen a woman blush," he said. "It's refreshing in this crazy era."

What's troubling him? Well, at least he's finally smiling.

During dinner, however, an imperceptible sadness seemed to take hold of him. His eyes turned dark and his shoulders sagged, as if he were carrying an unbearable burden. He stared out the window into the darkness. Perhaps, she thought, she could help him by listening . . . if he would trust her enough to confide later. In spite of his somber mood, she felt exhilarated around him, alive, even relaxed, and the convent was far away. Something about him made her feel free. Her words tumbled out naturally, and before she knew it, she began telling him things she hadn't told anyone in years. She spoke about her writing, her poetry, the textbooks she was creating for her students. He listened carefully. She wasn't used to such attentiveness.

The meal over, they decided to relax in the living room of the old lodge, but as they got up from the table, a strange dizziness seized Celie, and she grabbed at the table to steady herself. Not noticing, Tony stopped the tiny nun and tried to persuade her to give him some leftovers. When she nodded yes, he excused himself and followed her to the kitchen. He was back in a few moments.

"For the dog," he said, looking sheepish. Then he noticed. "You look pale. Are you okay?"

"I'm fine. Really." She faked a smile and straightened her shoulders. Her lightheadedness was subsiding. *It has to be all the stress.*

Rich oak bookcases jammed full of old books lined the walls of the room, and a green braided rug covered the worn mahogany floor. Tony settled into a tattered but comfortable wingback chair that faced the mammoth stone fireplace that took up almost an entire wall. But he was restless. A minute later, he got up and stoked the fire with a few logs and some kindling, then sat down again to admire the new blaze. Only the flames lit the room.

Celie sat down across from him in a large, padded rocking chair that also faced the fireplace. She covered her lap with a brown crocheted blanket. Thoughts of Sister Gerald suddenly forced their way into her mind again, and a faint wave of dizziness returned. She pushed images of the older nun out of her thoughts, and the dizziness passed. Tony was so quiet that she thought he'd fallen asleep. Then she heard him move and heave a slow sigh.

"It must be a release for you to soak up this cozy serenity," she said in a quiet voice.

"Serenity? Yeah. Right." He was silent for a minute. "Lately I don't know what peace is! My life's turned me inside out. It's my turn to struggle. Maybe you know what I'm talking about."

"Well, yes. This year's been full of challenges for me, too. Problems I didn't expect. That's partly why I came back here. This place soothes me." She clenched her teeth, trying not to cry. *Better to let him talk.*

"I understand," he said. "I feel like I'm sitting in a family room, and somehow I belong here. It's strange—I don't feel this way in my own living room at home. That's probably why I avoid it. I always end up in my kids' rooms, talking to them about school or helping them with their homework. Or I wind up in the basement, working on all my projects. But soon I might not be living there at all." He sighed and shook his head as if to clear it. "Well, I'll have to get used to the idea."

Celie sucked in her breath. *He's married!?* She sat up straighter and twisted her fingers through the gaps in the crocheted blanket. "Oh? How old are your children?"

"Michael is almost six, and Tony Jr. is eight. They're both characters. And quite different. They fight like crazy, but they're really good friends underneath. I'm glad. Someday when they're grown, they're going to need at least one good friend. I hope they have each other."

She didn't know what to say, so she folded her arms over her chest and began rocking. She was feeling the vertigo again, so she took more deep breaths. She noticed that the smell of the burning pine logs vaguely consoled her.

He was still speaking. "We love to camp. I'm planning a trip to Cape Cod, before the weather turns cold. Actually, I'm really looking forward to our taking a vacation together." As an afterthought, he added, "Anyway, I hope I can make it happen."

She stopped rocking. "If you want it that bad, you'll do it." She heard how sharp her tone was. Suddenly she felt upset, angry. Why had he asked to meet her here?

"I wish it were that easy," he was saying. "My wife is making everything tough for all of us, the boys, me."

The hush that followed was almost palpable. Celie knew he was hurting, but she couldn't speak. Nausea gripped her, and her stomach felt like she'd eaten stones for supper. *I have to get control of myself. He needs a friend. It's what I do.*

It was in the hoarseness of his voice. It softened as he spoke of his home and his young sons. She could feel his anguish.

He spoke again finally, as if he were speaking something out loud for the first time, "You see," he began, "I . . . I've just . . . I just discovered she's been seeing someone else. She's having an affair." He let the words hang, his voice hollow and empty, then he went on, as if now that he'd poked a small hole in the dam, his words could flow out freely, unmeasured and unjudged. "The part that's really hanging me up is, well, my boys have known about it for almost a year. They were afraid to tell me. Afraid of my reaction. The whole thing is a nightmare."

Empathy filled Celie, but she could only muster a few simple words. "Tony, I'm so sorry." Her body ached as she rocked in the shadows.

The fire was barely flickering now. The room had become a cave. Shrouded in darkness, she couldn't see his face. He and the wingchair had turned into a single dark silhouette. She sank down into her rocking chair and pulled the crocheted blanket up to her chin, trying to will his sadness away, along with hers.

He went on with his monologue, seemingly alone in his own universe. "Sometimes, when I let myself think about her and the boys, well, I just can't believe this is happening. You know? Me contemplating divorce? I've been a Catholic all my life. I'm not sure how the Church will view this!

"I was such a fool," he continued after a minute. "Why didn't I figure it out? I think about all the times she wasn't there when I came home from work. She was going to night classes, and I was the one who encouraged her to go back to college. I even helped her with her homework. I helped her study for her exams. So she was gone lots of evenings, but I didn't question it because that's what we were doing. Covering for each other on the home front. So we could build something for the future." He stopped.

"She went back to school to get her nursing degree," he said. "I did the same thing last year and the year before. Went back to school. I worked all day and took coursework at night to earn my MBA. It was my ticket to a better life. For both of us. For all of us. I thought she felt the same way about her degree. I even hired a housekeeper because she said there was no way she could carry a full load of classes and cook and clean and take care of the boys, too.

"But on some level, I must have known."

His voice turned harsh. "She'd been so cold to me for so long, I guess I got used to it. I figured that's the way it is when you're married for nine years."

His murky silhouette shifted in the shadows. Celie could barely see him. Then he sat forward and turned to face her. His face was half-lit by the fire. "The bottom line is, well, I probably didn't *want* to know what was going on. The more I think about it, the more I realize all the signs were there. I was so goddamned blind." He was reaching out. He wanted condemnation and understanding at the same time.

She tried to think of something to say to comfort him. Tears welled up in her eyes. "Sometimes things are too painful to see."

"That's right," he said. "You know about that too?" His voice showed surprise. Then it turned rough, as if he were angry at himself, at her, at the whole world. "How could you know?"

"I—"

"I'm sorry," he said. "I'm not myself. I shouldn't take this out on you. I've thought about you at lot in the last few months. That night I broke into your room. My joke about being a burglar. The morning we had breakfast together. You seemed to think so deeply about things that matter. That's why I had to come back here. To talk to you."

She finally found her voice. "Have you told all this to anyone else?"

"Of course not." His voice was low, depressed. "There isn't anyone else."

She waited. As weary as she felt, she had to say something to him, anything to console him.

"Several years ago," she began, hoping the uncertainty in her voice wasn't obvious, "back when I was a senior, the high school principal told someone I was way too intense, that I took everything too seriously. A friend told me what she'd said. I was really hurt. I thought I'd been insulted. I considered intensity a negative then. . . . But now that I'm older, well, I think there's a positive side to it. You know, thinking deeply about things, like you said. That's why I liked my college philosophy classes. My dad can be serious, too, sometimes, and he philosophizes about life, especially at family gatherings. Sometimes I think I take after him, but that sort of scares me, too, because his passion gets him into trouble. And I don't want that to happen to me."

"How?" He sounded interested in what she was saying.

"He broods. If he's in a bad mood, you never know why. It used to be kind of creepy to come home from school and see him sitting in the family room in the dark, sometimes for hours. We kids knew to stay away and leave him alone, because if you tried to talk to him, he'd say something mean or sarcastic."

"Is he still that way?"

"Yeah. Well, I guess so. I haven't been home in a while, of course. But what my mother and sisters say in their letters is that he comes home from work now and drinks way too much, and no one goes near him. My sisters are worried. Colleen was hellbent on getting away from home. I wonder if that's why she got married."

Darn, I'm rambling again. She wanted to steer the conversation back to Tony. "So, yes, I know about people who don't want to confront their demons. Sometimes they don't know how. Dad won't deal with his feelings. It's probably why he drinks. And my mom won't even talk about it. How can she? She's trying so hard to keep up a flawless front and pretend all of us are perfect. In fact, everyone at home is busy acting as if we're 'the model Catholic family.' I guess it's too big a risk to face things head-on. But I hope someday we will."

"Sometimes," he said slowly, "we don't meet things head-on until they're forced on us." He was sounding more forgiving now. "Where is home?" he asked.

"Sunny Southern California." Her tone was sarcastic. "They live in San Gabriel. It's about forty minutes east of L.A."

"Is that why you moved up north? San Gabriel's at least seven or eight hours from here." His question cut into her. He was blunt, but oddly, she liked his directness. It was so different from the way she'd been brought up.

"I guess that's part of it," she finally said, admitting it to herself for the first time.

They sat and watched the dying flames for a while, holding their shared moments in their hearts. The only sounds in the dark house were the sparks that flew up from the last pieces of brittle kindling. As a new blaze lit the room, she looked over at him. He was leaning back in the chair, his long legs stretched out in front of him, his feet on an old footstool. He was tall and muscular, she thought, and everything about him looked strong and competent.

And yet his heart is so wounded, she thought. *I guess we all are, in different ways.*

She had been almost awestruck at dinner when he'd talked about his job as an engineering manager at a large firm on the East Coast. He seemed young for so much responsibility. Maybe in his early thirties? She thought of his wife and the broken trust between them, and how his words revealed his love for his sons. What would happen to them? They were so young to learn about infidelity firsthand, and they'd tried to shield their father, too.

When the grandfather clock chimed, Celie counted to twelve. The fire was low now, and blue and orange flames wrapped themselves around the logs. Celie watched how the light flickered and played on the fireplace walls. Suddenly she began to wonder why she'd told Tony about her dad. She never shared private family details. Besides, what did her dad have to do with Tony's problems? She scolded herself for sharing her petty worries in the face of his insurmountable difficulties. Maybe she'd let him down.

Her nausea had disappeared, and now she felt spent and empty. She longed to tell him her own troubles. *But that'll never happen.*

All of a sudden, Tony rose from the chair. "Well, I think it's time. . . ." He came over to her, and put out his hand to help her up. She stood facing him, at a loss for words.

"Thank you, Celie. You've helped me," he said. "I knew you would." His hands gently closed on her shoulders as he leaned over and kissed her softly on her forehead.

She looked up at him as he stepped back. Tears gleamed in his eyes. But she couldn't say anything because her own eyes were full, too. She wanted so much to hug him, but instead she only nodded and tried to smile, as her own tears, seeping through the dam of her determination, began streaming down her cheeks. Pent up feelings were threatening to crack the shell of her composure, and now sobs began constricting her throat. She barely managed to say, "Good night."

"Wait," he said. "I've upset you."

He reached out again, but she shook her head and ran ahead of him up the stairs to her room.

CHAPTER 27

A FERRIS WHEEL DAY

All night long Celie had turned over and over in her bed, bombarded by dreams of Sister Gerald mixed with Tony. Now a blue-gray darkness filled Celie's room, the sheets felt hot, and a dog kept barking outside. Slowly lifting her feet out from under the covers, she sat up, then staggered over to the window to look out. The beach was an alabaster world, everything encased in fog. But where the sunrise had broken through, traces of glittery light shone on the ocean. Sure enough, there was the black Lab barking at the gulls overhead.

As she gazed outside, Celie's mood lifted, and a sense of freedom and peace began to fill her. Then she thought of Tony, and a thrill of excitement flowed through her, replacing the turmoil of her bad dreams. He had come here merely to find a friend, someone to confide in. She understood that now.

She wondered what this new day would bring. Why not take a morning walk? She found her jeans and T-shirt and put on the bulky ivory sweater she'd thrown into the suitcase as an afterthought. Only yesterday afternoon? So long ago.

When she reached a clearing a few yards from the retreat house, she saw Tony sitting on a large piece of driftwood under a grove of cypress trees, the black Lab sitting at his knees. Both were facing the ocean, their backs to her.

"Did you have insomnia, too?" she called as she trudged down the hill toward them.

Tony turned around and waved, holding on to the Lab's collar with his left hand. "I couldn't sleep, so I thought I'd spend some time with my friend here. He's been barking up a storm." He stroked the dog's throat as she approached.

"I know," she said. "I heard him. Have you named him yet?"

"I thought I'd call him Rags. What do you think?"

"That's a good choice. He's raggedy all right. I don't think he's had a bath in awhile." She came forward, tentatively approaching the dog, ready to fend off his advances.

Tony gripped his collar, "Don't worry. I've got him. He won't bother you." Nonetheless, she planted herself at least six feet away.

Tony chuckled. "You really are afraid of him, aren't you? He's harmless. Here, let me show you. Try to relax and stand still. Now just hold out your hand and let him sniff it first. Like this. Then scratch him under his chin." He demonstrated, and the dog began licking his forearm.

She took two or three reluctant steps forward. "Okay." But her shoulders tensed up and her teeth began to chatter, a response to childhood fear. The dog danced around her and stopped to lick her stiff, outstretched hand. She tried hard to calm herself as he sniffed her legs and shoes, then her upper thighs, but when he jumped on her, she pushed him away. "Go on, Rags. Go back to Tony. Go on!"

"Here, Rags, come here." Tony bent over to corral the dog with both arms. Then he let go and picked up a stick. "Go fetch, Rags!" He threw the stick far into the distance, and the dog scampered after it.

Celie was relieved to see the retriever stop to sniff a pile of kelp. "I'm a failure with dogs," she said. "Can't you throw the stick any further? To San Francisco, maybe?"

Tony's eyes searched her face. "That dog your father brought home must've seriously frightened you."

She nodded. "Yes. And I need to give my brain new information somehow, or I'll just keep holding onto those scary memories."

"Fear is strange," he said. "It keeps you frozen—the mind builds great defense mechanisms. It's the old horse story. If you fall off, you have to get back up and ride or you may never do it again. It works with bicycles, too." He smiled.

Celie tapped the side of her head. "It sounds easy up here, but I have a hard time when I'm scared. It overwhelms me, and I don't even know why I'm so frightened."

"You're not afraid of Ferris wheels, are you?" He pointed up the coast to a Ferris wheel that was barely visible in the lifting fog.

His question caught her off guard. "No, I'm not." She smiled back at him.

They headed up the beach toward the Santa Cruz Fun Zone, Rags trotting behind them.

"In a way," Tony said, "I was surprised you showed up this weekend, especially near a holiday. My secretary said you never called."

"I decided to come at the last minute," she said. "I needed a break, big time. Teaching plus drafting the new textbooks has been very demanding."

He nodded. "I was worn out myself, but the thought of staying here felt fantastic. After my meeting, the last thing I wanted to do was board another plane right away." They walked in silence for a minute. "Hey, I didn't recall that you were that serious about writing. I do remember your poem, though. In fact, I was planning to give it back to you, but I forgot it."

She laughed "So that's where I left it. Was that the surprise you mentioned in your letter?"

"Good guess. But now we have a reason to get together again, don't we?"

Celie felt her cheeks begin to burn. What could she say?

"Do you plan to sell your textbook manuscript to a New York publisher? If you do, I have a few friends in the publishing business, guys from my old neighborhood."

Celie wanted to shove every thought about school and the convent into a black hole in the far, far reaches of her mind. "The textbook project's going okay," she said, "but lately I've been feeling burnt out. Ideas flow like crazy, but then all of a sudden I run dry. Yes, I've been writing poetry since I was little. I always carry a journal with me to jot down my thoughts. The experts say we should let our artistic juices simmer for awhile. So after this . . . this vacation, I'm hoping I'll discover some new wells of creativity inside me. Does that ever happen to you?"

"Some," he said, "except I have to solve engineering and people problems. That's a whole different kind of creativity."

"What exactly is your job?"

"Right now, my company is working on a defense project out here. It's classified, so I can't talk about it. But I can tell you that we're heading up the design of a sophisticated electronics system. With the recent U.S. bombings in Cambodia, there's a serious need to get things up and running. Twelve-hour days were routine till this weekend."

Trying to keep up with him, she ran a few steps. "That sounds really demanding. You seem young to have that kind of responsibility."

He had to grin. "I guess I'm an old-timer at thirty-two. I've already seen a lot of life. Too much, maybe. I've worked all my life, one way or another, but I never made any real money until I earned my engineering degree. I got it when I was twenty, by skipping a couple of grades. After graduation, I landed a job working for IBM, but I hated it."

"Why?"

"It was incredibly boring. On my first day there, my boss offered me a design project. I had it solved by the end of the week. Then I had nothing to do for the rest of the month. I bothered him for more work, but when he finally acknowledged my requests, it was too late. I gave my notice. Two weeks later, I landed two job offers on Long Island for more money. I took the one that paid the most."

Celie marveled at his self-assurance. He seemed able to bend his career path at will, something a nun could never do.

As they entered the fun zone, he pointed at the Ferris wheel, its silver casements glinting in the morning sun. "I think it's open early. Wanna ride? It reminds me of Coney Island."

"Sure. I've only seen Coney Island in the movies. Does it really exist?" They paused in front of the Ferris wheel and watched it stop as the passengers ahead of them stepped into the lowest seat.

"You're kidding," he was saying. "'Course it's real. Coney Island isn't what it once was, though. When I was growing up in Brooklyn, I'd catch the subway for a nickel every chance I got in the summer. It was the place to be—and a dime would buy the famous meal at Nathan's."

"Nathan's? What's that?"

"Oh, come on! I can't believe you've never heard of Nathan's. You haven't lived until you've tasted a Nathan's hot dog."

She was becoming aware that Tony moved in a world totally foreign to hers. The more she learned about him, the more her curiosity grew.

Soon they were seated on the Ferris wheel. Celie gripped the bar in front of them as the music played and the big, whirling machine carried them up and around. The fog had burned off long ago, and now the horizon glowed with the bright coral streaks of a new day. From the top of the wheel, it was a glorious sight. They glimpsed waves that looked like rivulets washing the shoreline up and down the California coast and tiny sailboats that wavered on the ocean like toys. Tony pointed toward the cliffs, where Celie could barely make out the sprawling retreat house among the leaning cypress trees. Its windows shimmered in the bright sunlight.

She fell silent as they wound up and down, circling together over and over. Suspended in time on the Ferris wheel, she was overcome by the magical beauty all around them. When the wheel paused, Tony broke the spell. "Hey, where'd you go?"

"What? Oh, sorry. Daydreaming, I guess. The world looks so inviting from up here." Her nose and cheeks stung from the chill as her short hair moved in the breeze. She ran her hand through it and turned toward him, risking a connection with his magnetic eyes. "When I came to Santa Cruz last night, I was exhausted and troubled. And, I'll admit it, a little nervous. Now I feel exhilarated."

"I know. Up here, you're on top of the world. You feel powerful, like you just might be able to handle everything down there after all. A view from the top can't ever hurt, right?" He smiled.

His words seemed to penetrate the confusion she'd hidden deep inside.

The rest of the morning spun like the carousel they rode next, around and around, whizzing by in a multicolored dance of laughter and music. They were both eager to forget every part of their normal lives, to make precious, carefree memories of this day.

Rags followed them through the crowds of Fourth of July tourists, always waiting dutifully while they rode the merry-go-round and the bumper cars and tried their hand at the carnival games. Soon the sun had climbed high in the sky, and the dog whimpered as they sampled cotton candy and ate hamburgers for lunch. Tony fed him most of his french fries.

For Tony's sake, Celie showed some interest in Rags and cautiously laid her leftover hamburger on the pavement near the picnic table, then stepped away. He stroked the dog for a minute or two, then released him to eat his fill.

"Sometimes you have to climb back up on the horse one step at a time, right?" he kidded her.

Hearing Tony's voice, Rags wagged his tail. Celie bent over him, tentatively reached under his chin, and began scratching. But when he licked her wrist, she jumped back.

Tony closed his fingers over hers. "It takes time to conquer fear."

A shiver of excitement ran through her, but she pulled her hand away.

"Yes," she said, the warmth of his hand lingering on hers. Why did this seem like a beginning? It was a small one, but it was a beginning, nonetheless.

CHAPTER 28

AN UNEXPECTED RETURN HOME

The radio blared a popular tune, "All You Need Is Love," and Sister Celia Marie couldn't help it, she began singing along as she maneuvered the silver Pontiac back to San Francisco. But the lyrics of John Lennon's song gnawed at her. Her retreat by the sea had brought peace, happiness, and a place to hide away, but now she found herself dismissing the appealing thoughts that were whittling away at . . . at, yes, whittling away her denial like a chisel revealing an unwanted face in a piece of marble. Tony's face. Images of him kept flashing through her mind.

He's in desperate need for someone who cares, she told herself. She measured this thought, then pushed it away. Where was he going now? What was he thinking? After that first evening's conversation by the fire, he'd never mentioned his wife or his children again.

No! I can't dwell on him anymore. We both have our own confrontations to . . . to, well, confront.

But she couldn't face Sister Gerald tonight. Not yet. What could she possibly say or do?

It was strange. The time she'd spent with Tony had reassured her that she was still human, still a woman. Now she remembered the attraction and friendship she'd felt with Mike in high school, and her friendship with Dennis, too, and how he'd compared his induction into the Dodgers with her entrance into the Augustinian Order. But her relationship with Tony was altogether different. She liked Tony's blunt manner, his easy grip on all kinds of facts, his street smarts. She'd never known anyone from New York before, but he didn't seem to fit the stereotypes she saw on TV. He wasn't brusque or rude. True, he was direct and tuned into reality, and his confidence and assertiveness seemed unusually strong, but he could also be quiet and sensitive, even gentle. And he was so capable. Yes, she felt safe with him.

But would she ever see him again? Did she dare to consider it? She had no answers to her questions. Certainly not today. After all, he was struggling with the possibility of a divorce, something forbidden by the Catholic Church.

But there it was again. She wanted to get to know him better, share her thoughts with him. She couldn't deny it. A small spark of hope flickered somewhere deep inside her, like a candle that wouldn't go out.

No. Better not think about it. Not now.

Turning up the volume on the car radio, she sang louder as she sped up the freeway toward San Francisco. Entering Daly City, she saw clotheslines and trash barrels and dull block walls whizzing by as the music wailed. And now images of her Superior began flying through her mind like the pages of a book ruffled by the wind. Then she heard Sister Gerald's soprano voice rising in choir above the others, saw her olive skin and high cheekbones. And, as if she were seeing a film, memories converged on her of cocoa and Kahlua and wine and massage on that horrible night.

. . . her hands on my back and shoulders . . . and it felt so good . . . her breath on my cheek, her arms closing around me—oh, my God!

Her car swerved. She heard the honking of another car. She brought herself back to the freeway.

But . . . *did I invite it?* She had to admit that she'd felt the heat of old pleasures.

No, no, no!

But she'd always welcomed the older nun's friendship and hugs. After all, this was her Superior, the woman everyone admired. The one older woman Celie had trusted, since Sister Pauline in high school. What had gone wrong?

Nausea seized Celie as she turned into the fast lane. She ached inside with new layers of guilt. *I can't see Sister Gerald tonight.* Her knuckles were chalk-white as she gripped the steering wheel. *I've got to make a plan. Tomorrow.*

The cars in front of her swerved. Right. Left. She hit the brake. "Dear God!" The Pontiac whirled in a crazy pivot. Her heart thumped in her ears. Everything stopped. For a second, she leaned against the dashboard gulping air. She raised her head. No cars were damaged, but they were all facing in different directions.

Trembling, she followed the lead of those ahead and started the Pontiac. As she reached freeway speed again, she switched stations and turned the volume up. There it was again. They were playing that song, "All You Need Is Love. . . ."

Locking the Pontiac in the garage, Celie realized she was still wearing jeans and a sweater. Hopefully, everyone would be attending the parish picnic today at Golden Gate Park. To play it safe, she had to slip into the convent unnoticed. The house was deserted. She hurried to her cell, quickly changed into her religious habit, and set to work finishing her lesson plans for the upcoming week. An hour later, near dusk, she heard a knock.

"I saw the light under your door, dear." The creases between Sister Adele's graying eyebrows matched her somber tone. "I didn't realize you were home till now. I would've called you to the phone hours ago. I'll have to tell you. Sister Gerald's at the principal's conference." She extended her wrinkled hand as her frame filled the doorway. "There's no easy way to say this." Her voice fell. "Your father has had a heart attack."

"No!"

Sister Adele squeezed Celie's fingers. "Now, now, dear. Put your faith in the Lord. I've been praying ever since your mother called."

"What did Mom say?"

"He's stable now. He's in intensive care, but I'm afraid . . . well, she said the damage to his heart is significant. They're monitoring him and administering tests. Your mother requested that you come home for a few days."

Celie's head was spinning. "But—but who will take over my tutoring?"

"Don't worry your head one bit," Sister Adele replied. "I can do it. There's only two weeks left until August vacation anyway. Your children will be fine."

If anyone could fill in for her, it was Sister Adele. She'd propelled Celie through her first uncertain months of teaching last fall.

She was still speaking. ". . . and I'll see if I can get you a flight out immediately."

Celie nodded, then mustered a weak "Thank you."

153

Swiftly she repacked her suitcase, and an hour later Sister Adele was rushing her to the Oakland Airport, where she boarded a plane to Los Angeles.

Trying to ignore the pungent antiseptic smell that permeated the intensive care unit, she began fingering the large rosary beads that hung from her belt under her white scapular, but her hands were too clammy to grasp the beads with any firmness. She saw ten beds crowded into the small room, every patient motionless. Beside her father, monitors with neon lines and numerals were blinking. She moved closer to his bed.

Daddy's never looked so frail.

He lay sleeping, tubes and lines going from his arms to an IV bag and a large box that flashed indecipherable green codes. He opened his eyes as she came near.

"Dad, it's me. Celie."

"I know." His voice was faint. "Thanks for coming, hon." Then he shifted slightly and took a deep breath. Before she could think of anything else to say, he was asleep again.

She shivered, then pulled the blanket up over his shoulders. Had she said "I love you" the last time he'd phoned? Did he know how much she cared? He looked so small, so white and feeble. She stood there, not even thinking to pray, but worrying that he might not awaken, ever. Would this man who meant so much to her die without any idea of who she really was under the religious habit she wore?

All through her life, her father had presented a stern, almost unbending front to his children. Occasionally, his mood had lifted and he'd joked and laughed, his deep blue eyes shining wildly. But those times had been rare. She recalled how when she was little he had once wrapped Mom in a rousing hug in the middle of the kitchen, bending over her as if they were dancing, her long black hair skimming the floor. Mom had protested, "Let me go, Tom. You're acting crazy!" but they'd all heard the laughter in both their voices. Celie remembered the giddiness in her mother's face and the indefinable glee in her father's chuckle. But that was long ago.

Now Mom sat in a corner, as far from his bed as she could get, right against the windows, as if the bright L.A. sun might warm this frigid world.

"He's been sleeping since I arrived," she said. "Yesterday he was awake more often." Her voice sounded cheerful, but Celie could hear the familiar pretense. With Mom, everything was always fine. Her mother was a master at subterfuge. "Tomorrow will be better, sweetheart."

Celie flinched. There was that dreaded word Mom always used, "sweetheart." It was an endearment that invariably prefaced veiled criticism. She tried to hug her mother like she meant it, but everything inside her felt lifeless.

"I came as fast as I could," she murmured.

Her mother smelled of tobacco, and she felt fragile. But that wasn't new, either. "You needn't have worried, dear," Mom said. "Colleen and Maureen came right away. They've been by my side ever since it happened and they advised me to leave your younger brother and sisters at home till your dad feels better. They're so good. Taking off work to be with me. And Daddy too."

What could Celie say to this? Whatever she said or did, it was never enough.

Mom was still talking in her cheery tones. "You look so serious. Daddy'll be okay. Let me see you smile, sweetheart."

Mom's phrases from the past ricocheted in Celie's head like pinballs hitting familiar gates and barriers, battering the walls of her emotions. It had always been, "Why don't you smile more? You'll have more friends if you do. Others think you're stuck up, you're so solemn. So much like your dad."

What Mom had really meant, of course, was "Don't take after *him*." Over the years, her mother had made it plain that Celie was too intense, too curious, too direct. Now she was an adult, and a nun besides, and that still wasn't enough.

She finally spoke. "Of course I look serious, Mom. Dad's health *is* serious." She couldn't stuff her irritation away. Almost four years away from home had unearthed feelings she'd buried all her life.

Her mother sniffled and dabbed at her eyes with a wadded-up tissue. "Doctors say every hour your father lives strengthens his chances. It's already forty-eight hours since the heart attack. They say if he gets through seventy-two, he'll probably be out of the woods." She looked across the room at the figure in the bed, then back at her daughter. "Have you had anything to eat? How was your flight?"

"I'm not hungry. The flight was fine." Celie turned away. As always, she felt an invisible, insurmountable wall between them, a wedge that had separated them for as long as she could remember. But when she looked again at her mother's crumpled shoulders, her heart softened toward this woman who seemed to be a stranger. She reached down and touched her mother's hand. "C'mon, Mom, let's get something to eat. Want to try some soup?"

Mom nodded, and together they wound their way down the hall, found the cafeteria, and finally settled into a drab green booth. As they nibbled the saltine crackers served with chicken soup, Celie tried to penetrate her mother's facade. "How are you doing, Mom? Really? You must be exhausted."

"I'm fine, honey. Just fine. I think Daddy is progressing, too. Based on the doctor's report today. You'll see. We'll get better news tomorrow."

Celie listened, but all she heard were the same cheerful platitudes. "I suppose Monsignor Walsh came to visit."

Mom's eyes shifted toward the cafeteria entrance as if she wanted to bolt. "I haven't called him." She gulped a spoonful of soup, then took her time to swallow. "But Father Ambrose visited yesterday. Brought Daddy Communion—he was pleased. I think Father Ambrose is a true religious. Very kind. I've never seen your Daddy afraid before—" she looked as if she were going to cry but then turned away. She rarely allowed any negative emotions to show, and never in public. "He seemed much better after Father left." She straightened up, patted her hair, and swallowed half the water in her plastic glass.

"That's strange," Celie said. "Why hasn't Monsignor come? Is he out of town?" Her mother began to fidget, her eyes darting around the room. "Something's wrong, Mom. C'mon, you can tell me."

Mom patted her hair again and looked away. "I don't want him here." Celie strained to hear. "I . . . I . . . I've had enough of him! I don't want to be his secretary anymore, either. I don't want anything to do with him or . . . that . . . that *woman* he cavorts around with. But she asked for it! She led him on." Her index finger pointed at Celie. "She's close to your age. Young."

And suddenly her words began spilling out, non-stop. Mom had never opened up like this before. "Those kind of women," she drummed her fingers on the table, "those tramps—they know what they're doing. But I guess he *is* partially at fault. Men have such strong physical urges, you know. Much more than we do." Suddenly realizing what she'd just said, she looked away. But she didn't stop speaking. "Anyway, I told him it *had* to stop. The parishioners were getting wind of it. He's a priest. It's against his vocation, for heaven's sake. But he turned his back and walked away. Not a word! Last week he left me a note saying I should find another position. Didn't even have the nerve to fire me in person."

Celie clenched her hands under the table. She'd known Monsignor Walsh her whole life. How could he go on violating his vows after Mom noticed and warned him? A familiar lightheadedness took hold of her. "Mom, I'm so sorry. You worked long hours for him. You even organized those parish parties every time he was promoted." She reached out and put her hand over her mother's. They were clenched together and shaking. How well Celie remembered the first parish celebration. It had happened the same time as her trip to San Francisco, the one time she'd won an award for academic achievement in high school—and her first time away from home—but Mom had been too busy planning Monsignor Walsh's party to notice. Celie had gone with the chaperoned group and come home after four glorious days, eager to share her outing. Eating at Fisherman's Wharf. Riding the trolley cars. Crossing the Golden Gate Bridge. But when she'd entered a dark house, Mom was gone, and Dad was sleeping it off in the bedroom.

Much later at dinner, she'd been mute as stone while Mom babbled on about her decorations, the caterers, the band she'd hired. Oh, occasionally she'd interrupted herself to ask, "Sweetheart, how was your trip? Why so solemn? I thought you'd come home smiling for a change." But she hadn't listened to anything Celie had said.

Now her mother was wrapping the cellophane package from the saltines around one finger. Her eyes cast down, she scraped the empty soup bowl with her spoon. "I always looked up to Monsignor. My mistake. Such a mistake. That's why I always told you not to put people on pedestals, sweetheart. To accept people for who they are, not what you want them to be. They'll always disappoint you. Now it's happened to me. But it won't happen again."

Celie was amazed. There was no manipulation, no innuendo. Was this the *real* person behind her mother's mask? A vulnerable, middle-aged woman who rarely allowed herself to expect anything positive . . . for fear of being crushed by disillusionment? But Mom had warned her over and over, "You must put up with disappointments, Celie, and God will reward you. Pray. Pray every day. He'll give you strength. Life's all about giving, not getting. You'll be a success, depending on how much you make a difference in others' lives. Be content only with what life gives you. Make the best of it."

Celie suddenly felt sad for her mother. *Yes, I must put up with life's disappointments.*

Mom drained the glass of water and swept the cracker crumbs into one hand, "Well," she said, her bright voice restored, "that's it. Luckily, there aren't many of *those women* around. They thrive on driving men wild with their sexual perversions. It's a power thing, too, you know." She looked up. "Or maybe you don't know. Anyway, she was coming around the rectory every day. No wonder he finally succumbed." She dropped the cracker crumbs in her empty bowl. "By the way, have you seen those mini-skirts the young women are wearing now? They're asking for it. And God sees them." Her eyes pierced her daughter.

Confused, Celie stood up. Why was Mom asking her about mini-skirts? Her cheeks stung. Guilt weakened her knees, stabbed her heart. Hurrying toward the restroom, she swallowed hard, trying to breathe. Why didn't Mom blame Monsignor Walsh for his sin? He had the power and authority. He was admired by everyone, for God's sake. He should've cut that flirtatious woman off right from the start!

Rage welled up inside her, from her toes up through her legs, geysering into her stomach and lungs. She inhaled in gasps, feeling like she would suffocate. Finally reaching the ladies' room, she turned on a faucet full-blast, bent over, and splashed water on her face, drenching the white coif that hid her hair.

"How did Dad look to you?" Colleen asked as she eased her pregnant frame into the rocking chair facing Celie. They were alone on the back porch of her rented home. She poured lemonade into two glasses from a green plastic pitcher. It was late, almost eleven, and Celie could hear faint snoring from the bedroom. Colleen's husband Don had crashed a couple hours earlier. His workday began at four a.m., stocking shelves at the store his father owned.

Celie's voice quavered as she replied. "Dad looks so fragile. But I'm pretty sure he recognized me."

"I felt the same way," Colleen said.

Celie thought she saw her sister's eyes well up. Her voice wobbled, then she reined it in. "Thank God, Mom called the EMTs right away. He's totally sedated right now. They're trying to get him stabilized. One thing's in his favor, though. Forty-eight is young to have a heart attack."

Celie sipped her lemonade and nodded.

"I'm glad you're here," Colleen continued. "Somehow, I knew you wouldn't want to stay with Mom. That's why I suggested you come here, and she bought it. This way everybody's happy, right?"

"Thanks. I try with Mom, you know, but it's so hard for me. I don't think she even realizes it." Celie drank more lemonade.

Her older sister smiled. "That's the way I feel about Dad. He'll never forgive me for this," she said, pointing to her stomach. Celie remembered what Mom had written—*Dad's furious with Colleen. Don, of all people. Just married and pregnant so soon.*

"But Mom is Mom," Colleen went on, "It's scary, though. Sometimes I think my life is turning out just like hers. But she tries to be good to us. Always has."

Celie swished the liquid back and forth in her glass. "You and Mom have always gotten along. She loves your crazy sense of humor. Me? That's another story. I'm too intense for her, too idealistic, too something. . . ."

Colleen leaned forward. "You think so?"

"Yes." She hadn't confided in Colleen in a long time, hadn't risked trusting her. But now she went on. "I can't imagine what her life is like. A convert to the Church, with six kids and Dad for a husband. It's more than *I* could handle. I've always wished Mom and I were closer, but her life is so . . . so compartmentalized. So enclosed in all those trite sayings of hers."

"Really?"

Celie nodded. "Really. Don't tell me you never noticed. I'm much more direct than anyone else in the family when I do open up, and I've always questioned everything. It puts Mom off and she closes down. And you know how I hate her fake-cheery talk. I can't stand it. She was doing it at the hospital this afternoon. I tried to have a *real* conversation with her. And you know what? I was shocked when it actually worked for once. She told me about Monsignor Walsh. But then that fell apart, too."

Colleen took a sip of her lemonade before she spoke. "Wow, Celie, you're awfully upset. You and Mom have your differences, but I never realized—"

"That I don't view life the way she does? I never have."

Colleen rocked back and forth. "Don't forget, though. She puts up with a lot. Dad hasn't been himself for a long time. And now she has to deal with Monsignor's hypocrisy and rejection of her."

Celie drained her glass. "Well, she sure looked overwhelmed. I've never seen her like that. I was surprised how she finally opened up to me, but she blamed most of it on 'that woman.'"

"Yeah. The woman is a manipulator, for sure. The whole sordid affair is such a disappointment for Mom," Colleen put her swollen ankles up on a patio chair. "Plus Dad's gotten much worse since your last visit. You know how he and I always fought. I'd disagree with him a little, and then his sarcasm cut me to ribbons. You rarely said a word around him, so of course he didn't punish you the way he did me."

Her sister began wrapping a blanket around her bulky frame as she talked on. "Well, it's really bad now. Remember how he used to give us the silent treatment? Now he arrives home, starts drinking right away. Hardly ever comes to dinner. Barely says one word. Just sits in the dark. When the TV is off, it's sort of a relief because you know he won't talk. But you have to put up with his surliness. It's been tough on all of us. Especially Mom."

Celie put her glass on the table, staring at it for a moment. "Maybe I'm unloading, because . . . because things are bothering me." She reached for the glass again, averting her eyes, and set it on the tray.

"Can I help?"

"No. I have to figure this out for myself." She pushed herself up and wandered to the other end of the porch, where she picked a pink rose from the climbers entwined through the lattice. "Remember the wreaths Mom always made when we were in grade school?"

"For the May procession? I'll never forget *that* ritual, and all those flowers we placed in front of Mary's statue. Jeez, we spent so much time at church when we were young, didn't we? Funerals practically every Saturday. 'Helping out' in the choir." Colleen began singing the words of a familiar funeral dirge, *Dies irae, dies illa*, but after the first line, she ended it with her famous grin.

Celie smiled and walked over to pat Colleen's stomach. "How're you doing? You're six months along, right?"

"Yes. We're okay, now that Don and I have gotten used to the idea. To make matters worse, we're trying to make sizeable payments on the hardware store. We want to buy it from his dad." She smiled again. "The 'rhythm method' the Church sells sure isn't what it's cracked up to be. I should've known, though. Mom tried it and ended up with eight pregnancies."

"No wonder you think you're turning into Mom," Celie said. "That *would* be scary."

"Well, Don and I are *not* going to end up with six little mouths to feed like Mom and Dad. We've decided."

"What's the answer?"

"Sheesh, Celie! You're so completely cut off from everything, shut up in that convent. Haven't you even *heard* about the new birth control pill?"

Celie flashed back to years before, when Colleen used to corner her with that same mocking tone. It reminded her of Dad. She hated the family sarcasm. She kept silent now. That was the best thing to do when her sisters' moods turned mean.

Colleen ranted on, "'Course, the Church forbids it, but there's no other way. Believe me, when this one's 'out of the oven,' I'm going to start on the Pill." She pressed her teeth onto her bottom lip. "Thing is," she muttered, "I feel torn because of the Church's stand—"

"The Pope has to become more lenient," Celie broke in. "Not everyone can afford six kids or more. Mom and Dad had to scrape together every penny they had to raise us. It must be hard on you two, too, with the store."

"That's an understatement! But the most difficult part is that Don isn't Catholic, so he doesn't see anything wrong with birth control. I'm the one who'll wrestle with the guilt. And forget Communion if you go on the Pill! You can't take it one day, go to confession and get forgiven, and receive the Eucharist the next, then start over again. It's impossible."

"Well, then, just don't go to the same Sunday Mass as Mom and Dad."

Colleen smirked. "Yeah, if I do, I can't receive Communion because I'll be in the 'state of mortal sin,' as the catechism states, so I'll get Mom's stare at church and her famous hints afterwards. I'll never be able to let on that I'm taking the Pill." She paused. "This must all sound foreign to you, being a nun. You're so protected from the real problems of life."

Celie stared silently at the shadows in Colleen's backyard.

Oblivious, Colleen drank the last of her lemonade. "Sorry," she said. "I shouldn't be loading you down with my worries. Which reminds me. Did you hear Mike and his bride-to-be finally set a date? It's next summer."

"You told me he was engaged last Christmas." Celie knew her sister's comment was an opening, but suddenly she felt incredibly tired and, yes, depressed.

It had been a long day. Colleen would never understand the problems facing her, and Celie secretly wondered when she'd ever be ready to deal with them herself. She lifted the tray of glasses and pitcher and turned toward the back door. "Shouldn't we get to bed?"

Colleen hauled herself out of the chair. "Yeah. Dad's doctors want to have a consultation with us at 10 o'clock. Mom's an early bird. She'll be calling us first thing." She opened the screen for her younger sister and led her to the foldout couch in her tiny living room.

CHAPTER 29

CONFRONTATIONS

Engrossed in their conversation, the two doctors entered the hospital office and stopped, still talking, behind a large mahogany desk. Celie, Colleen, and Maureen were sitting across from them, hovering around their mother. Maureen, the eldest, initiated the lead question. "How is our dad? Please be candid."

Dr. Phelps, the head cardiologist, stepped forward as Dr. Page, a general practitioner, sat down. Phelps' eyes studied the trio of women. His air of authority impressed Celie. Colleen had already told her about his impeccable reputation and forthright manner.

"Your dad's case is more complicated than when I first diagnosed it," he began. "His prognosis is dependent not only on the condition of his heart, but on the serious physical effects caused by the pills he's been taking. Keep in mind that this has been going on for a very long time. Right now, his body is exerting tremendous energy ridding itself of the drug simultaneously with his heart's attempt to heal."

"What do you mean?" Celie asked. "What drug? The medication to thin his blood?"

"Celie." Mom waved one hand in front of Celie's face, trying to silence her, but her questions hung in the air.

The doctor turned to her. "Sister, you may not know that your father has been taking increasing doses of Valium, as prescribed by another doctor, for several years. I'm sure I don't need to emphasize that such heavy amounts of medication along with chronic alcohol abuse can have life-threatening effects, both on your father's mind and on his body." He cleared his throat, almost apologetically, and added, "I'm afraid he has a monumental battle ahead."

Celie's shock didn't quite register. "How long will he be hospitalized?" She could see Maureen shaking her head, but she went on anyway, "What do you recommend, doctor?"

"If no more coronary problems occur," he said, "I'll keep him here for at least three weeks. After that, I propose that he enter a drug rehabilitation facility. I'm ordering more rest for him than the other occupants, due to his recent heart attack."

Silence again.

As Celie sat there, staggering under this new information about her father, Dr. Phelps continued to talk. She saw his mouth moving, but his words had become unintelligible. She held herself rigid, arms folded tight under her scapular, and willed her tears to disappear. She wanted to cry, but she was a nun. *Nuns do not break down.*

After several minutes, she noticed that still no one was speaking.

"What can we do for him?" Her voice was so tiny she wondered if anyone heard it.

Dr. Phelps faced her again. "He needs encouragement right now. Lots of it." He looked at the rest of the family. "You all need to be honest with him. Stand by him. We'll do everything we can regarding his physical problems, but you must assure him you love him and will support him. Every day. When his heart is stable and he can leave here, he'll be in a rehab facility for quite a while. I suggest family counseling, too. I'm sorry. It won't be easy."

With the doctors gone, the four women huddled together, as if to ward off a deadly cold seeping through their clothes, through their skin. After a silent minute, Celie said, her voice still tiny, "Mom, I had no idea." She put her arm around her mother, whose cheeks were wet. Celie had never seen her mother cry.

"We have to do what he says." Her mother's voice was breaking up. "We have to support him. You girls can make a big difference."

Maureen turned to Celie. "You just *had* to ask those questions, didn't you!" Her hands were on her hips. "Before I could even get a word in, you had to go on and on asking the doctor for all the private details about Dad's condition."

"I didn't know—"

"C'mon, Celie! You can't be as blind as you pretend to be. He was always taking the pills. Even when you came home last Christmas. Don't play innocent! You always expect people to be so perfect so you don't have to face the reality that's right in front of you."

Mom raised a hand and shook her head. "Maureen, honey, don't get upset. Celie's always been one to ask lots of questions. It's just that . . . well, sometimes it's appropriate. Sometimes it's not. Celie, don't you start quarreling with your sister, *please*. What's important now is your Dad. We have to help him get well."

Why is it always my fault?

Once, when she was barely four and had kept holding their new Cocker Spaniel puppy in her arms, Colleen had complained all day to Mom, who took the dog away, giving Celie a stern look, and handed him over to her sister. Weeks later, when the puppy died in his sleep, Colleen began blaming her. "*You* killed him! If you hadn't carried him around night and day, he wouldn't be dead now!" Celie remembered how she'd gone to sleep sobbing, wondering if she'd really been the cause of the dog's death. For years, she believed it.

She had to speak up to Maureen now, she suddenly decided, even if it might upset Mom again. She wasn't going to put up with the family blame game anymore. "I didn't 'go on and on,'" she said. "I asked questions that needed to be asked. For the sake of us all."

Maureen didn't bother to reply, and Colleen was buzzing around her mother like a bee protecting its queen.

"Here, Mom, let me help you with your coat. It's nearly visiting time. Let's go over and see Dad now, okay?"

The threesome walked arm-in-arm down the hospital corridor, and Celie trailed behind. It was a formation she knew well. By ignoring her, they rendered her invisible. Once again she'd asked questions and demanded the truth. She shouldn't have. Her stomach churned.

There's no such thing as truth in this family! I just hope to God Dad can break this pattern! He'll have to.

CHAPTER 30

OPPORTUNITY AND A REVELATION

Alone on Colleen's porch again, Celie finished whispering the psalms of Vespers, laid her breviary gently on the table, and stirred her tea. Two weeks had passed, and her return flight to San Francisco was scheduled for tomorrow. Almost every day of her visit, she'd hoped to open up a dialogue with her father, but it had never happened. Was it her fault? Did she lack nerve? But how could she talk to him about his problems when she wasn't facing her own?

She checked her watch as Colleen's car pulled up. *Here goes.* If she didn't try to talk to Dad today, she'd never forgive herself. She climbed into the passenger seat of the old Ford station wagon, noticing how her sister's face glistened with perspiration. Colleen looked over at her.

"How can you stand to wear that long skirt and long sleeves and veils in such hot weather?" she asked. "It's over a hundred degrees today. Look at me. Shorts and all, and I'm still dripping!"

"I'm used to it," Celie said in a calm voice. "But changes are coming. When you see me next year, I'll be wearing a modern, short habit. And no coif." Celie touched the white cap that framed her face and covered her hair.

"Really?"

"Yes, the Vatican II Council in Rome is making sweeping changes. Nuns don't *have* to modify their dress, but we can if we want to." Celie told her sister more about the upcoming modifications that Pope John XXIII and the Ecumenical Council had instigated until Colleen interrupted her.

"Oh—I forgot to tell you—"

Celie clenched her hands together. Colleen, like everyone else in the family, rarely listened to her.

"Someone named Sister Lupe phoned before you and Mom got home yesterday. I promised her you'd call her back. Maybe you can reach her from the hospital. Her number's somewhere in here." Colleen dug into her purse with one hand as she gripped the steering wheel with the other.

"Sister Lupe?"

"Yeah. Said she wanted to talk to you right away. A summer course is starting next week at a place called . . . I think she said Maryvale. It's located in a town called Boulder Creek in the Santa Cruz Mountains. Something like that, anyway. She wanted you to enroll with her, and 'the other girls in your set.' I guess Rosemary's going, too. Uh, I mean Sister John Marie."

"Maryvale's gorgeous," Celie replied. "Off in the wild. Near a creek that's surrounded by enormous trees, and a rustic chapel. I spent a week there last year."

"Seems weird," Colleen muttered. "A college course in the mountains."

"Maryvale is owned by our Order. Courses were offered there last summer, too. We hire instructors from UC Berkeley. The Augustinian college is an accredited branch of the university."

"Wow, I'm impressed." Celie wondered if her sister was really impressed. She didn't sound like it. "UC Berkeley has a fantastic reputation," Colleen went on. "Even though students are demonstrating against the Vietnam War all the time. I heard on Walter Cronkite that they're demanding a ton of curriculum changes, too. Lots of hippies up there. I know you don't get out much, but haven't you read about it?"

Celie nodded and fibbed. "I'm not *that* out of it." Although access to TV and newspapers had been forbidden when she was a Novice and limited during her first year as a Postulant, she still never seemed to find much time to watch the nightly news broadcasts now.

"Well, Sister Lupe seemed eager for you to enroll."

"Really? I'd like to, but it depends."

"On what?"

"Permission from my Superior." Celie's stomach caved in.

Colleen shrugged and shook her head, then turned back to face the traffic and turned right into the hospital parking lot. "Give Dad my love, okay? I'll be back to pick you up. Tell him I'll swing over here to visit him after dinner. And keep cool."

Celie walked toward the hospital entrance, her mind churning excitedly over the unexpected chance to study with her friends. She'd bring another bathing suit so she could slide down the slick boulders with the others. Last year her old navy suit went threadbare from her skimming over the rocks, then plunging into the chilly river under the redwoods.

But her stomach lurched again when she pictured herself asking Sister Gerald for permission. She hadn't slept much in the last two weeks. Even in the quiet of Colleen's living room, her worries about Dad had given way to the fragmented, loathsome scenes of that night with her Superior. When she tried to decide why it had happened or what to do, no answers came. All she could do was ask for God's forgiveness again and again. She repeated her prayers until she was exhausted.

An intense dread had grown inside her as the time for departure drew near. Now a door was opening, offering her a way out. Instead of returning to Immaculate Mary Convent, she could postpone seeing Sister Gerald for a while longer.

Reaching the elevator, she spied a public telephone and dialed the number for the Sacred Heart Convent. When Lupe came to the phone, her first words were, "Hey, how're you doing? How's your dad?"

"My sister told me you called," Celie said. "He's been through an awful lot." She wrapped a curl of the phone cord around her finger. "But he's stabilized now, thank God. He might be coming home in a few weeks." *No need to reveal Dad's private hell to Lupe.* "Thanks for asking, and especially for your prayers. I really think he's going to be okay now."

"I'm sure glad," Lupe said.

"So what's this about some course at Maryvale?"

"I hope you want to attend 'cause I already called Sister Gerald for you. The sign-up deadline was yesterday, so I decided to put your name on the roster. Just in case you might get talked into it."

Lupe's tone was full of teasing, and Celie loved her for it. Could she possibly grasp how much her friendship meant? Her call now seemed nothing short of a miracle. Celie's voice quavered. "I'd love to take the class."

"Wow, you're not a hard sell at all!" Lupe paused. "Hey, you don't sound too good, though. Are you okay?"

169

"I'm fine. There's just lots of things going on. I've got a flight back to San Francisco tomorrow morning. Once I can get Sister Gerald's permission, I can pack right away and drive up to Maryvale in the afternoon."

"Don't worry about Sister Gerald. I talked to her yesterday and filled her in on the course. She didn't sound terribly happy, but she finally said if you wanted to, you could enroll. So, like I said, I signed you up. You won't be able to get in touch with her today anyway. She's left town. Went to Ukiah. Up where the Indian reservation school is. She's going up there to meet a new nun and give her some training so she can transfer to IME and teach in the fall."

"Lupe, you're fantastic!"

"I've always thought so. Glad you agree." Lupe's banter spilled over Celie like a warm shower.

"I can't wait," she said. "Lupe, we're going to have so much fun!"

"Can't think of a better place to earn three credits. Besides, Teach, you've got to help me with my writing assignments."

"If you could just stay focused during class, my dear, you'd have plenty of time to compose your papers after we roam through the woods. See you tomorrow. I'm excited!"

"Me, too! Bye."

Celie hung up, pressed the elevator button, and stepped in. As the elevator rose, so did her feelings of trepidation. Dad could be distant and difficult to talk to. He often turned a simple discussion into an argument, and Celie hated the derision he could dish out. But she made herself pause. *Lord, instead of worrying myself sick, I'll savor this moment. What a wonderful gift!* She let images of Maryvale flood her mind, the green splendor of the immense trees, the sparkling rush of the creek as it grew into a clear river. If she closed her eyes, she could almost smell the pine needles and the rushing water.

The elevator opened and she headed toward her dad's room.

Though he was still dreadfully pale, he was sitting up. He turned away from the television set on the wall and watched her as she strode toward his bed. His face was blotchy and lined, but his dark blue eyes were bright. "Can you turn the game off?" he asked.

She nodded, reached up and turned the off knob, then came to his bed and kissed him first on the lips, then on his forehead. "So, Dad, how're you doin' today? You seem kind of hot." She laid a hand on his brow for a moment, then pulled a chair up next to his bed and settled herself in it, one hand reaching out to hold his. He had never been demonstrative, but he quietly lit up when she summoned up the nerve to show him affection. Back when she was small, it had always been this way between them, an unspoken though infrequent camaraderie.

"No fever," he said. "They just took my temperature a couple minutes ago. Not a good day, though. My skin feels crawly. It goes away, but it comes back. The TV helps." His voice sounded hollow. "The Dodgers just won by nine runs, though, so I can rest easy." He tried to smile. "So you're going to fly away again tomorrow, huh?"

"Yeah. I hate to leave you, but you're going to pull through, Daddy. I'm sure of it. I'll call you lots. I promise. And guess what? A friend called to tell me about a college course starting up in the Santa Cruz Mountains. She already enrolled me. The place is like Blue Jay, where you used to take us every summer."

"That's good." He turned his face away and started to push himself up. "Uh, do you think you can lend a hand to your ol' Dad? I need help to get to the john." His voice sounded like gravel.

"Are you sure you're okay?"

"Yeah."

His progress across the room was painfully slow. He closed the bathroom door behind him and quiet filled the room. Alone, Celie wondered why he'd made such an abrupt exit. Then it dawned on her. She'd upset him when she mentioned leaving.

He'll never let on, though. He always hides his feelings. Why had she shared her excitement about the mountains?

The door opened, and she helped him back to bed. "Sorry," he said. "Not feeling so well. Your mom called the doctor to change my heart medication."

"Can I do anything?"

"No."

He edged onto the high mattress, his progress slow. Celie reached to help him, but he resisted. When he was settled, she covered him with the two thin, white hospital blankets.

"The doctors say it's going to take time," he said. "Lots of time till I feel like myself again."

She massaged his brow and temples. "You've been through so much."

He nodded vaguely and went on. "Appreciated you coming to see me like you have. And staying so long. I know you left your job up there. So you're excited to go back? That's good." His voice cracked. "That's all that counts, that you're happy."

She was shocked. He also never spoke about personal things.

"When your mom and I decided to send you girls to Catholic school, you know, I never thought you'd decide to become a nun."

Silence. Celie held her breath.

"But like I've said all along, if that's what you want, you should do it. I just want you to be happy. You understand?"

She moved behind him, straightening the pillows that propped him up. "Yes, Daddy. Now don't worry about me, okay?" She laid a hand on his shoulder. "You need to get well. That's the most important thing. You have to take good care of yourself. Promise?"

"Yeah." He managed a hesitant smile. "I have a lot of changes to make. I started talking to a counselor today. That's part of getting well. I never thought I'd do that. Not *this* old Marine, not in a million years! But after that counseling session, well," his voice suddenly changed. "Celie, I have to say . . . I have something to say to you. Before you go."

She sat down next to his bed again, studying the pattern of black and white squares on the linoleum floor as if they held the answers to the questions she ached to ask. She didn't have the courage to reply.

When she looked up again, he was staring at her. His blue eyes still scared her, even though she was a grown woman now. She realized he was desperate to express himself. He was struggling. "I think I've really . . . really let you down, Celie. All you kids. Your mother, too." She could see his hands curling into fists. "I have to work this out and get it under my control, you know what I mean? It's not going to be easy in the weeks and months ahead. They say only one in ten people will beat this for good, but I want to be that one. For myself and all of you. You understand what I'm saying?"

She couldn't summon the words to tell him how much she wanted him to overcome his addictions. But now that he'd opened up, she found herself tongue-tied. Helpless to hide her emotions, she looked into his eyes and, without a word, she nodded, tears filling her eyes. She leaned closer and hugged him, feeling his thin shoulders, then resting her cheek against his unshaven one. "Oh, Daddy, you won't let anybody down. You're gonna be the one guy who beats it. I'm so glad you want to. Daddy, I love you so much." Her arms tightened around him.

"I love you too, hon."

"Time for meds!" A plump blonde nurse barged into the room. "Doctor's making his rounds, Sister. Mr. O'Rourke, he'll be here to see you in a minute." She bustled over to check the blinking monitors then drew the curtains around his bed.

Celie pulled away from her dad, her cheeks still wet. "I'll go down the hall for a bit while the nurse finishes here. See you in a few minutes."

Colleen drove her to the airport early the next morning. Celie didn't feel like talking, so she listened to her sister's chatter and learned new truths about her dad.

"Yeah," Colleen said, "he's determined to overcome this thing, all right. Mom told me he's in the middle of some horrible withdrawal effects. Partly from the alcohol, but mostly from the Valium. They say it's a deadly combination. And he was taking such large doses when it happened. He told the counselor at his first session yesterday he's determined to conquer this substance abuse, even if it's the last thing he does. You know Dad! When he says he's going to do something, he puts out a hundred and fifty per cent."

"That's what he said to me," Celie replied. "I was stunned when he talked so openly . . . he even apologized."

"That's part of the whole rehab process, Mom says. What they call a twelve-step program." As she talked, Colleen swung the steering wheel around to make a turn, her tummy lodged snugly in front of it. "Besides, he would definitely want to talk to you." She hesitated. "You know, Celie, I've always thought you were his favorite."

"What do you mean? He's never treated me any different. In fact, after watching all your fights with him over the years, I always steered clear of him."

"Yeah, but you're still . . . his Beautiful Dreamer."

"What?"

"That's what he calls you. His Beautiful Dreamer. It's always been your nickname."

"I never knew."

"Aw, c'mon."

"No! I *never* knew. I remember him singing that song, along with the other ones, but—"

"You gotta be kidding. He's called you that for years. You didn't have a clue till now? Really?"

"No." Her tears began spilling over, dropping on her white habit. Why would Dad call her his Beautiful Dreamer? It sounded wonderful, but, no . . . no, he couldn't possibly mean it. It was just his way of explaining away her annoying childhood tendency to live in a fantasy world.

Over the years, she'd caused lots of trouble, getting so lost in her thoughts that all kinds of things happened that always riled him. She'd forget her lunch or leave her best sweaters and books on the bus. Mom even took her to the doctor once to have her hearing tested because she didn't respond when they talked to her. And her fainting spells worried them, especially when the doctors couldn't figure out why she did it. One time, when they were on a family vacation in the mountains, she'd wandered away for hours. Hiking among the tall pines, happily engrossed in her own world, she'd composed a poem that day. She couldn't wait to share it with them when she arrived back at the cabin. But by then Mom and Dad were frantic. They were so livid about her roaming alone on the mountain roads, they grounded her for a week.

With these memories crowding her mind, she murmured aloud, "That's probably what he meant."

"What?" Colleen asked.

"I was always drifting off, forgetting things, wandering away, getting caught up in my dreaming and causing them grief. That must be why he gave me that nickname."

Colleen had reached the airport parking garage and finally found a parking space. She switched the ignition off and turned toward her younger sister. "Celie," she said, her tone unusual because it was so gentle, "quit being so hard on yourself. It's not that at all. C'mon. Take a compliment for once in your life, even if you are a nun." She put her hand on Celie's, a rare gesture. "You know what I think? Dad knows you have dreams. He thinks you're going to make them come true. You remind him that he used to have dreams, too, a long time ago. And he loves you for it."

Celie's jumbled emotions began to tangle up her thoughts. She tried to suppress a sob, aware that Colleen could hear it. She couldn't believe this new reality.

Colleen gave Celie a Kleenex and turned away. "By the way," she said in her most offhand voice, "did Mom tell you she's going to counseling with Dad? Off and on until he leaves rehab?"

"I figured she would." Celie wiped her cheeks. "But the doctor said the whole family should be going. I talked to a psychiatrist recently about one of my students. He said if one person is emotionally stressed, it's usually a symptom of a complex family problem."

"I've heard that, too. But Mom keeps telling me, 'You don't need to be involved.'" Colleen's voice was thick with frustration. "I don't know, sometimes I think all Mom wants is to shove everything under the rug. That's the way their generation deals with things, you know?"

"That's Mom, all right. But, well, I hope she changes. And I sure don't want to bury things like her."

Colleen smiled. "Don't worry. You'll never hide from the truth."

Celie drew in a deep breath. "Not anymore, at least."

An hour later, Celie sat in the large Boeing jet, staring out the window, watching the morning sun draw bright outlines around the endless billows of white clouds. It looked like bronze glitter.

She inhaled all the way down to her toes, leaned back in her seat, closed her eyes, and began to hum an old Southern tune she'd heard her dad sing many times, "Beautiful Dreamer, queen of my song. . . ."

CHAPTER 31

FEAR OR COURAGE?

An unusual chill drifted under the eaves of the mountain cabin and slipped through the cracks of the window casements. In spite of the cold, Celie peeked out the window. The gray darkness revealed fog wrapped around the tall pine trees. Still tired, she punched her pillow and considered going back to sleep. Burrowing under her wool blanket again, she waited for the chapel bell to ring.

She'd wrestled with a nightmare earlier and awakened to find herself clammy with perspiration. Now she lay still, sorting out the disturbing images still imprinted on her consciousness. It had been so real. She'd been packing her suitcase in a room like the one she'd shared with Maureen and Colleen when she was young. The lights had been low, and suddenly the filmy outline of a face and shoulders had appeared beside her. The face had moved closer and began slamming orders at her in a voice she didn't recognize. She screamed, then tried to shout back, but no matter how she tried, she couldn't form the words. Instead, she'd begun spitting out weird, guttural pleas. Finally, all her energy spent, she'd awakened and lain exhausted for an hour or more.

Now Sister Lupe, who was sleeping on the cot next to her, pushed herself up, her eyes half-open. "Hey, Celie, what's the matter? You were making so much noise a while ago, you woke me up."

"I had a bad dream. Really bizarre."

"You sounded awfully upset."

Celie didn't answer.

Lupe shrugged her shoulders and started getting out of bed. "I have an idea. Why don't we get dressed and walk by the river before it's time for Mass. We've got an hour."

Celie looked at the windup alarm clock for the third time in an hour. "Lupe, we finally get to sleep late here, and you want to get up and hike around! And we're breaking the Profound Silence rule again too."

"Oh c'mon," said her friend. "Get up and meet the sun and shoo the ghosts away." Wrapping a blanket around herself, she shuffled toward the bathroom. Two minutes later, she was back beside Celie's bed. "Do I have to venture out there all by my lonesome? Hurry up! I'm outta here in five minutes."

"You're incorrigible!" Celie found her underwear, then put on the long, blue-checked dress that nuns wore when they worked or hiked in the woods. After tying the sash, she bent over to put on her tennis shoes. Minutes later, donning their black capes for warmth, the two young nuns closed the cabin door carefully so as not to awaken anyone else.

The fog still hovered among the tall trees as they picked their way around the grove of giant redwood trees and walked to the creek that surged from the unusually heavy snows in the Santa Cruz Mountains this year. Deep blue waters swirled around the granite boulders they'd used as slides the summer before, and clouds of mist shifted in blankets above the foliage. A long silver streak in the sky pierced through the dark trees. The sun was trying to penetrate the gloom.

Celie and Lupe gathered up smooth, round pebbles, lifting the hems of their floor-length dresses to hold them, then they began a silent contest to see who was better at skipping stones across the pond. Lupe was a master at this game. Every stone she threw ricocheted across the surface like a tiny water skier, deftly cutting small waves in its wake. At last Celie gave up and just admired Lupe's expert wrist motion and watched the rocks dance then disappear under the sparkling water.

"So," Lupe whispered, "are you gonna tell me?" She settled on a knurled log by the water's edge and motioned for Celie to sit beside her.

Celie looked out at the water. "Tell you what?"

Lupe's voice grew louder. "You know what."

Celie nodded. "It was so strange. I haven't had a dream like that in a long time. You know, the kind that seems so real? I woke up churning inside, and hot and sweaty even though it's freezing in that cabin."

"What do you remember about it?"

"I wish I could forget the whole thing."

Lupe laid one hand on Celie's arm. "Out with it."

"Well, I was in my room back home packing my suitcase. There was a ghost standing next to me. It kept ordering me around. It had such a strange, powerful voice that, well, it magnetized me."

"Oh, yeah? What did this magnetic ghost say?"

"'Put that bag down. You're not going anywhere!'"

"Wow." Lupe shook her head.

"And get this," Celie said, "the ghost's face, when I could even see it, kept changing. First, it was Mom, and then it sort of dissolved into Sister Gerald. I was trying to make go away. I yelled to try to make it leave me alone, but you know what? I couldn't get the words out."

"What were you trying to say?"

"Just 'Get out!' Over and over."

"Hmmm. That must've been when *I* woke up. I heard you, but I couldn't make out your words."

"The words wouldn't come. All I could do was make sounds. It was horrible."

"Well, did the ghost go away?"

"I don't remember. That's when I woke up."

They both gazed at the water, then Lupe said, "Strange. What do you think the nightmare means?"

"I've been feeling lots of pressure lately." Celie rubbed her eyes with her fingers.

"Yeah, I know." Lupe's voice was sympathetic. "You think you can fool me, but I've noticed. You haven't been yourself lately. What's eating you?" When Celie gave her a look, she said, "You know you can trust me, I'd never tell a soul. C'mon, level with me. It might help to talk about it."

As if shaking herself out of a reverie, Celie opened her eyes wide and faced Lupe. "Uh . . . to be honest, I'm pretty . . . confused. If you must know, it's . . . it's Sister Gerald. I'm really uncomfortable around her."

"She's putting too much pressure on you to finish those textbooks?"

"No. That's going okay. In fact, I love the whole project." She grinned. "I might even get the textbooks published next year. Sister Gerald's actually sending me to a conference to meet New York publishers in October."

With an answering grin and a nod, Lupe steered the conversation back to the nightmare. "Well, I can understand why your mom appeared in your dream. You told me a long time ago that you've never been close to her, like you always wanted. And you saw her a lot this month. So that fits." She measured her words. "But why would you tell Sister Gerald to get out of your room?"

Celie threw a stone half-heartedly into the creek.

Lupe wasn't finished. "If I've learned one thing about dreams," she said quietly, "it's that it's important to look at what happens. But it's more important to figure out how they make you feel. The unconscious is a very mysterious thing. Some believe it's God talking to us. I think dreams can tell us a lot about ourselves. So tell me how you felt right after you woke up."

"Totally exhausted and frustrated because I couldn't get the words out. But incredibly relieved, too, because I told them both off. It took a lot out of me. I felt like I'd been in a huge fight."

"Who won?"

"I think, uh. . . ." She laughed. "I think I *almost* did—and, even though I couldn't say what I wanted to say . . . come to think of it, the ghost *did* disappear right before I woke up."

"Great! That's a good sign."

Barely hearing Lupe, Celie went on. "And you're right about my mom. I tried and tried to get through to her during my last trip home, but it's no use. Sometimes I doubt we'll ever communicate, even though I wish it weren't so. But she's on a totally different wavelength from me. My sisters know how to relate to her, but I don't." She paused. Did she want to go on? She took a deep breath. "And . . . Sister Gerald? Well, that's another story." Another pause, as she noticed Lupe looking away. She figured her friend didn't want to appear to be prying. "I can't deny it," she was barely whispering now, "our relationship bothers me a lot. Still, she's done so much for me." She began talking louder again, more to herself than to Lupe. "I'm with her a great deal because of the manuscripts we're working on. She wants to be my friend, not just my Superior. But, uh, I—" She stopped and faced Lupe squarely, guarding her words. "Our relationship doesn't feel right. Not right at all. Maybe God *is* speaking through my dream."

"Uhhh, how friendly is she?"

180

"Too friendly. I can't figure out how to handle it. Do you—?"

"Yeah. I've watched her get close to others. She monopolizes first one nun, then another. It's never seemed right to me. She's certainly not a group person, unless it's a large gathering. Think about it, Celie. She's always part of a twosome. That's why I told you to steer clear of her. Remember? It just never looked right."

Celie raised her hands to her cheeks. "I wasn't aware . . . but now . . . now that you're pointing it out—but Lupe, it's gone way beyond—way beyond—" She shook her head.

"Way beyond what?"

"I just can't handle it, and I keep wondering if it's my fault. If I'm to blame. Oh, Lupe, I'm so mixed up. I don't know what to do."

"Celie, please. Why would you think what she does is your fault? I won't allow you to keep blaming yourself. And we all struggle with things in this life. You're only human."

As the chapel bells rang out, signaling the nuns' first wakeup call, Celie leaned forward and accepted her friend's hug. Lupe's arms were so comforting. "Thanks," she said quietly. "I'll figure something out. Just talking to you has helped."

Lupe gave her an extra squeeze then placed her hands on Celie's shoulders. As usual, she didn't mince words. "Don't dismiss this dream or how you feel about it. You've got to get to the bottom of it. Why don't you talk to a counselor?"

Celie's whole body tensed up. She folded her arms over her breasts as Lupe stood up and looked down at her.

"Seriously, Celie, I talked to a counselor a year ago, and she really straightened me out. I was scared at first, but after a couple of sessions, I discovered I had lots more options than I ever thought I had. And I realized not everything was my fault. The best part was, well, I didn't feel so crazy and mixed up. I'm much better."

Celie opened her mouth and tried to form a reply, but nothing came out.

"It's no big deal," Lupe went on. "You get permission and they arrange it. I bet you could go see someone while you're up here studying. Then you won't need to get Sister Gerald's consent. Come on, get up."

Celie stood up. "It's a good idea. I'll think it over." But her thoughts were still thick with doubt.

Lupe grabbed her hand and pulled her toward the path. "Promise me you'll at least consider it. We'd better hustle now. C'mon! I'll race you."

They ran along the dirt path through the trees. Lupe won the foot race, but as they arrived back at their cabin, Celie's doubts returned. *What a relief to tell her . . . at least part of it. But why am I still so afraid?*

Eleven young women in floor-length, blue-checked dresses and veiled heads sat in comfy overstuffed chairs or sat at tables, poring over books, making copious notes. They were studying for their philosophy midterm. The wrought-iron lamps glowed, and when the weathered grandfather clock in the corner chimed four times, they all looked up in surprise.

Celie was rereading a section of the *Summa Theologica* by St. Thomas Aquinas. Her professor had briefly discussed the writings of St. Augustine but seemed to prefer Aquinas, the renowned 13th-century Dominican teacher and philosopher. To prepare for their midterm essay, she'd asked her students to apply Aquinas' ideas to their own lives. Celie had been reading his treatise on passions and virtues over and over for two days, trying to digest the true meaning of the work, struggling to relate to his principles. Now, as she reread a paragraph, something finally clicked.

> The Philosopher says . . . we take counsel on great matters, because we distrust ourselves. Things that make us afraid are not simply evil, but have a certain magnitude . . . because they seem difficult to repel. . . . Consequently, when fear is intense, man does indeed wish to take counsel, but his thoughts are so disturbed he can find no counsel.

Incredible! Seven centuries ago, this learned Doctor of the Church had described the overwhelming fear gripping her now. She *did* distrust herself. Her opinions of Sister Gerald were chaotic and muddled. Lupe had been right that morning. She needed to talk it out, even if she *was* petrified about opening up. She went back to the text.

> . . . fear hinders action. If fear increases so much as to disturb reason, it hinders action even on the part of the soul.

Her fingers tightened on the book. Hungry for answers, she scanned the page to see if Aquinas offered any practical solutions.

> The Philosopher says courage is contrary to fear *[and they are]* farthest removed from one another . . . since fear turns away from future hurt . . . but courage turns on threatened danger, because of its own victory over that same danger.

"Future hurt." Was that why she felt so anxious? Was that her stumbling block? Would she feel even more wounded and worthless after she admitted her sin to a counselor? But then the comfort of Lupe's words sifted through her thoughts. *It made me realize I had lots of options and everything happening to me wasn't all my fault. I didn't feel like I was so crazy.*

What Lupe had said seemed to echo St. Thomas' treatise. Yes! They were both encouraging her. A little shiver of excitement raced through her. She'd endured a frozen powerlessness, not only now, but—she suddenly realized—she'd been silent and powerless for most of her life. Could she summon up enough inner strength now to overcome a lifetime of silence?

She turned to the next paragraph of the *Summa*.

> The Philosopher says that those *[who are]* hopeful are full of courage . . . *[and]* the cause of courage is the . . . imagination of hope that safety . . . *[is]* near.

Celie mulled over the idea of hope. She *did* have options. Like Lupe, she could find a protective shelter. Now it was up to her to "visualize a means of safety and to trust it." Her hope was the key. It would trigger the courage she needed!

She reread the final paragraph, focusing on the wise friar's summary.

> Men of fortitude who face danger according to . . . reason, face the danger not from passion but with due deliberation. . . . *[So]* when they are in the midst of danger, they experience nothing unforeseen, . . . therefore they are more persevering . . . *[and]* they face the danger on account of . . . *[hope]* which is . . . abiding.

Aquinas' words reminded her of her father. When he'd hugged her in the hospital, he hadn't underestimated his trials and the pain he would face in the weeks and months ahead. With reason and calm, he'd told her that he knew his journey would be extremely difficult. In a way, he'd already faced the hardships to come. *I have to try*, he'd said. *They say only one in ten people will beat it forever. I want to be that one.*

His hope-filled words still echoed in her memory. Only a month ago, Dad had shown her an incredibly determined awareness mixed with courage, plus a rare glimpse of open honesty. Celie would never forget it. He'd assessed his challenge. Knowing fully that he would suffer embarrassment, guilt, and pain in the future, knowing he was facing difficult odds, he had already visualized victory over his past. How utterly brave!

Could she, his Beautiful Dreamer, follow his lead? Would her hopes arm her with the protection she needed?

And then she remembered how Colleen had reassured her with words she would never forget. *Dad knows you have a lot of dreams and he thinks you're going to make them come true. You remind him that he used to have dreams too, long ago. And he loves you for it.*

CHAPTER 32

MOUNTAIN TREASURES?

August, 1967

Light had ebbed early, and although it was only two o'clock in the after-noon, the air hung saturated with moisture, but not even the sounds of distant thunder distracted Celie and the other young nuns. It was too warm to stop playing. They dove into the creek and careened down the slick boulders, eager to splash each other and cool themselves. Midterm exams were over, and they were celebrating.

Celie slithered underwater in the clear pond, enjoying the feel of the rivulets playing with her auburn hair. Swimming was the one time the Order allowed the nuns to take off their veils. She surfaced to float on her back and survey the gray clouds overhead.

They had two more golden summer weeks at Maryvale. Celie had pulled A's on both of her midterms, but her grades weren't the reason why she was finally feeling more serene. As she lay in the fresh, cool water, she let her mind settle again on the ideas she'd discovered in the *Summa Theologica*. The words of St. Thomas Aquinas had sparked new energy in her. She'd never thought much about "courage or daring" before, let alone considered them as virtues. Oh, as a child she'd watched plenty of old war movies with Dad, but how could John Wayne's gutsy achievements apply to *her* life? She'd also read tons of stuff about hope, especially since joining the convent, but what Aquinas wrote was different. *Courage and daring are the opposite of fear.*

She paddled to a quiet spot under an overhanging tree. *So,* she said to herself, *if I get up enough courage, then my fear will gradually disappear.* But how could she make it happen?

Aquinas wrote that "imagining some means of safety" could bolster hope.

What security net did she have? Could she transfer to another convent? But, she wondered, wouldn't that be running away? Besides, she loved the parishioners and the children she taught at IME.

Lost in thought, she side-stroked across the water. A counselor might help her figure things out. But would she have the nerve to tell her what had actually happened? Was it safe? The years of sickening guilt she'd felt after confessing her private sins clouded her resolve. Talking to a therapist meant revealing her weaknesses in the light of day. *But I felt much better after confiding in Lupe,* she reassured herself, *and, besides, everything I say to the counselor has to be kept confidential.*

Suddenly she was interrupted by a shout. "Sister! You need to come with us. See those dark clouds? They say it's a thunderstorm." It was cousin Rosemary, Sister John Marie, calling her to follow the rest of the nuns up the hill. Celie had been so preoccupied she hadn't noticed everyone vacating the creek and the pond.

"Are you okay, Sister?" Her cousin's voice was tinged with concern.

Why does she always act so formal? Such a perfect nun! Celie's irritation went back a long way. During her high school years, Mom had constantly raved about her cousin and what a "wonderful, thoughtful person" she was. But Celie had never seen things the way her mother did. She looked at Rosemary again. *She's so emotionless—like a cardboard mannequin.* Even so, her mother's words invaded her thoughts again. *Don't be so judgmental.*

"Sister?" Rosemary was standing at the edge of the pond. "Did you hear me, Sister Celia Marie?"

"Rosemary," Celie used her civilian name on purpose, "I'm doing fine. I'm just thinking." She scrambled out of the water and accepted the towel her cousin offered.

"Sometimes you worry me, Sister Celia Marie."

"I do?"

"Yes. It's as if you're somewhere else." A trace of a smile tugged at Sister John Marie's lips. "What if I hadn't seen you there? Hours could go by, and you'd still be in the water. What if lightning struck the water?"

Celie smiled. "You sound like my mom and dad, always saying I'm dreaming and lost in my own little world. You heard them nag me enough when we were growing up."

"I'm sorry. I didn't—"

"That's okay. I'm used to it."

"Well, I'm glad you were just thinking and it's nothing serious," Rosemary said. "Sometimes we can get too intense in this religious life. There's so much solitude."

"Really? But you always look so serene."

Rosemary started. "Oh." She started to say something, but instead folded her arms and shrugged. "I can have bad days, too, you know."

Celie was surprised by her cousin's hint of honesty. She always appeared so perfect. Or was that a mask? Did she grapple with problems, too? Celie brushed away her surprise and pressed on. "Do you ever struggle? With . . . with problems?

Rosemary looked down at the ground. "Sometimes."

"How do you pull yourself out of it?"

Her cousin turned away. "Well, I wait it out and . . . and, well, talking helps sometimes."

"Yes, I've considered that. The tough part is finding the right person to listen."

"Come on, Sister Celia Marie. It's starting to rain."

Celie persisted. "Rosemary, who do you talk to?"

Rosemary was already a dozen steps ahead. "The scripture says, 'If we knock, it shall be opened.'"

"Yes but . . . Thanks, Sister. That's a big help."

"Well, if you ever want to talk, I'm here for you, Sister."

Sure thing. Talking to my stuck-up cousin will solve everything. Rosemary had always irritated her, and here it was again, the famous Nun Voice. Celie couldn't stand it. She took a chance anyway. "Rosemary, can't you call me by my secular name once in awhile? Just for old times' sake? We've only known each other all our lives. I hardly ever call you Sister John Marie."

"Sure, Celie. I can do that." Rosemary's blue-green eyes flicked downward. A second later, though, she met Celie's gaze, but her lips weren't smiling.

As they stood facing each other, large drops of rain began to splatter them. A minute later, lightning flashed in the distance. There was nothing to do now but climb the hill and take cover.

The downpour rattled at the cabin's windows and lightning lit up the sky. As another thunderclap sounded, some of the nuns looked out the window. Leaves swirled up and sailed off, carried by the storm as it thrashed the oak and pine trees. How long would it last? Would lightning strike any of the old trees around the cabin? Were they safe?

All of the nuns had changed back into their shapeless, navy-checked dresses, white coifs and black veils, and sneakers. Even though they were forced to stay inside, it was still afternoon recreation time, so they were gathered around the fireplace, sitting in the sagging chairs and couches. A dusty, stuffed moose head with glass eyes stared down at them from the wall above the stone fireplace.

Celie was trying to bring some life into their listless gathering. "I've always loved thunderstorms," she said. One or two of the others agreed with her, but most shook their heads.

Lupe looked away from the fire. "Sister John Marie," she said, "why don't you play for us?

When the others echoed her request, Rosemary picked up her guitar and settled herself on the floor in front of the blaze. She tested the strings, turned two or three of the tuning pegs, then started strumming. Within two or three bars, the other young women began to chime in, altos and sopranos blending their voices in the song: "Where Have All The Flowers Gone?"

Moments like these brought tears of happiness to Celie's eyes. She'd never felt so close to a group of women before. For almost four years, she'd studied, taken exams, and suffered through the frustrations of student teaching with these other young nuns. She'd slept next to them in the Motherhouse dorm, eaten the spare meals they were served, sung and prayed with them in the chapel, and joked, laughed, and hiked with them in the hills of Santo Domingo. She'd even gotten to know their parents on visiting days at the Motherhouse. They'd all entered together, and now they seemed like true sisters. *They're even more my sisters than Maureen and Colleen.* She had never considered this before.

The young nuns hummed along as Sister John Marie segued into another folk song, and once they identified it, they started singing. "Hang Down Your Head, Tom Dooley" again, and a minute later, "Puff, The Magic Dragon. . . ."

Even as she sang along, Celie could hear a conversation on the other side of the room.

"Have you seen Soeur Sourire? Her name means Sister Smile," someone was saying. "She's called the Singing Nun, you know. I saw her on TV. She's a cloistered Dominican nun from Belgium. She sings that song about St. Dominic. It's so catchy!"

"I like it," one of the other nuns said, "but all I hear are negative comments about her."

"Why?"

"The older Sisters say all the publicity is bound to go to her head. How could she possibly go back to a life of solitude and prayer after being on TV? There are articles about her in magazines and newspapers all over."

"You mean she *was* the Singing Nun," said another voice. "She calls herself Luc Dominique now. She left her Order. She wants to be famous."

"I know." This was a shocked whisper. "Lots of nuns are leaving. Maybe it's due to all the changes."

"I don't understand it," another added.

The room suddenly became hushed as the old oak grandfather clock in the corner chimed three times, competing with the wind and rain outside.

Celie knew what they were saying was true. Too true. She'd read about nuns leaving their convents and finding new professions in the outside world. It was happening right here among the Augustinians, too. One morning she'd see a friend of hers praying in her chapel stall, and the next day the stall was empty, and in the refectory the silverware wrapped in her special napkin was gone, too. No announcements, no way to say goodbye—that's what hurt the most. How could her Superiors assume they were keeping these departures secret when everyone whispered about them for days, wondering why this nun or that one had left?

Celie peered out the window and thought she saw two small figures moving through the trees. Yes, two nuns heading for the lodge. They were shielding their faces from the wind and rain and holding large black umbrellas over their heads. One was tiny, the other tall.

Celie pressed her fingers against the cold window pane. "Is that Sister Pauline?" She hadn't seen her favorite high school teacher, and, yes, her friend, since the day she and Rosemary had said goodbye to her. That was a long time ago. Too long. Back then, Sister Pauline had been the only woman Celie had trusted, the teacher who had encouraged her to play sports and enter writing contests. She'd even brought Celie an armful of daisies the day Celie learned she'd won the top prize in a writing contest.

Yet when Celie had entered the convent, communication between them stopped. Sister Pauline had never come to visit her at the Motherhouse. She'd answered a couple of Celie's letters, but with such terse, impersonal notes that Celie had eventually given up. Why was she here now? Why was she walking up the hill in the rain? Celie was bewildered. She couldn't wait to talk to her, yet she felt a searing kind of hurt, too.

She strained to make out who Sister Pauline's companion was. "And it's Sister Adele!" she announced.

"Really?" Sister Lupe and the others crowded around the window as Sister John Marie ran to unlatch the door.

Sister Pauline swept into the room, dropping her battered umbrella. As she spied the guitar in Rosemary's hand, she exclaimed, "Aha! You're singing away in here while that wild wind is pushing us every which way except up the hill." She stopped to wipe off her soaked veil with a towel someone handed her. "I never thought we'd make it here in one piece!" The drama Sister Pauline created when she entered a room always amazed Celie.

Sister Pauline went immediately to the fireplace and whisked off her wet black cape, shaking raindrops into the crackling fire. Then she turned. "Okay, Sister John Marie, start strumming again or I'll do it for you."

While most of the young nuns gathered around to hug the new arrivals, Sister John Marie began to play another folk tune they'd all learned as Postulants. Everyone joined in the singing as Sister Pauline chose a seat and added her rich soprano to the chorus. When they finished, she seized the guitar and started another song, "Michael, Row Your Boat Ashore." Their impromptu recital went on and on until the rain dried up and it was suppertime. They assembled around the dining table and ate spaghetti and meatballs, still joking and laughing until eight o'clock. Shortly thereafter, they filed out under a cloudless night sky filled with stars and entered the small chapel next door, where they knelt together to sing the evening prayers of Compline and Matins.

Celie cherished this tiny, rustic church. The scents of fresh rain and pine wafted through the room on the cool breeze and the chanting of her sisters rose and fell in waves around her. She sang too, but her thoughts wandered back again to St. Thomas' words: *Hope leads to courage . . . when it is strong. Courage turns on threatened danger.*

She stopped singing and fixed her eyes on the sanctuary light. "Lord of my heart," she prayed in a whisper, "fill me with hope. Give me the nerve You gave my dad. I *must* take control of this fear and find the courage to go forward. Open a door for me and find a wise listener. Force me to tell the 'truth that will make me free.'"

Psalms ended, each nun dipped her fingers in the holy water, made the sign of the cross, and filed out of the chapel. Sister Pauline stood near the entrance and whispered good night to each. As Celie passed, she said, "Sister Celia Marie, may I speak to you for a minute?"

Celie stopped and they stepped outside the door.

"I heard that your father was seriously ill a few weeks ago," the older nun said. "How is he doing now?"

"Thanks for asking, Sister. Dad's doing much better. Mom phoned me yesterday to say he's finally leaving the hospital."

"Oh, I'm so glad." She pressed Celie's fingers. "He's such a good man. I was hoping your news would be positive. And, my dear, how are you doing? It's been so long since I've seen you."

"I've been," Celie's voice faltered in mid-sentence, "I've been okay."

"Child, you don't sound okay."

"No, really, Sister, I'm fine."

Sister Pauline smiled. "Can we get together tomorrow? I have time right after breakfast. We have lots of catching up to do. Please?"

"Okay," Celie answered as the Profound Silence bell began to toll.

Beginning in her freshman year in high school, Celie had gotten to know this sprightly, good-natured nun very well. Whether she was practicing volleyball or rehearsing for a choral performance or writing a story, Sister Pauline had kidded and goaded her on to greater achievements. Celie had never expected to win the state writing competition, but Sister Pauline had said, "I'm not surprised. You have a gift, Celie. Many gifts. When I met you, you didn't even know it."

These were memories Celie would never forget.

"So, my dear, what gives? Why such a tense look when I asked how you were last night?" As always, Sister Pauline was as direct as she was caring.

"I can't—I mean, I'm not sure about some things right now."

"I'm sorry to hear that. I'm surprised, too." The older nun's eyes softened as she studied Celie's face. "I've heard nothing but wonderful things about you this year. You were even the topic of conversation as we drove up here; Sister Adele raved about your work with your students. Has she mentioned that she's considering asking you to lead a new parish program helping immigrants? And when I've seen Sister Gerald at our principals' meetings these past few months, she's always praised you to the skies. The religion textbooks you're writing with your *own* lesson plans, your class's response to them, plus their parents' enthusiasm, well, they're the talk of the congregation." She patted Celie's hand. "I always ask about you, you know. But I'm sure you know that."

"No, I didn't know. I haven't heard anything. About you or . . . from you, either. In a long time." She couldn't help the way her voice cracked.

"You're upset. I'm sorry. I had no idea how troubled you were. I assumed from everything I heard, you were doing great, as always." Sister Pauline smiled brightly.

Celie tried to return a smile, but her heart sagged. Worst of all, she knew her feelings were transparent to Sister Pauline.

As if reading her thoughts, Pauline touched Celie's cheek. "I can see you're not yourself. You must be feeling down. Please, is there anything I can do?"

Celie's voice was tight, "I think . . . Sister, I think I need to talk to a counselor."

"Of course. I can arrange that for you. Right away. I don't want you to continue in this troubled state."

"Please don't tell anyone."

"You can trust me. I'll make a telephone call today. I know a wonderful woman counselor who's not far from here."

Celie stood up. "I can't talk anymore right now. Please understand, Sister. I hope the counselor will help. But I'm tired. I need to rest."

"By all means, my dear. I'll arrange everything for you. You'll have the information before I leave, and don't worry, this will be just between us."

Sister Pauline hugged her, but Celie's arms hung at her sides. Then she walked away without another word, wondering why the older nun had shown no surprise.

CHAPTER 33

SECRETS REVEALED

A tall, middle-aged woman, Mrs. Charlotte Fields had counseled several Augustinian nuns over the years. Though she was a life-long Christian, she told Celie, she was not a Catholic. She wore immaculate suits and glasses with tortoise shell frames. When she occasionally took her glasses off, her gray eyes seemed friendlier, making Celie feel more comfortable, as if the counselor had removed a screen between them.

Because school would start in six weeks, Mrs. Fields scheduled their sessions for three times a week. Gradually, during August and September, she managed to elicit the primary details of Celie's past attachment to Sister Gerald. Her calm, businesslike, but friendly manner reassured Celie and gained her trust. As the weeks wore on, she began to probe more, asking Celie about her adolescent contacts with boys. Eventually, Celie began sharing her past and talking about her family and the isolation and loneliness she'd always felt at home, plus her long friendship with Dennis and her two-year attraction to Mike. The only secrets Celie kept hidden were her sins of impurity and her fantasies about Tony. In fact, she decided she couldn't tell Charlotte anything about him. Not yet. Maybe not ever.

Their previous session had become exceptionally emotional, as Charlotte gently provoked Celie to plunge forward and describe the night she had found herself caught in the web of Sister Gerald's sexual intimacy. At last Celie was able to pour out feelings she hadn't expressed to anyone else— her guilt caused by the indefinable pull she'd felt toward her Superior, her confusion about whether she'd caused Sister Gerald's overtures, and all her self-condemnation.

"Worst of all," she concluded, "I violated my Vow of Chastity, and I feel utter disgust about that evening."

Today, as Celie sat in the waiting room, she mulled over Charlotte's words of the week before. *You admire Sister Gerald quite a bit,* she'd said. *I hear that. And you had to spend an unusual amount of exclusive time with her this summer. But don't be so hard on yourself. A warm and loving heart such as yours will naturally seek intimacy and love.*

Suddenly the door opened. Celie stepped forward, and Charlotte enveloped Celie's hand in both of hers.

"How are you today, Sister? Well, I hope?"

"I guess. So far, so good." As Charlotte closed the door and took her seat, Celie sat in the blue easy chair across from Charlotte in her leather recliner. Only a box of Kleenex and a tape recorder sat on the coffee table between them. After each visit, Charlotte gave Celie the tape of their session. "Play it back for yourself during the week," she'd said, "so you'll absorb some of the points you missed while we were talking. As you listen, the breakthroughs you've experienced here will sort of marinate inside you," she pointed to her head, then her heart, "and help you understand the new ideas we've discussed."

Now Charlotte pressed the Record button and sat back, her smile inviting Celie to speak. "You don't sound too sure about yourself today," she said. "What's going on with you? Share your mood with me."

"I feel sort of dull, I guess. Not particularly happy or sad. Just blah."

"Can you describe it some more?"

"Bleak. Barren."

"That's an intriguing word, 'barren.' Close your eyes for me, Sister, and share the pictures that word conjures up in your mind. What do you see?"

"I can't see anything yet."

"Breathe in deeply, as I taught you. Take your time. Relax."

After several minutes, Celie said, "I see a desert. There's nothing growing in it."

"Is anyone there?"

"A woman."

"Tell me about her."

Celie hesitated. "Well, she's wearing white clothes . . . oh, they're in shreds, so most of her body is revealed. She's wandering around. And it's sweltering hot."

"Is she wandering alone?"

"Yes. And she's thirsty."

"Open your eyes, Sister, and tell me what you think this image tells you about your feelings."

"I'm . . . I'm," she wasn't sure how to say it. "I'm alone. Completely alone. Wandering around. Lost. And stripped down."

"And?"

Celie turned away, gripping one arm of the chair with both hands. "I'm yearning for something. It's a terrible yearning." She stopped and thought about what she'd just said. "But I can't identify it. I don't know what will satisfy me."

"That's normal, Sister. It's normal for you to struggle with emptiness and depression, even a kind of nakedness after you told me about so many chaotic emotions last Thursday. You took a huge risk telling me. I admire you for it."

Celie's eyes were burning. "But it hurts. More than I've ever felt." She found a handkerchief in her pocket.

Charlotte's voice was gentle. "That's okay, dear. Go ahead and cry if you want to."

Celie kept silent. She couldn't allow her feelings to overcome her. Instead of crying, she blew her nose.

"Let me change the subject for a minute," Charlotte said. Celie turned to face her again. "I want to ask a few questions, if I may. They may be difficult to answer, so just share the first thoughts that come to mind, okay?" She took off her horn-rimmed glasses.

"Okay." Even to herself, Celie sounded like she was about ten years old.

"Have you given any thought about your religious vocation?" Charlotte asked. "Do you think you can continue living as a celibate nun? Have you ever thought about the possibility of going home?"

Celie took a deep breath and heaved a sigh. "Yes, last spring before I renewed my vows. But, no, I don't think I'm ready to go home yet. I'm involved in a lot of projects at IME. My teaching—the children are making such good progress. Also, the refugee project is just getting underway. And I love relating to the parish families. The religion textbooks I've been creating will be published pretty soon. I'm really excited about that. I . . . well, I *think* I'm having an impact on my students. And their parents, too.

No, I *know* I am. So . . . even with all the worry and regret still weighing me down, no, I'm not ready to give up. Not yet."

Charlotte nodded. "Okay, then. Give yourself more time to sort things out. All these worthwhile activities sound like you are inspiring and uplifting many people as a nun. That's a desire you stated very strongly last week. I can see you are still very genuinely committed. Let me ask you another question now. What areas of your life right now give you the most doubt and heartache?"

That's easy! But it was hard to put it into words. "This . . . this . . . *this thing* with Sister Gerald. I don't know what it is! What her intentions are. . . . I've never experienced anything like that. I just want it to go away. I wish so much that it had never happened. What can I do?"

Charlotte folded her hands and leaned forward a little. "How does this situation fit into your vocation?"

Celie gnawed on her lower lip. "It makes it a mockery."

"What can you do?"

"Stay away from Sister Gerald."

"Is that what you want?"

"Absolutely! I can't stand the thought of going near her again. I don't feel safe around her."

"I agree. From what you've told me, I don't consider her safe, either."

"But she's my Superior, and she's highly respected in our congregation. I can't be . . . can't be. . . ." She paused to think how to frame her reply. "Why did I let her get so close to me? She wasn't like that before, but then everything changed. I wonder if . . . if what I felt was abnormal or why I let her—" Celie hid her face behind her hands.

Charlotte's voice was soft and calm. "You must not keep blaming yourself. After hearing about your adolescence, I think it's quite unlikely you prefer intimacy with those of your own gender, as some women do. Often as we grow into adulthood, feelings for our own sex emerge, especially in an enclosed environment. Psychological studies also show that when intimacy with the opposite sex is impossible, tendencies toward emotional and sexual activity emerge in convent life just as they do in women's prisons. And in men's prisons and other environments, too, where there are no women for the men to engage with."

Celie pursed her lips. "Really? I had no idea! It's such a relief to hear you say that."

"Please listen to me carefully now. From now on, when you begin reproaching yourself, you must call a halt to those guilty thoughts. I'm telling you with conviction that I think Sister Gerald's actions were way out of line. I believe she is a lesbian who has not or will not come to grips with her own sexual preferences."

"A what?"

"A lesbian. It's a word you may not know. However, throughout history there have been many famous and successful lesbians and male homosexuals. The well-known authors Willa Cather and Edna Ferber, for example, and Alexander the Great. In this case, though, Sister Gerald has chosen to hide her desires quite effectively, but she also uses them to wield illicit power. More troubling is her hypocrisy as a celibate nun." Charlotte paused to put her glasses back on. "Her actions should even be construed as a type of assault, since she is your Superior. You'll have to decide, Sister Celia Marie. You have to decide if it might be important to report her to those in authority."

Celie eyelids flew open as she gripped the arms of her chair. "Oh, no! I couldn't—"

"Okay, okay. Let's not deal with that issue right now. Let's focus on your needs. I want to ask you more questions. Your sexual feelings, your desire for intimacy—this seems to be a side of yourself you haven't dealt with. Tell me more about your decision to be chaste. Did you spend time considering chastity before you entered the convent? Did you know what that vow meant? You told me about your past attraction to Mike, and Dennis, too, when you were an adolescent. You're twenty-two now. How do you think convent life will affect you as you grow into womanhood? Will it become easier or more difficult?"

"All I remember about sex in high school is that almost *everything* was a mortal sin and that meant going straight to Hell. I was so scared of getting involved with sins of impurity, so afraid of leading boys into sin. They warned us about it all the time."

"Who warned you?"

"All the nuns. And the priests, too. I wanted to stay pure, so I never let a boy touch me or," she closed her eyes and blushed in spite of herself, "or French kiss me. One guy I dated wanted to do that. And more! But I wouldn't let him, so he dumped me."

Celie did not see Charlotte's understanding smile. "So you thought the convent would be a haven from what the Church calls sins of impurity?"

"No! I never thought of it that way. I just thought since I'd remained chaste while I was dating, I'd have enough control to stay pure as a nun. I knew it wasn't going to be easy. It wasn't easy in high school, either. But I thought I could do it here. With God's help."

"And have you been able to?"

"I . . . it's hard. Harder than I ever thought it would be. But so far, I've been able to keep my feelings under control. For the most part." Celie couldn't bring herself to tell Charlotte about her inability to stop her private sins of impurity.

"I hear that you want to challenge yourself regarding chastity," Charlotte said, "but I think you're reaching a crossroads. You're going to have decide in future months whether or not you can renounce the expression of your sexuality. Your high school years were one thing, but you will spend your lifetime as a nun. You won't be able to ignore your emotions as you grow into womanhood, not the way you did as a teenager." She paused and shifted in her chair.

"Let me switch topics a little," she said a minute later. "I think you understand what we've been trying to do here together during these weeks. Unlock your feelings. Right?"

Celie nodded. "Yes. You want me to try to *feel* things instead of 'stuffing it all away.' I've never cried this much before or felt such anger and sadness."

"Yes. You need to face your feelings, passions, and sexual stirrings, face them honestly now and in the future, too. From what you've shared so far, I can see that even expressing irritation, not to mention rage or deep sadness, was not something ever talked about or encouraged while you were growing up. We have work to do, my dear. We have work to do to uncover *all* your emotions. Remember, Celie, God gave them to you.

"And," she continued, "in the months ahead, you'll have to weigh your sexual needs and emotional desires against your conviction to live as a religious nun."

Aware that she'd twisted the handkerchief in her lap into not one knot but three while the counselor talked, Celie looked up.

"Don't be afraid of your feelings," Charlotte was saying. "They're telling you that you can't trust Sister Gerald. You were sickened by her overtures. Let your feelings continue to tell you the truth about your inner life and your relationships with others. Remind yourself, too, that Jesus told us, 'If you know the truth, the truth will make you free.'"

Celie looked at her knotted handkerchief. *Will I ever feel free?*

CHAPTER 34

SURPRISES

The musty air lay like a stifling blanket over the dim classroom. Celie's back ached as she bent over her desk, and trickles of sweat ran down her face. She'd already opened the windows to encourage afternoon breezes, but neither the flag that hung near her desk nor the eucalyptus trees outside even moved. This morning's news had hailed the heat wave as "blazing and dangerous, and highly unusual for San Francisco in late September."

In spite of her discomfort, Celie was engrossed in her students' arithmetic test results. After four solid days of intense instruction on the concept of addition as a way to check subtraction, her efforts had paid off. Most of her second graders had scored well. Yes, days like this made teaching worthwhile.

Last year, she told herself, standing up straight to relax her back, *the children found this difficult. Either I'm getting better or this class is smarter. Maybe both.*

She looked around the room and imagined the children's expectant faces on Monday. *They're going to be so proud! I'll hang their papers up for Open House.*

Suddenly noticing how quiet it was, and out in the schoolyard too, she checked the clock. Everyone else had left school long ago. The Vespers bell would ring in half an hour. Following prayers, a celebration of Sister Adele's feast day was planned for tonight, and they were going to serve an authentic Mexican meal with Sister Adele's favorite dishes. Celie could almost smell Sister Rosarita's specialty, homemade tamales. She loved the cook's guacamole sauce and enchiladas, too. Most of these dishes were new to Celie, as her mother had never made them and eating out had been way too expensive. And Lupe was coming to dinner tonight. She'd promised to bring her mother's refried beans with spicy *chorizo*. Lupe was also indebted to Sister Adele, as the older nun had mentored both of them during their first year of teaching.

Celie began shutting the windows when a sharp knock interrupted her. She turned around to find a tall visitor standing just inside the doorway.

"Oh, hello, Sister," the man said. "Sorry to bother you. I'm looking for Celia O'Rourke. She teaches here."

It was Tony. He surveyed the classroom as he talked, then his eyes settled on her again. Suddenly his body stiffened. "Celie? It's you, isn't it?"

Celie stationed herself behind her desk to protect herself from the confused expression she saw on Tony's face. "Yes. It's me."

Silence. And more silence that dragged on, forming what seemed like a solid wall between them as they stared at each other. Worry and guilt began to spread through Celie as Tony's stance and scowl reflected his astonishment, maybe even silent rage.

"You lied to me," he finally said. "But why am I surprised by another lie? I should be used to deception by now."

"Tony, don't. Please don't be angry." She moved around the desk as he turned toward the door. "Tony. Please wait."

"Wait? For more lies?" His hand pulled on the doorknob. Suddenly he paused and turned around. "No. I can't deal with this. After all that's happened? Not now." He pulled the door open and rushed out of the classroom.

Celie hurried after him. "Tony, let me explain. I didn't lie. I just—"

He stopped and turned. "Omitted who you were. *What* you were?"

She watched him dash down the dark hall and lunge at the glass doors. Then he was gone. She followed him out and stood by the door, limp and forlorn, knowing she could never catch up with him. Minutes later, a black Thunderbird swerved up the street, curving recklessly in a U-turn. Next, the car sped past the school and turned onto Army Street. She caught a glimpse of him at the wheel. He was facing straight ahead, his chin jutting out, his back rigidly straight, his mouth a straight line.

She ran to the curb and stood there for a long time, gazing at the intersection long after his car had disappeared. Two students playing kickball down the block waved to her, and she absently raised her hand, but all she could think of was Tony. She'd wounded him, and he didn't deserve more pain. She must find a way to see him and explain.

"Look at the sky," Celie said.

Lupe looked up. "Yeah," she said, "it's quite a sunset. But you look like death warmed over. What's eating you? Were the beans and *chorizo* that bad?"

They were walking through the schoolyard together. Celie knew her friend was trying to joke her out of her gloomy mood. "They tasted okay," she replied. Images of Tony kept penetrating her thoughts, but she couldn't share them with Lupe.

They exited through the chain link gates and walked up the street. Lupe pointed to the hill in the distance. "That looks like a good place to view the city lights."

Reaching the crest of the slope, they noticed candy wrappers and empty soda cans left by kids who had played there after school. This vacant lot was a small oasis among the peeling clapboard houses that crowded Trenton Street, which gradually curved up the slope to overlook San Francisco. Celie absently picked up a torn baseball glove lying near the base of a leaking drinking fountain and put it on. Without thinking, she molded its pocket with her fist.

Lupe nodded toward the mitt. "You look like you know what you're doing."

"Huh? Oh, yeah. I used to play softball. I thought you knew. Sister Pauline coached us."

"Really? You sure don't sound excited about it. What position did you play?"

"Second base, but mostly I liked to hit. I even pulled off a couple home runs with the bases loaded." Celie paused. "It seems like centuries ago."

They sat down together on a worn stone bench and gazed out over the sparkling city. The sun's glow had disappeared now and the dark streets were filled with strings of white and red lights, vast necklaces spread in parallel lines as evening commuters headed home to the cities around the Bay.

"Speaking of Sister Pauline," Lupe began, "she asked about you the other day. She sounded concerned. She was at Sacred Heart to oversee the new music program. Have you been in touch with her?"

"No. Not since her visit to Maryvale. She's busy with her own duties. And who knows what else. But I did write her a letter. I hope I didn't bother her too much with my little life. But you know what? She actually wrote back. That was a shock."

"Hmm. Do I detect a touch of resentment? You're usually so mild mannered and sweet. Don't tell me you're letting your emotions out like the rest of us."

Celie had to grin a little. They both knew how many lectures Lupe had endured from her Superiors about "her unreasonable displays of emotion." She'd often used Celie as a sounding board to vent her frustrations. In turn, Celie had always urged her friend to control her feelings, especially her temper. Now the tables were turning.

"Okay," Celie admitted, "if the truth be known, I guess I *am* miffed. It's just that Sister Pauline and I were pretty close in high school. I was with her every day at volleyball practice, then softball, too, not to mention chorus. I considered her a good friend. And my mentor, though I didn't know the word then. But when I entered the convent, guess what? I never saw her again! Recently, when I finally asked her about it in my letter, she told me the Augustinian Rule cautions against familiar friendships. Against a familiar friendship with me. She wrote something strange about how she 'had to step aside so the Holy Spirit could direct me on the path of my vocation.'" She didn't both to hide the sarcasm and the bitterness in her voice.

"Wow, you are upset."

"Lupe, in these last four years, I haven't even gotten a phone call from her! It bothered me during our Postulancy year. During the Novitiate, too, but I didn't say anything, not even to myself, I guess, because I decided I was in training. You know what I mean? But when I saw her this summer—"

"It was like old times?"

"As far as *she* was concerned it was, but not for me. I mean, she seemed to care about me like before, but . . . well, I finally admitted—"

"What? Say it."

"I don't trust her. She hasn't initiated any contact with me, not even once, since I entered the convent. What kind of a relationship is that? I thought she was more than my mentor. I thought she was a real friend, despite the Augustinian Rule!"

"Well, I don't think I ever told you, Celie, but I was close to Sister Rose in high school, along with all the other girls that entered the convent from St. Cyril's High. And we've all compared notes since then. None of us heard from Sister Rose after we entered either. It's like, 'out of sight, out of mind.'"

"Really? I didn't know that. Friendships are really bizarre in the convent, aren't they?" Lupe nodded and Celie went on. "Family relationships, too. Think about it. Even Sister Marion can only visit Sister Veronica *one* afternoon a month. And they're *real* sisters!"

"Family visits are definitely limited," Lupe said, "but friends here are something totally different. It has to do with all those lectures we have to listen to on 'forbidden particular friendships.' I never heard that term before I entered the convent. They certainly go on and on about it—how we should be 'watchful and never spend much time with *one* person.'"

Celie nodded, thinking about what Charlotte had said to her. She laid her hand on her friend's shoulder. "Well, I'm very happy I'm doing just that, right now. You're the best."

"Ditto. Other than spouting off to you once in a while, the only other woman I can confide in is that counselor I told you about, and she gets paid to listen to me."

"I'm glad."

Lupe continued. "She's helped me quite a bit and she's supportive about my commitment to stay a nun, too. That's a relief! I thought she'd try to talk me out of it, like my folks."

"And thanks to you," Celie said, "my counselor's given me a lot to think about, too."

"Oh? You found a counselor? Good for you. I'm glad. I felt terrible seeing you struggling last summer."

"Thanks for your advice. You were right. I've been going to counseling for a couple months, three times a week, and it's helped. In fact, Sister Pauline arranged it. So I guess I shouldn't be too mad at her." Celie went on, trusting Lupe as she trusted no one else. "The counselor is trying to help me sort out my feelings. I've buried them for so long; it'll take forever for me to figure things out. That's probably why you hear my anger exploding all over the place."

"I was only kidding. You *need* to let your feelings out. You're pretty intense." Lupe softened her words by taking Celie's hand. She tipped her head to one side and Celie watched a wry grin spread across her face. "I *have* to say it. You know how blunt I am. I've always thought you were sort of repressed, Celie—it must be your Irish blood. But look at it this way, if you don't feel your emotions, you won't find out who you are. You'll never know what you hate or who you love."

Lupe turned to face the twinkling lights. "In my family," she said more quietly, "it was pretty crazy growing up. Chaos going on all the time, but one thing was always clear. We knew about feelings—they were like little bombs always going off in all directions. But that's important."

The two friends slipped into silence, watching the lights flicker far off against the dark sky and the Bay, the quiet between them as comfortable as a cozy blanket.

Images of Tony began to invade Celie's thoughts again, but she knew she'd confided enough for one night. She didn't dare tell her friend about meeting this man, especially not about her wish to see and apologize to him. Her friendship with Tony just couldn't end on such a hostile and bitter note. Nor could she tell Lupe the truth about her experiences with Sister Gerald. What would Lupe think of her? Celie found more comfort in Lupe's honest friendship than anywhere else, and she didn't want to tarnish that friendship. She knew, more than ever now, that real friendship was rare.

She let her thoughts drift again to her last session with Charlotte.

"Your hardest challenge," the counselor had said, "will be to determine in the months ahead if your life of chastity can withstand your need for intimacy. With some individuals it can; with others it cannot. Start by letting your feelings surface. Becoming aware of them doesn't mean you won't be able to control them. Once you're clear about what your anger or desires are telling you, you can learn how to manage them. It will become a life skill."

"But what can I do about my relationship with Sister Gerald?" she'd asked.

"For now, do not spend time alone with Sister Gerald. Above all, avoid any physical contact with her. Will you find that difficult?"

Celie recalled her careful reply to Charlotte's question. "No," she'd said, "but I miss the friendship we shared, even if I know that can't be anymore. I really have no desire to go near Sister Gerald again."

Before Charlotte could say anything, she'd added, "This summer, I was especially lonely. Sister Gerald and Sister Adele were the only other nuns who lived with me at IME besides Sister Rosarita, and she speaks only Spanish. Generally, I don't crave to be with one person, but I know I need friendships. Healthy ones."

"Do you think you can summon up your nerve to face your Superior and confront the feelings you'll have about it?" Charlotte had asked.

"Luckily, I haven't seen her since that horrible night. Right after, I rushed home to L.A. because of my dad's heart attack. Then I left to take a summer course in the Santa Cruz Mountains. When I returned to IME, I found out Sister Gerald had gone up north to our convent school in Ukiah. But I'm not sure how it will go when she comes back."

"Try not to worry about it too much," Charlotte had said.

"But she's my Superior! I'm not sure how to respond when we work on the textbook project again. She and I are the only ones creating it."

Celie wouldn't forget Charlotte's firm response. "You'll *have* to handle it, and with lots of tact. Eventually, you may even have to confront her. Or those in authority. For now, you must insist that others work on the textbooks with both of you or you must always work with Sister Gerald in a public place. A library, perhaps. Others *must* be present whenever you're with her. Make sure!"

Now Lupe nudged Celie, "Hey, quiet one! I think we'd better get back. I want to say goodbye to Sister Adele before I leave. She was such a goldmine for me. I was really fumbling around in the classroom until she stepped in to help me."

Celie stood up. "I know what you mean. You're filled with hopelessness, then Sister Adele shows up and explains how to turn everything around with her creative ideas—and they work because she's so experienced. All the kids at IME love her."

As they started down the hill, Lupe said, "I guess your schedule's going to tighten up real soon."

"Why?"

"Sister Adele told me at dinner that Sister Gerald's coming home tomorrow. You'll be diving back into that textbook project with her, right?"

Celie swallowed hard. "Really?"

Celie felt Lupe scrutinizing her as they walked toward Trenton Street. "Remember, I'm going to need a break," she said when the silence lasted too long. "These first few weeks of school are always stressful. Let's plan on stealing away to our favorite place under Golden Gate Bridge one day this week. Deal?"

"Deal."

As they hurried toward the convent entrance, Celie pushed her frantic thoughts about Sister Gerald out of her mind. Images of this afternoon replaced them. The black Thunderbird wheeling down this street. Tony's grim face. Where was he now, and how could she find him? She had to make amends. *Tomorrow.*

CHAPTER 35

NEW HONESTY

"**M**r. De Stefano's office. May I help you?"

"Yes, I have sort of a small emergency. This is Celia O'Rourke. Mr. De Stefano and I were supposed to meet this morning in San Francisco. I think I'm near his hotel, but I can't locate it without an exact address. Can you help me?"

"Certainly, Miss O'Rourke. It's right here on my desk. He's at the Princess Hotel, 4600 Army Street."

Celie thanked the secretary, copied down the address, and tucked it into her pocket. After leaving a note for Sister Adele, she picked up the keys to the Pontiac, which no one else would be using today since everyone was awaiting Sister Gerald's arrival from Ukiah.

She easily found the famous Princess Hotel, a historical landmark in the city, and searched for a parking space, wondering if Tony had chosen this hotel because of its proximity to Immaculate Mary Convent. Although she'd never ventured inside the hotel, she had often glimpsed its extravagant chandeliers as she drove by on her way to Sacred Heart, where Sister Lupe taught.

As she locked the Pontiac and caught sight of her reflection in the car window, she wondered again if her decision to wear jeans to make Tony more comfortable was the right one. She ran her fingers through her hair, its cinnamon highlights shining in the sun, and pinched her cheeks before straightening the teal plaid blouse she'd found in the rummage sale box.

This visit's going to be difficult. I dread it. But I have to speak to him.

Tony's brusque tone when she phoned him from the lobby unnerved her. "DeStefano."

"Hello, Tony? This is Celie. I'm here, at your hotel. I was hoping you'd agree to meet me so we can talk."

"In the lobby?"

"Yes. Downstairs."

Silence.

"Tony? Are you still there? Please allow me to explain—"

"I don't have to *allow* anything." His voice sounded cold, almost brutal. What could she say to persuade him to see her? To talk to her? She tried to steady her voice.

"Tony, I've been dealing with some serious problems since I met you . . ." She rushed on to get the words out. ". . . but I figured, why bother you with *my* troubles? You're wrestling with so many demons of your own. At least consider the fact that I've been pretty mixed up, like you, but for different reasons. Please come down and talk. I'll wait here."

Silence. *Click.*

She laid the receiver in the cradle and walked to the lavish seating area to the left of the hotel's main entrance and chose a velvet wingback chair. To distract herself, she admired the lustrous sheen on the marble floor, then examined the pattern woven into the elegant Persian rug under her feet. Next, she studied the sumptuous red and gold brocade curtains that framed the huge windows and the stately palms growing in large ivory Chinese pots. She had never seen such luxury before. The sparkling chandelier lit the main lobby, but the shadowed seating area where she waited was lit only by smaller lamps.

He must have a generous expense account to stay here. She looked at her watch. Had she only been waiting ten minutes? It seemed like ten hours. *Will he come?*

At last the elevator door opened, and Tony stepped forward, alone. He was wearing a blue oxford shirt and gray pants. He was tanned from the last weeks of summer sun, his collar open, and his dark hair slicked back, so he looked more professional than she remembered. He stood for a moment in front of the elevators, looking around the lobby. When he finally spotted her and strode forward, his face was a mask.

"You couldn't look more different than the last time I saw you." His laugh was as sarcastic as the tone of his voice.

When she rose to greet him, he merely gestured for her to sit down, avoiding her eyes, and chose a chair nearby.

"Thank you for coming," she said.

He stared at his clenched hands.

She tried again. "Tony, please accept my apology. I know I've made a mess of things. I really wanted to be your friend, but . . . but, well, I . . . I realize now I've betrayed your trust. God knows, you don't deserve that." She paused, but he neither looked at her nor replied. "You don't need any more pain." She paused again, afraid of more silence, then pushed on. "Please forgive me. I was so busy protecting myself. I was so worried about keeping my own life private, that I didn't consider your feelings."

Still without a word, he leaned forward and rubbed his eyes, as if to wipe away all the disillusionment pressing on his mind from these past months. She noticed that his wedding ring was missing from his left hand.

"I guess you were one person I thought I could confide in." His voice sounded beaten. "You knew about the lies I'd been hearing at home." He glanced up at her. "And then you betrayed me, too." He sat back and closed his eyes. "What else are you hiding from me?"

She squirmed in her luxurious velvet chair. "I . . . uh. . . . Nothing." The lobby was filling up with tourists, several of whom sat in chairs near them. "Tony, please, can we take a ride together?" she asked, lowering her voice. "This isn't a comfortable place to talk. What if we go to a park and take a walk? I might be able to talk more freely and . . . well, try to explain why I've never told you much about myself. I want to do that now."

He didn't answer, but stood up, made an ironic bow, and gestured for her to take the lead. She led him to the Pontiac outside, unlocked the passenger door, and slipped into the driver's seat.

As she exited the parking lot, she took a deep breath. "There's a spot where I often go with my friend. She's a teacher too. We go there to get some perspective on our lives . . . well, sometimes . . . we also share our classroom woes." She stopped the car for some pedestrians and then turned a corner. "The view of the Golden Gate Bridge is spectacular there. I think you'll like it. It's a small park and sometimes I take a little picnic with me, even when the weather is cold." She finally realized she was babbling. She maneuvered the silver sedan up Army Street and headed for San Francisco Bay, but she was so agitated she couldn't stop talking. "Sometimes it's so foggy you can hardly see the bridge, but on clear days I've seen Alcatraz and the hills of Sausalito. I love to watch the sun set, too. It's so uplifting. Have you ever driven across the bridge?" She turned to see if he was listening.

His eyes were stone cold, his face impassive. "No."

"Well, maybe we could try it! You might like it. The weather's bright today, and since you aren't driving, you'll be able to take in a panoramic view of the whole bay. Would you—?"

"Fine."

She glanced at him again before she made a right turn toward the wharf. Still no expression. "Well . . . let's just find the park first."

She gave up on trying to speak sensibly and silently drove into the lot next to the park. After locking the Pontiac, she led the way down a dirt path bordered by large forsythia bushes bursting with huge golden blooms. The park was compact, neatly tended, and hidden from the road. An arbor filled with yellow and coral roses framed some park benches that faced the bridge in the distance. She selected an ornate iron bench nearby and motioned for him to sit beside her. He sat at the other end, so close to the edge that she wondered if he would fall off. The silence continued as he glanced at the view and then stared down at his feet.

I guess he's in no mood to talk. She looked at him again and noticed the dark circles under his eyes, new worry lines in his forehead. *He probably doesn't even know we can see the bridge from here.*

She could feel his emotion, but was it despair or rage? As far back as she could remember, she'd been intimidated by others' anger, especially her father's. But today she was determined to forge ahead. Would he forgive her? Where was the man she had met all those months ago? The Tony who had burst into her room and apologized, the Tony who had "adopted" the dog on the beach, the Tony with whom she'd ridden on the Ferris wheel and the carousel. She tried to reassure herself. *If he'd written me off completely, he wouldn't have come here with me. Would he?*

Deciding to give him time, she studied the boats in the harbor—tugboats, oil tankers, sailboats of all sizes, and fishing vessels. Looking up, she could see the gulls trailing after them and mewling for fish scraps. Traffic on the bridge, she noticed, seemed light for a Saturday. Then she leaned back and simply gazed at the choppy azure whitecaps. The sight calmed her.

At last she grew impatient. It was time for them to talk. Shifting toward him, she summoned up her nerve. "Tony," she said, "I want to apologize again for my thoughtlessness. For my deception."

His hand waved at her angrily, as if swatting away a swarm of bees. His words exploded in loud chunks, each one battering her. "Enough! Don't. Keep. Apologizing!"

Celie flinched as if he'd slapped her. Tears welled up in her eyes, wetting both cheeks, but she didn't dare wipe them away. She turned away, hiding her face and trying to control herself, but this time she couldn't hold it all back. Months of worry, guilt, and self-loathing had built up inside her, and now the dam of self-control she'd constructed so carefully was giving way. Tears streamed down her cheeks. *Why now?* She hadn't cried in—she couldn't remember how long. She tried to muffle the sobs that broke in waves over her, but his bitter silence and angry blast had finally swept away her walls.

And then he surprised her. He leaned a little closer and pulled his folded white handkerchief out of his pocket. Still not speaking, he thrust it into her hand.

She accepted it, but turned away, trying to regain her composure. "Thank you," she managed in muted tones. But her shoulders heaved and she couldn't restrain her sobs.

And now he slid across the bench until he was sitting next to her. "Celie, I—please . . . I didn't mean to . . . please don't cry." He touched her shoulder.

She couldn't turn to face him. His handkerchief was now soaked with her tears as she held it to her face. "I'm trying . . . not to." But she cried all the harder, losing all restraint.

He placed both hands on her shoulders. "Celie," she could hardly hear him, "Celie, I had no idea. Maybe you need to go ahead . . . and cry."

She turned around, suddenly found his arms around her, and leaned into him.

"That's it, let it all out," he said.

Hiding her face in his shoulder, she continued to sob. All her reserve was dissolving. "I'm so sorry. Please forgive me." She heard the deep despair in her voice. "I can't do anything right. I try. I try so hard. But nothing I do seems to work. I don't think I can . . ." she hiccupped, "I can't . . . make anything work . . . anymore."

"No," he said, "that isn't true! Celie, you know it's not true. You've done lots of things right. You . . . you helped me the last time we were together. Just by listening. Remember?"

Encircled in his arms, she felt his gentle touch, stroking her back over and over as she tried to stop crying. His warmth was so comforting that she wanted desperately to prolong this moment. Finally, her sobs spent, she sighed, closed her eyes, and simply rested against him. An incredible feeling of unreality came over her, as if he had held her for a long, long time, as if within his arms she was absolutely, unequivocally safe, safer than she'd ever been before.

"Better now?"

She wiped her face and blew her nose in the soggy handkerchief, then looked at it as if she had no idea what to do with it. "Yes. I'm okay. I'm sorry I—"

"No, Celie, not again." His voice was lighter. He took the handkerchief out of her hand and stuffed it into his pants pocket. "If you apologize one more time—" He grasped both her shoulders, his soft brown eyes egging her on. "C'mon, where's the smile I remember? The one I saw when I invaded your room that night? You wanted to make me feel better about my terrible mistake, so you smiled. To reassure me."

She gave him the best smile she could muster. "It seems like a long time ago, doesn't it? That night you broke into my room."

Straightening up, she took a deep breath and turned to look out at the Bay. After a few silent minutes, she turned back, and tried to smile. "Even if you're determined not to accept my sixth apology, I want to buy you a clean hankie. Will you accept that?"

She watched him laugh. "Deal," he said. "Have you had breakfast? My stomach's griping. I think it's empty."

"Emotions stir up the appetite, I guess. Now that you mention it, yes, I'm hungry, too." But she suddenly felt timid about appearing with him in public. "I'm trying to think where we—"

As if reading her thoughts, he said, "Want to take that drive across the bridge you were plugging a while ago? There must be a restaurant along the highway over there."

"Good idea. And if we drive a few minutes beyond the bridge, we'll come to a place called the John Muir Woods. I've never been there, but I've read about it. It's supposed to be impressive. All those wonderful big trees, lots of hiking paths. I'm sure they sell snacks and sandwiches somewhere inside the park."

CHAPTER 36

EXPOSING ANGUISH

The travel article Celie had read about the Muir Woods had promised a stunning locale, and it was right. Mammoth redwoods overshadowed the picnic grounds, sheltering their table with a welcome coolness. Dappled sunlight illumined green Australian ferns nearby, their plumes waving in every direction. Celie admired it all as she ate a hamburger with Tony. Though she was weary from so much crying, she couldn't wait to hike down one of the paths leading away from the concession stand. Perhaps they'd come upon deer or squirrels or chipmunks.

"How was your burger?" Tony asked a few minutes later.

"I hated it!" She grinned and put the last bite into her mouth. Standing up, she held out her hands. "Would you like to try one of the trails? We could talk while we hike."

"Okay by me, but let's get a couple of things before we start." He disappeared for a few moments, returning with two red apples wrapped in napkins and a large bag of peanuts.

"You read my mind." Celie accepted an apple.

"I saw you hovering on that side of the gift shop earlier. It didn't take a genius to figure out you wanted to feed the wildlife."

"Am I that transparent?" she asked, trying to meet his eyes.

He studied her for a moment, but instead of replying, he abruptly turned away, picked up their lunch wrappings and dropped them in a trash barrel. "Let's go," was all he said. He pointed to a wooden sign that said *3-Mile Hiking Trail*. "I guess these loafers can handle it."

"Oh," she looked at his fine business shoes, "you didn't come prepared for a hike. I'm sorry."

"Celie, why do you keep apologizing? I'll manage fine."

Hearing the impatience in his voice, she drew back, but he pointed at the trail and she hurried to take the lead. *Why is he so short with me? I'd better explain fast. And be as honest as I can.*

When the path widened, she slowed down, falling into step with him. "I never expected to be hiking this trail with you," she said.

"Did I hear a complaint?" he asked. She couldn't tell whether he was joking or not, but when she looked at him, she saw he was smiling again.

"No," she said. "It's just . . . well, after we first met, I never thought I'd see you again."

"Yeah. Why bother to tell him I'm a nun?" His sudden cynicism cut through her.

She took a deep breath. "We were just two strangers at first. We connected . . . in an unusual way, and then we went our separate ways. It didn't seem necessary to . . . to say. . . ."

"An open-and-shut case, huh? No need for deliberation. Life's never simple, though, is it?"

What could she say? Finally she managed, "I'm finding that out."

"And I spoiled things by contacting you again, didn't I?" She could hear the tension in his voice. "By asking you to meet me again at the retreat house. But you could've turned me down, you know." Suddenly he was walking ahead of her, not looking back.

"There were lots of reasons why I showed up the second time." She tried to keep up as his pace quickened. "I can't possibly tell you what they all were. The point is, I came. Even though I never intended to. I was there on the beach to meet you. And I don't regret it. It was exactly what I needed at the time."

"Well, good." He sounded angry again. "I'm glad you got exactly what you needed."

"Wait a minute. You're dishing out anger and sarcasm at me because I misled you, but, well, if I'm not mistaken, you *thanked* me for coming that weekend. And I know you meant it."

"You don't know anything about me."

She stood still and waited until he stopped walking. He was several yards ahead of her, but he didn't turn around. "Listen," she said, "I'm not denying I kept my life private and it hurt you. I've apologized already, but you keep demanding that I *stop* saying I'm sorry. So why do you insist on . . ." she flipped her wrist at him, "flinging more anger at me?"

Now he turned to face her. "Maybe I 'fling a lot of anger' towards anyone who thinks they can put something over on me. What's wrong with that? In my book, you have to defend yourself against people who lie. Unfortunately, I've met plenty!"

So he'd been wounded more than once. She was sorry for him, but she also wanted him to realize he wasn't completely blameless this time. She took one step forward. "Tony, I don't know about *all* the people who've hurt you. I can only deal with this situation, right here, right now. I do know one thing, and I'll admit it again. I misled you by omission, and it caused you pain." She softened her tone, trying to sound calmer. "But you aren't totally innocent, either, you know. You thought I was a young, single woman, and you came to meet me that weekend as a married man, which was a pretty important detail to keep from *me.*" She lowered her voice as two hikers passed by, making a wide detour around them. "So weren't we both at fault?"

Holding back words they both might regret, they stood silently on the path facing the canyon where chaparral and sage covered the scorched hills. She heard blue jays calling to tiny finches flitting from tree to tree and children's voices floating in the distance. The dust of California's autumn, like finely sifted silt, coated the leaves and boulders all around them, and her freckled arms felt hot with a new burn.

Tony turned again, veering ahead of her, charging down the steep grade with a vengeance, and rounding a hairpin turn. Dust rose up around her as she followed him, breathing in the dry, parched air, her cheeks and lips gritty. As she made her way down the incline, the tall redwoods shrouded him in their shadows and she lost sight of him. She slipped on the gravelly path, picked herself up, slapped loose dirt off her jeans, and went on. *I've done it. He's furious. I was too outspoken. Even if I catch up with him, his silence will bury my nerve. No. I can't let myself be afraid anymore.*

She cut between two massive trees, then two more, then found the path again as it wound downward toward a shallow cave in the irregular sandstone.

She was almost at ground level now. Rounding the last steep curve, she saw him sitting on a wide, flat rock in front of the boulders she'd seen from the pinnacle. His back was to her, and he was washing his hands in the creek that trickled along the center of the parched riverbed.

She reached the trail's end and stopped, not knowing if it was safe to speak.

He turned his head and motioned to her. "Want to wash up?"

Warily, she moved forward. "Sure."

"Not much water, but enough." He doused his tanned face, now tinged with red from the blazing sun, then rolled up the sleeves of his blue shirt, damp from sweat and creek water. Layers of dust streaked the knees and cuffs of his gray pants, and beige silt covered his black loafers.

He saw her staring at him. "If I'd known where you were planning to take me. . . ."

Was his voice lighter? "Is that my cue to say—?"

"You're sorry? What do *you* think? No. I knew what I was doing. I just didn't plan on a hiking expedition. But that's my problem, okay?"

"Okay." She wanted him to keep talking.

"Anyway," he added, his voice softer than before, "it's my turn to apologize now." He glanced at her, then his eyes flitted away quickly, and he leaned over to dust off his shoes with his wet hands, then dipped them into the creek again.

"Do you mean it?"

He straightened up and faced her, penetrating her soul with his dark eyes. "Yes. What do you say we call a truce?" He held out his hand and she took it. He moved close to her then, and putting his fingers under her chin, he hesitated for a second, then kissed her forehead.

For a moment she couldn't breathe. She dared to look up at him. "You're sealing the truce?"

"Yes. Let's find a shady place to sit for awhile."

He set off on another path, holding her by the hand, until they found a bench situated on an overlook and shaded by the trees. After a few minutes of silence, Celie bent to gather several pine cones, setting several beside her on the bench.

"Still collecting treasures? Are you going to write any poems about them?"

"No, I don't think so. But I can use them for Christmas decorations. We usually make wreaths and sell them to raise money for classroom supplies."

He stared off in the distance. "Yeah." He looked away. "I'd almost forgotten you're a nun. It's difficult for me to even imagine you—"

"Some people have weird notions about nuns. You told me your experiences weren't exactly positive."

"That's an understatement. Maybe California breeds a different kind of nun. The Irish Sisters I knew in Brooklyn were stern. Mean. And I was just a smart-aleck kid. A wop." He looked at her. "You certainly don't look like any of them. You don't fit that mold."

"I guess I don't understand what 'that mold' is," she said. "It sounds like they treated you horribly. My teachers weren't like that. The nuns I knew growing up were positive role models. They were dedicated and strict, but really enthusiastic. Well, maybe a few of them shouldn't have been teachers, I'll admit that, but most of them encouraged us to excel in our studies. Sports and music, too."

She saw the surprise on his face. "That's why I thought religious life might suit me," she explained. "The nuns who taught me seemed to make such a difference in others' lives."

"You thought it *might* suit you? You don't sound too sure." He paused as she shot him a cool stare, then said, "Hey, prying isn't my thing. But I'm a New Yorker, and when I think it, I say it. Some people don't appreciate it." He grinned. "So don't hesitate to tell me to shut up if I'm out of line."

"No, no, no. It's okay. I like your honesty. But, well, your anger and sarcasm are another story."

He nodded. "Yeah. I unloaded on you pretty hard back there. Guess it's my turn to apologize again. One of the toughest things I've had to deal with lately is my anger. It gets out of control. And sometimes I unleash it on the wrong people. Forgive me?"

"Apology accepted. But you need to know that I'm not used to your directness, the way you let out your feelings. My dad used to be mean and sarcastic, too, and I hated it. I think he's changed now. But most of the time, everyone in my family is very *in*direct. Even manipulative." She thought for a minute. "Actually, it's sort of a relief—you saying exactly what you think. I don't have to spend time guessing. That's new for me."

He got up and leaned over to pick up the sack of peanuts he'd set down on the ground. "Want some?"

She tore open the bag with her fingernails and scattered the nuts among the redwood needles. Then they both pulled their apples out of their pockets and bit into the crisp fruit as they watched the squirrels scamper up for the peanuts. A minute later, she walked around the grove of trees, scattering more.

"You may be right," she said. "I'm not sure about being a nun for the rest of my life. I've been in training for almost four years. I've tried to make it work, but I still have doubts. It was those uncertainties that brought me to the retreat house last March. I was trying to decide whether to stick it out and make my vows for one more year."

"Did you make your decision?"

"Yes. At least I thought so. But it's been rocky ever since," she said. "Situations have come up in the last couple months, things I never could have expected. . . ."

"I hear you. Life decisions can be extremely difficult. Emotions get all stirred up. It puts you through the wringer, up one day and down the next. I know about it."

She emptied the bag and came back to sit by him. "You have strong feelings, like you said." She took the last bite of her apple and went on. "Mine are finally coming to the surface, too. Sometimes I can't deal with them." She looked up at him, seeking an answer.

"You can't stay bottled up forever," he said. "Emotions need an outlet. It's probably the engineer in me, but normally I rely on," he tapped his forehead, "my God-given brain to sort things out. I have to analyze a problem rationally in order to fix it. It's helped me see my way out of lots of craziness in my life, especially recently. But sometimes it takes weeks or months to figure things out."

"How do you do it? Rationalize it, I mean? I'm always going around in circles. I mean, how do you sort out your confusion like that?"

"I have a lot to learn, I admit. But one thing I do know." He ran a finger down her cheek, and his tenderness made her heart pound. "You have to start by being up front with yourself. You can't be any good for anyone else until you settle things inside." He tapped his chest. "You have to face up to what you honestly think and feel, not what you're *supposed* to think and feel. It's not easy."

"But *how* do you figure things out?" she asked again. "How do you get out from under all the expectations and really face things?"

"Hey, since writing's your thing, why don't you put all your thoughts down on paper? See what comes out. I think they call it journaling. Sure, it can be scary, but once you write it down and read it back, things will look more obvious. You'll feel better, too, because you're doing something to solve your troubles. It'll give you confidence to move forward."

"I've journaled since I was young," she replied, "and you know I write poetry—it calms me. But I've never used it to sort out my problems. Has writing helped you?"

"I'm not much of a writer," he said. "Especially when I'm on the road, I go over all kinds of possibilities in my head, then I draw up a little chart and list the pros and cons. Then I can make a decision."

Celie scuffled the dirt at her feet, giving herself some time to think.

Strangely enough, she decided, she and Tony were similar. Like her, he found it difficult to confide his problems to anyone. And he wanted to achieve on a grand scale, too. They were both trying to face life head-on and make major decisions that could turn their lives in totally new directions. The terrain ahead, though different, presented a quiet terror because they both wanted desperately *not* to fail.

Her voice was soft. "How *is* everything with you?"

He exhaled slowly. "Worse than when I saw you last. I've got very few choices if I want to protect my boys."

"What do you mean?"

"You probably don't know much about divorce. Why would you? In New York, it's almost impossible. It takes years sometimes. Unless you can prove infidelity."

"But I thought. . . ."

"No question. I found out she's been having an affair for over a year and using our credit cards to finance their . . . their trysts. People in our neighborhood have a lot more details about it than I do. But proving it in court is another story. I'd have to drag my boys and neighbors in to testify. I won't put my kids through that."

"How awful. I've seen a couple of my students torn apart by divorce. You could never ask your boys to turn against their mother."

He nodded. "Right. So if I try to end the marriage, it'll mean a long and bitter struggle with my wife and her lawyers. She's made that clear."

Celie couldn't help noticing how his demeanor had changed, how hollow and empty he looked as he spoke about his life.

"I know her," he was saying. "Financially, she'll take me to the cleaners and then turn around and ask for more. It'll be 'for the sake of the kids,' but who knows whether she'll ever spend the money on them. In her strange, mixed-up mind, I owe her. I've always owed her, big time. That's what our marriage was about."

"But that's so unfair," Celie protested. "As if money could buy the love and family ties your boys need!"

"Yeah, that's the real point. The boys. It's always been my boys I care about most. At some level, I knew how weak our marriage was, but I hung in for them. If we ever split up, gaining custody would be impossible. Fathers hardly ever get that chance in New York. I wanted to be near them as they grew up." He clasped his hands tight, leaning forward, looking at the ground where squirrels were still snatching nuts, but she knew he didn't see them. "It's a good thing I was, too. So many nights, I'd drive hours to get home and find a note on the kitchen table. She'd be off somewhere preparing for a college exam, supposedly with a study group. Yeah, right!" He picked up the empty bag, wadded it up, and threw it at a tree. Crackling noises filled the quiet—squirrels chattering and racing through the woods.

He went on. "So I'd cook up something for the boys and me to eat. I'd help them with their homework, break up their fights, too, and finally get them to bed. Most of the time, I'd fall asleep exhausted. I look back now and wonder how I put up with it. Why? The whole time she was probably out partying with that guy! I feel so much rage. It's tearing me up inside."

Celie stared at the redwoods encircling them. She understood now. His outbursts came from deep within. The world seemed to be twisting both of them up in a strange web of desperation. These last months had been difficult enough for her. Tony had been so patient to listen the few times they'd been together. She saw now that his problems were monumental compared to hers, and she ached to comfort him. Was there any small piece of advice she could offer? How could she help him tame his fury? Feeling helpless, she reached out and took his hand, stroking it, searching for the right words.

"I wish I could think of something to say to help you. I can't even imagine the anger and despair you must feel. When you said just now how overwhelming emotions can be and how they'd battered you in the past, I had no idea how much pain you were going through. I'm so sorry I complained about my problems. Yours are mind-boggling compared to mine. If there's something, anything, I can do to help, please tell me and I'll do it."

The pause lengthened between them.

"Celie, you've done it again. You used those words again."

She looked up at him. What words?

"You have a thing about those two words, don't you?" Though he was smiling, he pointed his index finger at her, a twinkle in his enigmatic eyes. "Do yourself a favor. Strike the words 'I'm sorry' out of your vocabulary. And while you're at it, put them on a shelf somewhere to rot!"

"I promise."

His eyes drew hers, and again she saw the lines that etched shadows under them.

"Seriously," he said, "I really appreciate your concern. It helps more than you know to talk to someone, to someone who cares enough to listen. There hasn't been anyone to talk to for a long time."

Without warning, he put his finger under her chin, then pulled her to him and kissed her full on the lips.

His lips were soft, and they triggered a hunger in her she'd never felt before. Before she knew it, she'd pulled back, casting her eyes downward. Her heart banged against her ribs, her body was hot. A fierce longing to kiss him again raged inside, but she sucked in her breath and turned away.

"I shouldn't have done that," he murmured. "But I'm not sorry. Even if you *are* a nun."

227

CHAPTER 37

PLUNGING IN

On Sunday afternoons, the nuns at Immaculate Mary Convent welcomed family visitors and worked on parish projects or school lesson plans. When the noon meal was over, they usually chatted together during recreation before they set off again to accomplish their individual tasks. Today was no different, except that Sister Gerald had returned after a lengthy absence.

As soon as she saw her Superior, Celie edged near the door. All she could think of was to rush off to join Sister Adele in the church hall, where a group of parishioners was meeting to plan how to aid needy refugee families.

Sister Gerald crossed the room. "Sister Celia, wait."

Celie forced herself to turn around.

"It's been so long!" the older nun said. "Seven weeks, I believe. I haven't seen you since you flew down south."

Celie could hear longing in her voice, though she knew no one else would. She tried to be cautious with her reply as she stood near the hallway leading to the schoolyard. "That long? I didn't realize—"

"I know you're heading for the meeting now, but can you spare me a couple of minutes? I want to introduce you to Sister Theresa. You and I can meet separately later. We need to get back to work on the religion manuscripts." Sister Gerald gestured for a diminutive nun to step forward.

Celie looked down at a round face with an ivory complexion and thick blond lashes framing baby blue eyes. *She doesn't look over sixteen.* Standing up straighter, she held out her hand, grasping the nun's delicate fingers. "So nice to meet you."

The smaller nun smiled, then lowered her eyes. Her cupid's bow mouth and her chubby cheeks reminded Celie of the Russian *matryoshka* dolls that had lined the shelves in an antique shop near her grandfather's house in San Gabriel.

Sister Gerald smiled again. "I've recruited Sister Theresa to help us finish our textbook manuscripts," she explained. "She's in her third week of teacher training and will visit your classroom on Tuesday to study your teaching methods. I also want her to team teach with me this semester. I can certainly use the help." She stretched her arm out above her head and gave a mock grin. "The piles on my desk are this tall. They grew like weeds while I was gone."

Celie composed her face, attempting nonchalance. Underneath her scapular, though, her nails dug into her palms. "Of course. If there's anything I can do to help, please let me know."

"Of course we'll need you, won't we, Sister Theresa?" Sister Gerald's eyes sucked at Celie as she closed in to give her a hug.

Celie took a step back, then caught herself. Her shoulders tightened, but, taking a quick breath to tame her feelings, she raised her arms to give the older nun a cursory hug. Then she stepped back and assumed a rushed look. Glancing at her watch, she mumbled, "I'm sorry to hurry off like this. Actually, I think the parish meeting has already started. Please excuse me."

Sister Gerald nodded, giving her permission, and Sister Theresa lowered her eyes again, her murmuring unintelligible. As Celie sped away, she heard them speaking in Spanish with Sister Rosarita.

Whew! Round one. Celie exhaled aloud as she hurried to the school auditorium, where Sister Adele was waiting. She tried to be positive, but her heart was full of dread. How would she handle Sister Gerald at their meeting later?

A group of parishioners filled the first two rows of seats. Mr. and Mrs. Cruz, Manuel's parents, sitting alone further back, raised their hands to greet Celie. She smiled at them and found a seat next to Sister Adele. They faced the parishioners.

Signaling for quiet, Sister Adele stood up. "Let's begin now. Sister Celia Marie and I are very gratified that so many of you have come out today to lend a hand. At least eight new refugee families will need our assistance immediately. So we have lots of work to do. Let's get started."

Murmurs arose, then the group settled down again and Sister Adele resumed. "To be perfectly candid," she said, "you all know more about this subject than we do. Many of you have recently fled from your own countries. So your suggestions are invaluable to us. Please help us formulate some practical plans. Let's start by listing the essentials these families will need now that they've entered our country. Then we'll designate individuals to take on each task. Please, don't hold back. We welcome all your ideas." She gestured for Celie to swing the large blackboard forward.

Grateful to dive into this new assignment, Celie wiped the board clean and picked up the chalk. She watched the rapid rise of hands and heard suggestions spill out one by one. *Sister Adele definitely knows how to motivate everyone.* Though images of Sister Gerald still crowded her mind, she pushed them away and forced herself to concentrate on translating the parishioners' proposals into a concise list. Soon more than a dozen ideas filled the blackboard and everyone was agreeing that their top priority was to find immediate housing for the refugees.

"Cuban friends live near my street," Manuel's mother shouted above the hum in the room. "Maybe Sister Celia and I go visit? We find room."

"That's a splendid idea, Mrs. Cruz," said Sister Adele. "Sister Celia Marie, what do you think?"

"I'll meet with Mrs. Cruz right after away, Sister. We can start this afternoon."

The petite Cuban mother nodded her head enthusiastically. Celie hadn't seen such a dazzling smile in weeks.

JOURNAL ENTRY, MONDAY, OCTOBER 12, 1967.

Up before dawn to write the textbook draft. Got quite a bit done. Such a joy to see it all coming together! Lessons from the Book of Matthew—my second graders love Christ's parables. I told them Jesus' story of the leaven, how His coming was unexpected, not like a kingly show, but nonetheless a vibrant hidden strength buried within all of us. With faith, I told them, our strength and love will grow and grow. I felt the power of God mirrored in the children's eyes.

I'm excited too about my new ideas for follow-up projects. Making bread with them was so special! As the dough rose up almost like a pastry balloon, the students' eyes grew so large.

I'll never forget it. They loved beating it down, learning how to knead, and seeing it rise even higher. At the lesson's end, they clasped their small hands, eyes shut tight in prayer, as we asked for God's gifts. When I remember images like these, I want to plug on and finish the textbooks. So much work to go.

The publishers' conference in Santa Barbara is only weeks away! I'll approach Sister Gerald about it today—where I'll stay, etc. The thought of rubbing shoulders with professionals who are passionate about publishing sends a thrill through me every time I think about it. I wrote Dad and told him—he's the only one in the family who's ever encouraged me to write—but he's always said it could never be my real career. "No money in it," he says, though I wonder what that means now that I'm a nun?

Tonight we'll meet again on the textbook project. In one way, I'm relieved Sister Theresa has joined our group. Thank you, God! Sister Gerald's eyes follow me relentlessly as we go over the chapter drafts. Eerie! A sinking hollowness fills me whenever I think about her or go near her. But it's strange how much I miss the discussions we used to have last summer. She had such unusual insights! She can be brilliant. But I have to be cautious—I will not get close to her again.

What were Tony's words? "Writing's your thing, so why don't you put your confusion down on paper? It can be scary, but things will become clearer. It'll give you confidence to go forward. But you must be honest."

Yet all my feelings stay bottled up. But, yes, mysterious stirrings have increased. They surface—when I let them, but wonderful images of him dance in my mind when I think of his gentle, capable ways. I wish I could talk to him! His wisdom was a healing salve on my wounds of guilt and worry last week. His kiss? Dear God, I can't allow myself to think about it.

Sister Gerald looked up from the textbook drafts spread out on her desk. "Sister Celia Marie, what are you planning for the final chapters?"

"I want to cover all the various metaphors of seeds and plants that Jesus used. He refers to them so many times that I think the children would benefit if they understood what He actually meant. I want to create a whole section. We can follow up with related planting projects. My second graders just completed a two-week religion and science project where they watched roots eventually sprout from kidney beans wrapped with a moist paper towel inside a glass. Then we planted them, and now bean plants are growing all over my classroom. They loved it."

"That sounds wonderful," Sister Gerald replied. "Oh, and Sister, can you spare some time after our session this evening?"

Celie kept her eyes glued to the manuscript and started nervously turning pages at random. Then she picked up her Bible and opened it to the Book of Matthew. "Where is the parable about the seeds?" she asked Sister Theresa. "You know the one I mean, 'Look at the birds of the air, they neither sow nor reap nor gather into barns . . .'"

"Sister," the younger nun said, "I don't think that's the selection you want. It has nothing to do with Christ's seed metaphors. The allegory of the seedlings begins here." She leaned across the table with her open Bible. "In Mark, Chapter 4. Or Chapter 13 in Matthew, and I believe you'll find seed references in John's gospel, also. I remember because Sister Adele read the passage in John in the refectory this morning." She paused, then asked, "Weren't you paying attention?"

Celie flushed. Obviously, she hadn't been listening during breakfast. Her thoughts were elsewhere.

But she had to correct this younger nun. After all, she could enumerate *all* the scripture references on seeds; she'd already compiled several lists. Instead, she decided to hold her peace. Why try to one-up the younger nun? It certainly wouldn't help her grow in the virtue of humility, would it?

Sister Gerald, still waiting for a reply, said, "You're right, Sister Theresa. Your command of Scripture is impressive. May I ask where you took your classes?"

Celie couldn't miss Sister Theresa's demure smile. "Thank you, Sister. I've always loved the New Testament, especially Matthew. Last semester, while I was taking a scripture course at St. John's University, I joined a study group. We all became so curious about different interpretations of the Bible verses we decided to meet more often. I researched Greek translations of some pivotal Gospel texts refined from Aramaic sources, then we pored over them together. Afterwards, God's words took on a much deeper meaning. I'd love to enroll in a scripture course here in San Francisco."

"Of course. We can definitely arrange that for you," Sister Gerald said. "Perhaps you should not only proofread our manuscript, but help us evaluate the content. What do you think, Sister Celia?"

"Yes. It might help." Celie's stomach tightened as she folded her arms over her chest.

When the clock in the hall chimed eight times, Sister Gerald straightened the papers on her desk and handed them to Sister Theresa. "Please evaluate this new portion of the curriculum after night prayers," she said. "We'll meet tomorrow night and go over your suggestions."

Sister Theresa beamed. "Thank you. Do you want me to share the Greek and Aramaic translations of the scriptural verses as well?"

"Certainly. We'd welcome your ideas. It will add a new dimension to our project. Don't you think so, Sister Celia Marie?"

"Yes."

"Now, Sister Theresa, if you'll excuse us, I'd like a brief meeting with Sister Celia Marie alone. We don't have much time before the Profound Silence bell rings."

Her heart drumming in her chest, Celie planted herself at the table across the room and began stacking her reference books in front of her. Her breath started coming in short spurts. *I have to calm down. She mustn't detect anything. I need to cut this short.*

Sister Gerald moved forward, taking a chair within inches of where Celie was standing. "So tell me, my dear, how are you? We haven't spoken in *so* long. How is your father? I was so sorry about his heart attack. Here, sit down."

"He's doing much better," she replied as she sat next to her Superior. "The flowers you sent were in his room when I arrived at the hospital. Thank you. It was very thoughtful. That seems so long ago now." She could feel the older nun studying her face. *Am I blushing? Dear God, help me!* "Mom tries to keep me posted on his doctor's reports because Dad's just never been one to pick up the phone." She had to keep going. "I've been receiving conflicting news, though. Mom says he's slowed down a lot, but the doctor reports he's recuperating rapidly. I finally spoke to him last week, and I was relieved when—"

"What did he say?"

"He said he's making real progress. I guess I shouldn't be surprised. When Daddy decides to do something, he usually doesn't allow anything to get in his way."

"That's good. But, Celie, what about you? You managed to add some more credits to your college transcript this summer."

"Yes, I did. By the time the session was scheduled to begin, you'd already left for Ukiah, and I couldn't reach you, so Sister Lupe told me you'd cleared my way to enroll. Thank you for giving me permission, I loved every minute of it—"

"Well, I had some second thoughts about it, I must admit. Sister Lupe is very persuasive, isn't she? Have you been friends with her long?" Sister Gerald's lips looked pinched, her eyes penetrating.

"Why, uh, no . . . just since we both entered the convent. We got to know each other during my first year as a Postulant. Why?"

"She has problems, or so I've been told," the older nun said. "Did you know she's been seeing a psychiatrist? Quite regularly, I understand. The words I've heard are 'impetuous, rowdy, even unstable.' Frankly, I was surprised she made temporary vows last year." As Sister Gerald cleared her throat, Celie selected another thick book to the stack in front of her. "Anyway," her Superior said, "that's not why I asked you to meet with me this evening. We need to plan for the publishing convention at the end of the month. There aren't any Augustinian convents in Santa Barbara, so I've tentatively planned that we share a room in the hotel from Wednesday until Sunday. I need to lock in our reservations."

What? Share a room? "Oh. I didn't know we'd be going together," she said aloud, holding a book against her chest. "Will any other Sisters be attending?"

"Of course I'll be coming with you." Sister Gerald let out a laugh. "You didn't think I'd send you alone, did you? No, just you and I will attend. Up to now, no one in our congregation has ever attempted to create their own textbooks—that's part of the excitement of this project! Why, my dear, what's the matter? You don't look yourself."

"Nothing, Sister," Celie said. "I'm just not feeling well tonight, that's all. I'm sure it's not serious, just a temporary stomach problem. . . ."

The older nun moved her chair nearer. "Are you sure? I've been wondering why you seem so distant. But if you're ill, well, that explains it. We should continue this conversation tomorrow then. Go on now and get some rest."

"Thank you, Sister." Celie put the book down and got up, crossing the room without another word. Eager to find refuge upstairs, she shut the door behind her and rushed down the hall, momentary dizziness causing her to stop and lean against the wall.

My stomach is upset, that's not a lie. Oh, God, infuse a quick solution into my weary brain. I need a way out. Soon.

Climbing the circular stairs to her cell, she repeated the derogatory words Sister Gerald had used to label Lupe. "Rowdy. Unstable."

What's she got against Lupe? She doesn't have a clue what Lupe's like. How dare she condemn her!

Then, as she reached her cell door, a new perspective on the conversation hit her. *She's trying to distance me from Lupe!*

JOURNAL ENTRY, TUESDAY, OCTOBER 13, 1967.

I overslept. Great! Now I'll never get my curriculum drafts done.

Didn't sleep soundly all night—this rain matches my mood.

Morning prayers don't begin till six. No time for the textbook manuscripts. I'll try to journal my feelings instead—hard as it is. Tony's idea. He keeps invading my thoughts. I wonder what he's doing right now? It's nine a.m. New York time. He must be at work, tackling some major defense project. He's probably wonderful at directing the people who report to him. Such a quiet, capable man. So thoughtful and intelligent. And at home? How can he possibly live in the same house with his wife? And how are his boys?

Prisoner
Rain batters at my window like relentless tears.
Can't figure why—I feel so low.

Anchor pulls my insides, chained to ocean floor,
Afloat but held captive,
No freedom to explore.

Tonight's meeting will bring tons of corrections, I know what's coming. Sister Gerald's so impressed with Sister Theresa's knowledge of scripture. They'll make drastic changes in my manuscript. Will my voice be lost? Am I selfish and full of pride to want my writing to stay whole and untouched by others?

The publishing conference looms ahead. It's another storm. I see the unremitting raindrops washing the windows now and an impending doom overwhelms me that I can't explain. I have to hide my aversion when Sister Gerald comes near. But she looks inside me, as if she's examining my soul.

The chapel bells began to chime, signaling the morning Hour of the Divine Office, to begin in five minutes, and then Mass. She stuffed her journal into a nightstand drawer and rushed downstairs. Usually she enjoyed blending her voice with the others as they sang the Latin psalms, but today the waves of Gregorian chant did not soothe her heart. Sister Gerald's words had robbed her of sleep last night, and now they began pummeling her brain again.

How could she avoid sharing a hotel room with this woman? She didn't want to make it obvious or cause a scene, and the last thing she wanted was to make Sister Gerald angry. She'd wrestled with the problem all night.

As the hymns rose around her, Celie lost herself in silent, desperate prayer. *Lord, please show me your wisdom, your light. I must preserve my vow of chastity, but my vow of obedience is at stake, too. But is it? Sharing a room with my Superior out of submission cannot be—O Lord, I won't risk being with Sister Gerald! The feelings I remember from that night repulse me, even as I somehow miss her friendship. She used to seem so wonderful, so strong. Please, Lord, show me how to resolve this mess. I'm desperate. Please, please help me.*

Later, as Mass ended, Father Carmine faced them with his blessing of peace. As required by the new Vatican Council rules, he asked the congregation to offer greetings of peace to each other in English. Used to the old, familiar Latin rituals, the nuns were clumsy and unprepared for any personal demonstrations. Nonetheless, every nun turned to another and said, "Peace be with you." Celie found Sister Theresa leaning toward her. *Of all people.* Even as she inwardly scolded herself for her lack of charity and feelings of, yes, rivalry (she had to admit it), she looked down into Sister Theresa's luminous eyes and repeated the words of peace. At that second, an idea lit up inside of her.

I'll ask Sister Gerald to bring Sister Theresa to the publishing conference. That'll solve everything! But she'll get totally involved in the textbook project if she comes. Well, I'll have to take that chance.

"Lord," she whispered, "thank you! Now give me insight on how to make it happen."

The lesson plan meeting was not going well. Sister Theresa and Sister Celia Marie sat on either side of their Superior. The redlined manuscript lay on the table in front of them. No one had ever used red to correct Celie's work before. An hour of conversation filled with corrections and modifications had crept by, and there were still mountains of curriculum pages to discuss. When a sharp knock interrupted their discussion, Celie couldn't have been more relieved.

Lupe's coifed, pixie face leaned around the door, her hand on the knob. "Sister Gerald, I'm sorry to interrupt, but Sister Adele said it would be okay. She wanted me to come and find Sister Celia Marie. Some members of your parish's immigrant group are outside. They came by mistake to Sacred Heart parish, so I phoned Sister Adele and brought them down here to Immaculate Mary."

"What's the problem, Sister?" Sister Gerald's voice was sharp.

"Our pastor notified us today that a new unit of Cuban refugees arrived in San Francisco over the weekend. A bunch of them. He expects them to settle in both Sacred Heart and IM parishes. When I finished dinner, some members from your parish group came to *our* convent. Apparently the leader is a Mrs. Cruz?"

Celie nodded to Sister Gerald, "Yes. Mrs. Cruz is heading up our search for housing."

"Well," said Lupe, "I guess she couldn't reach Sister Celia Marie or Sister Adele this evening, but she knows several families in our parish who can temporarily house the new refugees and—"

"Get to the point, Sister," Sister Gerald said.

Lupe nodded. "Sister Adele said just now that our two parishes should join forces."

"Are you telling me that everyone is out in the sitting room and they want to have a meeting on housing the immigrants this minute?"

"Well, yes, Sister Gerald. It certainly wasn't planned, but this Mrs. Cruz seems very certain we can solve their lodging problem. Supposedly, these new refugees have nowhere to sleep tonight. That's why it's so urgent."

Sister Gerald looked at Celie. Her eyes were dark and her voice strained. "I guess you must go, Sister. You know Mrs. Cruz better than anyone. We'll have to carry on here without you and make corrections as we see fit."

"Can't we go over the corrections tomorrow?" Celie asked.

"There's no time left. If we plan to have partial galleys ready for the publishing conference, we have to give the changes to the printer by Friday. The rest of my week is booked except for Thursday. I have meetings every evening. Don't worry. Sister Theresa will fill in for you."

"But, Sister, I can work with Sister Theresa after dinner while you're at your meetings," Celie protested. "I'd like to have a chance to review her markups myself."

"Sister, did you hear what I said? You have enough to do. This new parish group is going to demand your time, and you also promised to draft the last section of the textbook this week. I bet you haven't even started it yet. You'd better have it ready for Sister Theresa by Thursday morning so we can revise it that night and turn it over to the printer."

Stung, Celie forced herself to show a calm acceptance she didn't feel.

"Go on, Sister Celia Marie," said Sister Gerald.. "I can hear your Mrs. Cruz jabbering from here." She turned to Lupe. "Sister, I don't believe we'll need your services beyond tonight. I think it's best that Sister Celia Marie take over the entire refugee group. If Sister Adele or Sister Celia Marie need to coordinate with Sacred Heart parish, they'll phone your pastor."

Reluctantly, her heart wringing with trepidation, Celie handed over the textbook pages to Sister Theresa, stood up, and left the room.

The door was no sooner shut than Lupe pulled her aside. "Wow! She's ripping mad!" But a grin pulled at her mouth.

"I'm not thrilled, either," Celie fumed.

"What's eating you?"

"Oh, nothing, except if Sister Theresa has her way, my entire manuscript will be scrapped and she'll 'correct' it and it'll become a completely new book. And I won't be there to salvage the lessons I've worked so hard on all these months! Sister Gerald is convinced Sister Theresa's scripture study at St. John's gives her pre-eminent authority. Theresa scrawled red lines everywhere! We spent the last hour squabbling over her innumerable changes to my first seven chapters."

"Celie, I'm sorry. It's rotten timing for a parish emergency. I'd stand in for you with Mrs. Cruz, but Sister Gerald doesn't want *my* help. That's clear."

"So I noticed. She sure didn't shower you with Sisterly love. Don't take it personally, though. She's unpredictable. And I found out not too long ago, her opinion of you is completely skewed."

The famous twinkle in Lupe's eyes turned into a wink. "Well," she said dryly, "I hate to override her directives, but our pastor explicitly asked *me* to lead the Sacred Heart parish group and find homes for these people. 'Course, it wasn't exactly the right time to inform your eminent Superior, if you catch my drift. I'll ask Father Sullivan to inform her himself."

"Lupe, you're priceless!"

"Thanks. Don't you wish we had one of those wire-tap bugs so we could listen in on that phone conversation?"

Celie put her arm around her friend as they hurried toward the parlor where the visitors waited. A heated discussion in both Spanish and English drifted down the hall toward them, Mrs. Cruz's voice rising above all the others.

CHAPTER 38

MARVELS, PUBLISHING AND OTHERWISE

Celie crept down the convent stairs fully dressed. The grandfather clock near the refectory chimed five times, then quiet descended again. *I can't believe I'm sneaking around here like a criminal,* she thought, looking around, *but there's no other way.* Reaching the hallway, she lifted the telephone receiver and dialed the New York number.

"DeStefano speaking."

The sound of his voice sent an unexpected shiver through her. Suddenly she couldn't form any words.

"Hello? Who's calling?"

"Hello," she whispered. "Tony?" She moved into the recreation room, dragging the phone cord behind her, then pushed the door almost shut. "Tony, it's me, Celie. How are you?"

"What a surprise. And a very welcome one at that."

"I just wanted to hear how things are going."

"Celie, what time is it there? Five a.m.?"

"Yes. I always get up this early."

"You do?"

"Yes, I write as soon as I wake up. Mostly poetry. Lately I've been following your advice and writing in my journal."

"Good. Has it helped?"

"To tell you the truth, I'm not sure yet. I mean, I'm discovering things about myself I never knew, but not . . . not what I expected."

He chuckled. "We can be quite a mystery to ourselves, can't we? We're in for surprises when we start unraveling all the secrets we've hidden."

"That's exactly it! How did you know?"

"I was a master at burying stuff," he said. "Much better at it than you'll ever be."

"You seem to be a master at avoiding my questions, too. How are you?"

"Well," he paused, and she heard his chair squeak. "I guess I'm not any worse than when you saw me last. Just more certain of the future. Resigned to it, I guess."

"You don't sound happy."

"She made the decision for me. She refuses to go to a marriage counselor. Just wants a divorce so she can marry her . . . boyfriend. She broke the news to me last week. But she won't discuss the kids. Not yet."

"Oh, I'm so sorry." Thinking she heard footsteps in the hall, Celie flattened herself against the wall. Maybe whoever was coming wouldn't notice the phone cord trailing through the door.

"Yeah," he said. "Well, maybe I'll be able to put some pieces of my life back together eventually. Right now, the boys are reacting . . . in unpredictable ways. Me, too." His tone changed. "Hey, Celie, you have a knack. You always get me talking about myself. I never talk about myself. Except with you. But what's up with you?"

"I don't even know your boys, but I feel for them," she said. "They're not much older than my students."

"Celie, you're not answering me. How are you?"

There it was. "Well, the truth is, things aren't any better. In fact, I think they're getting worse." She forced herself to sound more upbeat. "But I'm determined to hang in."

"Have you figured out why you want to stay? That's important."

"I've begun a new project," she said. "My best friend and I are leading a new parish group. We're trying to help Cuban immigrants acclimate themselves to the U.S. So far, we've managed to find them temporary housing, food, and supplies, plus enroll their children in school. I really love helping them. It's kept me busy, too. And another exciting thing is going to happen in two weeks."

"What's that?"

"Remember those textbooks I've been writing? Using the lesson plans I created? Well, I'll be attending a conference at the end of the month in

Santa Barbara. Lots of New York publishers are coming. McCabe Hall and Hilton Moss and—"

"Celie, I told you a long time ago, I have friends in those circles. Two guys I grew up with in Brooklyn. They'll treat you right."

"Yes, now I remember."

"I'll phone one of my buddies. His name is Peter Ferraro. He attends every publishing conference in the country. I'll give him your name. It won't be hard for him to spot you in that crowd."

"Oh, Tony, you don't have to—"

"Celie, he'll give you valuable advice. Show you the ropes. Know what I mean? It wouldn't hurt for you to talk to him. Why don't you bring along your collection of poems, too? He's my friend, but he'll tell you the truth."

"Well . . . I'll think it over. Oh, gee, the others will be gathering for prayers in a few minutes. I hate to rush off so fast, but I'd better. Please take care of yourself. Your boys, too."

"Thanks. It's great to hear your voice. You're such an unusual, caring person. Your call sure surprised me." He cleared his throat. "Please, Celie, keep at it, the journaling, I mean. And don't forget to bring your poetry to the conference. Promise me."

"I will. Bye, now."

She carefully opened the door, peered out, saw that the hallway was empty, and replaced the receiver. The convent was still mantled in gray light. The clock showed 5:30 and no one else had stirred yet. Going to the window, she noticed that the fog was thick and filmy outside. Hearing the foghorns bleating in the distance, she sighed, then suddenly felt as if a dead weight had lifted from her shoulders. Folding her arms under her scapular, she walked to the chapel, where she quietly slipped inside and knelt in her stall.

Time to meditate. Time to commune with God, her friend.

The only light was the sanctuary candle, a sign of God's faithful presence. She watched the candle flicker, listened to the birds twittering outside, and breathed the familiar aroma of burning wax mingled with incense. The scent of night-blooming jasmine on the altar permeated the air, too. Quieting her thoughts, she reached down inside herself to find God's presence.

"Jesus," she whispered, "I feel your peace. You fill me up and surround me now, as You have during so many long weeks of worry and struggle. But why do You offer me such serenity, right after I've phoned someone I'm not supposed to openly talk to or meet? Lord, he's become a good friend to me. He's like no friend I've ever had. Why does he always understand whenever I explain my thoughts or feelings? Why did You bring him into my life? His marriage is so hopeless now. Do You condemn him, as the Church does? I can't believe You do.

"Please, Lord, You know the mysteries of the universe. You know the mysteries of my soul. Lead us all in the ways of Your heart. Your will, not mine."

CHAPTER 39

REPLACED?

The silver Pontiac inched along in the rush-hour traffic, covering only a mile in ten minutes. At the wheel, Celie wiped perspiration from her brow and tucked a loose strand of hair inside her white coif, then reached for the glove compartment to find her sunglasses.

"Sister, I'll do that for you." Seated in the passenger seat, Sister Theresa found the glasses and handed them to her.

"Thank you, Sister. The sun's blinding me. This traffic is brutal, and we're only halfway to Santa Barbara. There's no way we'll arrive on time for the opening dinner."

"Don't worry, Sister," Sister Gerald said from the back seat. "Take your time. The dinner isn't that important. Tomorrow's seminars are the valuable part of this conference."

But Sister Gerald's reassurance didn't soothe her. Her thoughts reeled with possible solutions to a problem that had been brewing in her mind for weeks. Sister Theresa was slated for a single room in the hotel, whereas she had to share a room with Sister Gerald. How could she gracefully switch rooms?

As red brake lights lit up as far ahead as she could see, Celie stopped the Pontiac again and rubbed her eyes, then grabbing her stomach, she let out a slow moan.

Sister Gerald leaned forward. "What's the matter, Sister?"

"I don't know. Sharp pains. In my stomach and abdomen."

"Sister Theresa, you'd better drive. Sister Celia, quick, get out while the traffic is stopped. Change places, Sisters."

As Celie got out, the chubby younger nun dutifully eased herself over to the driver's seat, adjusted the rearview mirror and, after Celie had settled herself in the passenger seat, stepped on the accelerator. The traffic slowly moved forward a few more feet.

Celie knew her feigned illness would have to be ongoing and convincing. Sister Gerald's keen ability to read people was well known. She hadn't been promoted to the positions of the congregation's youngest Superior and principal for nothing.

Remembering how her brother Stevie used to double over and wail when he suffered from tummy aches, Celie laid both hands flat on her stomach and crouched down. "Perhaps the pain will pass," she whispered just loud enough for Sister Gerald to hear. Now real knots were beginning to form in her stomach as a fit of jitters seized her. Ever since she was little, whenever she was really nervous, her teeth began to chatter. Well, she'd just have to incorporate it into her act.

"Sister Celia, you're shaking." Gathering up her own long black cape, Sister Gerald spread it over Celie like a blanket.

"I'm suddenly freezing!" she fibbed. "Thank you, Sister." Then she planted the next seed. "I just hope this isn't contagious."

She timed her groans at five-minute intervals after that.

I can't prolong this drama too long. She'll catch on. Half an hour later and maybe a mile further up the freeway, she closed her eyes behind her sunglasses and pretended to go to sleep.

An hour later, when they checked into the hotel, Celie took the key Sister Gerald handed her.

"Maybe you'd better isolate yourself," the older nun said. "In case you're contagious. Take Sister Theresa's room."

I'm safe! Feeling no remorse for her deceit, but only a grand sense of liberation, Celie unlocked her single room. Her nervous jitters and stomach pains had miraculously disappeared.

Throngs of businessmen milled around the hotel lobby, their striped and paisley ties the only spots of color in a sea of starched white shirts and navy suits. Celie felt as if every eye was turning in her direction as she stepped off the elevator. *Why didn't I wait for the others?* She lowered her eyes, uncomfortable with the attention her white Augustinian habit was causing, and walked as sedately as she could to the conference table to register. Within minutes, a tall, stocky man ventured toward her. "Sister Celia Marie?"

"Yes? How did you know my name?"

She noticed large kind eyes under thick black brows. "I guess I took a colossal chance," he replied with a chuckle. "I was told to look for a nun in her twenties. You're the only nun I've seen so far, and I bet you're not pushing thirty yet. Am I right?"

The large hand he extended reminded her of a boxer she had met long ago when her father took her to the Friday night fights. "Let me introduce myself, Sister. My name is Peter Ferraro. I believe we have a mutual friend. Tony DeStefano?"

Her hand was lost in his, even as she tried to offer him a firm grip. "Yes," she said. "Tony told me he had contacts in the publishing business."

"You teach in San Francisco, right? Tony said you've recently completed a manuscript of poetry and you've tested it out in the classroom."

"Well, I often read poetry to my second grade class. Once in awhile I squeeze in one of my own poems, too. Sometimes I visit the higher grades during their literature classes, too, and once in a while, I share my work with them."

"And how do the children respond?"

His interest made her relax. "I've been surprised. At first, they yawned and looked bored when I read them *any* poems, famous ones or mine. But I think it's kind of like classical music or Shakespeare. If you keep exposing kids to poetry, they begin to like it. Pretty soon, they're begging for more."

He nodded. "Sister, do you have any free time today?" He handed her his business card. "I'd like to review your manuscript. I represent McCabe Hall in New York, and I have some colleagues who might be interested in your work. They work in our educational division. Apparently there's a push on right now to expose kids of all ages to poetry."

To ease her nervousness, Celie swallowed before she spoke. "Yes. I believe I could meet with you after lunch. Before the afternoon workshops begin."

As crowds of attendees swarmed around them, moving toward the conference room for the opening session, Celie glimpsed Sister Gerald and Sister Theresa stepping out of the elevator.

"I'm looking forward to it." Peter's voice was smooth and professional as he flashed another grin. "Shall we meet right here? Please bring an extra copy of your manuscript. I might want to show it to a couple of our editors."

She nodded, slipping his card into her pocket, and he turned away to join the throng filing through the doors while she stood still and waited for the other two Sisters.

Sister Gerald was businesslike, almost brusque. "Good morning, Sister Celia Marie. Let's find some seats before the whole room fills up." She led the two younger nuns to the back of the large auditorium to avoid attention. As they found three seats, she turned to Celie. "Are your stomach problems gone, Sister? You don't look as pale as you did last night. Did you rest well?"

"Yes, thank you, I did. The pains come and go, but luckily they've subsided for now."

"Why was that man talking to you?" Sister Gerald asked as she settled herself between Celie and Sister Theresa.

"Oh, uh . . . he stepped on my toe when someone in the crowd accidentally pushed him. He stopped to apologize, that's all." *How many lies will I have to tell before this weekend is over? Please God, forgive me!*

"I'm not an expert in the poetry field, but you've certainly included some original, lyrical work in these pages. I'm impressed." Peter Ferraro talked fast as he reread a few poems and flipped through the pages of Celie's manuscript.

A thrill ran through her. *Does he really mean it?*

"Would you mind if I showed your work to the colleagues I mentioned? I promise I'll get back to you as soon as they review it."

"Yes, I guess so. Of course!" She could hardly contain her excitement.

"Thank you, Sister. I see you've included your address and phone number in San Francisco. You'll hear from me within four weeks."

He stood up, offered his hand to her again with a smile, and she looked up into the bluest eyes she'd ever seen, then she had to look away. He nodded then turned, and soon he'd disappeared into the crowd gathering for the afternoon breakout sessions.

She found the workshop she'd signed up for and a seat near a window. Checking her watch, she searched the room for Sister Gerald and Sister

Theresa. What an exhilarating day! But as thrilled as she was, she decided she would not say a word about Peter Ferraro or McCabe Hall Publishing to Sister Gerald or Sister Theresa. At least not yet.

As the speaker began to introduce the afternoon topic, "Revising Your Manuscript for Final Publication," Celie scanned the crowd again for her companions. It wasn't like Sister Gerald to miss an opportunity to learn about the textbook business. Besides, she had specifically asked Celie to meet her here at this seminar. Celie turned around to look for the older nun. No sign of her. Puzzled, she settled down to take extensive notes so she could share them with Sister Gerald at dinner.

But dinner came and went, and Celie still did not connect with her companions. Eventually, she called room service and ordered a modest meal, then she phoned Sister Gerald's room for the fourth time.

"Hello?" Sister Gerald's voice sounded strange.

"Sister, I've tried calling you several times," Celie said. "And I've looked everywhere. Are you two all right? Has anything happened? I was afraid something had—"

"Of course everything's all right. I tried to find you and couldn't, so Sister Theresa and I were forced to have dinner downstairs without you. By the way, are you feeling any better? Or are those strange stomach pains attacking you again?"

Does she suspect? "Uh, no, they haven't disappeared . . . but they aren't as sharp now. It only hurts every couple of hours. So I'm having soup tonight. Sister, thank you for your concern."

"Good. I'll call a doctor when we get back to San Francisco. I think you've been sick too often lately, don't you? You need to be checked thoroughly. Well, Sister, we'll talk in the morning. I'm afraid I'm quite tired tonight. We're both going to turn in. Good night."

Click.

Celie sat there, staring into the phone for a whole minute before she replaced the receiver. *How strange, she cut me off. And her voice was so abrupt. And I checked the hotel restaurant several times. I didn't see either of them all day, and I'm sure neither of them showed up all evening.*

The next day, feelings of both relief and abandonment beset Celie. Although the other two nuns sat with her at breakfast, she felt invisible in their presence. It was a reminder of her childhood so many years ago. The women deferred politely to her if she spoke, but most of the time they talked around her, laughing together as if they alone were sharing the punch lines of secret jokes.

As the morning session wore on, she watched them sitting together, their shoulders touching, pressing their heads together to share each other's notes. When she tried to join their conversation, pauses multiplied, and she soon realized that she might as well be speaking to an empty room. Finally, she gave up and decided to fold up into silence. At break time, they excused themselves to wander outside around the hotel grounds, leaving Celie to sit by herself and watch the streams of businessmen make their way to the telephones in the lobby.

Conversation in the car the next night verified Celie's worst nightmare. She sat in the back seat as Sister Theresa maneuvered the Pontiac up the freeway toward San Francisco. Sister Gerald, in the passenger seat now, chatted on and on with the younger nun about the scriptures and their various translations and finally they brought up the topic of completing the religion textbooks. *Her* project.

"We must forge ahead," her Superior said, "or we won't make the deadline. Sister Theresa, perhaps you could revise Sister Celia's final chapters since she's so busy with the new refugee assignment. Then we'll proofread the whole manuscript at the end of this week before it's sent off to the publisher."

Sister Theresa nodded. "Of course, Sister, I'd be happy to."

Turning back toward Celie, Sister Gerald raised her voice. "I know your time is limited now, Sister, so Sister Theresa can take over your job and give us the helping hand we need. You'll be able to help proofread, though, won't you, Sister? Surely, you'll have time for that."

Celie felt like Sister Gerald had lunged at her, punching her hard in the stomach and knocking her down. She had never felt so wounded. *No! You can't give my lesson plans to Theresa! They're mine. I created them. Don't let her carve up all my precious experiences with my class, the ones I've stayed up nights and risen at dawn to add to the textbooks.*

But it was useless. Sister Gerald didn't even wait for Celie to answer. She turned back to Sister Theresa, and their conversation hummed along non-stop as the car sped through the night.

Huddled alone in the back seat, Celie shivered in the evening chill and wrapped her thin black cape around her. She stared at the ebony night outside, pierced by icy, silver lights.

She'd been replaced.

"Lord, help me . . . help me make this sacrifice. Dear God, turn this into a blessing," she whispered over and over.

CHAPTER 40

TIES THAT BIND

"No, Mrs. Cruz, we can't allow twelve people to stay in that tiny house. I'll call a few more families tonight and ask them. Yes, let's meet at nine o'clock tomorrow morning at the parish hall."

Celie hung up the phone and pulled a sheet of paper out of her file. She'd crossed off at least thirty names and phone numbers. Only twelve remained. She picked up the phone again and dialed.

"Mrs. Ortiz? This is Sister Celia. Your daughter Rosa is in my class."

"Hello, Seester, she like you so much. I hope she not in trouble."

"No, no. Rosa's doing very well this year. Mrs. Ortiz, I'm calling you for another reason. We're trying to find temporary homes for an unusually large group of refugees who have recently come from Cuba. Mrs. Cruz suggested I call you. Do you think you could help?"

Ever since she'd met the Cuban immigrants, Celie had thrown herself into the new parish project with Sister Adele and Sister Lupe. It was the only way she could ignore the gaping hole in her heart.

After leaving the textbook manuscript with Sisters Gerald and Theresa that night five weeks ago, she and Lupe had interviewed dozens of new families, with Lupe as their interpreter. They had also scheduled a meeting with the pastors of the Immaculate Mary and Sacred Heart parishes the following day. Next, with Sister Adele's help, they had borrowed enough blankets and pillows from several local convents to set up a makeshift dormitory in the Immaculate Mary auditorium. They'd no sooner set up cots for the sixty refugees who had no housing than Mrs. Cruz had called to offer Celie twelve names to contact in the days ahead, households that might temporarily take in a few people. Staying up until midnight, she and Lupe had also begun pulling together as much warm clothing as they could from the boxes targeted for the annual parish rummage sales. The refugees had escaped from Castro's Cuba with only the clothes on their backs. Many stayed in south Florida, but some made their way across Mexico to western states like California; eventually their leaders connected with relatives who worked in social services in the Bay Area.

The next morning, the families had awakened to their first dawn in the crowded parish auditorium and the nuns served them coffee, juice, and rolls for breakfast. Mrs. Cruz had called Celie that day too, adding new names to her list of possible host families. Celie began phoning these generous people, a task that would continue as the days wore on. So far, she was elated with her success. After two weeks, she'd found homes for forty immigrants, but finding housing for the last twenty had proved more difficult.

Children had willingly given up their rooms and doubled up with their parents so a whole family could move into their bedroom. Celie marveled at the generosity of these people from the twin parishes in San Francisco's Mission District. Mrs. Cruz had also collected casseroles from numerous families to feed the refugees during these past weeks, while Celie worked every day with Sister Rosarita to supply meals to the remaining twenty people in the parish hall who still had nowhere to go.

As the days passed, Sister Adele took on the legal and administrative tasks, meeting with each family to fill out necessary paperwork for entrance into the United States as well as school enrollment papers. Both Lupe and Celie had also tackled the problems of bus transportation and carpools for the children, and Lupe gathered even more blankets, pillows, clothing, personal supplies, plus cast-off school uniforms. If permanent housing opportunities finally opened up, these reserves would become the refugees' possessions. In addition, the three nuns planned to pick up furniture that several prominent San Francisco families had promised to Sister Adele as soon as stable housing came through from the city's social services agencies.

One of the most difficult parts of the refugee project was finding jobs for the immigrant parents because, although many had been highly skilled professionals in Cuba, they lacked English. Celie left this concern to the older nun, but she offered to type job application forms and tutor the adults in the evening.

Sister Adele's wide-ranging experience continually amazed Celie. Originally, she'd regarded her mentor as nothing more than a quiet but talented master teacher who taught fifth grade. Now Celie was beginning to realize the broad dimensions of Sister Adele's expertise. She was a powerhouse of efficiency, Celie was learning, and revered by a number of political and social organizations in the Bay Area.

The weeks had raced by since the publishing conference, claiming most of Celie's time and energy. On top of her responsibilities with the refugees, her new second grade students were creating new challenges, as more than a third of the children struggled to read English because they spoke only Spanish at home.

In the early weeks of the term, Celie had borrowed several first grade textbooks to supplement her second grade texts. She was determined to achieve the same success with these new children that Manuel had attained the year before. Now one of the top students in the third grade, he often stopped by Celie's classroom after school to clean her blackboards. His academic progress buoyed Celie's spirits and gave her confidence that, with time, the children in her new class would excel, too.

Just this morning, she'd read *The Little Engine That Could* to her students. She wanted to encourage them to try harder to understand all the new English words they were hearing in and out of class. She also tried to ease their transition to English by teaming the Spanish-speaking children with American-born pupils. Step by step, her buddy program began to succeed. Yesterday she'd measured the children's progress again. Yes, they were doing better! She was delighted.

After a long day of teaching and correcting papers today in her classroom, she rushed to the convent kitchen at four-thirty, to help Sister Rosarita prepare Italian meatballs and sauce for the nuns plus the twenty Cuban refugees still living in the parish hall. She'd had no time in these past few weeks to slip out to the yard after dinner to hit tennis balls. In fact, she barely had time to think or rest.

Maybe it was better this way, she thought, as she laid her head on the pillow each night and whispered the words of St. Paul,

Do not be anxious, but in everything, by prayer
and petition with thanksgiving, let your requests be

made known to God. And the peace of God, which
surpasses all understanding, will guard your hearts
and your thoughts in Christ Jesus (PHIL 4:6,7, WEB).

Now she checked her watch. Twenty-five minutes before nine. Not too late for more phone calls. She wanted to reach the remaining prospects on her list before the Profound Silence bell tolled. Hearing a busy signal, she hung up and was startled a minute later when the telephone rang.

"Hello?"

"Hi, how's it going?" Lupe's voice held an excitement Celie didn't feel tonight.

"Oh," she said, looking at her list again. "It's going okay. I managed to talk Mrs. Ortiz into taking a family for a couple of weeks. We're down to sixteen people on cots now."

"Great! Make it twelve. I just found another family. They can house four more. Don't worry, we'll get there. Hey, you sound exhausted. Try to get a good night's rest tonight, for a change."

"If I can." Celie yawned in spite of herself. "I can't seem to unwind at night lately."

"Yeah, I've noticed the circles under your eyes. But it doesn't do any good to lie awake stewing about things. Remember, everything will still be there when you wake up: teaching, writing, tutoring English, cooking for extra people, etc., etc. Just a few meager things to accomplish in our dull, boring lives." Lupe's familiar banter felt as warm as a big hug at the end of a tiring day.

"Yeah, right." Celie smiled, but reached up to massage away the pain in her neck.

"I mean it! You've been driving yourself too hard lately. Why don't you try my tried-and-true sleeping remedy? Take hot milk with a dose of Ovaltine . . ." she lowered her voice ". . . and try a jigger of whiskey in it, too. That'll make you sleep like a baby. Or snore like my dad. Honest."

"Really?"

"Yeah. It works for me every time. Promise?"

"Promise." Celie hung up the phone with a smile. *Dear Lord, what would I do without Lupe? Thank you, God, for this treasure.*

Finished in her office, Celie mounted the stairs to return to her cell and opened the door to find two letters. Sister Gerald must have slipped them under her door after dinner. Both were sealed. Celie was glad. But why would her Superior bother to read them anyway?

During the past few weeks, Celie had barely seen her Superior, let alone talked to her. Sister Gerald and Sister Theresa were totally engrossed in completing the textbook manuscripts. They'd met with the publishers numerous times, but invited Celie only once. After that single meeting, they had closed her out of the project. The initial stabs of disappointment she'd felt had turned into a throbbing, intolerable ache whenever she saw the two nuns huddled over *her* manuscripts. But what could she do? Nothing, except busy herself even more with the Cuban refugees. Now she tried to dismiss her obsessive thoughts, as she had so many times before, but it didn't do any good. Her dream of publishing her precious lessons was completely out of reach now and the wound in heart refused to heal.

She picked up the letters. One was from Florida. The handwriting sparked her curiosity. Who did she know there?

November 6, 1967

Dear Red,

Don't faint. Yeah, it's me after too many months. Eight, to be exact. I know, I promised to write. Haven't been very good about keeping my word, have I?

So how are you? Last time I saw you, you weren't yourself at all. I've thought about that day many times. I hope things have straightened out for you by now.

I'd like to talk to you more often, but we move to a new town every few days. Excuses, excuses, right? But, I just might be in California again soon and if I am, I will definitely call you. Some things have come up and I guess this time, I'm the one who needs to talk.

Keep on plugging for your dream, Celie. We're like sharks. They can't ever be still. Unless we keep moving towards something, we die.

So long for now,
Dennis

Celie reread it three times. So few words, but so much meaning between the lines. She wondered if her friend was in trouble. He had never written to her, had hated writing as long as she'd known him. The last paragraph especially puzzled her; Dennis never talked about death. He was the eternal optimist. So, she asked herself, why his strange reference to sharks?

Then she tore open the second envelope. The cursive script she saw was artistic and perfectly straight, a model of the penmanship she'd learned back in grade school. Skipping to the next page, she saw Sister Pauline's signature. Her shoulders slumped and she gnawed on her lower lip as she read the letter.

November 10, 1967

Dear Sister Celia:

Although the Rule of the Order frowns on me sending letters to those I've taught and mentored in the past, I felt your particular situation warranted communication.

I've wondered, since I saw you last summer, how you've been doing. I know you were deeply troubled then. I hope the counselor I suggested helped you clear up your doubts and confusion.

Celie, we all, even the most committed, go through periods of darkness. It's a temporary lull or a period of dryness when God seems far away. But usually, with time, those arid months pass and we regain our spiritual base, and become more dedicated than ever. It has been so in my life these past fifteen years. Many of those whom you have met and live with have weathered these internal storms as well. Read Saint Augustine's life or the lives of other saints. If this "dark night of the soul" didn't happen, I suppose our commitment to our religious life wouldn't be much sacrifice.

More importantly, I wanted you to know you are in my prayers daily. I've sensed, since I met you back in high school, that you would become a model Augustinian Sister. From the reports I hear of your progress, I believe I was right. Word is, your teaching is exemplary and the people of Immaculate Mary parish love you more every day.

There is no need to contact me. Our Rule is right and must be followed. Vigilance and prudence regarding friendships is the best practice. But be assured, I pray for you often, Celie. Be patient also, and everything will come together for the greater honor and glory of God.

Sincerely,
Sister Pauline

Celie stared at this letter for a long time. She heard boys yelling to one another outside and absently wondered why they weren't safe in their homes, their parents sending them off to bed. Then, all of sudden, she picked up Sister Pauline's letter and ripped it in half, then in half a second time, then again. Her hands came up to cover her eyes, and along with her tears, tiny pieces of paper fell to her lap. What good did it do to have a friend who would always be so distant and far away? What kind of peculiar friendship was this? Even correspondence was forbidden. Pauline had finally admitted it, saying that the Rule was right. Yes, she was grateful for the older nun's kindness and advice, but she also knew there wouldn't be another letter, nor even a phone call.

Why, Lord? Every day I try to love Your children, the people of our parish, the new immigrants, and all my Augustinian Sisters. I try so hard. Why do You offer me such loneliness and disappointment in exchange for my love?

CHAPTER 41

GOOD NEWS OR NOT?

Rosa and Manuel were standing in the door of the classroom. The girl's shiny chestnut hair was shorter than usual, and the wide red ribbon binding her topknot bobbed as she spoke.

"Seester, why no Christmas tree? My father knows where to get one. Cheap. Tomorrow he bring one to you."

The two children leaned against Celie's door as the wind rattled the windows. In third grade now, they often stopped by after school to help their former teacher. Today they'd decorated Celie's Christmas bulletin board and now they were prattling away as they buttoned up their rain jackets and pulled on their rubber boots for the walk home.

Celie took a moment to study them before she answered. She remembered the mute little boy and the animated, distracted girl who had gazed up at her last year from these same desks, both of them struggling to speak and read English. They'd grown and learned so much. She felt so proud of them.

"Seester, did you hear?" Rosa's pert little face gazed up at the nun, demanding a response.

"Yes, Rosa, I heard you. I guess I was thinking how much you've both grown up."

"Oh, Seester, you sound like Mama." Rosa's impish grin contrasted with Manuel's big, serious eyes. "When are you—?"

A slight dizziness forced Celie to sink back into her chair. "Oh, the Christmas tree—well, I haven't planned on one. I've been spending so much time getting donated trees for the refugees that I haven't even thought much about decorating my classroom."

Manuel spoke up. "Yes, Seester, my mama has many boxes. Food ees all over our house—eet's going to new im-grant families, too."

"Both your parents have helped so much. Thank them again for me."

As Manuel nodded, Rosa persisted. "Seester, you no answer."

"You *didn't* answer, Rosa," Celie corrected.

"Okay. You didn't answer. Don't you want a tree? My father, he bring you one. Tomorrow."

Someday Rosa will make a wonderful manager, Celie told herself with an inner smile. She forced a reply. "Are you sure? I don't want to impose on your father's generosity. He's done so much already."

"Seester, you gotta have tree," Manuel insisted.

Rosa gave a vigorous nod. "Don't worry, I fix everything, Seester," she said. "My father come, okay? C'mon Manuel, les go. Mama wants me home. Bye, Seester."

The two children began walking together down the deserted school hall, then turned around to wave at Celie. She watched Manuel help Rosa put up her red umbrella as they stepped out into the wet afternoon. The little boy and girl crossed Trenton Street and made their way up the hill as drizzle turned to rain, and the wind began whipping at their umbrellas.

Celie gazed after them, unexpected tears rimming her eyes. *Such beautiful children.* She distracted herself by admiring the Christmas lights framing the windows of the houses across the street, lights of every color flickering like neons. She wrapped her arms around her waist to lessen the chill as she watched the lights dance in the wind. A clap of thunder startled her. Staring at the charcoal sky, she shivered again, and suddenly she realized it wasn't just the storm that made her feel so cold.

Christmas is coming, yet I feel so empty. I feel all dull and dark. It's like I have no feelings left.

Shadows descended on her classroom as she turned off the lights and checked the clock. She was late for Vespers, but today she didn't care. Gathering up her books, she draped her black cape over her shoulders and walked swiftly across the playground to the convent. The wind blew her skirts and sprayed icy raindrops on her face, but she didn't bother to open her umbrella.

Sister Rosarita greeted her at the kitchen door. "Sister, is good you home. Call from New York."

At the words New York, Celie's mouth went dry. Absently, she noted how good Sister Rosarita's cooking smelled as she stepped into the hall to pick up the telephone.

"Hello? This is Sister Celia Marie."

"Hello, Sister. Peter Ferraro here. Do you remember me? The publishing conference in Santa Barbara?"

"Oh, yes! Of course, I remember." Stunning blue eyes under unruly black brows, his oversized hands enveloping hers.

"Well, I said I'd get back to you but you probably gave up on me." She listened to his warm chuckle. "It took a little longer than I'd planned to get my colleagues to review your manuscript. I was right, though. They liked your work. A lot!"

Surprise turned her speechless. All she could manage was, "Yes?"

He went on. "Poetry is hot with young people right now—Silverstein is big in the elementary grades and Rod McKuen's latest book of poems was a smash. Publishers want to offer poetry to kids *and* adults. The market's wide open. So your timing couldn't be better."

She wanted to respond, but words still eluded her.

"Are you still there, Sister?"

"Um . . . yes."

"Okay. Just checking our connection. To get to the bottom line, McCabe Hall Publishing is very interested in your manuscript. They loved your zany poems and the profound ones, too. Have you written any others? For kids in the higher grades? We want to reach the adolescent and teenage markets, too. Introduce a series to schools and national bookstores."

Celie felt a thrill race right through her whole body. She could hardly form a reply. "You really . . . really like my poetry . . . that much?"

He laughed out loud. "Tony told me you'd be flabbergasted. Yes, we really liked your poems that much. Everyone here is *very* interested. Enough to ask for more. Do you think you could manage another manuscript by June? That should give you plenty of time. We won't need the third one till next November."

Blinking and gasping for breath, Celie was very aware now of the aroma of tamales, the lighted windows across the street, the twinkling Christmas lights waving in the wind, blinking on-off, on-off. Suddenly everything looked ultra-festive. Was God answering her prayer? *Peace that defies understanding will infuse your mind and heart.*

"Sister, you've gone quiet again. You still there?"

"Mr. Ferraro, to tell you the truth, I guess I'm so thrilled I can hardly speak. I needed to pray for a moment. I am just so grateful to you."

"Sister, don't thank me. Your work is wonderful. We're awfully glad Tony found you for us. Consider it an early Christmas present, okay?"

"It's the best news I've had in . . . in a long, long time."

"Hey, that's great. You've made my day, too. Well, it's nearly eight here, so I'd better sign off. I need to get home. They're predicting five inches of snow tonight in New York. So long for now, Sister. I'll phone you again in a few days. After you've received our contract in the mail."

"Yes." What could she say? "I can't thank you enough, Mr. Ferraro."

"Sure, Sister. Talk to you soon. So long."

Celie gripped the receiver, the dial tone still buzzing in her ear as she leaned against the door just inside the kitchen.

"Good news, Sister?" Sister Rosarita dug a large spoon into the steaming pot on the stove and pulled out three tamales, nestled in their cornhusks, setting them on a hefty serving tray. The spoon went back into the pot for more.

"Yes," she whispered. "Yes. Life-changing news."

But now it was time to be quiet. The other nuns were already in the chapel chanting Vespers.

Sister Rosarita gave her a wide smile. "Sister," she whispered, "are you still on phone or do you talk to me?"

Celie jumped and grinned and shook her head, then put the receiver into its cradle. She smiled back at her tiny wrinkled friend. "I was talking to you, Sister."

"I think, but I no sure. Sister, you put food on table? We must eat when they good an' hot, right?"

"Oh, of course. The tray's bigger than you are. Let me help you. Your tamales always make my mouth water!"

As the chapel bells began to toll, Celie moved quickly back and forth from the kitchen to the refectory and set the large food trays out. Vespers was over, and the ten Sisters with whom she lived were lined up at their places in the dining room. Sister Theresa took her place at the lectern to read the life of Saint Augustine during the meal. With a nod from Sister Gerald, the nuns recited a prayer of gratitude for their food, then sat down to begin dinner in silence.

Celie took a bite of the bland lettuce and tomato salad and dreamed of a sprinkle of salt and pepper. But, again, they were out of her reach, and she was forbidden to ask anyone to pass them. *I guess everyone's into their tamales. Or they're immersed in this exhilarating story of St. Augustine's conversion. Oh, well.*

As Sister Theresa continued reading, Celie nodded to Sister Adele, who was offering her the platter of the steaming tamales. She put her half-finished salad aside and dug into the main dish. As she relished the spicy cornmeal and beef, she tried again to fully grasp the impact of Peter Ferraro's news. Was it really true? A New York publisher wanted to turn *her* poetry into a published book! Plus they wanted more? A series?

She was dying to tell someone . . . but who? Of course, she'd call home. She'd tell her father first. *He'll be so proud.* Should she call Colleen and Maureen? *Well, they might not be so thrilled.* Would Mom be happy? *Better not get my hopes up.* She'd definitely write to Tony to thank him. *He'll be so happy for me.* If it weren't for him. . . . And she had to call Lupe tonight, too.

But, she told herself, maybe she should talk to Sister Adele first. About the details. Right after dinner. It was safer to meet with Sister Adele than Sister Gerald, to get the official Augustinian perspective on this new turn in her life.

"Sister Adele? Can I have a word with you?"

"More housing for the immigrant families?"

"No. For the moment, that's all handled," Celie said. "This is a completely different matter. I need your advice."

"Of course, Sister. Meet me in the recreation room after night prayers. That should give us about a half-hour before Profound Silence. Can it wait till then?"

"It will have to."

Sister Adele's eyes turned curious. "You look so excited. Okay, we can talk now. Come into my office."

As Celie settled herself in front of the older nun's desk, fidgeting with the rosary beads hanging from her belt, Sister Adele closed the door.

"So? Out with it, child. You look like you're going to burst."

"Sister, I've just had the most wonderful offer!" She leaned forward across the desk. "A representative from one of the New York publishing houses I met at the Santa Barbara conference phoned me this afternoon. They want to publish a small book of my poetry! I can't believe it's true. But that's not the whole story. They also want me to submit two more manuscripts in the coming year for teenage readers. I'm so excited, I can't wait to call my parents and tell them, and—" She stopped. A troubled expression was clouding Sister Adele's kind face. "What is it?"

"Well," the older nun began, "don't think I'm not thrilled for you, Sister Celia. I truly am."

"I hear a 'but' coming. What's the matter?"

"It's just, well, although changes are happening unusually fast due to the Vatican II Council, I'm not sure Mother Mary Lucretia—"

Celie controlled her voice, but she couldn't hold back. "Are you saying the Order won't allow me to publish?"

"No, Sister, I'm not saying that. I'm sure your poetry is exquisite and well worth publishing. It's just, well, you're going to have to be patient. We're making lots of changes these days—our attire and the relaxation of the Rule regarding home visits and all. But although other congregations have allowed personal preferences as far as new professions, ours has not. At least not yet."

Celie blinked. "But I'm not asking to change my profession. I want to teach. I love teaching."

"Yes. And you're a wonderful teacher. What I'm trying to say is, well, I'm just not sure that an individual nun in our congregation would be able to publish her own writing at this time. Certainly in the future it might be acceptable, but right now, it's questionable. What I mean is . . . it might take at least several months. Umm, perhaps even a year for you to obtain permission."

"A year? Permission from whom?"

"Well, first, you must gain Sister Gerald's consent, which shouldn't be a problem, except—

"Except what?"

"Oh, nothing really, Sister, but that may take a considerable amount of time. You should write to the Vicaress General, Mother Mary Lucretia. However, she's working with our congregation in Austria at present, so the process will take a little while because she will want to personally review your manuscript of poetry with Sister Gerald." Sister Adele paused. "Child, your face looks like a storm has wiped away the sunshine."

Celie's stomach was churning. Her shoulders wilted as she sank back in the chair. *How could this be?*

The older nun leaned forward. "Sister, it isn't a no. Please, you look so disappointed. Listen, you're young and, naturally, you want everything to happen immediately. What I'm trying to say is this. Our religious community does not always move at great speed."

"But *we* moved fast, didn't we, Sister?" She couldn't help the scorn in her voice. "The Church wanted us to help the homeless refugees and get them settled, so we moved with *incredible* speed. It took us only eight weeks."

Sister Adele nodded slowly and looked down, avoiding Celie's angry face. "Sister," she said, her voice soft, "you must not judge us too harshly. Keep in mind you joined the Augustinian Order, a monastic institution dating back to the twelfth century. Traditions in our Order are highly cherished. Our Rule does not change rapidly, even in times like these."

Celie's voice was leaden. "So what you're saying is no one in this congregation has ever published a book under their own name?"

"No one I know of in the thirty-five years I've been an Augustinian nun. It doesn't mean it will never happen, though. Actually, the textbooks and curriculum you've been working on with Sister Gerald—"

"Don't forget Sister Theresa."

"Uh, yes, And Sister Theresa, also. But you see, it's the first time, to my knowledge, that *anyone* within our congregation has formally published anything. Sister Gerald, uh, of course, uh, obtained permission a long time ago from Mother Mary Lucretia. But the whole project hinges on the idea that other teachers in the Order would be able to use our—your—curriculum in their classrooms and add to it. Because . . . because that would solve. . . ." She shook her head. "Suffice it to say, the authorship question was scrutinized extensively."

"No one ever told me the other teachers would add to my, er, to *the* textbooks. What do you mean, 'the authorship question'?"

"Well, after many months of lengthy discussion, it was finally resolved, and Mother Mary Lucretia gave permission."

"So whose names will appear as authors of the new textbooks?"

The older nun looked flustered now and suddenly stood up as if to end the meeting. "Well, Sister, I'm sorry, but I'm not authorized to tell you more than this."

"Sister Adele, whose names will appear as authors?" Though she kept her voice level and low, Celie's persistence sprang from the anger that had smoldered inside her for months. The project was no longer hers, and that was insufferable enough. But she'd assumed that her name would at least be printed on the textbook's title page along with Sister Gerald's and Sister Theresa's. Would it be too much to ask, after her endless hours of teaching the lessons, then writing them down and adding more information? After all, *her* ideas and *her* classroom experiences were the nucleus of the books.

"Well, Sister?"

Sister Adele concentrated on gathering up stray pencils, straightening up a desk that was already immaculate and almost bare. "I'm not at liberty to say right now."

"Please, Sister!"

"Well, maybe I can divulge . . . something. But, please, don't let on to anyone. . . ." She sat down again. "Sister Celia Marie, numerous meetings took place last year between Sister Gerald and Mother Mary Lucretia on the authorship issue. Mother kept reminding Sister Gerald that pride was a factor, and she warned her about the danger of the open individual acknowledgment of selected nuns within the Order. She believed it might become too overwhelming in the end. Because we've seen it happen to other nuns. A few years ago, Sister Dominique, the famous Belgian singing nun, the one who made that hit record, left her Order. Mother believes public recognition is too great a temptation for any of us. So she decided that instead of the text bearing individuals' names, something more general should be used."

"General? Like what?"

"I'm not exactly sure, but I'm guessing Mother Lucretia will approve a generic byline like 'The Augustinian Sisters of Santo Domingo.' It's more communal. Gives our congregation recognition, but avoids the dangers of individual pride."

"I see." Celie pushed herself up out of her chair. Without another word, she turned to go.

"Sister, please wait."

Celie had never heard Sister Adele use a tone so strong and forceful. She made herself turn around.

The older nun was standing again, clasping her hands in earnest. "Sister," she said, "I've worked for many months with you. You already know how much I admire your efforts and your talents. Please think carefully about this . . . this opportunity you've told me about. Evaluate it against the vocation you've embraced. I doubt that this way of life will ever include the individual recognition that publishing your poetry might entail. You must weigh the desires of your heart versus the reality of the life you have chosen."

Celie stood quietly, repeating the nun's last sentence over and over in her mind. *You must weigh the desires of your heart versus the reality of the life you have chosen.* What did that mean? She wanted to ask, but she couldn't find the strength to say one word. She crossed the office and reached for the silver doorknob. It felt like ice. She jerked the door open and rushed out, then climbed the stairs, barely hearing the fragments of laughter and conversation floating up from the recreation room. When the bells began to sound, she knew she should join the other nuns in the chapel for night prayers. But she had no heart for it tonight. Though she tried to will her feet to turn and descend the steps and obey the Rule, her legs still carried her upward. Reaching her cell, she closed the door behind her. For tonight, at least, she must lock out a world seemed bent on crushing her.

Kneeling by the window, Celie sobbed for hours, then eventually dried her eyes to consider Sister Adele's words. Deep down, she understood that the older nun was right. She couldn't blame the Rule of the Order. It was she who had freely taken vows to obey, no matter what.

Furthermore, she had to accept the reality that the recent changes the Augustinian congregation was implementing were very uncommon and usually took years to achieve. And she must face the devastating fact that this Order might never relax its Rule enough to allow her to publish under her name. And even if Mother did modify her decision, would it be enough? Celie seemed to be standing outside herself, looking in. What were her deepest desires? What was most important to her? To publish? To see her name in print? To gain recognition? Or to sublimate her talents and choose humility instead of pride? To turn down this opportunity and work simply to make a difference, to work solely within this congregation's guidelines? If she refused this offer from McCabe Hall, she'd remain an anonymous teaching nun, one single nun dedicated to hundreds of her students and their communities.

As she struggled in the dark, verses she'd read over and over to her class kept echoing in her mind:

> *You are the world's light—a city on a hill, glowing*
> *in the night for all to see. Don't hide your light! Let*
> *it shine for all to see . . . so they will praise your*
> *heavenly Father* (MATTHEW 5:14–16, NLT).

"Dear God," she whispered, "do You want me to follow the dream I've wished for since I was a little girl? You gave me this talent and a passion to create poems. Do You want me to reach others with these gifts? Would I be following Your will if I ignored this opportunity? 'Not my will, but Thine be done.'"

CHAPTER 42

QUESTIONS

The sharp ring of the phone awakened Celie. She'd been kneeling by her bed in the shadows for over an hour and had dozed off. Knowing that recreation was over and the other nuns were praying in the chapel, she opened her cell door and rushed to the telephone booth to pick up the receiver.

"Immaculate Mary Convent."

"May I speak to Sister Celia O'Rourke?" said a male voice that sounded somehow familiar.

"This is Sister Celia."

"Hey, Celie!" She heard a laugh, then, "I bet you can't guess who this is—a voice from your long lost past."

"Dennis?"

He sighed and laughed again. "I'm a dead giveaway, huh? No use trying to be a mystery man."

Celie faked a cheerful reply, "That's for sure."

"Hey, are you okay?"

Feeling suddenly dizzy, she leaned against the wall. She was learning that faintness always descended on her when her feelings overwhelmed her. But why now? She tried to maintain the cheerful tone Dennis expected. "Who wouldn't recognize that famous Massachusetts accent?" she said. "You always did talk funny."

"I asked for that one, didn't I? Hey, Red, how the heck are you? You don't sound like yourself."

"I'm fine, Dennis. Fine."

"You don't sound too convincing," he said. "You never could fake it, though. This is Dennis, remember? I know you. Sorry to call so late. I must've caught you at a bad time."

He always detected her moods. She'd never been able to hide her emotions from him. She smiled in spite of the misery that gripped her and tried again. "Well, you don't quite sound yourself, either."

"Touché!"

"What's up?" she asked. "I didn't hear from you for months, then I got your letter."

"Well, I happened to be in San Francisco," his voice faltered, "and since tomorrow's Saturday, I thought you might have a few minutes to see an old friend. What d'ya say?"

"That sounds great. Want to meet around noon?"

"You're on. But, Celie, I'm not exactly comfortable sitting in convent parlors, so can you meet me at the sandwich shop on the corner of Trenton Street and Army? Is that okay? And, Red, try to be on time, just this once." He'd always loved to tease her, and if he discovered any small weakness, he would harp on it forever.

She slipped into the banter they'd shared so long ago. "I'm *always* on time."

"Yeah. Right. See you Saturday."

As Celie went back to her cell, memories of Dennis made her smile in spite of her mood. When they'd walked to school together, no matter how hard she'd tried to hurry, she was invariably tardy and Dennis never let her forget it. She pictured him as he'd looked years ago, waiting on the corner for her, standing next to his bike.

"Hey, Red, you're late," he always called out. "For the umpteenth time."

She always ignored him and walked on ahead. It had worked every time. Dennis hated to be ignored. Soon he was riding up behind her.

"Red, why're you mad at me?"

And then she'd turned around and given him a smile and they'd resumed their teasing the rest of the way to school.

Now, alone in her cell, she sat on her bed, picturing him. Of all people, she'd never expected Dennis to call. As she put on her nightgown, she realized how much she'd missed him, even his relentless teasing. He'd always had a way of joking her out of her down moods. And that grin of his was irresistible. No way could she stay depressed around him. Her heart lifted at the thought of seeing him tomorrow.

Dear God, maybe You sent Dennis to rescue me. Thank you.

They went through the old ritual. Timing her entrance, Celie made sure she was several minutes late, and when she finally arrived at the restaurant, he was pacing. She surveyed him through the glass door as she reached for its handle. He'd filled out. Months of pitching had toned his arms and shoulders into a healthy, muscular hardness, and he was pacing back and forth in the vestibule, his head leading his body, both hands in his pockets.

She couldn't help giggling. *He looks like he's in the dugout waiting to go to bat, and judging from the look on his face, the bases are loaded.*

She breezed in. "Hey, you, why so serious?"

His puckered brow disappeared as he grinned. "You did it on purpose, didn't you? Don't deny it."

"I just wanted it to be like old times," she said innocently. "I wanted to make you feel at home."

"Yeah, right." He grinned again. "Well, I hate to rush you, but I'm kinda hungry. Let's find a place to sit and order a good, ol'-fashioned hamburger 'n' fries."

"Great!"

They settled in a booth toward the back of the restaurant and Dennis ordered for them both. Within minutes, he was biting into his burger and saturating his french fries with ketchup, just the way she remembered. As usual, Celie picked at her sandwich.

"Why so glum?" he asked between bites. "Last time I saw you, you were almost as happy as my mom at an Irish wake. I see you've donned your nun robes again, but you look like you're contemplating a new profession. Funeral director?"

"Ha-ha. You don't look on top of the world yourself. It's strange how when our own lives aren't going too well, we detect the same pain in others."

"Whoa! Your Irish is raring today! But lay off me. I haven't seen you in a blue moon, so I can't be the problem."

"I know. I'm sorry. I guess I am in a dark mood."

"That's an understatement. What's eating you? I don't think I remember you ever being this upset. But, then, you're such a master at concealing your feelings."

"That's the trouble," she said. "I'm learning that I not only hide things from everybody else, but I've been hiding things from myself, too. Important things."

"Like what?"

"My passion for writing. Oh, Dennis, everything's going wrong."

As he reached for more fries, she felt him scrutinizing her. "Hey," he said, "it can't be that bad."

"No. It's worse. But let me tell you the good news first. You're not going to believe this! Yesterday morning, a New York publisher phoned me. Their educational division wants to publish my poetry!"

Dennis whistled. "Wow!"

"And that's not all. They want me to produce two more manuscripts in the next twelve months so they can sell a trilogy. *My* trilogy. They plan to market the books nationwide to schools, libraries, even bookstores. *My* poems! Can you believe it?"

"That's fantastic!" His green eyes gleamed as he gave her a thumbs up. "Congrats. Red, I always knew you could do it. You didn't get those A's in school for nothing. Next thing I know, you'll be on Ed Sullivan. They'll call you the Poet Nun—you'll give both Timothy Leary and the Singing Nun a run for their money."

Celie was beaming. His exaggeration buoyed her spirits.

He pressed her. "So? Give me the rest of the story. I know—the publisher's pleading with you to write two mystery novels, too. Not to mention the fact that you've signed a contract to create a religious cookbook."

She laughed. "Dennis, don't go there. You'll never let me forget my kitchen disasters, will you? I thought you'd forgotten all those recipes gone wrong."

"*Recipes Gone Wrong* by the Right Nun. Yeah. It has a ring to it. It's better than the Poet Nun. Say, let's collaborate on that cookbook."

I'm feeling better already. She tried to swing the conversation back to the original topic, but she wasn't feeling glum anymore, at least not now. And Dennis was still laughing as he enumerated her cooking adventures. In the old days, he'd arrive at the O'Rourkes on a weekend afternoon and, invariably, she'd be in the middle of trying out a brand new recipe, determined to succeed. But just as invariably, when the meal came out of the oven, and everyone, including Dennis, was gathered around the table . . . well, the new recipes just never seemed to work. Usually it was Stevie, her little brother, who put his two cents in first.

"What *is* this stuff?"

Dennis was still grinning at her. "Those were the good old days, weren't they?"

Suddenly uncomfortable, she straightened her veil and silently gazed into his laughing eyes. "Yes, and it's not easy growing up."

"So get on with your story," he said. "What's so bad about a big New York publisher who loves your poetry?"

"Well, it's not quite that simple." She fiddled with her napkin. "I went to Sister Adele last night. She and I have worked together in the parish a lot, and she's been with the Augustinians for over thirty years, so I figured I'd broach the subject with her first and—"

"Don't tell me. They aren't going for it."

"Well, she didn't say—"

"But it's what she meant. Right?"

She had to be honest with herself and with him. "Well, yes. I guess so. Unless I want to wait and see if—"

"Wait? How long? Since when does a New York publisher wait?"

She was ripping the paper napkin in her lap to shreds. "That's exactly the problem. There's no telling how long the Order will take to review this, and even after they do, they might not grant me permission. If I don't take this offer . . . well, it'll be gone." She heard herself wind down to a whimper. "Do you understand?"

Dennis leaned forward and touched her hand. "'Course I understand, Red. This is it—this is your chance. It may not come again. The real question is, well, how much do you want it?" He waited silently as the clatter and conversation in the restaurant eddied around them.

Celie let out a deep breath. "I want it very badly. And I was so close! Earlier this year, my Superior asked me to write several textbooks using the lessons I created for my classes. So I wrote them all. The Augustinians were going to use them in classrooms throughout the Order. I was to be the author of a whole series of religion textbooks for the primary grades. But then my Superior took the project away from me—"

"What? How can they do that? That's terrible." His remaining french fries lay ignored on his plate. "Why? What happened?"

"It's a long story . . . and it'll upset me way too much to go into detail." She paused, then rushed on, "Dennis, I realize now that I've yearned to be a published author since I was a child. Remember fourth grade, when Sister Elizabeth read *Little Women* to us, a chapter a day, and she finally finished the book?"

He nodded.

"That's when I decided I was going to write a book someday. Remember? I told everyone I knew. Anything seems possible when you're nine years old, right?"

He nodded again and smiled.

"I think I got the idea because Sister Elizabeth had praised a story I'd written a week before. She raved about it to my parents. My mom actually phoned my aunt and my grandparents and bragged about my writing talent. Though she never said a word to me. But," she felt like a wounded child now, "but I can't remember her ever praising me or singling me out for anything. So, of course, I was overjoyed. After that, my dream was to someday get my stories and poems published."

"I never knew." His hand closed over hers.

"Well, as the years went on, I just got quieter and quieter about it. So many things got in the way. And I kept hearing over and over, 'You can't make a living as a writer, especially if you're a girl.'" Her voice trailed away.

"What did they suggest, the ones who told you you couldn't be a writer?"

"Not much, really. Marry and raise a bunch of kids. Become a nurse, a teacher, a secretary. Or a hairdresser. Those were my choices. My family always said I'd make a good nurse because I was so calm in a crisis. But, well, when they gave us career testing in high school, I always scored in the top percentile in teaching."

"So, then . . . where'd you get the idea of becoming a nun?"

"My cousin Rosemary talked incessantly about it. So did Mom. You must have heard them. And to me, being a nun seemed like it was a chance to be a force for good in a troubled world, a way for me to inspire people. Back then, I thought it was the ultra profession as far as helping people."

"I always thought you wanted to be at the top of the heap."

"Yes. But I wanted to make people's lives better, like the nuns I'd known in school. That's what really drove me."

"Well, Red, I'm sure you *have* helped lots of people."

"Yes, I know, but—"

"But what?"

"But there's. . . . It's hard to explain. After trying everything, trying so hard, for years . . . and, yes, I've succeeded in many ways, but. . . ." She put one hand over her heart, "There's still a hole somewhere inside me, and no matter what I do, it won't go away."

"So, you're saying the life you've chosen isn't enough?"

Celie didn't answer. Instead she turned her face to the window. "I've wanted to be a writer for a long time, but it was more like a childhood fairy-tale daydream, not a realistic goal. Now there's a possibility my dream will come true! You can't imagine how thrilled I was when the publisher called."

He squeezed her hand. "Yes, I can, Celie. But I have to tell it to you straight. They're not only taking away your job, but your soul as well! Why do you put up with it? Don't let it happen. Go for it, Red. Go for the brass ring on that merry-go-round. Don't turn away from yourself and your dream. Writing is what drives you. I can see it. It's who you *are*."

Tears started creeping down her cheeks. "You do understand, don't you? You wanted to play baseball and you made it. I—I saw it in your face last Christmas and I heard it in your stories. It shook me up then. It made me start asking myself questions."

"Yeah. Baseball is my dream, my passion—since I was six years old. I'll never give it up unless they force me out or I'm totally injured." He looked down. She noticed his white knuckles.

"What, Dennis? What's wrong?"

"Well, when we last talked, you were trying to decide whether to change your life. So I thought of you when rumors started making the rounds on the team. I called you because I thought you wouldn't mind if . . . if I unloaded on you for once."

"What rumors? You shouldn't be listening to gossip."

"It's not a rumor. Not gossip. The word is, cuts are coming, and they say I'm gonna be part of it."

"No! They won't let you go. My dad's constantly quoting your pitching and batting stats. He saves headlines in the paper about you."

"Not lately." He hung his head. "I've been on a losing streak for the last few months, and now they're starting to think I'm on the way out, that I don't have the stamina or strength to be a pitcher. The bottom line is . . . my life might be turning a corner, too. I hope the buzz isn't true," he lifted his head and tried to smile, "but I guess there's nothing more definite in this world than change. Right?"

She took his hand. "Yes, and it's scary. I'll pray hard the cuts don't touch you."

He pulled his hand away and brushed back his hair. "Thanks, Red, I'll keep you posted. Just seeing you has helped. A lot. It seems we're both at a crossroads, right? But I don't want to talk about me anymore. Besides, the cuts aren't scheduled till the end of the season, so there's really no use worrying about it now. Worrying won't improve my game, that's for sure. We need to concentrate on you. The timing is critical."

Conflicting emotions wrestled inside her. "I feel so selfish focusing on myself. How can I possibly give up being a nun just because I want to publish and see my name on a book? It seems so egotistical. And so at odds with everything I've been trying to achieve in the last four years."

"You're missing the point," he said gently. "You don't have to stop doing what you're doing. Helping people, I mean. You're good at it. You've proven that. Plus, the kids and their parents love and appreciate you." A shadow crossed his face as he continued. "I wish I'd put together a plan when I went for my dream, but college was something I never considered. Now if they do let me go, I have nothing to fall back on. I can't even teach P.E. in a public school. Plus I don't know if I'd be any good as a teacher. But you? You've achieved a career as a teacher and you've worked to earn your degree. You'll graduate in a year or so, right? And now they're offering you the icing on the cake, a publishing opportunity. If you take their offer, you don't have to give up teaching."

"But I may have to give up being a nun."

It seemed as if suddenly the whole room went silent.

Dennis formed his words with care. "Yes, you may have to give up being a nun. But I'd like you to consider two questions."

"What?"

"Who created you, Celie? Who put this seed of a dream inside of you?"

278

She waved to Dennis as he took off in his shiny blue Mustang. For the moment, his grin had vanished, and his green eyes looked into hers as he swung the car out of the driveway. Then he raised his hand in a salute and smiled and waved at her. A minute later, he was speeding down the street toward the freeway.

Minutes later, Celie was locking the Pontiac in the garage. The sun shone almost silver-white in the gray sky as she hurried toward the schoolyard. The cold air chilled her cheeks and eyes, and her veil fluttered every which way as she braced herself against the wind. Her mind raced with chaotic thoughts, crowding out everything around her, so much so that she didn't notice Mrs. Cruz waving to her until she heard her name being called. She finally waved back and, still in a fog, closed the school door behind her. Entering her dark classroom, she switched on the lights, and settled at her desk where her teacher's satchel full of papers and books sat.

Out came the children's tests. She had to correct them this weekend. She shoved her hand into her briefcase again to find her math manual, but she touched her journal instead. She opened the blue cover. On the first page was a poem she'd written over a year ago:

The Habit
As if I'll become accustomed
   to this life,
     this role,
     this costume.
As if by putting on a long white robe day after day,
I'll don a white existence:
   white like sand, pummeled into purity
     white like paste, gluing rules to people
       white like . . . snow,
        empty space,
          vacant worlds . . .
  thin ivory cloth,
  ensuring respect, pedestals personified.

Underneath—
I am
   have always been
    scared,
     sinful,
      resolute,
       restless,
        and wanting . . .

She slammed the journal closed.

Minutes later, still breathing hard, she opened it again and turned the pages, one by one, reviewing all her journal entries, pondering words written during the past years.

She'd been so naive in the beginning, revering Sister Pauline, waiting so patiently to hear from her "precious friend." Or so she had thought. Then she had given all her admiration to Sister Gerald, hanging on every word the older nun uttered, every gesture. Both nuns had used her . . . and both had abandoned her, too. But Sister Gerald's "massages" were unforgivable! She turned more pages. Her journal entries after she'd spoken with Tony were more revealing. Her loneliness, her longing to connect with someone who understood her. Her notes following her counseling sessions with Charlotte made everything so obvious. The counselor had told her that she'd been a victim of sexual assault, and when she didn't submit to the relationship Sister Gerald wanted, the lesbian nun had taken up with a more compliant Sister Theresa. But not before she punished Celie by turning her publishing project over to her new protégée.

It was all so plain now, laid out in black and white. No wonder she'd felt so depressed, so utterly hopeless.

The prospect of publishing her religion lessons and sharing them with teachers plus hundreds of children had seemed so fulfilling. Once. Her entries from last June seemed to dance across the page with childlike excitement. Yes, the religion texts, probably modified significantly, would still be published by the Augustinian Sisters, but *her name* would not appear on *her work*. The elation she'd expressed months earlier had been quashed. She turned more pages. Her recent journal entry describing the publisher's offer had infused her with new joy. Yes, she longed to accept this chance to reach thousands with her poetry. Published with *her own name.*

Scanning the pages, she noticed that she'd mentioned Mike a number of times, Dennis, too, but so many more pages were overflowing with Tony. She couldn't ignore what had flowed through her pen day after day. Like a record, playing over and over, her desire for real friends and her deep need for intimacy kept repeating. Did she want an exclusive love? Marriage? Maybe not with Tony—his situation was so full of obstacles, but still . . . her journal entries both concealed and hinted at her secret longing for marriage and children.

Celie sat in her classroom, trying to digest the thoughts and emotions she'd just read. *What shall I do now?* Feeling dizzy, she decided to take a break and wandered out into the school hall, then headed to the faculty room for a cup of stale coffee. So much had happened in the last year. Her head ached, and for a few minutes nausea almost overwhelmed her as she climbed the staircase.

It will pass, she assured herself as she had so many times before. But these dizzy spells were increasing. *I have to get hold of myself.*

Finding the faculty room open and empty, she made her way toward the adjoining bathroom.

If I could just sit for a minute.

She splashed water on her forehead and wet two paper towels, then locked herself into a stall and sat down, bending forward and holding her head in her hands. She bent further down. *I have to get my blood flowing again.* She remembered something her mother had said, something about blood rushing to her head. Taking deep breaths and holding the cold, wet paper towels to her temples, she began to feel almost normal. Then the nausea took hold again, and she fought to control the urge to heave.

Trying to stifle the waves of vertigo, she covered her face with the moist towels. A minute later, she heard something in the stall next to her. She jumped when she heard a small crash on the tile floor—a bottle?

She stood up, determined to banish her swirling nausea, opened the stall door, and stumbled to the sink, hoping more wet paper towels would relieve her lightheadedness.

"Sis-TER, wass wrong?" Sister Adele came out of the other stall.

Celie got a glimpse of a bottle in her hand before the older nun stuffed it away into her pocket and leaned closer to inspect Celie's pale face.

"Chile, you look as white as yer habit. What'd you say wass wrong? Here, I'll help you back." She grappled with Celie's arm.

Smelling alcohol, Celie pulled away.

Sister Adele took a step and weaved a little. "Wassa matter?"

Suddenly feeling clearer, Celie turned toward the towel dispenser. "I'm okay, Sister Adele. But I should ask . . . what's the matter with you?"

The older nun didn't seem to hear her. As she staggered forward, Celie backed away from the sour smell of liquor. Sister Adele's eyes were glazed and she held on to the sink to maintain her balance.

"Sisser, what'd you say? You don look well. Here—lemme help you."

"No!" Celie pulled away from Sister Adele's grasp, "No!" The word exploded. Screaming the word again, she ran through the faculty room, down the hall, and out into the schoolyard, welcoming the cold air against her skin.

How can I trust any of them? Adele, I admired you so much . . . and now . . . and now. . . .

Clutching the wet paper towels in her hand, she ran until she hit the chain link fence. "That's it," she said aloud. "No more." Tears streamed down her face. "Please, God, no more!"

CHAPTER 43

SPEAKING UP

Celie's hand was shaking as she gripped the receiver. Willing herself to sound calm, she said, "Dad? How are you?" She felt suffocated in the convent telephone booth.

"I'm pretty good, hon. But what's up with you? Why are you calling?"

"Nothing. I just wanted to hear your voice."

"Are you sure? I can't hear you very well. You okay?"

"I'll speak louder," she said. "Yes, I'm okay. Of course I'm okay. How're things going with you? I haven't called you in a while. Sorry."

"No need to apologize, honey. Things are the same—I'm still trying to beat this thing, but I'm making progress. The program's working so far. That's what counts. Taking each day at a time. That's the AA mantra. One day at a time. I'm going to the meetings."

"I'm glad, Daddy. How's Mom?"

"She's okay. She's not home at the moment. You want me to have her call you?"

"No, Dad. I guess . . . I guess I just wanted to talk to you. How are you, really?"

"Well, if I said this was easy, I'd be lying. That's a fact. But I never expected it to be. Rehab is finally over. It was difficult. But AA seems to be a good thing for me. The right thing now. Your mom even came with me a couple times. I never thought so many other fine people had this problem, too. It surprises me how much the meetings help. I'm even getting up and sharing. How about that? My generation's not very good at that, you now, but I feel better afterwards. I think it's because I'm helping others with their problems. Keeps me going."

Tears flowed down her cheeks as she listened. When he paused, she asked, "Have you been back to the doctor?"

"Yeah. Doc says I'm doing pretty well. My ticker seems in better shape. I still get those ugly prickly feelings sometimes, like my skin is crawling all over with something—it's part of the Valium withdrawal—and I don't feel great every day. But I'm sure better than I was! Your mom and I even get out once in a while now, to visit friends. She likes that. We miss you, honey."

She could hardly swallow. She wiped her eyes, but the tears kept coming. The pause lengthened. She couldn't speak.

"Celie? You still there, Celie?"

"Yes."

"You don't sound right," her father said. "Something's wrong and you're not telling me. Talk to me, honey."

Unable to suppress the trauma that had built up over the past year, she was sobbing now. She had to tell him the truth. She took a deep breath. "Dad, things haven't been going well. I just can't seem to. . . ."

"Honey, you don't sound good at all."

"Dad, I can't seem to—to . . . no matter . . . no matter what I do, well . . . it isn't going anywhere. I can't seem to . . . to. . . ."

"How long have you been feeling this way? You don't sound like yourself at all. What's wrong? Tell me what's wrong."

"Almost the whole year." She blew her nose. "Ever since I came home at Christmas. I've been trying so hard. . . . Daddy, I couldn't tell you. I know you wanted me to have my dream—"

"Honey, haven't I always said if you're not happy, you can come home? I've always told you that. Always. Ever since you left."

"Yes, Daddy, you always told me. Well, I've finally admitted I'm not . . . not as happy here as . . . as I thought . . . and I might be ready to come home."

"That's fine, honey. We'd love to have you home again. Think seriously about it. Promise me."

"I will."

"Please. Whatever you decide, I'm in your corner. You hear me? In your corner."

"Yes. Dad, don't mention this to Mom yet, will you?"

"No, of course not. Now calm yourself down. Take it easy. And for the next few days, try to think things through. Will you do that? Jot down all the things that are bothering you. Put everything in that journal you always write in. Write down all the things that make you happy, too. It's a good way to weigh everything. Then you can call and tell me your final decision when you're ready to. Mom and I will be okay with whatever you want."

"Okay, Dad. I promise. Thanks for listening. I'm glad you're doing better. And . . . Daddy? I've never told you before . . . I love you. I admire the work you're doing on yourself. You have so much courage. I love you more than I can say."

His voice was hoarse. "I love you, too, Celie."

She'd avoided this meeting for days. Her letter to Mother Mary Lucretia requesting she be released from her vows was finally finished. She'd been working on this letter for a week, explanations of why she must leave the Order had poured out, filled whole pages, then she'd revised and recopied the letter, which had then lain in her bedside drawer for two more days. The strange thing was, she kept telling herself, after she'd listed all her reasons on paper, she felt not only relieved, but, yes, even justified.

After rereading the letter again last night, she had become even more certain. Everything seemed absolutely right on paper. She didn't fit in here. But she *could* fit in somewhere else. As a teacher, she could work with children and their parents, too, even immigrants. On the outside. In public or parochial schools. During the last few days she had allowed herself to consider her long-suppressed thoughts of marrying someday and having children of her own, desires she'd entertained early in high school and then relinquished.

After making her decision, she'd phoned her parents. They'd both been unequivocal in their response. "Come home as soon as you can."

Now she stood in the hallway, holding the letter under her scapular and waiting for Sister Theresa to come out of Sister Gerald's office. It seemed so long ago that she'd been Sister Gerald's confidante, babbling away with her Superior, creating wonderful plans for next year's religion lessons.

Today she'd set up a formal appointment with Sister Gerald. She couldn't chicken out again. Yesterday she'd lingered here for almost an hour, her heart in her throat, afraid to knock, waiting for the door to open and her Superior to greet her. Finally, she had stolen away to her cell. Her chest was pounding, and her head was throbbing, but she stood resolutely, watching the clock. *I have to get through this.* She was determined to obtain dispensation from her vows so she could be at home on Christmas day.

The door opened. Sister Theresa came out. She nodded and walked away. They hadn't spoken in weeks.

Celie took one step forward. *Lord, help me choose the right words.* She took another step. She was standing in the door. *I will confront her. I will speak the truth.* She took another step. She was in Sister Gerald's office. *Then I'll be free, as You promised.*

The older nun motioned for Celie to sit down. She was standing behind her desk, looking out at the noisy schoolyard full of children playing with balls and jump ropes. "So, Sister Celia Marie, what brings you here?" she asked. "I haven't seen you in weeks, except in the chapel or across the refectory table." Her voice sounded both frigid and forlorn.

"Sister, I—" Celie stared up at the older nun, whose eyes remained fixed on the window. "I've been thinking about things very carefully in the last several months. I've even recorded most of my inner thoughts and feelings in my journal."

"Yes? Go on."

"You know I've been struggling for a long time with my vocation."

"Oh. That again." The Superior sounded relieved. "I've told you before, we all struggle here. You're not the only one."

Celie's temper suddenly flared. "Well, perhaps those of us who struggle so hard should leave. Maybe it's a sign God wants us elsewhere."

Sister Gerald blinked in spite of her self-control. "Is that what you came to tell me?"

"Yes. After months—*years* of stress and tension, I've decided I don't belong here. I truly believe God created me to spend my energy in another kind of life. Not as an Augustinian nun."

"Well, I can't stop you." Sister Gerald's voice was cold. "But I must tell you that I believe you're throwing away a great opportunity to help hundreds, even thousands, of people. You'll never be able to achieve that in a secular life."

"Sister, do you really believe the life of a nun is completely about helping others?"

"Yes, of course. I wouldn't be here if I didn't. Furthermore, I wouldn't be true to my own convictions as an Augustinian Superior if I did not warn you of the pitfalls of the life you're now choosing. The world is a very difficult place, Sister Celia, very unforgiving and full of temptations. You will not be able to serve God and help people out there the way you would if you remained a religious Sister of God and St. Augustine."

Celie felt heat rising through her chest to her neck and spreading across her face. She was vibrating with rage. "Sister," she held her voice steady, "what right do you have to talk of the temptations 'of the world'? You, of all people! You're leading a secret, forbidden life, Sister Gerald. You may be reaching hundreds of people and children with your good works, but you haven't faced your own truth deep inside your own body . . . and your soul. Don't talk to me about fidelity to this life and helping millions. The vows here are about poverty, obedience *and chastity*." Her voice went quiet. "You need help." She was almost pleading now. "Both of us know it. You need to seek help. A counselor. At a minimum."

"Are you finished, Sister?" Sister Gerald stood tall, not moving, not blinking. She glared at Celie, her eyes dark coals. Celie felt like arrows were shooting right through her. She shifted her gaze. It was no use.

Sister Gerald straightened her scapular. "I said, is that all, Sister?" Her voice was deathly quiet. "You'd better resume your teaching now. Your class is waiting." She turned her back again and laid one hand on the blinds, staring out at the schoolyard and continuing in a lifeless monotone, "As far as your plans, I assume you've composed a letter to Mother Mary Lucretia asking to be released from your vows? Dispensation should take less than two weeks."

"Yes. I have it here."

Sister Gerald turned around. Celie showed her the letter.

"Fine. Send your request as soon as possible. As for your departure, I'm sure I don't need to remind you it must be done with absolute secrecy. Do not tell anyone—your fellow Sisters, your students, the parishioners. It's customary for me to obtain money for your flight home and a small amount for a going-away outfit. I'll place an envelope under your cell door when I receive your dispensation." She paused, but her expression did not change. "And make sure you leave all of your religious belongings behind. Your Augustinian habit, your rosary, your prayer books. You may take home only the items and bedding you brought with you on entrance day. And your Bible. You are dismissed."

Celie stood up, but she couldn't go yet. She looked into her Superior's eyes again. "Sister Gerald, in the name of God, please seek help. You are living a lie. We both know it. Even worse, you're assaulting others too innocent to understand what you're doing and leading them into your web of so-called friendship. Don't you care at all about them? You're luring them and poisoning those around you with your power and hypocrisy! You must face your own truth before God. You should leave the convent, too."

There. She'd said it. Her conscience before God was satisfied.

She couldn't leave fast enough.

CHAPTER 44

JOURNEY WITH GOD

Sunset and shadows had descended on the chapel. The glossy floor reflected the remaining amber light as Celie knelt alone in the back pew, absorbed in the beauty of the waning day. The glow from a fading sun played on the stained glass windows, creating a kaleidoscope of blues, greens, and yellows on the mahogany benches and marble floors. But it was the sanctuary light that soon drew Celie's eyes. As always, for her it was a beacon of God's presence. She stood up and walked quietly forward, then knelt in the first pew and watched the small flame flicker and shine. She felt at home here. How many times in these last four years had she prayed near the altar here?

Shutting her eyes for a few silent moments, she held herself very still. *I'll miss this time and this place.* "Dear God," she said aloud, "don't let me lose my sanctuary of peace. No matter where I go, I believe what You said long ago, 'The kingdom of God is within you.'"

But everything else will change now. The scope of her religious vocation that had always seemed so vast and all encompassing was now narrowing to her own individual choices. *Should I get married?* she wondered. *Have children? Almost everyone does.* She doubted she would ever again devote her life to a greater cause than the needs of her own family. Well, maybe her writing could reach hundreds of people. Her teaching too. *I don't know what you have in store for me, Lord, but I welcome whatever You bring to me.*

Would her new secular life change her faith? Her mission in life? The last thing she wanted was to lose her relationship with God. Even amid all the uncertainties of the last year, she still felt His abiding Presence.

I know deep inside You are part of my decision, she prayed, still gazing at the sanctuary light. *You made me who I am. You know the inner searchings of my heart. But how will this work out? The days ahead frighten me. Please, You must lead me in my future choices. It won't be easy. Lord, I promise to visit You often in private and regular prayer and whenever I find a church, I will come in and pray, even if it's only for a few minutes. I want to keep You close to me as I journey on to discover my new life.*

The sunset was giving way to night. Celie watched the sanctuary candle glowing brighter in the deepening twilight. She put her head in her hands, feeling the silence, holding herself still to allow God's peace to enter her heart.

Very slowly, the peace she sought came over her. The twinkling light seemed to reach out to her, to comfort her with the reality that God was within her. The little flame reassured her that God would be present with her, no matter where she traveled in her unknown future. Feeling stronger now, sure that God would walk beside her, she rose from the pew, genuflected in the aisle, and made her way back to the chapel doors. Before she closed them, she turned to look at the small beacon flickering in this chapel refuge.

Then, for almost the last time, she climbed the stairs to her cell.

Crossing the schoolyard the next morning, Celie looked up into an azure sky filled with billowing clouds. All at once, she wanted to shout, sing, dance. She twirled, impetuously clapping her hands together, feeling the breeze on her face, smelling the cold, sharp air that matched the tingling that raced through her limbs. Her joy seeped out, making her giddy. She rushed down the familiar hall, skipping the last couple of steps, noticing the children peeking around the classroom door and grinning from ear to ear. Their bright smiles mirrored hers. She heard giggling as she came into the room. It *was* funny, wasn't it? It was wonderful, too. She laughed aloud and clapped her hands as she breezed into the room.

"Okay, boys and girls! I've decided to do something different today. We'll get out our favorite records and sing Christmas carols! What do you think about that? We'll spend the rest of the day playing games. They'll all be learning games, of course."

The children squirmed in their seats. "Which ones, Sister? Scrabble? Checkers? Clue?"

"Who wants to set up the record player? Where are the Christmas records?" she asked them.

Hands shot up all around the room. The classroom buzzed with merry commotion.

"I need to speak to Dennis Malone." Celie held the phone to her ear and listened to sounds of cheering and shouting in the background. She wondered what the team was celebrating.

"Hello?"

"Dennis, what's going on there? What a racket."

"We're partying big time. First win we've had in weeks."

"Great! You're at the top of your game, as usual?"

"Oh, I don't know about that," he said. "I didn't pitch tonight."

She tried to cheer him up. "When will you? Soon?"

"Actually, I pitch tomorrow night. I sure hope this win's contagious."

"It will be," she said. "Think positive."

"Hey, Red, what gives? You *never* call me. To what do I owe this exalted privilege?"

"I want to tell you my news."

"Oh?"

"It's probably no surprise to you, but I've decided to try my wings in the outside world. I gave my notice today. In a few weeks I'll be on my way home to Southern California."

He whistled. "You're leaving? Wow! You sound so happy about it, too."

"I am. Now that my decision's made, after so many months of struggle, I'm at peace . . . and incredibly relieved."

"Way to go, Red! I couldn't be happier for you. Have you gotten back to the New York publisher?"

"Not yet. My parents were first on my list to tell. You're second. I'll call the East Coast next. I can't wait to take them up on their offer. It's funny," she added. "Now that I've made my decision to leave, I can't wait to get on with the rest of my life. I even started writing again. I wrote a new poem last night."

"Way to go!" he said again. "You're going for the brass ring after all. You won't regret it. And keep writing. There's no telling where it might lead you now."

"I will," she said. "The days ahead will be uncertain. Dennis, I have to admit I'm really scared, but I think I can figure things out if I take it one step at a time. Dad keeps telling me that's what he's learned at AA. It's helped him a lot."

"The future's always scary, Red. You don't have a monopoly on fear, believe me. But your dad's right, we all need to take each day as a challenge. It's simple, but we forget it. I'm relieved he's doing better, by the way. When I'm back in California, I'll stop by and see him—and you. That's where you'll be staying, right?"

"Yes, for the time being. They both sounded happy to have me back home. Well, I should go now, but before I do, I wanted to thank you again. The way you listened to me a week or so ago? That was the best gift you could've ever given me. I'll always be grateful."

"Red, it was nothing."

"It was *something*. Something wonderful, and I'll never forget it."

Feeling the tears begin, she changed the subject. "Hey, maybe now I can come to one of your games. To cheer you on, like old times. What do you say?"

"That'd be great, *really* great. Keep in touch, Red."

CHAPTER 45

A SHOPPING SPREE

The envelope Sister Gerald had promised appeared under Celie's cell door at six o'clock on Saturday morning. Already dressed and ready for prayers, she ripped it open to find a signed Vatican document releasing her from her vows, a plane ticket to Los Angeles, and $50 to spend on clothes to wear home. Incredibly relieved, yet still feeling overwhelmed, she slipped the items back into the envelope when she heard the chapel bell toll. She had to get ready for Lauds, Mass, and then breakfast. She drew her black cape around her shoulders, knowing very soon she would no longer be wearing it. In two days, her life would take a completely different shape. She would be free from the relentless Augustinian Rules, her responsibilities as a nun, and her white nun's habit. In only forty-eight hours, she would become a new Celia O'Rourke.

As the nuns filed out of the refectory an hour later, Sister Gerald tapped Celie on the shoulder, her face still a stern mask.

"Sister Adele won't be able to accompany you on your shopping trip, after all," she said. "She's—um, she's indisposed this morning and sends her sincere regrets about your decision. But I'm sure you can find the department stores on your own. The Pontiac will be available today until two o'clock." Her mission completed, she turned and walked away.

Celie stood alone in the hall, watching Sister's Gerald's back until she disappeared. Was this the same nun she had admired so much? Only a few months ago, she'd looked up to this talented and unusually mystical woman. Or so she had thought. *Now I pity her,* she thought with a sigh. *But I pray she will seek God's help to mend her soul.*

Then she skipped up the stairs two at a time and headed for the hall phone near her cell. She dialed a familiar number.

"Sister Lupe, please."

"Hello?"

"Hi, Lupe. Surprised I phoned you so early?"

"Yeah, I sure am. What's up? You sound like you just won the lottery." She laughed. "You can't keep the money, though—our Vow of Poverty, remember?"

"I've never even bought a lottery ticket." She mimicked Lupe's tone, "Our vow of Poverty, remember? But I called to ask if you can meet me in an hour. I'm on a special mission and I need your help."

"I don't know," Lupe said. "This is pretty short notice. I have a lot of important work to do. Sister Rose has increased my Obedience Work."

"Because of your exceptional behavior, I presume?"

"Not quite. But you're close. She's given me an *unusual* opportunity—to become a *model* for all the nuns here."

Celie couldn't help but hear the italicized words in her friend's voice. "Well, I'm impressed."

"Don't be. This weekend, I get to scrub every bathroom from top to bottom. Then I get to wash the windows and buff all the floors, including the chapel. And I've got the kitchen cupboards to rearrange, too, besides polishing all the silverware. Plus my classroom is a complete mess, and I need to—"

"Okay, okay. I'm thoroughly impressed at your sacrificial enthusiasm. Or is it your hefty penance? But I don't need a model nun right now. I need a special friend. Surely you can get it all done on Sunday. Besides, what if I told you I was offering you the opportunity to steal off with me to do something a little illicit?"

"Illicit? How alluring!"

"Thought so. I'll pick you up at nine-thirty, sharp."

"I'm rearranging my schedule even as we speak. And I'm dying of curiosity!"

"You look like the cat that ate the canary," Lupe said, as she settled herself on the park bench beside Celie. "I haven't seen your face glow like that in, well, months."

They were facing the Golden Gate Bridge, watching the morning sun burn off the fog hovering over the hills of Sausalito. The cables that suspended the bridge were shimmering orange and silver as the sun's rays broke free of the mist.

"I have some news," Celie began. "I hope you'll think it's good news." She turned toward her friend and took her hand. "I've finally made my decision."

Their gaze connected and Lupe sighed. "You're going to leave, aren't you?" Her eyes smiled, though tears glistened at the base of her dark lashes.

"Yes." Celie leaned in closer and hugged her tight. "I've finally realized that as valuable as this way of life is, I'm just not cut out for it. I've figured out what God created me to do at last. Write and publish and teach. Later, maybe get married and have a brood of kids."

Lupe gave Celie another squeeze. "I've known for a long time how much you were struggling. I guess I'm not surprised."

"Lupe, you're such a wonderful friend. And I wasn't kidding this morning. You *are* a model nun."

"I have conflicts, too, you know."

"But under your joking, you're at peace," Celie said.

Lupe nodded. "You know what? Strange as it seems, I think this life does fit me, though the congregation isn't changing as fast as I'd like. And sometimes those in authority just don't consider me their best asset. But they'll eventually see the light. For the time being, I feel comfortable here with my work in the parish and the classroom. And you're right, I am at peace . . . with God and myself."

She moved back a little, and laying both hands on her friend's shoulders, she fixed her brown eyes on Celie's. "I know you haven't been happy for a long time, but today I see something new in your face. You have to give yourself credit, Celie. You've been a wonderful nun," she broke into her usual grin, "well, maybe not a 'model' one like me, but you'll touch the world much more as a writer and a teacher." Her fingers clasped Celie's shoulders. "Promise me something, Celie O'Rourke. Someday soon, I want to be invited to your wedding and be a godmother to your kids."

"Of course," Celie whispered and hugged her again.

Unable to say anything more, the two friends turned to survey the boats in the harbor and listen to the gulls and the foghorns honking in the distance.

Lupe finally broke the silence. "So what now? What illicit trouble can we get into today?"

"Well, I've already broken one command of Sister Gerald's," Celie said. "My leaving was supposed to be a secret, with my departure in the wee hours, tomorrow morning. I'm to be whisked away by a taxi and take a flight to L.A., never to be heard of again. I won't even get to say goodbye to Sister Adele, though I'll definitely write to her. Maybe on the plane tomorrow."

"How sad," Lupe said. "I don't understand why they can't embrace the fact that you've simply chosen another pathway to God. They must want to make sure no one talks to you and decides to run away, too." She softened her words with a pause and a grin. "I think you've been a wonderful nun. But now you've turned into a bad example. Not a model for the rest of us!" She squeezed Celie's hand and beamed. "I'm *so* glad you broke their departure rule. Now I can hug my best friend goodbye." After another hug, she added, "So you were talking about doing something illicit. What did you have in mind?"

"You have to go shopping with me. Sister Adele cancelled out, and I don't want to go alone. I'm sure you can guess why. How's your taste in going-away outfits? I need honest advice, and I know I can depend on your opinions."

"Don't mind if I do. Wow, I feel like a conspirator already." Lupe rubbed her palms together, her eyes glistening. "Fashion consultant, huh? That sounds lots more exciting than being a model nun. C'mon, let's get started."

"What's going on in there?" Lupe said to the dressing room curtain. "You're much too quiet. Open the curtain at least a crack. Let me see what the first dress looks like."

Inside the fitting room, Celie was carefully folding her Augustinian habit and veil in a pile on a chair. "Just a minute," she said as she lifted an olive green and orange flowered dress over her head. Peeking around the curtain, she spied Lupe leaning against a nearby wall. A middle-aged saleslady wandered by within hearing distance, casually straightening a stack of sweaters on a table and trying not to look at the two nuns. Lupe began to smile.

Celie pushed the curtain back so Lupe could get an eyeful. "So? What do you think?"

"Wow!"

"Shhhh, not so loud!"

Lupe lowered her voice. "That dress is a knockout. It fits you perfectly. But I'm not sure orange is your color."

"I'm not sure, either," Celie said. "These colors seem sort of gaudy. And the skirt's so short! It must be the latest fad. You know, I have no clue what the styles are these days. But I know one thing. Dresses are much shorter than they were four years ago."

"Well, try on the other dresses. We have plenty of time."

Celie stole a look at the saleslady, who was definitely hovering closer to the dressing room now, then nodded at Lupe, who raised her eyebrows. Then, eyes twinkling, she raised her voice, "Well, Sister, we'll need to survey all the styles. You might as well try them all on."

The saleslady couldn't help it. She turned and gawked at them as she straightened every single sweater on the table.

Back inside the fitting room, Celie struggled with the next outfit. She could hear Lupe speaking to Mrs. Snoop.

"No, I think we're doing fine, thank you."

She peeked through the slit to see Lupe standing with her hands clasped demurely under her snowy white Augustinian scapular.

The plump saleslady sidled forward, smiling and nodding at the tall, olive-skinned nun. "Are you *sure* your companion doesn't need any help, Sister?" she asked. "Because if you want me to bring you any more dresses, I can. Don't hesitate. She's a size ten, isn't she?"

"Yes. Thank you," Lupe said. "She's got six dresses now, and it'll take a bit of time to sort them out. But if you have any others after that—"

"Yes. I'll come back and see how you're doing in a few minutes."

Celie watched the nosy saleslady amble off, then she closed the curtain and faced the mirror as she zipped up the new dress.

"Celie," Lupe hissed through the curtain, "she sized you up, even with your habit on." She giggled. "I can't wait to see the styles she picks out now. How does the next one look? Does it fit?"

Celie opened the curtain again. "Ta-da!" She looked more closely at her friend. "Why are you laughing? Do I look that pathetic?"

"Stop begging for compliments. You know you look wonderful in that dress."

Celie turned one way, then another, in front of the wall mirror. "Then wipe that smirk off your face, okay?"

"I can't help it. You heard me a minute ago, didn't you?"

Celie nodded, but let Lupe explain anyway.

"Mrs. Snoop has just moseyed back over here for the third time. She can't figure out what's going on. But she's determined to find out. She's decided you're a size ten and wants to bring you more dresses."

Celie laughed. "Behave yourself, Lupe. Don't offer her any explanations. She might be in touch with someone at Immaculate Mary parish, and I'm under orders to keep this whole going-away thing a secret. Remember, it's a small world." She turned and twisted in front of the mirror to get more views of the dress she was wearing. "This one's the best so far," she finally said. "The color is really different. Apple green. I think it fits pretty well, too, don't you?" She pulled at the hem with both hands. "But it's so short! An inch above my knees. I feel sort of naked."

"Stop pulling at it, then. Besides, it's the style. They call them miniskirts. My sister always wears them when she visits. You worry too much."

Lupe grabbed at the tag hanging from the three-quarter-length sleeve. "It's a new fabric, too. Polyester knit. Doesn't need ironing. Wash it and hang it up to dry. Amazing! It fits you perfectly. And that color is a smash with your auburn hair. It's tons more flattering on you than black and white." Their eyes smiled at each other in the dressing room mirror.

"But you definitely need new shoes," Lupe said. "Somehow those clunkers just don't show off the dress." They both broke into a fit of giggles as Celie bent to pick up one of her black granny shoes. "You think so?" A smirk played at her lips. "Well, I have twenty dollars left, so I guess I can afford a pair of shoes. And maybe a small purse to match? Gosh—imagine. Carrying a purse again!"

Lupe nodded. "Try a few more outfits on first, just to make sure. In the meantime, I'll go find a new slip for you. This is going to be fun! I'll be in the lingerie department. Ha! I can't wait to see all the raised eyebrows there."

Celie watched Lupe roll her eyes before she marched off.

Meanwhile, the saleslady was laboring forward, at least half a dozen dresses folded over her arm. She met Lupe in the aisle.

"Oh, I think she's already found her favorite dress," Lupe told her, "but maybe she can try those on anyway. Just to make sure." She gestured back toward Celie's dressing room.

The saleslady, eyes hungry to see a nun out of her habit, made a beeline for Celie's dressing room, but Celie had disappeared behind the curtain.

"Sister, wait! I have six more for you!"

"Lupe, I love everything we bought today. Thanks so much."

Lupe giggled. "Even the lacy chartreuse pantaloons?"

"*Especially* the pantaloons! They match my dress perfectly. They were never in style before, except if you wanted to be Little Bo Peep for Halloween, so I've never owned a pair. Thanks for talking me into buying them."

"This illicit escapade has been so worth it, just watching that woman as she rang everything up made me want to burst out laughing," Lupe said. "And I could hardly keep a straight face when she mentioned the Ecumenical Council and how it's causing so many changes in our Order. She wanted so badly to ask us exactly what we were doing. But she never did. I have to admire her self-control."

"Yeah, but what's she going to tell her husband tonight?" Celie mimicked an outraged voice. "What's the world coming to these days, Harold? Can you imagine? Nuns wearing modern dresses with mini-skirts! Yes, Harold, I'm *sure*. I was their cashier. That's what they bought. An apple green mini dress with chartreuse pantaloons. Yes, pantaloons with lace! Of course, I'm sure."

Both nuns laughed until tears streaked down their cheeks. Suddenly, however, it hit Celie that this new step in her life meant she would hardly ever see Lupe again."

"You're so much fun and such a good friend," she said. "I'm going to miss you so much. We have to make a date to go shopping again. Next time you're in Southern California. Promise?"

Arms around each others' waists, they carried the packages up the hill. The two friends were on their last journey home together.

CHAPTER 46

THE CHOSEN SHELL

As the stewardesses, their nails and makeup impeccable, instructed the passengers to fasten their seatbelts, Celie looked around. Maybe the cabin didn't look any different than it had when she'd flown to Los Angeles earlier in the year, but everything else felt so unreal. She tried to calm herself by watching the trucks and people on the runway become smaller and smaller as the plane took off.

The manila envelope she'd tucked in the pocket in front of her seat began to tempt her again. She'd received it yesterday, but after noting the New York City postmark, she'd decided not to open it yet. Even now, she hesitated, biding her time by studying the handwriting. She knew it was Tony's, though his return address was new. She wrestled with her conflicting thoughts. She knew she wasn't ready for more complications—the changes ahead were enough for her right now—but he was her friend. A very special one. He'd helped her to find a publisher and suggested that she keep a journal. . . .

Only two or three minutes went by before she tore open the envelope. A small Christmas package fell out.

December 14, 1967

Dear Celie,

We haven't spoken in a while. I've missed talking with you, but I've been reluctant to write, since my life grows more complicated

301

every day. I hope you understand. No need to burden you with my troubles.

A few days ago, Peter Ferraro told me your first manuscript of poetry is being edited and prepared for printing. He said the publisher asked you to write more. You didn't mention that in your letter. Congratulations! What a fantastic opportunity. You must be thrilled.

With Christmas only ten days away, I'm remembering our hike through the Muir Woods and those pine cones you gathered to take home. I picture you at school with your kids, putting together Christmas wreaths to raise money for the refugees. I'd buy one myself if I weren't 3,000 miles away.

My business trips to California will resume in February. I hope you'll allow me another visit. Our friendship, strange as it seems, means more to me than you could ever imagine.

For now, all of my energy and efforts are focused on my two boys. Yes, Celie, I've decided to fight for custody of them in the courts after all. I wouldn't be able to face myself if I didn't at least try.

Please take a few minutes to drop me a note at my new address. I've moved out and am renting an apartment just two blocks away from the boys. The place is about as big as a closet but it'll have to do for now. My expenses, as you can imagine, are somewhat overwhelming—but enough said on the turmoil here.

I hope your life is turning around. May this Christmas season bring you peace. You certainly deserve it. I've enclosed a couple of gifts. Actually, the word "gift" is a misnomer because I'm giving these treasures back to you—the poem and shell you left on the table the day we first shared breakfast together last April. Remember?

You told me back then you weren't sure why you chose that particular shell. I found your poem, too, after you left. I've mulled over your words since then and I've come up with my own interpretation. Maybe I'll share it with you when we get next time.

Though I'll admit I was reluctant, I wanted to give these gifts back to their true owner. My guess is your future readers will cherish your poem as much as I did.

Until we meet again, Merry Christmas and Happy 1969!

Sincerely,
Tony DeStefano

As she reread the letter twice more, her heart went out to him. She knew he was suffering pain she couldn't possibly fathom. She folded the letter carefully and put it in her purse.

Should she answer him now? Call him when she arrived home? There was so much to explain. No, she'd wait and think things over. Tony's friendship would mean more challenges. But later, when she was settled, maybe she'd at least phone him.

She pictured his tanned face and his friendly eyes. Absently tracing her lips with her finger, she felt his kiss again, remembering that day in the Muir Woods. It seemed so long ago. No, she might call him after all—before Christmas.

She unwrapped the tiny package. The Sun-n-Moon shell was nestled there with her poem folded inside it. Picking up the shell, she reread the lines she'd written that radiant April morning on the beach. Lightly penciled, they'd seemed like only a rambling set of words then. She whispered them aloud:

Simplicity shell.
Only one half,
Bleached pure white inside and out.
Outside—rough and ribbed,
ridges curved,
forced into parallel paths.
Inside—satin smooth,
sea-shaped, cupped
Ready to hold—
what?

Yes, she knew the poem's true meaning now. Subconscious yearnings had emerged from her soul that day. The poem was both a statement of her rigid life as a nun and a prophecy of her deepest desires—to be open, soft and primed to embrace her future—to find and choose others and welcome them into her heart. More than that, to continue to choose her true self.

The End